DOUBLEDAY
CELEBRATES
100 YEARS OF
EXCELLENCE

L. M. Alcott

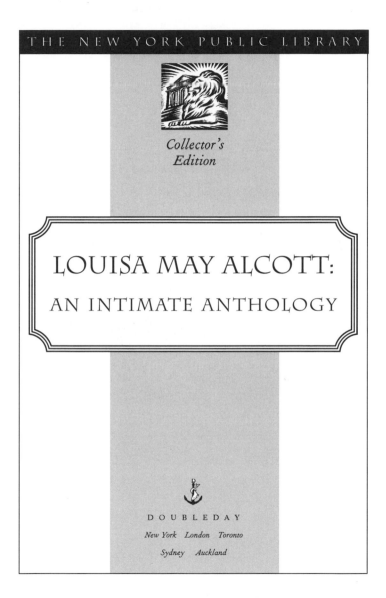

*Collector's
Edition*

LOUISA MAY ALCOTT:

AN INTIMATE ANTHOLOGY

DOUBLEDAY

New York   London   Toronto

Sydney   Auckland

FRONTISPIECE: *Louisa May Alcott, after a portrait photograph, ca. 1850.*

PUBLISHED BY DOUBLEDAY
a division of Bantam Doubleday Dell Publishing Group, Inc.
1540 Broadway, New York, New York 10036

DOUBLEDAY and the portrayal of an anchor with a dolphin
are trademarks of Doubleday, a division of
Bantam Doubleday Dell Publishing Group, Inc.

Book design by Marysarah Quinn

Library of Congress Cataloging-in-Publication Data
Alcott, Louisa May, 1832–1888.
[Selections. 1997]
Louisa May Alcott: an intimate anthology / Louisa May Alcott. —1st ed.
p.   cm. — (The New York Public Library collector's edition)
Includes bibliographical references.
1. Alcott, Louisa May, 1832–1888.   2. Women authors, American—19th
century—Biography.   3. Autobiographical fiction, American.   I. Title.
II. Series.
PS1018.A4   1997
813'.4—dc21   97-16454
                                                                    CIP

ISBN 0-385-48722-3

1   3   5   7   9   10   8   6   4   2

ACKNOWLEDGMENTS

This volume was created with the participation of many people throughout The New York Public Library. For their help in developing *Louisa May Alcott: An Intimate Anthology*, we are grateful for the contributions of the curators and staffs of the Henry W. and Albert A. Berg Collection of English and American Literature, the Miriam and Ira D. Wallach Division of Art, Prints and Photographs, the General Research Division, the Rare Books Division, and the Manuscripts and Archives Division. Special recognition and thanks go to researcher and writer Kenneth Benson; Anne Skillion, Series Editor; and Karen Van Westering, Manager of Publications.

The New York Public Library wishes to extend thanks to its trustees Catherine Marron and Marshall Rose, as well as to Morton Janklow, for their early support and help in initiating this project.

Paul LeClerc, President

Michael Zavelle, Senior Vice President

Marie Salerno, Vice President for Public Affairs

CONTENTS

III. FROM THE MAGIC INKSTAND:

Four Stories

IV. REMEMBERING LOUISA MAY ALCOTT:
Essays, Photographs, Drawings, and a Poem

ABOUT LOUISA MAY ALCOTT

WHEN *LITTLE WOMEN* WAS FIRST PUBLISHED IN 1868, JO March, its blunt-spoken, funny, independent, and irrepressible heroine, captivated readers across the land. Perhaps no one was more astonished by the novel's triumph than Louisa May Alcott, the woman who had brought Jo to life, the woman, as it turned out, who had *lived* Jo's life. In *Little Women,* Jo proposes her version of paradise. "I'd have," she says, "a stable full of Arabian steeds, rooms piled with books, and I'd write out of a magic inkstand." After years of struggling to shore up the finances of what one contemporary described as an "exceedingly impecunious household," she discovered that she had dipped her pen, at last, into that magic inkstand. Almost overnight, Alcott was one of the most famous and admired women in America.

From that time forth, whatever she wrote sold, and grateful Victorians heralded her as the "Benefactor of Households" and "Youth's Companion." Even the mighty Henry James dubbed her the Trollope of the nursery and schoolroom, and to this day she remains a sentimental favorite with children (or at least, with their parents). But there is another Louisa May Alcott—perhaps the real one—who was far more complex: a fierce and funny woman with a rapier wit who despised sham and loathed "gush" (as she called it), who irreverently mocked and satirized the moral and class pieties of her day. A woman who believed in hard work and fair pay, who groaned when she heard the word "metaphysics," and who had nothing but contempt for many of those who idolized her. This is the Alcott of "Transcendental Wild Oats," "Hospital Sketches," and "A Wail Uttered in the Woman's Club," three of the more hilarious pieces in this collection, which, together with her spirited and often acerbic letters and diaries, may serve to introduce many readers to an altogether more modern and vital Alcott. ("Boston," Seán O'Faoláin shrewdly observed, "imposed its own polite reticences and devious evasions on a novelist who, in her private life, hardly knew what those words meant.")

And she was a woman with a florid and sensuous imagination who wrote about hashish experimentation, psychosexual manipulation, interracial romance, murderous passion, and other "lurid" topics—for money, to be sure, but perhaps too for the range and freedom that such sensational themes granted her. Alcott had many gifts, of which she was absurdly modest; but her stance toward life was a fusion of the humorous and the warmhearted. Alcott looks so grim and sobersided in most of her photographs, but people who knew her intimately, and even those who had met her only briefly, were always struck by her eyes. They flashed and dazzled. They had *life*. Before she was hewn into a monument, Alcott was a woman who had led an extraordinary life by anyone's standards, but especially her own, which were very high.

LOUISA MAY ALCOTT WAS BORN ON NOVEMBER 29, 1832, IN GERMANtown, Pennsylvania, the second daughter of Amos Bronson Alcott and Abigail ("Abba") May Alcott, two of the more remarkable characters in the annals of nineteenth-century American parenting. There were four daughters in the family: Anna ("Nan") had arrived twenty months before Louisa; and Elizabeth ("Lizzie") and Abby May ("May") were to follow in 1835 and 1840, respectively. To the more

Louisa May Alcott, sometime in the 1870s. She took little satisfaction in her portraits. "When I don't look like the tragic muse," she told Maria S. Porter, "I look like a smoky relic of the Boston fire"—and in even the best of the bad photographs, as she wryly explained to an editor, one glimpsed but the "pensive invalid."

conventional souls of Concord, Massachusetts, which the Alcotts would one day make world-famous, this spirited troop of down-at-the-heel vegetarians, idealists, abolitionists, hoydens, and suffragettes probably seemed more than a little eccentric.

Born into very humble circumstances in Connecticut in 1799, Bronson Alcott was a self-taught philosopher and reform-minded educator whose theories of pedagogy were as unorthodox as they were unpopular. His daughters bore the burden—and the benefit—of his advanced methods of instruction. Unquestionably, Bronson was a singularly inept breadwinner; at times his unworldliness was almost breathtaking. It was Louisa who would one day define a philosopher as "a man up in a balloon, with his family and friends holding the ropes which confine him to earth, and trying to haul him down."

Abba May Alcott had a great deal of New England blue blood running through her Bostonian veins, including that of Samuel Sewall, the judge who presided over the Salem witch trials. By marriage she was connected to John Hancock; and the Mays, noted for their staunch support of abolition as well as their philanthropy, were one of Boston's most distinguished families. Abba was devoted to her husband—indeed, in the view of many, including her father, she was all too loyal. While she could have done without the metaphysics, she shared Bronson's passion for charity and social justice, and both were fervent supporters of abolition and women's rights. But unlike her husband, Abba was not completely devoid of a practical knowledge of life—while Bronson pondered the Oversoul and Harmonic Being, she held the family together. When she was twenty-eight, their daughter, Louisa, reflected on Abba in her journal: "All the philosophy in our house is not in the study; a good deal is in the kitchen, where a fine old lady thinks high thoughts and does kind deeds while she cooks and scrubs."

After the failure of his highly experimental Temple School in Boston in 1840, Bronson moved his family to Concord, drawn there by his friend and steadfast, if often exasperated, supporter Ralph Waldo Emerson. As usual, Bronson's plans were foggy, but he was an infinitely hopeful man who believed that he need only be true to his principles

*Amos Bronson Alcott, mystical idealist and begetter of the
unfortunate* Orphic Sayings, *which a wag of the day likened to "a
train of fifteen coaches going by, with only one passenger." Others
were fond of pointing out that Bronson's most important contribution
to literature was, of course, his daughter Louisa.*

"to get not only a useful name, but bread and shelter, and raiment." Abba was not so sanguine; and she and her daughters would learn, painfully, that Providence is not always providential. Above all, it was Louisa who took that lesson to heart.

Alcott and her sisters received what would now be considered an extremely haphazard education. But books at home were choice, even if they were not plentiful; and gifted instructors like Thoreau—for botany—were at hand. As a child, Alcott was rambunctious, strong-willed, energetic, full of fun, and given to "moods." No boy passed muster with Alcott until she had beaten him in a race, and "no girl if she refused to climb fences, and be a tomboy." She often said that her greatest grief was that she had not been born a boy. One childhood companion remembered a tall, slim, dark young girl, adding that "limbs predominated and were used freely." Perhaps not surprisingly, Alcott developed a keen sense of the ludicrous at a very young age.

In the spring of 1842, Bronson sailed for England, where he discoursed on "New Ideas and the New Time" with sundry reformers and visited an innovative school that had been named in his honor. Flush with the sort of success he had never known in Concord, he returned in the fall, bringing with him a handful of Englishmen, fellow devotees of the "Newness," with whom he planned to establish a utopian community in New England. And so on June 1, 1843, the "Consociate Family," a motley assemblage that included the not entirely enthusiastic Abba Alcott and her daughters, took possession of a run-down farm on the slope of Prospect Hill in the tiny hamlet of Harvard, Massachusetts. The ninety acres of rocky soil and the ramshackle farmhouse were christened "Fruitlands" by Bronson, whose admiration for the apple bordered on idolatry. All were secure in their faith that "the land awaits the sober culture of devout men." Emerson, who visited Fruitlands in the summer, was more astute. "They look well in July; we will see them in December." It was a fiasco.

Years later, in "Transcendental Wild Oats," her most amusing account of the rise and fall of the hapless Consociate Family, Alcott brilliantly skewered the linen-clad communitarians of Fruitlands. In that droll story, the shenanigans on Prospect Hill read as farce. But in fact, the disintegration of Fruitlands was terribly traumatic for Alcott and her sisters. On December 10, 1843, just after her eleventh birthday, she wrote in her journal, "In the eve father and mother and Anna and I had a long talk. I was very unhappy, and we all cried. Anna and I cried in bed, and prayed God to keep us all together." Long convinced that he was possessed of gifts "that the age needs to have put in exercise," Bronson actually discussed with Abba and the girls whether it would be best for all if he struck out on his own. The family remained intact, but the heretofore supremely self-confident Bronson collapsed into a suicidal depression.

Abba now took charge, securing three rooms and a kitchen—at 50 cents a week—in a village about a mile from Fruitlands, and on January 16, 1844, the Alcotts abandoned their New Eden. Louisa Alcott never forgot that debacle, and there was to be much more wandering and disappointment after Fruitlands; many more humiliating loans, harassing debts, and cadging from friends and family; illnesses and separations and years of toil and endless scrambling that always seemed to land the family back precisely where it had begun. And through it all, Alcott wrote, turning to her "Imagination Book" as both solace and "vent." As a child at Fruitlands, she had studied a picture of the great Swedish soprano Jenny Lind. "She must be a happy girl," she thought. "I should like to be famous as she is."

IN THE FALL OF 1844, THE ALCOTTS RETURNED TO CONCORD, AND the next spring, with a small inheritance that had come to Abba from her father, augmented by a five-hundred-dollar gift from the ever generous Emerson, they bought an old clapboard house on the Lexington Road. This unprepossessing structure Bronson enlarged, skillfully beautified, and landscaped, and baptized "Hillside." (In 1852, the place was purchased from the Alcotts by Nathaniel Hawthorne, who renamed it "The Wayside.")

In many ways, the years at Hillside were a magical time for Louisa

Alcott. There were the splendid amateur theatricals in the barn, in which she soared to melodramatic heights as playwright, designer, dramaturge, and actress, indulging her natural taste for the "lurid," so preferable to more wholesome fare, as long as it was "strong and true." She devoured Dickens, Shakespeare, Goethe (her "chief idol"), and, as always, the Alcott family favorite, *The Pilgrim's Progress.* When, at fifteen, the "book mania" descended on Alcott with full force, she boldly ventured into Emerson's library to ask him what she should read. "Wait a little for that," he said, as she looked at his treasures. "Meantime try this, and if you like it, come again." She opened a little school in the Hillside barn, with Emerson's children as her star pupils; she wrote flowery poetry and her first story; and she explored forest and field with that most romantic and enthralling of misanthropes, Henry David Thoreau, whose beautiful gray eyes "seemed to pierce through all disguises."

The idyll of Hillside could not last, for Concord had scant use for Bronson Alcott, the chronically unemployed schoolteacher whose generally incomprehensible "Orphic Sayings," which Margaret Fuller had published only reluctantly in *The Dial,* had made him a laughingstock. In the fall of 1848, the family moved to Boston, where, with the help of some influential patrons, Abba was launched into the working world as a "Missionary to the Poor." Bronson began to hold the philosophical "Conversations" that were to bring him both acolytes and ridicule, as well as—one day—a measure of fame as the "Sage of Concord."

For Louisa Alcott, now began what might be called her apprenticeship to life. Boston offered numerous enticements, especially, of course, the theater, and she was felled by more than one "stagestruck fit." But for the most part, life now meant work, and she turned her hand to almost anything she could in an unending, herculean effort to keep the "Alcott Sinking Fund" afloat. She took in mountains of sewing, taught kindergarten (hated it), tried governessing, and even worked as a servant in the household of an odious lawyer, earning the grand sum of four dollars for seven weeks of backbreaking labor. She continued to write, stories simmering away in her head as she stitched pillowcases into the night.

Alcott was twenty-two when her first book, *Flower Fables,* was published. This charming collection of fairy tales, which she had woven for Emerson's daughter Ellen, years before in the barn at Hillside, brought her $32. On Christmas Day in 1854, she presented a copy of her "firstborn" to Abba, telling her mother that she hoped "to pass in time from fairies and fables to men and realities." In the fall of 1857, the Alcotts left Walpole, New Hampshire, where they had settled for two years, and returned yet again to Concord. In the spring, Lizzie Alcott died after a long and tormenting decline, having contracted scarlet fever when the family lived in New Hampshire. Her death was not unexpected, but still it was a great blow to the family. In the summer, the Alcotts moved to a new home, a rather dilapidated affair that Bronson crowned "Orchard House." At last the wandering family was anchored, and indeed, this "pretty retreat" was to be the family mansion for twenty-five years. Alcott, who found "the proper grayness of Concord" stifling, spent much of her time in Boston, where she preferred to do her writing.

In November 1862, Alcott took the very bold step, for a young woman of her class, of volunteering as an army nurse in a Civil War hospital. She was not a man and could not enlist, but she would do her part. Marched to the station by her sister May and Hawthorne's son Julian, she felt for all the world as if she were "the son of the house going to war." She arrived at the almost unbelievably squalid Union Hotel Hospital in Georgetown just before the huge number of casualties from the Battle of Fredericksburg began to pour in. Here indeed was reality. "I never began the year," she wrote in January, "in a stranger place than this, five hundred miles from home, alone among strangers, doing painful duties all day long, & leading a life of constant excitement in this great house surrounded by 3 or 4 hundred men in all stages of suffering, disease & death."

Alcott's tour of duty was cut short after only six weeks when she

North Main Street, Concord, from a stereograph taken sometime in the 1870s.

contracted typhoid fever and, in a state of delirium, was brought home to Concord by her father. "Recovered my senses," she noted in February, by March, she was able to get about a little. But Alcott never fully recovered her health, her system poisoned by the doses of calomel (a deadly mercury compound—standard issue then) that she had been administered for her fever. The witty, vivid, biting, and moving *Hospital Sketches* (1863), cast from the letters she had written home from the Union Hotel Hospital, were Alcott's first real literary success. Much to her surprise and delight, she had "done a good thing without even knowing it."

While still in Georgetown, Alcott received word that her melodramatic shocker "Pauline's Passion and Punishment" had taken first place in a competition sponsored by *Frank Leslie's Illustrated Newspaper*. This is one of the first of the wonderful "blood & thunder" tales with which a certain "lady of Massachusetts" would illuminate the gaudy tabloids of her day. With her one hundred dollars in prize money, Alcott promptly paid off some bills, glad that her winter had born "visible fruit."

Throughout the 1860s, Alcott continued to churn out "rubbishy" tales, published anonymously or pseudonymously, that "paid the butcher's bill," "put down a new carpet," and generally blessed her family "in the way of groceries and gowns." Savvy editors like Frank Leslie were ready to snap up anything she wrote, but Alcott often claimed that she despised the sensational potboilers that kept the family "cosey," that she was in it just for the money. But she also once told an interviewer, "I think my natural ambition is for the lurid style. I indulge in gorgeous fancies and wish that I dared inscribe them upon my pages and set them before the public."

After the tremendous success of *Little Women* in 1868, Alcott abandoned, for the most part, the fiends, drug addicts, assassins, femme fatales, sumptuous settings, flaming passions, and grand catastrophes of her ever enticing sensation tales. In 1864, she had published her first novel, *Moods,* an intriguing and very romantic study of marriage (and mismarriage) inspired by a line from Emerson: "Life is a train of

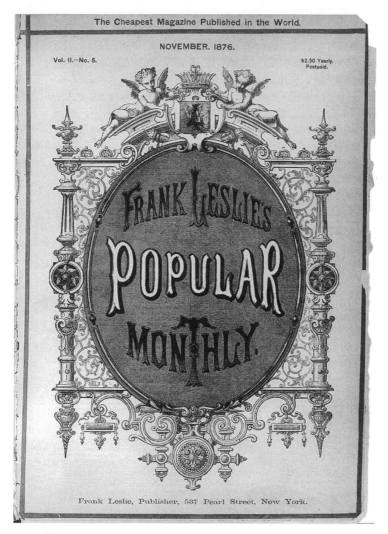

The Cheapest Magazine Published in the World.

NOVEMBER. 1876.

Vol. II.—No. 5.

$2.50 Yearly,
Postpaid.

Frank Leslie, Publisher, 587 Pearl Street, New York.

Frank Leslie's Popular Monthly *featured tales of royalty, wild animals, military and scientific expeditions, and general daring-do. This issue reprints "Perilous Play," Alcott's very odd sensation tale, for which she crafted one of her best closing lines—* "Heaven bless hashish, if its dreams end like this!"

moods like a string of beads, and as we pass through them they prove to be many-colored lenses which paint the world their own hue, and each shows only what lies in its focus." A work close to Alcott's heart, *Moods* scored a moderate success; but it did shock some readers, who accused its author of "speaking freely" of the bonds of holy matrimony. Ironically, it was *Little Women*, a book Alcott did not even want to write, that established her wealth and fame, and in short order, after it was published on October 1, 1868. The next spring, as the "sweet and wholesome influence" of the March family saga wafted across the land, Alcott exulted in her freedom: "Paid up all the debts, thank the Lord!—every penny that money can pay,—and now I feel as if I could die in peace."

As it frequently does, fame proved to be a dubious blessing. Reporters quickly converged on Concord for a look at the great "authoress," but like her old neighbor, the notoriously elusive Hawthorne, Alcott preferred to dodge into the woods to avoid capture. She was half amused and half furious to find herself besieged by the sort of "autograph fiends" who swore to treasure—for eternity—the grasshoppers they plucked from her front yard; and was infuriated that her family's privacy was constantly invaded. It often seemed as if fame and fortune brought her but little pleasure, except when she could employ those powerful possessions to assist the people she loved.

From 1870 onward, Alcott turned out a steady succession of "healthy and hearty" novels, tales, and sketches for a seemingly insatiable audience of children and young adults. "Though I do not enjoy writing 'moral tales' for the young, I do it because it pays well," she told a correspondent, well aware of the price she was paying to keep the "pathetic family" going. Her role as "Dear Aunt Jo" all too often left her unfulfilled, her brain "squeezed dry," and so she relished the writing of *A Modern Mephistopheles*, a steamy and powerful psychological thriller that was issued, anonymously, in 1877. She particularly relished the guessing games that ensued, not least when her friends said to her, "I know you didn't write it, for you can't hide your peculiar style."

To modern tastes, Alcott's cheerily energetic "moral tales," most with a salutary lesson neatly tucked in, can seem overly sentimental and simplistic. But often the lesson looked to the future, as when the heroine of *Rose in Bloom* (1876) takes up the banner for women's rights:

> We've got minds and souls as well as hearts; ambition and talents as well as beauty and accomplishments; and we want to live and learn as well as love and be loved. I'm sick of being told that is all a woman is fit for! I won't have anything to do with love until I prove that I am something beside a house-keeper and a baby-tender!

Temperance, vegetarianism, woman suffrage, educational and health reforms, abolition: she was, after all, an Alcott, and as Madeleine Stern has written, her parents had passed on to her a "legacy of iconoclasm." When women gained the right to vote for the Concord school committee in 1880, Alcott was first in line. And she was proud to pay the poll tax: "As my head is my most valuable piece of property I thought $2.00 a cheap tax on it."

Alcott's last years were devoted to the care of her father, who, after suffering a stroke in 1882, reposed placidly among his transcendental mists until his death six years later. She also assumed the burden (and joy) of raising her niece Lulu, the only child of her youngest sister, May, who died in Paris in 1879, six weeks after giving birth to her first child. Alcott was often in very poor health, and increasingly found it more and more difficult to write; her last novel, *Jo's Boys* (1886), took a very uncharacteristic four years to complete. Her journals and diaries chart, in poignant and painful detail, her myriad sufferings and an interminable round of dosings, quackery, despair, "cures," and, too rarely, relief. On March 6, 1888, she passed away in a convalescent home in Roxbury, near Boston, probably unaware that, two days before, at the family's home on Beacon Hill, Bronson had gone ahead of her.

ABOUT THIS EDITION

THE LOUISA MAY ALCOTT WHO HAS BEEN MESMERIZING LEGIONS of new readers during the past couple of decades is most definitely *not* the same Louisa May Alcott whose "life of beneficence and self-abnegation" was so admired by her contemporaries. Unquestionably, Alcott's days overflowed with generosity (hers) and self-denial (hers again), and noble-minded late Victorians were duly appreciative. But what *they* missed out on was the gutsy, acerbic, down-to-earth, powerfully driven woman and writer who has only recently begun to come into focus with the publication of her diaries and letters, and—most important—with the excavation of her long buried "blood & thunder tales." Madeleine Stern and Leona Rostenberg were the pioneering scholars who led the charge, with fresh brigades of Alcottians amassing in the rear. Critics and theorists have been quick to pounce, but "Invincible Louisa" is not only smarter than most of her evaluators, she is a far superior writer.

In this unprecedented collection of Alcott's most revealing public and private writings, a rich portrait of a fascinating woman emerges, but it is not—be forewarned—of "Aunt Jo." A shrewd Concordian once observed that Concord was large enough for Thoreau, but it could not suffice for the cosmopolitan Miss Alcott, who "had no proclivity for paddling up and down Concord River in search of ideas." Similarly, one can say that Alcott is far larger than *Little Women*, great as that book is. In these pages, one will find Concord's most famous daughter dipping her pen into a dazzling array of inkstands.

There is a lot of multifaceted literary virtuosity on display here, and it is accompanied by an intriguing selection of manuscripts, letters, photographs, and other treasures drawn from the special collections of The New York Public Library. Not only do these rarely seen artifacts vividly evoke the successful woman of letters, but they also afford intimate glimpses into the life of the very private woman who, unlike everyone else, was hardly impressed by her own great celebrity and for whom beloved family and dear friends were what truly mattered in life.

The portrait of the writer and her world that emerges in this volume is humorous, touching, surprising, varicolored, and gripping, and it may startle those who have long thought of Alcott as a sort of comforting, if rather fusty, overstuffed Victorian sofa. She in fact brandished a highly versatile pen that delivered both caresses and well-placed puncture wounds; and she was no granitic moralist (bearing the Jo Marches of the silver screen in mind, one might say that the *real* Jo was probably closer in spirit to Katharine Hepburn than she was to June Allyson). Alcott once joked with an interviewer that her dear old town of Concord "has never known a startling hue since the redcoats were there." But then, as she knew full well, Concord had not yet *really* read Louisa May Alcott.

SKETCHES FROM LIFE

Two of the "sketches" included here—"Transcendental Wild Oats" (1873) and "How I Went Out to Service" (1874)—are closely modeled on crucial (and painful) experiences in Alcott's life, but both can be savored even if one knows absolutely nothing about the Concord

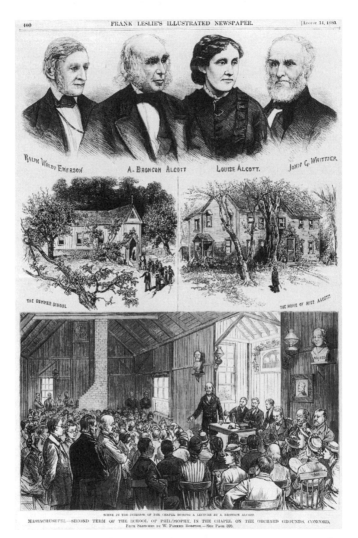

Four luminaries of American letters, from the August 14, 1880, issue of
Frank Leslie's Illustrated Newspaper. At the bottom of the page, Bronson
delivers a lecture at the Concord School of Philosophy while Emerson, just
four to his left, appears to be resting his eyes.

Scheherazade. In the former, Alcott, writing with sharpened quill, looks back to the Fruitlands debacle. It was meant to be a chapter in a projected work on her father's life—titled, tellingly, *The Cost of an Idea*—which, sadly, Alcott did not complete. For complex reasons, she found it difficult to write about her father (after all, Mr. March's most distinguishing characteristic in *Little Women* is his absence), a fact that has excited the analytically inclined as the flower does the bee. But in "Transcendental Wild Oats" he is there—and in all his glory—as Abel Lamb. Alcott's send-up of misty-minded idealists who dined on "bowls of sunshine for breakfast" must have offended *someone*, but apparently not her father. Bronson touchingly wrote in his journal that Louisa's "new story" surprised him by "the boldness and truthfulness of its strokes."

"How I Went Out to Service" is an acidly humorous recounting of what Madeleine Stern has called the "Humiliation at Dedham," the brief period when Alcott worked as a servant in that Massachusetts town. "Starved & frozen" was how she bluntly described it in her diary. Perhaps the worst of it, if one can credit the story, was that her employer, the Honorable James Richardson, attempted to seduce her with Hegel, an excruciating experience to be sure. One longs to know if Mr. Richardson somehow stumbled upon Alcott's story when it was published in *The Independent*.

In the simple and affecting "Recollections of My Childhood" (1888), Alcott sketched her life for *The Youth's Companion* not long before her death, recalling the girl who had thought she "must have been a deer or a horse in some former state, because it was such a joy to run." The tone of this romanticized version of a life that was often extremely difficult is achingly nostalgic and, for its young audience, suitably inspiring.

Alcott's flowering as a writer began truly to gather steam with *Hospital Sketches* (1863), her comic, vibrant, and pathetic—in the sense of the word her audience would have understood: that which excites pity or sadness—dispatches from a Civil War hospital. With its Dickensian gusto and sparkling style, *Hospital Sketches* scored a hit and "Tribulation Periwinkle" (Alcott's *nom de nurse*) entranced everyone, even the august Henry James, Sr. With characteristic drollery, Alcott wrote to her publisher:

> I had a visit from an army surgeon the other day who considered my mules striking likenesses, & the book "one to do no end of good both in & out of the army &c." I didn't quite see how but haven't the least objection to its revolutionizing the globe if it can. All is pleasant & looks promising. I have hope such a powerful work won't distract the mind of the nation from more useful matters.

Alcott never earned much from the book, but as she commented to herself in her journal, "The 'Sketches' . . . showed me 'my style,' and taking the hint, I went where glory awaited me." Even if it fails to revolutionize the globe, it is time this marvelous book was more widely known.

FROM THE MAGIC INKSTAND: FOUR STORIES

"I am trying to turn my brains into money by stories," Alcott told her father in an affectionate letter written from Boston on November 28, 1855, one day before his fifty-sixth birthday (and her twenty-third). It would be a number of years before she would make good on her declaration that "though an *Alcott*, I *can* support myself." But by 1863 she could write in her journal, "A year ago I had no publisher, and went begging with my wares; now *three* have asked me for something, several papers are ready to print my contributions, and F. B. S[anborn] says 'any publisher this side of Baltimore would be glad to get a book.' " She had more than earned the right to crow a little, and by any reckoning, 1863 was a banner year for Alcott. Not only did *Hospital Sketches* arrive, to general acclaim, but Alcott also placed a poem, one of her best ("Thoreau's Flute"), and two stories ("Debby's Debut" and "My Contraband") in *The Atlantic Monthly*, which really *was* something, even if, as she claimed, passing the *"Atlantic* test" wasn't worth "two straws." This collection features those two very different *Atlantic* stories (the latter, at the editor's insistence, was printed as "The Brothers") as well a third tale from the same year ("Pauline's Passion and Punishment"), which would seem to be the child of an altogether more sultry clime than that available to Alcott in either Concord or Boston. Taken together, these three gems of her fancy give an idea of what Alcott was capable of when she was "living in her inkstand."

In December 1862, after plowing through hundreds of manuscripts, the editors of *Frank Leslie's Illustrated Newspaper* selected the work of a certain "lady of Massachusetts" as their Prize Story. Her submission, "Pauline's Passion and Punishment," was judged to be of "exceeding power, brilliant description, thrilling incident and unexceptionable moral." Still, in spite of this last, Concord would probably have been aghast to learn that the author of this heavy-breathing, prize-winning potboiler was none other than Louisa May Alcott.

The other two tales from 1863 selected for this anthology— "Debby's Debut" and "My Contraband"—provide a vivid contrast to the grand histrionics of "Pauline's Passion and Punishment," showing, as Madeleine Stern has said, how, early in her career, Alcott "seesawed between the romantic and the plausible." Written with one eyebrow firmly arched, "Debby's Debut" is a romantic and most enjoyable comedy of manners in which Alcott, who very much disliked any kind of pretentiousness, has some fun with "Society." In the strange and powerful tale "My Contraband," two half-brothers—one a dissolute Confederate soldier, the other a handsome "contraband" (during the Civil War, a slave who had escaped behind Union lines or who had remained in territory captured by the Union Army)—are reunited, fatefully. "My Contraband" is an especially fascinating example of

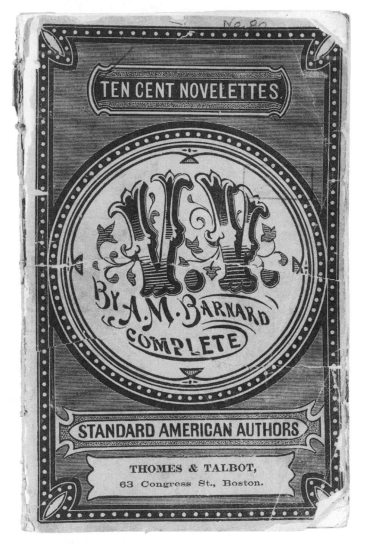

No. 80

TEN CENT NOVELETTES

BY A.M. BARNARD

COMPLETE

STANDARD AMERICAN AUTHORS

THOMES & TALBOT,
63 Congress St., Boston.

In 1864, Alcott dashed off this lurid shocker, which positively revels in the evil machinations of the thoroughly rotten Virginie Varens.

what one critic has described as Alcott's "violently partisan" war stories.

The briefest story included in this volume, "Perilous Play" (1869), is one of Alcott's last potboilers, and for many a modern sensibility, it may prove to be one of the more shocking of the shockers. For this ripe tale of hashish experimentation, which, surprisingly, appeared under Alcott's name when it was republished in *Frank Leslie's Popular Monthly* in 1876, seems to take as its motto: Just Say Yes.

A CHOICE COLLECTION OF POEMS

Alcott claimed to know little of poetry ("I never read modern attempts"), and as she told a friend, even so fine a poem as "Thoreau's Flute" was never meant to go beyond the pages of her scrapbook. It may well not have been her "forte," but Alcott in fact wrote a great deal of fluent, often very funny verse. In this anthology we have gathered together five of the best poems she wrote about her own life and the people who meant the most to her.

"The Hawthorne" (1862–63), Alcott's gracious tribute to her neighbors at The Wayside, closes by ranking the noble Hawthorne with "Emerson's pine & Thoreau's oak." According to Hawthorne's wife, Sophia, "Thoreau's Flute" (1862–63) was "an inspiration one Midnight at Georgetown," and was not actually written down by Alcott until she had recovered from the severe bout of typhoid fever that nearly killed her. It was Mrs. Hawthorne who brought the poem to the attention of *The Atlantic Monthly*, where it was published in September 1863. As was common at the time, "Thoreau's Flute" appeared without its author's name appended to it, and this leads to a lovely story that comes from Maria S. Porter, who knew Alcott well.

One day, as Mr. Alcott was calling upon Longfellow, the poet took up the last *Atlantic* and said, "I want to read to you

Emerson's fine poem on Thoreau's Flute." As he began to read, Mr. Alcott interrupted him, exclaiming with delight, "My daughter Louisa wrote that!" In telling me of this, Louisa said, "Do you wonder that I felt as proud as a peacock when father came home and told me?"

When her mother died on November 25, 1877, Alcott felt that a great warmth had gone out of life. "My only comfort," she reflected, "is that I *could* make her last years comfortable, and lift off the burden she has carried so bravely all these years." In February, she wrote the beautiful poem "The Transfiguration" (1878) to her mother's memory. It was first published in *A Masque of Poets* (1878), one of the volumes in Roberts Brothers' "No Name Series" (in which the authorship of each novel, tale, and poem chosen for the series was "to remain an inviolable secret").

May Alcott Nieriker, the youngest of the "little women," died in Paris on December 29, 1879. As a young girl, May was highly independent and spirited (after Louisa, one childhood friend would recall, she was "the biggest romp among her sisters"); and she is memorably reconstituted in *Little Women* as that "regular snow maiden" Amy, who "always carried herself like a young lady mindful of her manners." A gifted and ambitious artist whose copies after Turner were praised by Ruskin, at thirty-seven May married—very happily—a Swiss businessman fifteen years her junior. But she died less than two years later, just seven weeks after giving birth to her first child, a daughter who was christened Louisa May Nieriker. The loss of the family's "midsummer girl" was, Alcott wrote despairingly in her journal, "a very bitter sorrow for all." As she had done when Marmee died, Alcott poured her grief into words, and with "Our Madonna" (1880) lovingly sketched the life of the "bright soul" whose death was almost more than she could bear.

In a 1932 magazine article, the then quite ancient Julian Hawthorne fondly recalled his great friend Louisa May Alcott as a woman of

honesty, goodwill, and common sense, adding with the amiable condescension of a man of another era that she possessed "humor surpassing
the ordinary humor of women—an attitude of comedy in her daily
conversation, but poised and inwardly sparkling." Alcott generally
reserved her most glittering sallies for her intimate friends or family
(though one doubts that many of these penetrated the genial fog that
enveloped Bronson); but now and then, she went public. Maria S.
Porter has recorded that Alcott occasionally delivered her nonsense
rhymes (or "jingles," as she called them) at the Concord woman's
club; and that the effect produced by such priceless ditties as "A Wail
Uttered in the Woman's Club" (ca. late 1870s/early 1880s) was, inevitably, "shouts of merriment, followed by heartiest applause." These
stanzas take aim both at the pretensions of Concord's coterie of male
philosophers and at the fiends who, descending on Concord in search
of genius, made the author's life a living hell. "[T]he Alcotts are not
on exhibition in any way," Louisa was forced to remind an acquaintance who wanted to drop by Orchard House with some of *her* friends.
Fame had indeed proven to be an "expensive luxury," and beneath the
hilarity of Alcott's "Wail" lies an immense anger at a public which did
not understand that "the books belong to them but not the peace, time,
comfort and lives of the writers."

The Heart of Louisa May Alcott: Letters and Journals

To the common reader, the critical controversies that percolate in
academic coffeepots can seem arcane if not downright dull and beside
the point. (To quote Mrs. Gamp, "Them which is of other naturs
thinks different.") This is not to say that literary criticism, psychobio-
graphical sleuthing, and other forms of homage to an author do not
have their place, in or out of academe; but the best—and usually most
enjoyable—way into the heart of a writer's life is to be found in a

more luminous place, right there, quietly waiting within her private writings. With these, she seems to speak directly to the reader's soul.

Sadly, parts of Alcott's private voice and private world have vanished forever. "Sorted old letters," she noted in her journal in 1885. "Not wise to keep for curious eyes to read, & gossip-lovers to print by & by." (It should also be noted that families then were, in general, rather rigorous about burning most of the deceased's papers whenever a loved one "crossed over.") Alcott did maintain a journal faithfully for most of her life, supplementing the record of some years with small pocket diaries in which she jotted down brief summaries of her activities. But over the years portions of this autobiographical record were also lost; and even though it seems she may have contemplated the eventual publication of at least sections of her journal, Alcott probably destroyed some of it herself. (In 1882, following her mother's wishes, she also destroyed Abba's diaries—a great loss, for, to judge by what has survived of *her* private writings, Abba may well have wielded the most powerful pen in the family. Louisa Alcott did not take her style from Bronson.) But the letters and journals that have come down to us are choice.

This anthology is graced with a number of Alcott's most vibrant, interesting, and revealing letters; and these are nicely complemented by generous excerpts from her very moving journals. Alcott reread her journals periodically, and often added notes or commentary—alternately laconic, drily deadpan, or contemplative—to passages that had been written long before. In 1885, she reread her account of the day, forty years past, when she had torn out of the woods round Concord and come upon a meadow flooded in sunshine (adding a note, that on that day, the "little girl 'got religion' "):

> It seemed like going through a dark life or grave into heaven beyond. A very strange and solemn feeling came over me as I stood there, with no sound but the rustle of the pines, no one near me, and the sun so glorious, as for me alone. It seemed as

if I *felt* God as I never did before, and I prayed in my heart that
I might keep that happy sense of nearness in my life.

She was thirteen; her style, simple and direct. This, years before she
would forge her professional credo: "Never use a long word when a
short one will do as well."

In a perceptive and nuanced article published in *Vogue* in 1995
("Does *Little Women* Belittle Women?"), Mary Gaitskill speaks of the
"visceral tenderness" with which Alcott wrote of young women in her
work, of how she wrote "about a way of life that was congruent with
her gut-level principles." As we hope to show with this anthology,
tenderness and principle (along with, needless to say, some healthy
doses of the "fun and follies in every-day life") are woven bountifully
throughout Alcott's letters and journals.

She Stood Out: Remembering
Louisa May Alcott

"Louisa, when I first saw her, was a black-haired, red-cheeked, long-
legged hobbledehoy of 28, though not looking or seeming near that
age. But there was power in her jaw and control in her black eyes;
good nature in her generous mouth, and jollity in her laugh; in short,
she was a leader, and, in a place like Concord, she stood out." Thus
Julian Hawthorne, more than seventy years after he first met Louisa
May Alcott. *She stood out.* That may be the simplest and even the most
elegant way to express what was so remarkable about the genius who,
as a young girl, had so longed to do something splendid and heroic
with her life. "I don't know what," announces Jo in *Little Women*,
"but I'm on the watch for it, and mean to astonish you all, some day."
Most of Alcott's contemporaries would indeed be astonished by what
"Jo" was to accomplish (even if the precociously pompous Henry
James took it upon himself to explain to Alcott that she was *not* a

genius); but those who knew her well were not surprised by her achievement.

The reminiscences and ruminations gathered together in this volume overflow with candor, warmth, color, and life. Three of the writers (Emerson, Hawthorne, and Porter) knew Alcott intimately, and pay tribute to her with great affection (that perceptive and urbane raconteur Julian Hawthorne seems to have been especially smitten). Mrs. Wood was in fact closest to Lizzie among the Alcott girls, but late in life she looked back to her own childhood, and there was wild Louisa, who always seemed to be doing her best to scandalize "dull old Concord."

Two bracing originals—one American (Ives), one British (Chesterton)—take Louisa & Co. under consideration, and although neither ever met the Concord Scheherazade, after reading their musings one certainly wishes they had, as it is easy to imagine these three getting on splendidly. Bronson's loving poem to his daughter speaks—unforgettably—for itself.

OF THE YOUNG LOUISA, WITH HER MASSES OF CHESTNUT HAIR, HER sparkling eyes, her flyaway clothes, and her ink-stained hands, Madelon Bedell has written, eloquently, "She wished for greatness. In truth, she was already great, if by the word we mean large, expansive, ready to act at all times without regard for consequences in pursuit of a grand aim: in that sense Louisa had been great since childhood." When, just before her twenty-third birthday, Alcott finally decided to abandon her dream of a career as an actress, she wrote to her father:

> After being on the stage & seeing more nearly the tinsel & brass of actor life (much as I should love to be a great star *if* I could), I have come to the conclusion that it's not worth trying for at the expense of health & peace of mind, & I shall try to be contented with the small part already given me & acting that well try to mix the tragedy & comedy of life so wisely that

when the curtain falls I can jump up as briskly as the stage dead always do, & cheered by the applause of my little audience here, go away to learn & act a new & better part in the Lord's theatre where all *good* actors are *stars*.

She did not know that her "small part" had already placed her among the stars.

LOUISA MAY ALCOTT:

AN INTIMATE ANTHOLOGY

PART 1

SKETCHES FROM LIFE:
Autobiographical Stories and Essays

RECOLLECTIONS OF
MY CHILDHOOD

O NE OF MY EARLIEST MEMORIES IS OF PLAYING WITH BOOKS IN my father's study. Building towers and bridges of the big dictionaries, looking at pictures, pretending to read, and scribbling on blank pages whenever pen or pencil could be found. Many of these first attempts at authorship still exist, and I often wonder if these childish plays did not influence my after life, since books have been my greatest comfort, castle-building a never-failing delight, and scribbling a very profitable amusement.

Another very vivid recollection is of the day when running after my hoop I fell into the Frog Pond and was rescued by a black boy, becoming a friend to the colored race then and there, though my mother always declared that I was an abolitionist at the age of three.

During the Garrison riot in Boston the portrait of George Thompson was hidden under a bed in our house for safe-keeping, and I am told that I used to go and comfort "the good man who helped poor slaves" in his captivity. However that may be, the conversion was genuine, and my greatest pride is in the fact that I have lived to know the brave men and women who did so much for the cause, and that I had a very small share in the war which put an end to a great wrong.

Being born on the birthday of Columbus I seem to have something of my patron saint's spirit of adventure, and running away was one of the delights of my childhood. Many a social lunch have I shared with hospitable Irish beggar children, as we ate our crusts, cold potatoes and salt fish on voyages of discovery among the ash heaps of the waste land that then lay where the Albany station now stands.

Many an impromptu picnic have I had on the dear old Common, with strange boys, pretty babies and friendly dogs, who always seemed to feel that this reckless young person needed looking after.

On one occasion the town-crier found me fast asleep at nine o'clock at night, on a door-step in Bedford Street, with my head pillowed on the curly breast of a big Newfoundland, who was with difficulty persuaded to release the weary little wanderer who had sobbed herself to sleep there.

I often smile as I pass that door, and never forget to give a grateful pat to every big dog I meet, for never have I slept more soundly than on that dusty step, nor found a better friend than the noble animal who watched over the lost baby so faithfully.

My father's school was the only one I ever went to, and when this was broken up because he introduced methods now all the fashion, our lessons went on at home, for he was always sure of four little pupils who firmly believed in their teacher, though they have not done him all the credit he deserved.

I never liked arithmetic or grammar, and dodged these branches on all occasions; but reading, composition, history and geography I enjoyed, as well as the stories read to us with a skill which made the dullest charming and useful.

"Pilgrim's Progress," Krummacher's "Parables," Miss Edgeworth, and the best of the dear old fairy tales made that hour the pleasantest of our day. On Sundays we had a simple service of Bible stories, hymns, and conversation about the state of our little consciences and the conduct of our childish lives which never will be forgotten.

Walks each morning round the Common while in the city, and long tramps over hill and dale when our home was in the country, were a part of our education, as well as every sort of housework, for which I have always been very grateful, since such knowledge makes one independent in these days of domestic tribulation with the help who are too often only hindrances.

Needle-work began early, and at ten my skilful sister made a linen shirt beautifully, while at twelve I set up as a doll's dress-maker, with my sign out, and wonderful models in my window. All the children employed me, and my turbans were the rage at one time to the great dismay of the neighbors' hens, who were hotly hunted down, that I might tweak out their downiest feathers to adorn the dolls' head-gear.

Active exercise was my delight from the time when a child of six I drove my hoop round the Common without stopping, to the days when I did my twenty miles in five hours and went to a party in the evening.

I always thought I must have been a deer or a horse in some former state, because it was such a joy to run. No boy could be my friend till I had beaten him in a race, and no girl if she refused to climb trees, leap fences and be a tomboy.

My wise mother, anxious to give me a strong body to support a lively brain, turned me loose in the country and let me run wild, learning of nature what no books can teach, and being led, as those who truly love her seldom fail to be,

Through nature up to nature's God.

I remember running over the hills just at dawn one summer morning, and pausing to rest in the silent woods saw, through an arch of trees, the sun rise over river, hill and wide green meadows as I never saw it before.

Something born of the lovely hour, a happy mood, and the unfolding aspirations of a child's soul seemed to bring me very near to God, and in the hush of that morning hour I always felt that I "got religion" as the phrase goes. A new and vital sense of His presence, tender and sustaining as a father's arms, came to me then, never to change through forty years of life's vicissitudes, but to grow stronger for the sharp discipline of poverty and pain, sorrow and success.

Those Concord days were the happiest of my life, for we had charming playmates in the little Emersons, Channings, Hawthornes and Goodwins, with the illustrious parents and their friends to enjoy our pranks and share our excursions.

Plays in the barn were a favorite amusement, and we dramatized the fairy tales in great style. Our giant came tumbling off a loft when Jack cut down the squash vine running up a ladder to represent the immortal bean. Cinderella rolled away in a vast pumpkin, and a long, black pudding was lowered by invisible hands to fasten itself on the nose of the woman who wasted her three wishes.

Little pilgrims journeyed over the hills with scrip and staff and cockleshells in their hats; elves held their pretty revels among the pines, and "Peter Wilkins' " flying ladies came swinging down on the birch tree-tops. Lords and ladies haunted the garden, and mermaids splashed in the bath-house of woven willows over the brook.

People wondered at our frolics, but enjoyed them, and droll stories are still told of the adventures of those days. Mr. Emerson and Margaret Fuller were visiting my parents one afternoon, and the conversation having turned to the ever interesting subject of education, Miss Fuller said:

"Well, Mr. Alcott, you have been able to carry out your methods in your own family, and I should like to see your model children."

She did in a few moments, for as the guests stood on the door steps a wild uproar approached, and round the corner of the house came a wheelbarrow holding baby May arrayed as a queen; I was the horse, bitted and bridled and driven by my elder sister Anna, while Lizzie played dog and barked as loud as her gentle voice permitted.

All were shouting and wild with fun which, however, came to a sudden end as we espied the stately group before us, for my foot tripped, and down we all went in a laughing heap, while my mother put a climax to the joke by saying with a dramatic wave of the hand:

"Here are the model children, Miss Fuller."

A portrait of Ralph Waldo Emerson, the idol of Alcott's youth. When he died on April 27, 1882, she wrote in her journal, "Our best & greatest American gone . . . & the man who has helped me most by his life, his books, his society . . . Illustrious & beloved friend, good bye!"

My sentimental period began at fifteen when I fell to writing romances, poems, a "heart journal," and dreaming dreams of a splendid future.

Browsing over Mr. Emerson's library I found "Goethe's Correspondence with a Child," and was at once fired with the desire to be a second Bettine, making my father's friend my Goethe. So I wrote letters to him, but was wise enough never to send them, left wild flowers on the doorsteps of my "Master," sung Mignon's song in very bad German under his window, and was fond of wandering by moonlight, or sitting in a cherry-tree at midnight till the owls scared me to bed.

The girlish folly did not last long, and the letters were burnt years ago, but Goethe is still my favorite author, and Emerson remained my beloved "Master" while he lived, doing more for me, as for many another young soul, than he ever knew, by the simple beauty of his life, the truth and wisdom of his books, the example of a good, great man untempted and unspoiled by the world which he made nobler while in it, and left the richer when he went.

The trials of life began about this time, and my happy childhood ended. Money is never plentiful in a philosopher's house, and even the maternal pelican could not supply all our wants on the small income which was freely shared with every needy soul who asked for help.

Fugitive slaves were sheltered under our roof, and my first pupil was a very black George Washington whom I taught to write on the hearth with charcoal, his big fingers finding pen and pencil unmanageable.

Motherless girls seeking protection were guarded among us; hungry travellers sent on to our door to be fed and warmed, and if the philosopher happened to own two coats the best went to a needy brother, for these were practical Christians who had the most perfect faith in Providence, and never found it betrayed.

In those days the prophets were not honored in their own land, and Concord had not yet discovered her great men. It was a sort of refuge for reformers of all sorts whom the good natives regarded as lunatics, harmless but amusing.

My father went away to hold his classes and conversations, and we women folk began to feel that we also might do something. So one gloomy November day we decided to move to Boston and try our fate again after some years in the wilderness.

My father's prospect was as promising as a philosopher's ever is in a money-making world, my mother's friends offered her a good salary as their missionary to the poor, and my sister and I hoped to teach. It was an anxious council; and always preferring action to discussion, I took a brisk run over the hill and then settled down for "a good think" in my favorite retreat.

It was an old cart-wheel, half hidden in grass under the locusts where I used to sit to wrestle with my sums, and usually forget them scribbling verses or fairy tales on my slate instead. Perched on the hub I surveyed the prospect and found it rather gloomy, with leafless trees, sere grass, leaden sky and frosty air, but the hopeful heart of fifteen beat warmly under the old red shawl, visions of success gave the gray clouds a silver lining, and I said defiantly, as I shook my fist at fate embodied in a crow cawing dismally on the fence near by,—

"I *will* do something by-and-by. Don't care what, teach, sew, act, write, anything to help the family; and I'll be rich and famous and happy before I die, see if I won't!"

Startled by this audacious outburst the crow flew away, but the old wheel creaked as if it began to turn at that moment, stirred by the intense desire of an ambitious girl to work for those she loved and find some reward when the duty was done.

I did not mind the omen then, and returned to the house cold but resolute. I think I began to shoulder my burden then and there, for when the free country life ended the wild colt soon learned to tug in harness, only breaking loose now and then for a taste of beloved liberty.

My sisters and I had cherished fine dreams of a home in the city, but when we found ourselves in a small house at the South End with not a tree in sight, only a back yard to play in, and no money to buy any of the splendors before us, we all rebelled and longed for the country again.

Anna soon found little pupils, and trudged away each morning to her daily task, pausing at the corner to wave her hand to me in answer to my salute with the duster. My father went to his classes at his room down town, mother to her all-absorbing poor, the little girls to school, and I was left to keep house, feeling like a caged sea-gull as I washed dishes and cooked in the basement kitchen where my prospect was limited to a procession of muddy boots.

Good drill, but very hard, and my only consolation was the evening reunion when all met with such varied reports of the day's adventures, we could not fail to find both amusement and instruction.

Father brought news from the upper world, and the wise, good people who adorned it; mother, usually much dilapidated because she *would* give away her clothes, with sad tales of suffering and sin from the darker side of life; gentle Anna a modest account of her success as teacher, for even at seventeen her sweet nature won all who knew her, and her patience quelled the most rebellious pupil.

My reports were usually a mixture of the tragic and the comic, and the children poured their small joys and woes into the family bosom where comfort and sympathy were always to be found.

Then we youngsters adjourned to the kitchen for our fun, which usually consisted of writing, dressing and acting a series of remarkable plays. In one I remember I took five parts and Anna four, with lightning changes of costume, and characters varying from a Greek prince in silver armor to a murderer in chains.

It was good training for memory and fingers, for we recited pages without a fault, and made every sort of property from a harp to a fairy's spangled wings. Later we acted Shakespeare, and Hamlet was my favorite hero, played with a gloomy glare and a tragic stalk which I have never seen surpassed.

But we were now beginning to play our parts on a real stage, and to know something of the pathetic side of life with its hard facts, irksome duties, many temptations and the daily sacrifice of self. Fortunately we had the truest, tenderest of guides and guards, and so learned the sweet uses of adversity, the value of honest work, the beautiful law of compensation which gives more than it takes, and the real significance of life.

At sixteen I began to teach twenty pupils, and for ten years learned to know and love children. The story writing went on all the while with the usual trials of beginners. Fairy tales told the Emersons made the first printed book, and "Hospital Sketches" the first successful one.

Every experience went into the chauldron to come out as froth, or evaporate in smoke, till time and suffering strengthened and clarified the mixture of truth and fancy, and a wholesome draught for children began to flow pleasantly and profitably.

So the omen proved a true one, and the wheel of fortune turned slowly, till the girl of fifteen found herself a woman of fifty with her prophetic dream beautifully realized, her duty done, her reward far greater than she deserved.

HOW I WENT OUT TO SERVICE

WHEN I WAS EIGHTEEN I WANTED SOMETHING TO DO. I HAD tried teaching for two years, and hated it; I had tried sewing, and could not earn my bread in that way, at the cost of health; I tried story-writing and got five dollars for stories which now bring a hundred; I had thought seriously of going upon the stage, but certain highly respectable relatives were so shocked at the mere idea that I relinquished my dramatic aspirations.

"What *shall* I do?" was still the question that perplexed me. I was ready to work, eager to be independent, and too proud to endure patronage. But the right task seemed hard to find, and my bottled energies were fermenting in a way that threatened an explosion before long.

My honored mother was a city missionary that winter, and not only served the clamorous poor, but often found it in her power to help decayed gentlefolk by quietly placing them where they could earn their bread without the entire sacrifice of taste and talent which makes poverty so hard for such to bear. Knowing her tact and skill, people often came to her for companions, housekeepers, and that class of the needy who do not make their wants known through an intelligence office.

One day, as I sat dreaming splendid dreams, while I made a series of little petticoats out of the odds and ends sent in for the poor, a tall, ministerial gentleman appeared, in search of a companion for his sister. He possessed an impressive nose, a fine flow of language, and a pair of large hands, encased in black kid gloves. With much waving of these somber members, Mr. R. set forth the delights awaiting the happy soul who should secure this home. He described it as a sort of heaven on earth. "There are books, pictures, flowers, a piano, and the best of society," he said. "This person will be one of the family in all respects, and only required to help about the lighter work, which my sister has done herself hitherto, but is now a martyr to neuralgia and needs a gentle friend to assist her."

My mother, who never lost her faith in human nature, spite of many impostures, believed every word, and quite beamed with benevolent interest as she listened and tried to recall some needy young woman to whom this charming home would be a blessing. I also innocently thought:

"That sounds inviting. I like housework and can do it well. I should have time to enjoy the books and things I love, and D—— is not far away from home. Suppose I try it."

So, when my mother turned to me, asking if I could suggest any one, I became as red as a poppy and said abruptly:

"Only myself."

"Do you really mean it?" cried my astonished parent.

"I really do if Mr. R. thinks I should suit," was my steady reply, as I partially obscured my crimson countenance behind a little flannel skirt, still redder.

The Reverend Josephus gazed upon me with the benign regard which a bachelor of five and thirty may accord a bashful damsel of eighteen. A smile dawned upon his countenance, "sicklied o'er with the pale cast of thought," or dyspepsia; and he softly folded the black gloves, as if about to bestow a blessing, as he replied, with emphasis:

"I am sure you would, and we should think ourselves most fortunate if we could secure your society, and—ahem—services for my poor sister."

"Then I'll try it," responded the impetuous maid.

"We will talk it over a little first, and let you know to-morrow, sir," put in my prudent parent, adding, as Mr. R—— arose: "What wages do you pay?"

"My dear madam, in a case like this let us not use such words as those. Anything you may think proper we shall gladly give. The labor is very light, for there are but three of us and our habits are of the simplest sort. I am a frail reed and may break at any moment; so is my sister, and my aged father cannot long remain; therefore, money is little to us, and any one who comes to lend her youth and strength to our feeble household will not be forgotten in the end, I assure you." And, with another pensive smile, a farewell wave of the impressive gloves, the Reverend Josephus bowed like a well-sweep and departed.

"My dear, are you in earnest?" asked my mother.

"Of course, I am. Why not try this experiment? It can but fail, like all the others."

"I have no objection; only I fancied you were rather too proud for this sort of thing."

"I am too proud to be idle and dependent, ma'am. I'll scrub floors and take in washing first. I do housework at home for love; why not do it abroad for money? I like it better than teaching. It is healthier than sewing and surer than writing. So why not try it?"

"It is going out to service, you know though you are called a companion. How does that suit?"

"I don't care. Every sort of work that is paid for is service; and I don't mind being a companion, if I can do it well. I may find it is my mission to take care of neuralgic old ladies and lackadaisical clergymen. It does not sound exciting, but it's better than nothing," I answered, with a sigh; for it *was* rather a sudden downfall to give up being a Siddons and become a Betcinder.

How my sisters laughed when they heard the new plan! But they soon resigned themselves, sure of fun, for Lu's adventures were the standing joke of the family. Of course, the highly respectable relatives held up their hands in holy horror at the idea of one of the clan degrading herself by going out to service. Teaching a private school was the proper thing for an indigent gentlewoman. Sewing even, if done in the seclusion of home and not mentioned in public, could be tolerated. Story-writing was a genteel accomplishment and reflected credit upon the name. But leaving the paternal roof to wash other people's tea-cups, nurse other people's ails, and obey other people's orders for hire—this, this was degradation; and headstrong Louisa would disgrace her name forever if she did it.

Opposition only fired the revolutionary blood in my veins, and I crowned my iniquity by the rebellious declaration:

"If doing this work hurts my respectability, I wouldn't give much for it. My aristocratic ancestors don't feed or clothe me and my democratic ideas of honesty and honor won't let me be idle or dependent. You need not know me if you are ashamed of me, and I won't ask you for a penny; so, if I never do succeed in anything, I shall have the immense satisfaction of knowing I am under no obligation to any one."

In spite of the laughter and the lamentation, I got ready my small wardrobe, consisting of two calico dresses and one delaine, made by myself, also several large and uncompromising blue aprons and three tidy little sweeping-caps; for I had some English notions about housework and felt that my muslin hair-protectors would be useful in some of the "light labors" I was to undertake. It is needless to say they were very becoming. Then, firmly embracing my family, I set forth one cold January day, with my little trunk, a stout heart, and a five-dollar bill for my fortune.

"She will be back in a week," was my sister's prophecy, as she wiped her weeping eye.

"No, she won't, for she has promised to stay the month out and she will keep her word," answered my mother, who always defended the black sheep of her flock.

I heard both speeches, and registered a tremendous vow to keep that promise, if I died in the attempt—little dreaming, poor innocent, what lay before me.

Josephus meantime had written me several remarkable letters, describing the different members of the family I was about to enter. His account was peculiar; but I believed every word of it and my romantic fancy was much excited by the details he gave. The principal ones are as follows, condensed from the voluminous epistles which he evidently enjoyed writing:

"You will find a stately mansion, fast falling to decay, for my father will have nothing repaired, preferring that the old house and its master should crumble away together. I have, however, been permitted to rescue a few rooms from ruin; and here I pass my recluse life, surrounded by the things I love. This will naturally be more attractive to you than the gloomy apartments my father inhabits, and I hope you will here allow me to minister to your young and cheerful nature when your daily cares are over. I need such companionship and shall always welcome you to my abode.

"Eliza, my sister, is a child at forty, for she has lived alone with my father and an old servant all her life. She is a good creature, but not lively, and needs stirring up, as you will soon see. Also I hope by your means to rescue her from the evil influence of Puah, who, in my estimation, is a *wretch*. She has gained entire control over Eliza, and warps her mind with great skill, prejudicing her against *me,* and thereby desolating my home. Puah hates *me* and always has. Why I know not, except that I will not yield to her control. She ruled here for years while I was away, and my return upset all her nefarious plans. It will always be my firm opinion that she has tried to *poison me*, and may again. But even this dark suspicion will not deter me from my duty. I cannot send her away, for both my deluded father and my sister have entire faith in her, and I cannot shake it. She is faithful and kind to them, so I submit and remain to guard them, even at the risk of my life.

"I tell you these things because I wish you to know all and be warned, for this old hag has a specious tongue, and I should grieve to see you deceived by her lies. Say nothing, but watch her silently, and help me to thwart her evil plots; but do not trust her, or beware."

Now this was altogether romantic and sensational, and I felt as if about to enter one of those delightfully dangerous houses we read of in novels, where perils, mysteries, and sins freely disport themselves, till the newcomer sets all to rights, after unheard of trials and escapes.

I arrived at twilight, just the proper time for the heroine to appear; and, as no one answered my modest solo on the rusty knocker, I walked in and looked about me. Yes, here was the long, shadowy hall, where the ghosts doubtless walked at midnight. Peering in at an open door on the right, I saw a parlor full of ancient furniture, faded, dusty, and dilapidated. Old portraits stared at me from the walls and a damp chill froze the marrow of my bones in the most approved style.

"The romance opens well," I thought, and, peeping in at an opposite door, beheld a luxurious apartment, full of the warm glow of firelight, the balmy breath of hyacinths and roses, the white glimmer of piano keys, and tempting rows of books along the walls.

The contrast between the two rooms was striking, and, after an admiring survey, I continued my explorations, thinking that I should not mind being "ministered to" in that inviting place when my work was done.

A third door showed me a plain, dull sitting-room, with an old man napping in his easy-chair. I heard voices in the kitchen beyond, and, entering there, beheld Puah the fiend. Unfortunately for the dramatic effect of the tableaux, all I saw was a mild-faced old woman, buttering toast, while she conversed with her familiar, a comfortable gray cat.

The old lady greeted me kindly, but I fancied her faded blue eye had a weird expression and her amiable words were all a snare, though I own I was rather disappointed at the commonplace appearance of this humble Borgia.

She showed me to a tiny room, where I felt more like a young giantess than ever, and was obliged to stow away my possessions as snugly as in a ship's cabin. When I presently descended, armed with a blue apron and "a heart for any fate," I found the old man awake and received from him a welcome full of ancient courtesy and kindliness. Miss Eliza crept in like a timid mouse, looking so afraid of her buxom

companion that I forgot my own shyness in trying to relieve hers. She
was so enveloped in shawls that all I could discover was that my
mistress was a very nervous little woman, with a small button of pale
hair on the outside of her head and the vaguest notions of work inside.
A few spasmodic remarks and many awkward pauses brought us to
teatime, when Josephus appeared, as tall, thin, and cadaverous as ever.
After his arrival there was no more silence, for he preached all supper-
time something in this agreeable style.

"My young friend, our habits, as you see, are of the simplest. We
eat in the kitchen, and all together, in the primitive fashion; for it suits
my father and saves labor. I could wish more order and elegance; but
my wishes are not consulted and I submit. I live above these petty
crosses, and, though my health suffers from bad cookery, I do not
murmur. Only, I must say, in passing, that if you *will* make your
battercakes green with saleratus, Puah, I shall feel it my duty to throw
them out of the window. *I* am used to poison; but I cannot see the
coats of this blooming girl's stomach destroyed, as mine have been.
And, speaking of duties, I may as well mention to you, Louisa (I call
you so in a truly fraternal spirit), that I like to find my study in order
when I come down in the morning; for I often need a few moments of
solitude before I face the daily annoyances of my life. I shall permit
you to perform this light task, for *you* have some idea of order (I see it
in the formation of your brow), and feel sure that *you* will respect the
sanctuary of thought. Eliza is so blind she does not see dust, and Puah
enjoys devastating the one poor refuge I can call my own this side the
grave. We are all waiting for you, sir. My father keeps up the old
formalities, you observe; and I endure them, though *my* views are
more advanced."

The old gentleman hastily finished his tea and returned thanks,
when his son stalked gloomily away, evidently oppressed with the
burden of his wrongs, also, as I irreverently fancied, with the seven
"green" flapjacks he had devoured during the sermon.

I helped wash up the cups, and during that domestic rite Puah chatted in what I should have considered a cheery, social way had I not been darkly warned against her wiles.

"You needn't mind half Josephus says, my dear. He likes to hear himself talk and always goes on so before folks. I sometimes thinks his books and new ideas have sort of muddled his wits, for he is as full of notions as a paper is of pins; and he gets dreadfully put out if we don't give in to 'em. But, gracious me! they are so redicklus sometimes and so selfish I can't allow him to make a fool of himself or plague Lizy. She don't dare to say her soul is her own; so I have to stand up for her. His pa don't know half his odd doings; for I try to keep the old gentleman comfortable and have to manage 'em all, which is not an easy job, I do assure you."

I had a secret conviction that she was right, but did not commit myself in any way, and we joined the social circle in the sitting-room. The prospect was not a lively one, for the old gentleman nodded behind his newspaper; Eliza, with her head plumed up in a little blanket, slumbered on the sofa, Puah fell to knitting silently; and the plump cat dozed under the stove. Josephus was visible, artistically posed in the luxurious recesses of his cell, with the light beaming on his thoughtful brow, as he pored over a large volume or mused with upturned eye.

Having nothing else to do, I sat and stared at him, till, emerging from a deep reverie, with an effective start, he became conscious of my existence and beckoned me to approach the "sanctuary of thought" with a melodramatic waft of his large hand.

I went, took possession of an easy chair, and prepared myself for elegant conversation. I was disappointed, however; for Josephus showed me a list of his favorite dishes, sole fruit of all that absorbing thought, and, with an earnestness that flushed his saffron countenance, gave me hints as to the proper preparation of these delicacies.

I mildly mentioned that I was not a cook; but was effectually silenced by being reminded that I came to be generally useful, to take his sister's place, and see that the flame of life which burned so feebly in this earthly tabernacle was fed with proper fuel. Mince pies, Welsh rarebits, sausages, and strong coffee did not strike me as strictly spiritual fare; but I listened meekly and privately resolved to shift this awful responsibility to Puah's shoulders.

Detecting me in gape, after an hour of this high converse, he presented me with an overblown rose, which fell to pieces before I got out of the room, pressed my hand, and dismissed me with a fervent "God bless you, child. Don't forget the dropped eggs for breakfast."

I was up betimes next morning and had the study in perfect order before the recluse appeared, enjoying a good prowl among the books as I worked and becoming so absorbed that I forgot the eggs, till a gusty sigh startled me, and I beheld Josephus, in dressing gown and slippers, languidly surveying the scene.

"Nay, do not fly," he said, as I grasped my duster in guilty haste. "It pleases me to see you here and lends a sweet, domestic charm to my solitary room. I like that graceful cap, that housewifely apron, and I beg you will wear them often; for it refreshes my eye to see something tasteful, young, and womanly about me. Eliza makes a bundle of herself and Puah is simply detestable."

He sank languidly into a chair and closed his eyes, as if the mere thought of his enemy was too much for him. I took advantage of this momentary prostration to slip away, convulsed with laughter at the looks and words of this bald-headed sentimentalist.

After breakfast I fell to work with a will, eager to show my powers and glad to put things to rights, for many hard jobs had evidently been waiting for a stronger arm than Puah's and a more methodical head than Eliza's.

Everything was dusty, moldy, shiftless, and neglected, except the domain of Josephus. Up-stairs the paper was dropping from the walls, the ancient furniture was all more or less dilapidated, and every hole and corner was full of relics tucked away by Puah, who was a regular old magpie. Rats and mice reveled in the empty rooms and spiders wove their tapestry undisturbed, for the old man would have nothing altered or repaired and his part of the house was fast going to ruin.

I longed to have a grand "clearing up"; but was forbidden to do more than to keep things in livable order. On the whole, it was fortunate, for I soon found that my hands would be kept busy with the realms of Josephus, whose ethereal being shrank from dust, shivered at a cold breath, and needed much cosseting with dainty food, hot fires, soft beds, and endless service, else, as he expressed it, the frail reed would break.

I regret to say that a time soon came when I felt supremely indifferent as to the breakage, and very skeptical as to the fragility of a reed that ate, slept, dawdled, and scolded so energetically. The rose that fell to pieces so suddenly was a good symbol of the rapid disappearance of all the romantic delusions I had indulged in for a time. A week's acquaintance with the inmates of this old house quite settled my opinion, and further developments only confirmed it.

Miss Eliza was a nonentity and made no more impression on me than a fly. The old gentleman passed his days in a placid sort of doze and took no notice of what went on about him. Puah had been a faithful drudge for years, and, instead of being a "wretch," was, as I soon satisfied myself, a motherly old soul, with no malice in her. The secret of Josephus's dislike was that the reverend tyrant ruled the house, and all obeyed him but Puah, who had nursed him as a baby, boxed his ears as a boy, and was not afraid of him even when he became a man and a minister. I soon repented of my first suspicions, and grew fond of her, for without my old gossip I should have fared ill when my day of tribulation came.

At first I innocently accepted the fraternal invitations to visit the study, feeling that when my day's work was done I had earned a right to rest and read. But I soon found that this was not the idea. I was not to read; but to be read to. I was not to enjoy the flowers, pictures, fire, and books; but to keep them in order for my lord to enjoy. I was also to be a passive bucket, into which he was to pour all manner of philosophic, metaphysical, and sentimental rubbish. I was to serve his needs, soothe his sufferings, and sympathize with all his sorrows—be a galley slave, in fact.

As soon as I clearly understood this, I tried to put an end to it by shunning the study and never lingering there an instant after my work was done. But it availed little, for Josephus demanded much sympathy and was bound to have it. So he came and read poems while I washed dishes, discussed his pet problems all meal-times, and put reproachful notes under my door, in which were comically mingled complaints of neglect and orders for dinner.

I bore it as long as I could, and then freed my mind in a declaration of independence, delivered in the kitchen, where he found me scrubbing the hearth. It was not an impressive attitude for an orator, nor was the occupation one a girl would choose when receiving calls; but I have always felt grateful for the intense discomfort of that moment, since it gave me courage to rebel outright. Stranded on a small island of mat, in a sea of soapsuds, I brandished a scrubbing brush, as I indignantly informed him that I came to be a companion to his sister, not to him, and I should keep that post or none. This I followed up by reproaching him with the delusive reports he had given me of the place and its duties, and assuring him that I should not stay long unless matters mended.

"But I offer you lighter tasks, and you refuse them," he begun, still hovering in the doorway, whither he had hastily retired when I opened my batteries.

"But I don't like the tasks, and consider them much worse than hard work," was my ungrateful answer, as I sat upon my island, with the soft-soap conveniently near.

"Do you mean to say you prefer to scrub that hearth to sitting in my charming room while I read Hegel to you?" he demanded, glaring down upon me.

"Infinitely," I responded promptly, and emphasized my words by beginning to scrub with a zeal that made the bricks white with foam.

"Is it possible?" and, with a groan at my depravity, Josephus retired, full of ungodly wrath.

I remember that I immediately burst into jocund song, so that no doubt might remain in his mind, and continued to warble cheerfully till my task was done. I also remember that I cried heartily when I got to my room, I was so vexed, disappointed, and tired. But my bower was so small I should soon have swamped the furniture if I had indulged copiously in tears; therefore I speedily dried them up, wrote a comic letter home, and waited with interest to see what would happen next.

Far be it from me to accuse one of the nobler sex of spite or the small revenge of underhand annoyances and slights to one who could not escape and would not retaliate; but after that day a curious change came over the spirit of that very unpleasant dream. Gradually all the work of the house had been slipping into my hands; for Eliza was too poorly to help or direct, and Puah too old to do much besides the cooking. About this time I found that even the roughest work was added to my share, for Josephus was unusually feeble and no one was hired to do his chores. Having made up my mind to go when the month was out, I said nothing, but dug paths, brought water from the well, split kindlings, made fires, and sifted ashes, like a true Cinderella.

There never had been any pretense of companionship with Eliza, who spent her days mulling over the fire, and seldom exerted herself except to find odd jobs for me to do—rusty knives to clean, sheets to turn, old stockings to mend, and, when all else failed, some paradise of moths and mice to be cleared up; for the house was full of such "glory holes."

If I remonstrated, Eliza at once dissolved into tears and said she must do as she was told; Puah begged me to hold on till spring, when things would be much better; and pity pleaded for the two poor souls. But I don't think I could have stood it if my promise had not bound me, for when the fiend said "Budge" honor said "Budge not," and I stayed.

But, being a mortal worm, I turned now and then when the ireful Josephus trod upon me too hard, especially in the matter of boot-blacking. I really don't know why that is considered such humiliating work for a woman; but so it is, and there I drew the line. I would have cleaned the old man's shoes without a murmur; but he preferred to keep their native rustiness intact. Eliza never went out, and Puah affected carpet-slippers of the Chinese-junk pattern. Josephus, however, plumed himself upon his feet, which, like his nose, were large, and never took his walks abroad without having his boots in a high state of polish. He had brushed them himself at first; but soon after the explosion I discovered a pair of muddy boots in the shed, set suggestively near the blacking-box. I did not take the hint, feeling instinctively that this amiable being was trying how much I would bear for the sake of peace.

The boots remained untouched; and another pair soon came to keep them company, whereat I smiled wickedly as I chopped just kindlings enough for my own use. Day after day the collection grew, and neither party gave in. Boots were succeeded by shoes, then rubbers gave a pleasing variety to the long line, and then I knew the end was near.

"Why are not my boots attended to?" demanded Josephus, one evening, when obliged to go out.

"I'm sure I don't know," was Eliza's helpless answer.

"I told Louizy I guessed you'd want some of 'em before long," observed Puah, with an exasperating twinkle in her old eye.

"And what did she say?" asked my lord with an ireful whack of his velvet slippers as he cast them down.

"Oh! she said she was so busy doing your other work you'd have to do that yourself; and I thought she was about right."

"Louizy" heard it all through the slide, and could have embraced the old woman for her words, but kept still till Josephus had resumed his slippers with a growl and retired to the shed, leaving Eliza in tears, Puah chuckling, and the rebellious handmaid exulting in the china-closet.

Alas! for romance and the Christian virtues, several pairs of boots were cleaned that night, and my sinful soul enjoyed the spectacle of the reverend bootblack at his task. I even found my "fancy work," as I called the evening job of paring a bucketful of hard russets with a dull knife, much cheered by the shoe-brush accompaniment played in the shed.

Thunder-clouds rested upon the martyr's brow at breakfast, and I was as much ignored as the cat. And what a relief that was! The piano was locked up, so were the bookcases, the newspapers mysteriously disappeared, and a solemn silence reigned at table, for no one dared to talk when that gifted tongue was mute. Eliza fled from the gathering storm and had a comfortable fit of neuralgia in her own room, where Puah nursed her, leaving me to skirmish with the enemy.

It was not a fair fight, and that experience lessened my respect for mankind immensely. I did my best, however—grubbed about all day and amused my dreary evenings as well as I could; too proud even to borrow a book, lest it should seem like a surrender. What a long month it was, and how eagerly I counted the hours of that last week, for my time was up Saturday, and I hoped to be off at once. But when I announced my intention such dismay fell upon Eliza that my heart was touched, and Puah so urgently begged me to stay till they could get some one that I consented to remain a few days longer, and wrote post-haste to my mother, telling her to send a substitute quickly or I should do something desperate.

That blessed woman, little dreaming of all the woes I had endured, advised me to be patient, to do the generous thing, and be sure I should not regret it in the end. I groaned, submitted, and did regret it all the days of my life.

Three mortal weeks I waited; for, though two other victims came, I was implored to set them going, and tried to do it. But both fled after a day or two, condemning the place as a very hard one and calling me a fool to stand it another hour. I entirely agreed with them on both points, and, when I had cleared up after the second incapable lady, I tarried not for the coming of a third, but clutched my property and announced my departure by the next train.

Of course, Eliza wept, Puah moaned, the old man politely regretted, and the younger one washed his hands of the whole affair by shutting himself up in his room and forbidding me to say farewell because he "could not bear it." I laughed, and fancied it done for effect then; but I soon understood it better and did not laugh.

At the last moment, Eliza nervously tucked a sixpenny pocketbook into my hand and shrouded herself in the little blanket with a sob. But Puah kissed me kindly and whispered, with an odd look: "Don't blame us for anything. Some folks is liberal and some ain't." I thanked the poor old soul for her kindness to me and trudged gayly away to the station, whither my property had preceded me on a wheel-barrow, hired at my own expense.

I never shall forget that day. A bleak March afternoon, a sloppy, lonely road, and one hoarse crow stalking about a field, so like Josephus that I could not resist throwing a snowball at him. Behind me stood the dull old house, no longer either mysterious or romantic in my disenchanted eyes; before me rumbled the barrow, bearing my dilapidated wardrobe; and in my pocket reposed what I fondly hoped was, if not a liberal, at least an honest return for seven weeks of the hardest work I ever did.

Unable to resist the desire to see what my earnings were, I opened the purse and beheld *four dollars*.

I have had a good many bitter minutes in my life; but one of the bitterest came to me as I stood there in the windy road, with the sixpenny pocket-book open before me, and looked from my poor chapped, grimy, chill-blained hands to the paltry sum that was considered reward enough for all the hard and humble labor they had done.

A girl's heart is a sensitive thing. And mine had been very full lately; for it had suffered many of the trials that wound deeply yet cannot be told; so I think it was but natural that my first impulse was to go straight back to that sacred study and fling this insulting money at the feet of him who sent it. But I was so boiling over with indignation that I could not trust myself in his presence, lest I should be unable to resist the temptation to shake him, in spite of his cloth.

No, I would go home, show my honorable wounds, tell my pathetic tale, and leave my parents to avenge my wrongs. I did so; but over that harrowing scene I drop a veil, for my feeble pen refuses to depict the emotions of my outraged family. I will merely mention that the four dollars went back and the reverend Josephus never heard the last of it in that neighborhood.

My experiment seemed a dire failure and I mourned it as such for years; but more than once in my life I have been grateful for that serio-comico experience, since it has taught me many lessons. One of the most useful of these has been the power of successfully making a companion, not a servant, of those whose aid I need, and helping to gild their honest wages with the sympathy and justice which can sweeten the humblest and lighten the hardest task.

Fruitlands, the short-lived Utopia so memorably resurrected by Alcott in her satirical romp "Transcendental Wild Oats." The setting was gorgeous indeed, but while the brethren devoted themselves to metaphysics, all labor at Fruitlands seemed to fall to the female members of the family.

TRANSCENDENTAL WILD OATS

A Chapter from an Unwritten Romance

O N THE FIRST DAY OF JUNE, 184–, A LARGE WAGON, DRAWN BY A small horse and containing a motley load, went lumbering over certain New England hills, with the pleasing accompaniments of wind, rain, and hail. A serene man with a serene child upon his knee was driving, or rather being driven, for the small horse had it all his own way. A brown boy with a William Penn style of countenance sat beside him, firmly embracing a bust of Socrates. Behind them was an energetic-looking woman, with a benevolent brow, satirical mouth, and eyes brimful of hope and courage. A baby reposed upon her lap, a mirror leaned against her knee, and a basket of provisions danced about at her feet, as she struggled with a large, unruly umbrella. Two blue-eyed little girls, with hands full of childish treasures, sat under one old shawl, chatting happily together.

In front of this lively party stalked a tall, sharp-featured man, in a long blue cloak; and a fourth small girl trudged along beside him through the mud as if she rather enjoyed it.

The wind whistled over the bleak hills; the rain fell in a despondent drizzle, and twilight began to fall. But the calm man gazed as tranquilly into the fog as if he beheld a radiant bow of promise spanning the gray sky. The cheery woman tried to cover every one but herself

with the big umbrella. The brown boy pillowed his head on the bald
pate of Socrates and slumbered peacefully. The little girls sang lullabies to their dolls in soft, maternal murmurs. The sharp-nosed pedes-
trian marched steadily on, with the blue cloak streaming out behind
him like a banner; and the lively infant splashed through the puddles
with a duck-like satisfaction pleasant to behold.

Thus these modern pilgrims journeyed hopefully out of the old
world, to found a new one in the wilderness.

The editors of *The Transcendental Tripod* had received from
Messrs. Lion & Lamb (two of the foresaid pilgrims) a communication
from which the following statement is an extract:—

"We have made arrangements with the proprietor of an estate of
about a hundred acres which liberates this tract from human owner-
ship. Here we shall prosecute our effort to initiate a Family in harmony with the primitive instincts of man.

"Ordinary secular farming is not our object. Fruit, grain, pulse,
herbs, flax, and other vegetable products, receiving assiduous attention,
will afford ample manual occupation, and chaste supplies for the bodily
needs. It is intended to adorn the pastures with orchards, and to super-
sede the labor of cattle by the spade and the pruning-knife.

"Consecrated to human freedom, the land awaits the sober culture
of devoted men. Beginning with small pecuniary means, this enterprise
must be rooted in a reliance on the succors of an ever-bounteous
Providence, whose vital affinities being secured by this union with
uncorrupted field and unworldly persons, the cares and injuries of a
life of gain are avoided.

"The inner nature of each member of the Family is at no time
neglected. Our plan contemplates all such disciplines, cultures, and
habits as evidently conduce to the purifying of the inmates.

"Pledged to the spirit alone, the founders anticipate no hasty or
numerous addition to their numbers. The kingdom of peace is entered
only through the gates of self-denial; and felicity is the test and the
reward of loyalty to the unswerving law of Love."

This prospective Eden at present consisted of an old red farmhouse, a dilapidated barn, many acres of meadow-land, and a grove. Ten ancient apple-trees were all the "chaste supply" which the place offered as yet; but, in the firm belief that plenteous orchards were soon to be evoked from their inner consciousness, these sanguine founders had christened their domain Fruitlands.

Here Timon Lion intended to found a colony of Latter Day Saints, who, under his patriarchal sway, should regenerate the world and glorify his name for ever. Here Abel Lamb, with the devoutest faith in the high ideal which was to him a living truth, desired to plant a Paradise, where Beauty, Virtue, Justice, and Love might live happily together, without the possibility of a serpent entering in. And here his wife, unconverted but faithful to the end, hoped, and after many wanderings over the face of the earth, to find rest for herself and a home for her children.

"There is our new abode," announced the enthusiast, smiling with a satisfaction quite undampened by the drops dripping from his hat-brim, as they turned at length into a cart-path that wound along a steep hillside into a barren-looking valley.

"A little difficult of access," observed his practical wife, as she endeavored to keep her various household goods from going overboard with every lurch of the laden ark.

"Like all good things. But those who earnestly desire and patiently seek will soon find us," placidly responded the philosopher from the mud, through which he was now endeavoring to pilot the much-enduring horse.

"Truth lies at the bottom of a well, Sister Hope," said Brother Timon, pausing to detach his small comrade from a gate, whereon she was perched for a clearer gaze into futurity.

"That's the reason we so seldom get at it, I suppose," replied Mrs. Hope, making a vain clutch at the mirror, which a sudden jolt sent flying out of her hands.

"We want no false reflections here," said Timon, with a grim smile, as he crunched the fragments under foot in his onward march.

Sister Hope held her peace, and looked wistfully through the mist at her promised home. The old red house with a hospitable glimmer at its windows cheered her eyes; and, considering the weather, was a fitter refuge than the sylvan bowers some of the more ardent souls might have preferred.

The new-comers were welcomed by one of the elect precious,—a regenerate farmer, whose idea of reform consisted chiefly in wearing white cotton raiment and shoes of untanned leather. This costume, with a snowy beard, gave him a venerable, and at the same time a somewhat bridal appearance.

The goods and chattels of the Society not having arrived, the weary family reposed before the fire on blocks of wood, while Brother Moses White regaled them with roasted potatoes, brown bread and water, in two plates, a tin pan, and one mug; his table service being limited. But, having cast the forms and vanities of a depraved world behind them, the elders welcomed hardship with the enthusiasm of new pioneers, and the children heartily enjoyed this foretaste of what they believed was to be a sort of perpetual picnic.

During the progress of this frugal meal, two more brothers appeared. One a dark, melancholy man, clad in homespun, whose peculiar mission was to turn his name hind part before and use as few words as possible. The other was a bland, bearded Englishman, who expected to be saved by eating uncooked food and going without clothes. He had not yet adopted the primitive costume, however; but contented himself with meditatively chewing dry beans out of a basket.

"Every meal should be a sacrament, and the vessels used should be beautiful and symbolical," observed Brother Lamb, mildly, righting the tin pan slipping about on his knees. "I priced a silver service when in town, but it was too costly; so I got some graceful cups and vases of Britannia ware."

"Hardest things in the world to keep bright. Will whiting be allowed in the community?" inquired Sister Hope, with a housewife's interest in labor-saving institutions.

"Such trivial questions will be discussed at a more fitting time," answered Brother Timon, sharply, as he burnt his fingers with a very hot potato. "Neither sugar, molasses, milk, butter, cheese, nor flesh are to be used among us, for nothing is to be admitted which has caused wrong or death to man or beast."

"Our garments are to be linen till we learn to raise our own cotton or some substitute for woolen fabrics," added Brother Abel, blissfully basking in an imaginary future as warm and brilliant as the generous fire before him.

"Haou abaout shoes?" asked Brother Moses, surveying his own with interest.

"We must yield that point till we can manufacture an innocent substitute for leather. Bark, wood, or some durable fabric will be invented in time. Meanwhile, those who desire to carry out our idea to the fullest extent can go barefooted," said Lion, who liked extreme measures.

"I never will, nor let my girls," murmured rebellious Sister Hope, under her breath.

"Haou do you cattle'ate to treat the ten-acre lot? Ef things ain't 'tended to right smart, we shan't hev no crops," observed the practical patriarch in cotton.

"We shall spade it," replied Abel, in such perfect good faith that Moses said no more, though he indulged in a shake of the head as he glanced at hands that had held nothing heavier than a pen for years. He was a paternal old soul and regarded the younger men as promising boys on a new sort of lark.

"What shall we do for lamps, if we cannot use any animal substance? I do hope light of some sort is to be thrown upon the enterprise," said Mrs. Lamb, with anxiety, for in those days kerosene and camphene were not, and gas unknown in the wilderness.

"We shall go without till we have discovered some vegetable oil or wax to serve us," replied Brother Timon, in a decided tone, which caused Sister Hope to resolve that her private lamp should be always trimmed, if not burning.

"Each member is to perform the work for which experience, strength, and taste best fit him," continued Dictator Lion. "Thus drudgery and disorder will be avoided and harmony prevail. We shall rise at dawn, begin the day by bathing, followed by music, and then a chaste repast of fruit and bread. Each one finds congenial occupation till the meridian meal; when some deep-searching conversation gives rest to the body and development to the mind. Healthful labor again engages us till the last meal, when we assemble in social communion, prolonged till sunset, when we retire to sweet repose, ready for the next day's activity."

"What part of the work do you incline to yourself?" asked Sister Hope, with a humorous glimmer in her keen eyes.

"I shall wait till it is made clear to me. Being in preference to doing is the great aim, and this comes to us rather by a resigned willingness than a wilful activity, which is a check to all divine growth," responded Brother Timon.

"I thought so." And Mrs. Lamb sighed audibly, for during the year he had spent in her family Brother Timon had so faithfully carried out his idea of "being, not doing," that she had found his "divine growth" both an expensive and unsatisfactory process.

Here her husband struck into the conversation, his face shining with the light and joy of the splendid dreams and high ideals hovering before him.

"In these steps of reform, we do not rely so much on scientific reasoning or physiological skill as on the spirit's dictates. The greater part of man's duty consists in leaving alone much that he now does. Shall I stimulate with tea, coffee, or wine? No. Shall I consume flesh? Not if I value health. Shall I subjugate cattle? Shall I claim property in any created thing? Shall I trade? Shall I adopt a form of religion? Shall I interest myself in politics? To how many of these questions—could we ask them deeply enough and could they be heard as having relation to our eternal welfare—would the response be 'Abstain'?"

A mild snore seemed to echo the last word of Abel's rhapsody, for

Brother Moses had succumbed to mundane slumber and sat nodding like a massive ghost. Forest Absalom, the silent man, and John Pease, the English member, now departed to the barn; and Mrs. Lamb led her flock to a temporary fold, leaving the founders of the "Consociate Family" to build castles in the air till the fire went out and the symposium ended in smoke.

The furniture arrived next day, and was soon bestowed; for the principal property of the community consisted in books. To this rare library was devoted the best room in the house, and the few busts and pictures that still survived many flittings were added to beautify the sanctuary, for here the family was to meet for amusement, instruction, and worship.

Any housewife can imagine the emotions of Sister Hope, when she took possession of a large, dilapidated kitchen, containing an old stove and the peculiar stores out of which food was to be evolved for her little family of eleven. Cakes of maple sugar, dried peas and beans, barley and hominy, meal of all sorts, potatoes, and dried fruit. No milk, butter, cheese, tea, or meat appeared. Even salt was considered a useless luxury and spice entirely forbidden by these lovers of Spartan simplicity. A ten years' experience of vegetarian vagaries had been good training for this new freak, and her sense of the ludicrous supported her through many trying scenes.

Unleavened bread, porridge, and water for breakfast; bread, vegetables, and water for dinner; bread, fruit, and water for supper was the bill of fare ordained by the elders. No teapot profaned that sacred stove, no gory steak cried aloud for vengeance from her chaste gridiron; and only a brave woman's taste, time, and temper were sacrificed on that domestic altar.

The vexed question of light was settled by buying a quantity of bayberry wax for candles; and, on discovering that no one knew how to make them, pine knots were introduced, to be used when absolutely necessary. Being summer, the evenings were not long, and the weary fraternity found it no great hardship to retire with the birds. The inner light was sufficient for most of them. But Mrs. Lamb rebelled. Evening was the only time she had to herself, and while the tired feet rested the skilful hands mended torn frocks and little stockings, or anxious heart forgot its burden in a book.

So "mother's lamp" burned steadily, while the philosophers built a new heaven and earth by moonlight; and through all the metaphysical mists and philanthropic pyrotechnics of that period Sister Hope played her own little game of "throwing light," and none but the moths were the worse for it.

Such farming probably was never seen before since Adam delved. The band of brothers began by spading garden and field; but a few days of it lessened their ardor amazingly. Blistered hands and aching backs suggested the expediency of permitting the use of cattle till the workers were better fitted for noble toil by a summer of the new life.

Brother Moses brought a yoke of oxen from his farm,—at least, the philosophers thought so till it was discovered that one of the animals was a cow; and Moses confessed that he "must be let down easy, for he couldn't live on garden sarse entirely."

Great was Dictator Lion's indignation at this lapse from virtue. But time pressed, the work must be done; so the meek cow was permitted to wear the yoke and the recreant brother continued to enjoy forbidden draughts in the barn, which dark proceeding caused the children to regard him as one set apart for destruction.

The sowing was equally peculiar, for, owing to some mistake, the three brethren, who devoted themselves to this graceful task, found when about half through the job that each had been sowing a different sort of grain in the same field; a mistake which caused much perplexity; as it could not be remedied; but, after a long consultation and a good deal of laughter, it was decided to say nothing and see what would come of it.

The garden was planted with a generous supply of useful roots and herbs; but, as manure was not allowed to profane the virgin soil, few of these vegetable treasures ever came up. Purslane reigned supreme, and the disappointed planters ate it philosophically, deciding that Nature knew what was best for them, and would generously supply their needs, if they could only learn to digest her "sallets" and wild roots.

The orchard was laid out, a little grafting done, new trees and vines set, regardless of the unfit season and entire ignorance of the husbandmen, who honestly believed that in the autumn they would reap a bounteous harvest.

Slowly things got into order, and rapidly rumors of the new experiment went abroad, causing many strange spirits to flock thither, for in those days communities were the fashion and transcendentalism raged wildly. Some came to look on and laugh, some to be supported in poetic idleness, a few to believe sincerely and work heartily. Each member was allowed to mount his favorite hobby and ride it to his heart's content. Very queer were some of the riders, and very rampant some of the hobbies.

One youth, believing that language was of little consequence if the spirit was only right, startled new-comers by blandly greeting them with "Good-morning, damn you," and other remarks of an equally mixed order. A second irresponsible being held that all the emotions of the soul should be freely expressed, and illustrated his theory by antics that would have sent him to a lunatic asylum, if, as an unregenerate wag said, he had not already been in one. When his spirit soared, he climbed trees and shouted; when doubt assailed him, he lay upon the floor and groaned lamentably. At joyful periods, he raced, leaped, and sang; when sad, he wept aloud; and when a great thought burst upon him in the watches of the night, he crowed like a jocund cockerel, to the great delight of the children and the great annoyance of the elders. One musical brother fiddled whenever so moved, sang sentimentally to the four little girls, and put a music-box on the wall when he hoed corn.

Brother Pease ground away at his uncooked food, or browsed over the farm on sorrel, mint, green fruit, and new vegetables. Occasionally he took his walks abroad, airily attired in an unbleached cotton *poncho*, which was the nearest approach to the primeval costume he was allowed to indulge in. At midsummer he retired to the wilderness, to try

his plan where the woodchucks were without prejudices and huckle-
berry-bushes were hospitably full. A sunstroke unfortunately spoilt his
plan, and he returned to semi-civilization a sadder and wiser man.

Forest Absalom preserved his Pythagorean silence, cultivated his
fine dark locks, and worked like a beaver, setting an excellent example
of brotherly love, justice, and fidelity by his upright life. He it was
who helped overworked Sister Hope with her heavy washes, kneaded
the endless succession of batches of bread, watched over the children,
and did the many tasks left undone by the brethren, who were so busy
discussing and defining great duties that they forgot to perform the
small ones.

Moses White placidly plodded about, "chorin' raound," as he
called it, looking like an old-time patriarch, with his silver hair and
flowing beard, and saving the community from many a mishap by his
thrift and Yankee shrewdness.

Brother Lion domineered over the whole concern; for, having put
the most money into the speculation, he was resolved to make it
pay,—as if anything founded on an ideal basis could be expected to do
so by any but enthusiasts.

Abel Lamb simply revelled in the Newness, firmly believing that
his dream was to be beautifully realized and in time not only little
Fruitlands, but the whole earth, be turned into a Happy Valley. He
worked with every muscle of his body, for *he* was in deadly earnest.
He taught with his whole head and heart; planned and sacrificed,
preached and prophesied, with a soul full of the purest aspirations,
most unselfish purposes, and desires for a life devoted to God and
man, too high and tender to bear the rough usage of this world.

It was a little remarkable that only one woman ever joined this
community. Mrs. Lamb merely followed wheresoever her husband
led,—"as ballast for his balloon," as she said, in her bright way.

Miss Jane Gage was a stout lady of mature years, sentimental,
amiable, and lazy. She wrote verses copiously, and had vague yearn-
ings and graspings after the unknown, which led her to believe herself
fitted for a higher sphere than any she had yet adorned.

Having been a teacher, she was set to instructing the children in the common branches. Each adult member took a turn at the infants; and, as each taught in his own way, the result was a chronic state of chaos in the minds of these much-afflicted innocents.

Sleep, food, and poetic musings were the desires of dear Jane's life, and she shirked all duties as clogs upon her spirit's wings. Any thought of lending a hand with the domestic drudgery never occurred to her; and when to the question, "Art there any beasts of burden on the place?" Mrs. Lamb answered, with a face that told its own tale, "Only one woman!" the buxom Jane took no shame to herself, but laughed at the joke, and let the stout-hearted sister tug on alone.

Unfortunately, the poor lady hankered after the flesh-pots, and endeavored to stay herself with private sips of milk, crackers, and cheese, and on one dire occasion she partook of fish at a neighbor's table.

One of the children reported this sad lapse from virtue, and poor Jane was publicly reprimanded by Timon.

"I only took a little bit of the tail," sobbed the penitent poetess.

"Yes, but the whole fish had to be tortured and slain that you might tempt your carnal appetite with that one taste of the tail. Know ye not, consumers of flesh meat, that ye are nourishing the wolf and tiger in your bosoms?"

At this awful question and the peal of laughter which arose from some of the younger brethren, tickled by the ludicrous contrast between the stout sinner, the stern judge, and the naughty satisfaction of the young detective, poor Jane fled from the room to pack her trunk and return to a world where fishes' tails were not forbidden fruit.

Transcendental wild oats were sown broadcast that year, and the fame thereof has not yet ceased in the land; for, futile as this crop seemed to outsiders, it bore an invisible harvest, worth much to those who planted in earnest. As none of the members of this particular community have ever recounted their experiences before, a few of them may not be amiss, since the interest in these attempts has never died out and Fruitlands was the most ideal of all these castles in Spain.

A new dress was invented, since cotton, silk, and wool were forbidden as the product of slave-labor, worm-slaughter, and sheep-robbery. Tunics and trowsers of brown linen were the only wear. The women's skirts were longer, and their straw hat-brims wider than the men's, and this was the only difference. Some persecution lent a charm to the costume, and the long-haired, linen-clad reformers quite enjoyed the mild martyrdom they endured when they left home.

Money was abjured, as the root of all evil. The produce of the land was to supply most of their wants, or be exchanged for the few things they could not grow. This idea had its inconveniences; but self-denial was the fashion, and it was surprising how many things one can do without. When they desired to travel, they walked, if possible, begged the loan of a vehicle, or boldly entered car or coach, and, stating their principles to the officials, took the consequences. Usually their dress, their earnest frankness, and gentle resolution won them a passage; but now and then they met with hard usage, and had the satisfaction of suffering for their principles.

On one of these penniless pilgrimages they took passage on a boat, and, when fare was demanded, artlessly offered to talk, instead of pay. As the boat was well under way and they actually had not a cent, there was no help for it. So Brothers Lion and Lamb held forth to the assembled passengers in their most eloquent style. There must have been something effective in this conversation, for the listeners were moved to take up a contribution for these inspired lunatics, who preached peace on earth and good-will to man so earnestly, with empty pockets. A goodly sum was collected; but when the captain presented it the reformers proved that they were consistent even in their madness, for not a penny would they accept, saying, with a look at the group about them, whose indifference or contempt had changed to interest and respect, "You see how well we get on without money"; and so went serenely on their way, with their linen blouses flapping airily in the cold October wind.

They preached vegetarianism everywhere and resisted all temptations of the flesh, contentedly eating apples and bread at well-spread tables, and much afflicting hospitable hostesses by denouncing their food and taking away their appetite, discussing the "horrors of shambles," and "incorporation of the brute in man," and "on elegant abstinence the sign of a pure soul." But, when the perplexed or offended ladies asked what they should eat, they got in reply a bill of fare consisting of "bowls of sunrise for breakfast," "solar seeds of the sphere," "dishes from Plutarch's chaste table," and other viands equally hard to find in any modern market.

Reform conventions of all sorts were haunted by these brethren, who said many wise things and did many foolish ones. Unfortunately, these wanderings interfered with their harvest at home; but the rule was to do what the spirit moved, so they left their crops to Providence and went a-reaping in wider and, let us hope, more fruitful fields than their own.

Luckily, the earthly providence who watched over Abel Lamb was at hand to glean the scanty crop yielded by the "uncorrupted land," which "consecrated to human freedom," had received "the sober culture of devout men."

About the time the grain was ready to house, some call of the Oversoul wafted all the men away. An easterly storm was coming up and the yellow stacks were sure to be ruined. Then Sister Hope gathered her forces. Three little girls, one boy (Timon's son), and herself, harnessed to clothes-baskets and Russia-linen sheets, were the only teams she could command; but with these poor appliances the indomitable woman got in the grain and saved the food for her young, with the instinct and energy of a mother-bird with a brood of hungry nestlings to feed.

This attempt at regeneration had its tragic as well as comic side, though the world only saw the former.

With the first frosts, the butterflies, who had sunned themselves in the new light through the summer, took flight, leaving the few bees to see what honey they had stored for winter use. Precious little appeared beyond the satisfaction of a few months of holy living.

At first it seemed as if a chance to try holy dying also was to be offered them. Timon, much disgusted with the failure of the scheme, decided to retire to the Shakers, who seemed to be the only successful community going.

"What is to become of us?" asked Mrs. Hope, for Abel was heart-broken at the bursting of his lovely bubble.

"You can stay here, if you like, till a tenant is found. No more wood must be cut, however, and no more corn ground. All I have must be sold to pay the debts of the concern, as the responsibility rests with me," was the cheering reply.

"Who is to pay us for what we have lost? I gave all I had,—furniture, time, strength, six months of my children's lives,—and all are wasted. Abel gave himself body and soul, and is almost wrecked by hard work and disappointment. Are we to have no return for this, but leave to starve and freeze in an old house, with winter at hand, no money, and hardly a friend left; for this wild scheme has alienated nearly all we had. You talk much about justice. Let us have a little, since there is nothing else left."

But the woman's appeal met with no reply but the old one: "It was an experiment. We all risked something, and must bear our losses as we can."

With this cold comfort, Timon departed with his son, and was absorbed into the Shaker brotherhood, where he soon found that the order of things was reversed, and it was all work and no play.

Then the tragedy began for the forsaken little family. Desolation and despair fell upon Abel. As his wife said, his new beliefs had alienated many friends. Some thought him mad, some unprincipled. Even the most kindly thought him a visionary, whom it was useless to help till he took more practical views of life. All stood aloof, saying, "Let him work out his own ideas, and see what they are worth."

He had tried, but it was a failure. The world was not ready for Utopia yet, and those who attempted to found it only got laughed at for their pains. In other days, men could sell all and give to the poor, lead lives devoted to holiness and high thought, and, after the persecution was over, find themselves honored as saints or martyrs. But in

modern times these things are out of fashion. To live for one's principles, at all costs, is a dangerous speculation; and the failure of an ideal,
no matter how humane and noble, is harder for the world to forgive
and forget than bank robbery or the grand swindles of corrupt politi-
cians.

Deep waters now for Abel, and for a time there seemed no passage
through. Strength and spirits were exhausted by hard work and too
much thought. Courage failed when, looking about for help, he saw no
sympathizing face, no hand out-stretched to help him, no voice to say
cheerily,

"We all make mistakes, and it takes many experiences to shape a
life. Try again, and let us help you."

Every door was closed, every eye averted, every heart cold, and no
way open whereby he might earn bread for his children. His principles
would not permit him to do many things that others did; and in the
few fields where conscience would allow him to work, who would
employ a man who had flown in the face of society, as he had done?

Then this dreamer, whose dream was the life of his life, resolved to
carry out his idea to the bitter end. There seemed no place for him
here,—no work, no friend. To go begging conditions was as ignoble as
to go begging money. Better perish of want than sell one's soul for the
sustenance of his body. Silently he lay down upon his bed, turned his
face to the wall, and waited with pathetic patience for death to cut the
knot which he could not untie. Days and nights went by, and neither
food nor water passed his lips. Soul and body were dumbly struggling
together, and no word of complaint betrayed what either suffered.

His wife, when tears and prayers were unavailing, sat down to wait
the end with a mysterious awe and submission; for in this entire resignation of all things there was an eloquent significance to her who knew
him as no other human being did.

"Leave all to God," was his belief; and in this crisis the loving soul
clung to this faith, sure that the Allwise Father would not desert this
child who tried to live so near to Him. Gathering her children about
her, she waited the issue of the tragedy that was being enacted in that

solitary room, while the first snow fell outside, untrodden by the footprints of a single friend.

But the strong angels who sustain and teach perplexed and troubled souls came and went, leaving no trace without, but working miracles within. For, when all other sentiments had faded into dimness, all other hopes died utterly; when the bitterness of death was nearly over, when body was past any pang of hunger or thirst, and soul stood ready to depart, the love that outlives all else refused to die. Head had bowed to defeat, hand had grown weary with too heavy tasks, but heart could not grow cold to those who lived in its tender depths, even when death touched it.

"My faithful wife, my little girls,—they have not forsaken me, they are mine by ties that none can break. What right have I to leave them alone? What right to escape from the burden and the sorrow I have helped to bring? This duty remains to me, and I must do it manfully. For their sakes, the world will forgive me in time; for their sakes, God will sustain me now."

Too feeble to rise, Abel groped for the food that always lay within his reach, and in the darkness and solitude of that memorable night ate and drank what was to him the bread and wine of a new communion, a new dedication of heart and life to the duties that were left him when the dreams fled.

In the early dawn, when that sad wife crept fearfully to see what change had come to the patient face on the pillow, she found it smiling at her, saw a wasted hand outstretched to her, and heard a feeble voice cry bravely, "Hope!"

What passed in that little room is not to be recorded except in the hearts of those who suffered and endured much for love's sake. Enough for us to know that soon the wan shadow of a man came forth, leaning on the arm that never failed him, to be welcomed and cherished by the children, who never forgot the experiences of that time.

"Hope" was the watchword now; and, while the last logs blazed on the hearth, the last bread and apples covered the table, the new commander, with recovered courage, said to her husband,—

"Leave all to God—and me. He has done his part, now I will do mine."

"But we have no money, dear."

"Yes, we have. I sold all we could spare, and have enough to take us away from this snow-bank."

"Where can we go?"

"I have engaged four rooms at our good neighbor, Lovejoy's. There we can live cheaply till spring. Then for new plans and a home of our own, please God."

"But, Hope, your little store won't last long, and we have no friends."

"I can sew and you can chop wood. Lovejoy offers you the same pay as he gives his other men; my old friend, Mrs. Truman, will send me all the work I want; and my blessed brother stands by us to the end. Cheer up, dear heart, for while there is work and love in the world we shall not suffer."

"And while I have my good angel Hope, I shall not despair, even if I wait another thirty years before I step beyond the circle of the sacred little world in which I still have a place to fill."

So one bleak December day, with their few possessions piled on an ox-sled, the rosy children perched atop, and the parents trudging arm in arm behind, the exiles left their Eden and faced the world again.

"Ah me! my happy dream. How much I leave behind that never can be mine again," said Abel, looking back at the lost Paradise, lying white and chill in its shroud of snow.

"Yes, dear, but how much we bring away," answered brave-hearted Hope, glancing from husband to children.

"Poor Fruitlands! The name was as great a failure as the rest!" continued Abel, with a sigh, as a frostbitten apple fell from a leafless bough at his feet.

But the sigh changed to a smile as his wife added, in a half-tender, half-satirical tone,—

"Don't you think Apple Slump would be a better name for it, dear?"

HOSPITAL SKETCHES

Chapter I

Obtaining Supplies

"I WANT SOMETHING TO DO."

This remark being addressed to the world in general, no one in particular felt it their duty to reply; so I repeated it to the smaller world about me, received the following suggestions, and settled the matter by answering my own inquiry, as people are apt to do when very much in earnest.

"Write a book," quoth the author of my being.

"Don't know enough, sir. First live, then write."

"Try teaching again," suggested my mother.

"No thank you, ma'am, ten years of that is enough."

"Take a husband like my Darby, and fulfill your mission," said sister Joan, home on a visit.

"Can't afford expensive luxuries, Mrs. Coobiddy."

"Turn actress, and immortalize your name," said sister Vashti, striking an attitude.

"I won't."

"Go nurse the soldiers," said my young brother, Tom, panting for "the tented field."

"I will!"

So far, very good. Here was the will—now for the way. At first sight not a foot of it appeared, but that didn't matter, for the Periwinkles are a hopeful race; their crest is an anchor, with three cock-a-doodles crowing atop. They all wear rose-colored spectacles, and are lineal descendants of the inventor of aerial architecture. An hour's conversation on the subject set the whole family in a blaze of enthusiasm. A model hospital was erected, and each member had accepted an honorable post therein. The paternal P. was chaplain, the maternal P. was matron, and all the youthful P.s filled the pod of futurity with achievements whose brilliancy eclipsed the glories of the present and the past. Arriving at this satisfactory conclusion, the meeting adjourned, and the fact that Miss Tribulation was available as army nurse went abroad on the wings of the wind.

In a few days a townswoman heard of my desire, approved of it, and brought about an interview with one of the sisterhood which I wished to join, who was at home on a furlough, and able and willing to satisfy all inquiries. A morning chat with Miss General S.—we hear no end of Mrs. Generals, why not a Miss?—produced three results: I felt that I could do the work, was offered a place, and accepted it, promising not to desert, but stand ready to march on Washington at an hour's notice.

A few days were necessary for the letter containing my request and recommendation to reach headquarters, and another, containing my commission, to return; therefore no time was to be lost; and heartily thanking my pair of friends, I tore home through the December slush as if the rebels were after me, and like many another recruit, burst in upon my family with the announcement—

"I've enlisted!"

An impressive silence followed. Tom, the irrepressible, broke it with a slap on the shoulder and the graceful compliment—

"Old Trib, you're a trump!"

"Thank you; then I'll *take* something": which I did, in the shape of dinner, reeling off my news at the rate of three dozen words to a mouthful; and as every one else talked equally fast, and all together, the scene was most inspiring.

As boys going to sea immediately become nautical in speech, walk as if they already had their "sea legs" on, and shiver their timbers on all possible occasions, so I turned military at once, called my dinner my rations, saluted all new comers, and ordered a dress parade that very afternoon. Having reviewed every rag I possessed, I detailed some for picket duty while airing over the fence; some to the sanitary influences of the wash-tub; others to mount guard in the trunk; while the weak and wounded went to the Work-basket Hospital, to be made ready for active service again. To this squad I devoted myself for a week; but all was done, and I had time to get powerfully impatient before the letter came. It did arrive however, and brought a disappointment along with its good will and friendliness, for it told me that the place in the Armory Hospital that I supposed I was to take, was already filled, and a much less desirable one at Hurly-burly House was offered instead.

"That's just your luck, Trib. I'll tote your trunk up garret for you again; for of course you won't go," Tom remarked, with the disdainful pity which small boys affect when they get into their teens. I was wavering in my secret soul, but that settled the matter, and I crushed him on the spot with martial brevity—

"It is now one; I shall march at six."

I have a confused recollection of spending the afternoon in pervading the house like an executive whirlwind, with my family swarming after me, all working, talking, prophesying and lamenting, while I packed my "go-abroady" possessions, tumbled the rest into two big boxes, danced on the lids till they shut, and gave them in charge, with the direction,—

"If I never come back, make a bonfire of them."

Then I choked down a cup of tea, generously salted instead of sugared, by some agitated relative, shouldered my knapsack—it was only a traveling bag, but do let me preserve the unities—hugged my family three times all round without a vestige of unmanly emotion, till a certain dear old lady broke down upon my neck, with a despairing sort of wail—

"Oh, my dear, my dear, how can I let you go?"

"I'll stay if you say so, mother."

"But I don't; go, and the Lord will take care of you."

Much of the Roman matron's courage had gone into the Yankee matron's composition, and, in spite of her tears, she would have sent ten sons to the war, had she possessed them, as freely as she sent one daughter, smiling and flapping on the door-step till I vanished, though the eyes that followed me were very dim, and the handkerchief she waved was very wet.

My transit from The Gables to the village depot was a funny mixture of good wishes and good byes, mud-puddles and shopping. A December twilight is not the most cheering time to enter upon a somewhat perilous enterprise, and, but for the presence of Vashti and neighbor Thorn, I fear that I might have added a drop of the briny to the native moisture of—

"The town I left behind me";

though I'd no thought of giving out: oh, bless you, no! When the engine screeched "Here we are," I clutched my escort in a fervent embrace, and skipped into the car with as blithe a farewell as if going on a bridal tour—though I believe brides don't usually wear cavernous black bonnets and fuzzy brown coats, with a hair-brush, a pair of rubbers, two books, and a bag of ginger-bread distorting the pockets of the same. If I thought that any one would believe it, I'd boldly state that I slept from C. to B., which would simplify matters immensely; but as I know they wouldn't, I'll confess that the head under the funereal coal-hod fermented with all manner of high thoughts and heroic purposes "to do or die,"—perhaps both; and the heart under the fuzzy brown coat felt very tender with the memory of the dear old lady, probably sobbing over her army socks and the loss of her topsy-turvy Trib. At this juncture I took the veil, and what I did behind it is nobody's business; but I maintain that the soldier who cries when his mother says "Good bye," is the boy to fight best, and die bravest, when the time comes, or go back to her better than he went.

Till nine o'clock I trotted about the city streets, doing those last errands which no woman would even go to heaven without attempting, if she could. Then I went to my usual refuge, and, fully intending to keep awake, as a sort of vigil appropriate to the occasion, fell fast asleep and dreamed propitious dreams till my rosy-faced cousin waked me with a kiss.

A bright day smiled upon my enterprise, and at ten I reported myself to my General, received last instructions and no end of the sympathetic encouragement which women give, in look, touch, and tone more effectually than in words. The next step was to get a free pass to Washington, for I'd no desire to waste my substance on railroad companies when "the boys" needed even a spinster's mite. A friend of mine had procured such a pass, and I was bent on doing likewise, though I had to face the president of the railroad to accomplish it. I'm a bashful individual, though I can't get any one to believe it; so it cost me a great effort to poke about the Worcester depot till the right door appeared, then walk into a room containing several gentlemen, and blunder out my request in a high state of stammer and blush. Nothing could have been more courteous than this dreaded President, but it was evident that I had made as absurd a demand as if I had asked for the nose off his respectable face. He referred me to the Governor at the State House, and I backed out, leaving him no doubt to regret that such mild maniacs were left at large. Here was a Scylla and Charybdis business: as if a President wasn't trying enough, without the Governor of Massachusetts and the hub of the hub piled on top of that. "I never can do it," thought I. "Tom will hoot at you if you don't," whispered the inconvenient little voice that is always goading people to the performance of disagreeable duties, and always appeals to the most effective agent to produce the proper result. The idea of allowing any boy that ever wore a felt basin and a shoddy jacket with a microscopic tail, to crow over me, was preposterous, so giving myself a mental slap for such faint-heartedness, I streamed away across the Common, wondering if I ought to say "your Honor," or simply "Sir," and decided upon the latter, fortifying myself with recollections of an evening in a charming green library, where I beheld the Governor placidly consuming oysters, and laughing as if Massachusetts was a myth, and he had no heavier burden on his shoulders than his host's handsome hands.

Like an energetic fly in a very large cobweb, I struggled through the State House, getting into all the wrong rooms and none of the right, till I turned desperate, and went into one, resolving not to come out till I'd made somebody hear and answer me. I suspect that of all the wrong places I had blundered into, this was the most so. But I didn't care; and, though the apartment was full of soldiers, surgeons, starers, and spittoons, I cornered a perfectly incapable person, and proceeded to pump for information with the following result:

"Was the Governor anywhere about?"

No, he wasn't.

"Could he tell me where to look?"

No, he couldn't.

"Did he know anything about free passes?"

No, he didn't.

"Was there any one there of whom I could inquire?"

Not a person.

"Did he know of any place where information could be obtained?"

Not a place.

"Could he throw the smallest gleam of light upon the matter, in any way?"

Not a ray.

I am naturally irascible, and if I could have shaken this negative gentleman vigorously, the relief would have been immense. The prejudices of society forbidding this mode of redress, I merely glowered at him; and, before my wrath found vent in words, my General appeared, having seen me from an opposite window, and come to know what I was about. At her command the languid gentleman woke up, and troubled himself to remember that Major or Sergeant or something Mc K. knew all about the tickets, and his office was in Milk Street. I perked up instanter, and then, as if the exertion was too much for him, what did this animated wet blanket do but add—

"I think Mc K. may have left Milk Street, now, and I don't know where he has gone."

"Never mind; the new comers will know where he has moved to, my dear, so don't be discouraged; and if you don't succeed, come to me, and we will see what to do next," said my General.

I blessed her in a fervent manner and a cool hall, fluttered round the corner, and bore down upon Milk street, bent on discovering Mc K. if such a being was to be found. He wasn't, and the ignorance of the neighborhood was really pitiable. Nobody knew anything, and after tumbling over bundles of leather, bumping against big boxes, being nearly annihilated by descending bales, and sworn at by aggravated truckmen, I finally elicited the advice to look for Mc K. in Haymarket Square. Who my informant was I've really forgotten; for, having hailed several busy gentlemen, some one of them fabricated this delusive quietus for the perturbed spirit, who instantly departed to the sequestered locality he named. If I had been in search of the Koh-i-noor diamond I should have been as likely to find it there as any vestige of Mc K. I stared at signs, inquired in shops, invaded an eating house, visited the recruiting tent in the middle of the Square, made myself a nuisance generally, and accumulated mud enough to retard another Nile. All in vain: and I mournfully turned my face toward the General's, feeling that I should be forced to enrich the railroad company after all; when, suddenly, I beheld that admirable young man, brother-in-law Darby Coobiddy, Esq. I arrested him with a burst of news, and wants, and woes, which caused his manly countenance to lose its usual repose.

"Oh, my dear boy, I'm going to Washington at five, and I can't find the free ticket man, and there won't be time to see Joan, and I'm so tired and cross I don't know what to do; and will you help me, like a cherub as you are?"

"Oh, yes, of course. I know a fellow who will set us right," responded Darby, mildly excited, and darting into some kind of an office, held counsel with an invisible angel, who sent him out radiant.

"All serene. I've got him. I'll see you through the business, and then get Joan from the Dove Cote in time to see you off."

I'm a woman's rights woman, and if any man had offered help in the morning, I should have condescendingly refused it, sure that I could do everything as well, if not better, myself. My strong-mindedness had rather abated since then, and I was now quite ready to be a "timid trembler," if necessary. Dear me! how easily Darby did it all: he just asked one question, received an answer, tucked me under his arm, and in ten minutes I stood in the presence of Mc K., the Desired.

"Now my troubles are over," thought I, and as usual was direfully mistaken.

"You will have to get a pass from Dr. H., in Temple Place, before I can give you a pass, madam," answered Mc K., as blandly as if he wasn't carrying desolation to my soul. Oh, indeed! why didn't he send me to Dorchester Heights, India Wharf, or Bunker Hill Monument, and done with it? Here I was, after a morning's tramp, down in some place about Dock Square, and was told to step to Temple Place. Nor was that all; he might as well have asked me to catch a humming-bird, toast a salamander, or call on the man in the moon, as find a Doctor at home at the busiest hour of the day. It was a blow; but weariness had extinguished enthusiasm, and resignation clothed me as a garment. I sent Darby for Joan, and doggedly paddled off, feeling that mud was my native element, and quite sure that the evening papers would announce the appearance of the Wandering Jew, in feminine habiliments.

"Is Dr. H. in?"

"No, mum, he ain't."

Of course he wasn't; I knew that before I asked: and, considering it all in the light of a hollow mockery, added:

"When will he probably return?"

If the damsel had said, "ten to-night," I should have felt a grim satisfaction, in the fulfillment of my own dark prophecy; but she said, "At two, mum"; and I felt it a personal insult.

"I'll call, then. Tell him my business is important": with which mysteriously delivered message I departed, hoping that I left her consumed with curiosity; for mud rendered me an object of interest.

By way of resting myself, I crossed the Common, for the third time, bespoke the carriage, got some lunch, packed my purchases, smoothed my plumage, and was back again, as the clock struck two. The Doctor hadn't come yet; and I was morally certain that he would not, till, having waited till the last minute, I was driven to buy a ticket, and, five minutes after the irrevocable deed was done, he would be at my service, with all manner of helpful documents and directions. Everything goes by contraries with me; so, having made up my mind to be disappointed, of course I wasn't; for, presently, in walked Dr. H., and no sooner had he heard my errand, and glanced at my credentials, than he said, with the most engaging readiness:

"I will give you the order, with pleasure, madam."

Words connot express how soothing and delightful it was to find, at last, somebody who could do what I wanted, without sending me from Dan to Beersheba, for a dozen other bodies to do something else first. Peace descended, like oil, upon the ruffled waters of my being, as I sat listening to the busy scratch of his pen; and, when he turned about, giving me not only the order, but a paper of directions wherewith to smooth away all difficulties between Boston and Washington, I felt as did poor Christian when the Evangelist gave him the scroll, on the safe side of the Slough of Despond. I've no doubt many dismal nurses have inflicted themselves upon the worthy gentleman since then; but I am sure none have been more kindly helped, or are more grateful, than T. P.; for that short interview added another to the many pleasant associations that already surround his name.

Feeling myself no longer a "Martha Struggles," but a comfortable young woman, with plain sailing before her, and the worst of the voyage well over, I once more presented myself to the valuable Mc K. The order was read, and certain printed papers, necessary to be filled out, were given a young gentleman—no, I prefer to say Boy, with a scornful emphasis upon the word, as the only means of revenge now left me. This Boy, instead of doing his duty with the diligence so charming in the young, loitered and lounged, in a manner which proved his education to have been sadly neglected in the—

How doth the little busy bee,

direction. He stared at me, gaped out of the window, ate peanuts, and gossiped with his neighbors—Boys, like himself, and all penned in a row, like colts at a Cattle Show. I don't imagine he knew the anguish he was inflicting; for it was nearly three, the train left at five, and I had my ticket to get, my dinner to eat, my blessed sister to see, and the depot to reach, if I didn't die of apoplexy. Meanwhile, Patience certainly had her perfect work that day, and I hope she enjoyed the job more than I did. Having waited some twenty minutes, it pleased this reprehensible Boy to make various marks and blots on my documents, toss them to a venerable creature of sixteen, who delivered them to me with such paternal directions, that it only needed a pat on the head and an encouraging—"Now run home to your Ma, little girl, and mind the crossings, my dear," to make the illusion quite perfect.

Why I was sent to a steamboat office for car tickets, is not for me to say, though I went as meekly as I should have gone to the Probate Court, if sent. A fat, easy gentleman gave me several bits of paper, with coupons attached, with a warning not to separate them, which instantly inspired me with a yearning to pluck them apart, and see what came of it. But, remembering through what fear and tribulation I had obtained them, I curbed Satan's promptings, and, clutching my prize, as if it were my pass to the Elysian Fields, I hurried home. Dinner was rapidly consumed; Joan enlightened, comforted, and kissed; the dearest of apple-faced cousins hugged; the kindest of apple-faced cousins' fathers subjected to the same process; and I mounted the ambulance, baggage-wagon, or anything you please but hack, and drove away, too tired to feel excited, sorry, or glad.

Chapter II

A Forward Movement

A S TRAVELLERS LIKE TO GIVE THEIR OWN IMPRESSIONS OF A JOUR-
ney, though every inch of the way may have been described a
half a dozen times before, I add some of the notes made by the way,
hoping that they will amuse the reader, and convince the skeptical that
such a being as Nurse Periwinkle does exist, that she really did go to
Washington, and that these Sketches are not romance.

New York Train—Seven P.M.—Spinning along to take the boat at
New London. Very comfortable; munch gingerbread, and Mrs. C.'s
fine pear, which deserves honorable mention, because my first loneli-
ness was comforted by it, and pleasant recollections of both kindly
sender and bearer. Look much at Dr. H.'s paper of directions—put my
tickets in every conceivable place, that they may be get-at-able, and
finish by losing them entirely. Suffer agonies till a compassionate
neighbor pokes them out of a crack with his pen-knife. Put them in the
inmost corner of my purse, that in the deepest recesses of my pocket,
pile a collection of miscellaneous articles atop, and pin up the whole.
Just get composed, feeling that I've done my best to keep them safely,
when the Conductor appears, and I'm forced to rout them all out
again, exposing my precautions, and getting into a flutter at keeping
the man waiting. Finally, fasten them on the seat before me, and keep
one eye steadily upon the yellow torments, till I forget all about them,
in chat with the gentleman who shares my seat. Having heard complaints of the absurd way in which American women become images of
petrified propriety, if addressed by strangers, when traveling alone, the

inborn perversity of my nature causes me to assume an entirely opposite style of deportment; and, finding my companion hails from Little
Athens, is acquainted with several of my three hundred and sixty-five
cousins, and in every way a respectable and respectful member of
society, I put my bashfulness in my pocket, and plunge into a long
conversation on the war, the weather, music, Carlyle, skating, genius,
hoops, and the immortality of the soul.

Ten, P.M.—Very sleepy. Nothing to be seen outside, but darkness
made visible; nothing inside but every variety of bunch into which the
human form can be twisted, rolled, or "massed," as Miss Prescott says
of her jewels. Every man's legs sprawl drowsily, every woman's head
(but mine,) nods, till it finally settles on somebody's shoulder, a new
proof of the truth of the everlasting oak and vine simile; children fret;
lovers whisper; old folks snore, and somebody privately imbibes
brandy, when the lamps go out. The penetrating perfume rouses the
multitude, causing some to start up, like war horses at the smell of
powder. When the lamps are relighted, every one laughs, sniffs, and
looks inquiringly at his neighbor—every one but a stout gentleman,
who, with well-gloved hands folded upon his broad-cloth rotundity,
sleeps on impressively. Had he been innocent, he would have waked
up; for, to slumber in that babe-like manner, with a car full of giggling,
staring, sniffing humanity, was simply preposterous. Public suspicion
was down upon him at once. I doubt if the appearance of a flat black
bottle with a label would have settled the matter more effectually than
did the over dignified and profound repose of this short-sighted being.
His moral neck-cloth, virtuous boots, and pious attitude availed him
nothing, and it was well he kept his eyes shut, for "Humbug!" twinkled at him from every window-pane, brass nail and human eye
around him.

Eleven, P.M.—In the boat "City of Boston," escorted thither by
my car acquaintance, and deposited in the cabin. Trying to look as if
the greater portion of my life had been passed on board boats, but
painfully conscious that I don't know the first thing; so sit bolt upright,
and stare about me till I hear one lady say to another—"We must

secure our berths at once"; whereupon I dart at one, and, while lei-surely taking off my cloak, wait to discover what the second move may be. Several ladies draw the curtains that hang in a semi-circle before each nest—instantly I whisk mine smartly together, and then peep out to see what next. Gradually, on hooks above the blue and yellow drapery, appear the coats and bonnets of my neighbors, while their boots and shoes, in every imaginable attitude, assert themselves below, as if their owners had committed suicide in a body. A violent creaking, scrambling, and fussing, causes the fact that people are going regularly to bed to dawn upon my mind. Of course they are! and so am I—but pause at the seventh pin, remembering that, as I was born to be drowned, an eligible opportunity now presents itself; and, having twice escaped a watery grave, the third immersion will certainly extinguish my vital spark. The boat is new, but if it ever intends to blow up, spring a leak, catch afire, or be run into, it will do the deed tonight, because I'm here to fulfill my destiny. With tragic calmness I resign myself, replace my pins, lash my purse and papers together, with my handkerchief, examine the saving circumference of my hoop, and look about me for any means of deliverance when the moist moment shall arrive; for I've no intention of folding my hands and bubbling to death without an energetic splashing first. Barrels, hen-coops, portable set-tees, and life-preservers do not adorn the cabin, as they should; and, roving wildly to and fro, my eye sees no ray of hope till it falls upon a plump old lady, devoutly reading in the cabin Bible, and a voluminous night-cap. I remember that, at the swimming school, fat girls always floated best, and in an instant my plan is laid. At the first alarm I firmly attach myself to the plump lady, and cling to her through fire and water; for I feel that my old enemy, the cramp, will seize me by the foot, if I attempt to swim; and, though I can hardly expect to reach Jersey City with myself and my baggage in as good condition as I hoped, I might manage to get picked up by holding to my fat friend; if not it will be a comfort to feel that I've made an effort and shall die in good society. Poor dear woman! how little she dreamed, as she read and rocked, with her cap in a high state of starch, and her feet comfortably cooking at the register, what fell designs were hovering about her, and how intently a small but determined eye watched her, till it suddenly closed.

Sleep got the better of fear to such an extent that my boots appeared to gape, and my bonnet nodded on its peg, before I gave in. Having piled my cloak, bag, rubbers, books and umbrella on the lower shelf, I drowsily swarmed onto the upper one, tumbling down a few times, and excoriating the knobby portions of my frame in the act. A very brief nap on the upper roost was enough to set me gasping as if a dozen feather beds and the whole boat were laid over me. Out I turned; and, after a series of convulsions, which caused my neighbor to ask if I wanted the stewardess, I managed to get my luggage up and myself down. But even in the lower berth, my rest was not unbroken, for various articles kept dropping off the little shelf at the bottom of the bed, and every time I flew up, thinking my hour had come, I bumped my head severely against the little shelf at the top, evidently put there for that express purpose. At last, after listening to the swash of the waves outside, wondering if the machinery usually creaked in that way, and watching a knot-hole in the side of my berth, sure that death would creep in there as soon as I took my eye from it, I dropped asleep, and dreamed of muffins.

Five, A.M.—On deck, trying to wake up and enjoy an east wind and a morning fog, and a twilight sort of view of something on the shore. Rapidly achieve my purpose, and do enjoy every moment, as we go rushing through the Sound, with steamboats passing up and down, lights dancing on the shore, mist wreaths slowly furling off, and a pale pink sky above us, as the sun comes up.

Seven, A.M.—In the cars, at Jersey City. Much fuss with tickets, which one man scribbles over, another snips, and a third "makes note on." Partake of refreshment, in the gloom of a very large and dirty depot. Think that my sandwiches would be more relishing without so strong a flavor of napkin, and my gingerbread more easy of consumption if it had not been pulverized by being sat upon. People act as if early travelling didn't agree with them. Children scream and scamper;

men smoke and growl; women shiver and fret; porters swear; great truck horses pace up and down with loads of baggage; and every one seems to get into the wrong car, and come tumbling out again. One man, with three children, a dog, a bird-cage, and several bundles, puts himself and his possessions into every possible place where a man, three children, dog, bird-cage and bundles could be got, and is satisfied with none of them. I follow their movements, with an interest that is really exhausting, and, as they vanish, hope for rest, but don't get it. A strong-minded woman, with a tumbler in her hand, and no cloak or shawl on, comes rushing through the car, talking loudly to a small porter, who lugs a folding bed after her, and looks as if life were a burden to him.

"You promised to have it ready. It is not ready. It must be a car with a water jar, the windows must be shut, the fire must be kept up, the blinds must be down. No, this won't do. I shall go through the whole train, and suit myself, for you promised to have it ready. It is not ready," &c., all through again, like a hand-organ. She haunted the cars, the depot, the office and baggage-room, with her bed, her tumbler, and her tongue, till the train started; and a sense of fervent gratitude filled my soul, when I found that she and her unknown invalid were not to share our car.

Philadelphia.—An old place, full of Dutch women, in "bellus top" bonnets, selling vegetables, in long, open markets. Every one seems to be scrubbing their white steps. All the houses look like tidy jails, with their outside shutters. Several have crape on the door-handles, and many have flags flying from roof or balcony. Few men appear, and the women seem to do the business, which, perhaps, accounts for its being so well done. Pass fine buildings, but don't know what they are. Would like to stop and see my native city; for, having left it at the tender age of two, my recollections are not vivid.

Baltimore.—A big, dirty, shippy, shiftless place, full of goats, geese, colored people, and coal, at least the part of it I see. Pass near the spot where the riot took place, and feel as if I should enjoy throwing a stone at somebody, hard. Find a guard at the ferry, the depot, and here and there, along the road. A camp whitens one hill-side, and a cavalry training school, or whatever it should be called, is a very interesting sight, with quantities of horses and riders galloping, marching, leaping, and skirmishing, over all manner of break-neck places. A party of English people get in—the men, with sandy hair and red whiskers, all trimmed alike, to a hair; rough grey coats, very rosy, clean faces, and a fine, full way of speaking, which is particularly agreeable, after our slip-shod American gabble. The two ladies wear funny velvet fur-trimmed hoods; are done up, like compact bundles, in tartan shawls; and look as if bent on seeing everything thoroughly. The devotion of one elderly John Bull to his red-nosed spouse was really beautiful to behold. She was plain and cross, and fussy and stupid, but J. B., Esq., read no papers when she was awake, turned no cold shoulder when she wished to sleep, and cheerfully said, "Yes, me dear," to every wish or want the wife of his bosom expressed. I quite warmed to the excellent man, and asked a question or two, as the only means of expressing my good will. He answered very civilly, but evidently hadn't been used to being addressed by strange women in public conveyances; and Mrs. B. fixed her green eyes upon me, as if she thought me a forward huzzy, or whatever is good English for a presuming young woman. The pair left their friends before we reached Washington; and the last I saw of them was a vision of a large plaid lady, stalking grimly away, on the arm of a rosy, stout gentleman, loaded with rugs, bags, and books, but still devoted, still smiling, and waving a hearty "Fare ye well! We'll meet ye at Willard's on Chusday."

Soon after their departure we had an accident; for no long journey in America would be complete without one. A coupling iron broke; and, after leaving the last car behind us, we waited for it to come up, which it did, with a crash that knocked every one forward on their faces, and caused several old ladies to screech dismally. Hats flew off, bonnets were flattened, the stove skipped, the lamps fell down, the water jar turned a somersault, and the wheel just over which I sat received some damage. Of course, it became necessary for all the men to get out, and stand about in everybody's way, while repairs were made; and for the women to wrestle their heads out of the windows, asking ninety-nine foolish questions to one sensible one. A few wise females seized this favorable moment to better their seats, well knowing that few men can face the wooden stare with which they regard the former possessors of the places they have invaded.

The country through which we passed did not seem so very unlike that which I had left, except that it was more level and less wintry. In summer time the wide fields would have shown me new sights, and the way-side hedges blossomed with new flowers; now, everything was sere and sodden, and a general air of shiftlessness prevailed, which would have caused a New England farmer much disgust, and a strong desire to "buckle to," and "right up" things. Dreary little houses, with chimneys built outside, with clay and rough sticks piled crosswise, as we used to build cob towers, stood in barren looking fields, with cow, pig, or mule lounging about the door. We often passed colored people, looking as if they had come out of a picture book, or off the stage, but not at all the sort of people I'd been accustomed to see at the North.

Way-side encampments made the fields and lanes gay with blue coats and the glitter of buttons. Military washes flapped and fluttered on the fences; pots were steaming in the open air; all sorts of tableaux seen through the openings of tents, and everywhere the boys threw up their caps and cut capers as we passed.

Washington.—It was dark when we arrived; and, but for the presence of another friendly gentleman, I should have yielded myself a helpless prey to the first overpowering hackman, who insisted that I wanted to go just where I didn't. Putting me into the conveyance I belonged in, my escort added to the obligation by pointing out the objects of interest which we passed in our long drive. Though I'd often been told that Washington was a spacious place, its visible magnitude quite took my breath away, and of course I quoted Randolph's expression, "a city of magnificent distances," as I suppose every one does when they see it. The Capitol was so like the pictures that hang opposite the staring Father of his Country, in boarding-houses and hotels, that it did not impress me, except to recall the time when I was sure that Cinderella went to housekeeping in just such a place, after she had married the inflammable Prince; though, even at that early period, I had my doubts as to the wisdom of a match whose foundation was of glass.

The White House was lighted up, and carriages were rolling in and out of the great gate. I stared hard at the famous East Room, and would have liked a peep through the crack of the door. My old gentleman was indefatigable in his attentions, and I said "Splendid!" to everything he pointed out, though I suspect I often admired the wrong place, and missed the right. Pennsylvania Avenue, with its bustle, lights, music, and military, made me feel as if I'd crossed the water and landed somewhere in Carnival time. Coming to less noticeable parts of the city, my companion fell silent, and I meditated upon the perfection which Art had attained in America—having just passed a bronze statue of some hero, who looked like a black Methodist minister, in a cocked hat, above the waist, and a tipsy squire below; while his horse stood like an opera dancer, on one leg, in a high, but somewhat remarkable wind, which blew his mane one way and his massive tail the other.

"Hurlyburly House, ma'am!" called a voice, startling me from my reverie, as we stopped before a great pile of buildings, with a flag flying before it, sentinels at the door, and a very trying quantity of men lounging about. My heart beat rather faster than usual, and it suddenly struck me that I was very far from home; but I descended with dignity, wondering whether I should be stopped for want of a countersign, and forced to pass the night in the street. Marching boldly up the steps, I found that no form was necessary, for the men fell back, the guard touched their caps, a boy opened the door, and, as it closed behind me, I felt that I was fairly started, and Nurse Periwinkle's Mission was begun.

Chapter III

A Day

"THEY'VE COME! THEY'VE COME! HURRY UP, LADIES—YOU'RE wanted."

"Who have come? the rebels?"

This sudden summons in the gray dawn was somewhat startling to a three days' nurse like myself, and, as the thundering knock came at our door, I sprang up in my bed, prepared

To gird my woman's form,
And on the ramparts die,

if necessary, but my room-mate took it more coolly, and, as she began a rapid toilet, answered my bewildered question,—

"Bless you, no child; it's the wounded from Fredericksburg; forty ambulances are at the door, and we shall have our hands full in fifteen minutes."

"What shall we have to do?"

"Wash, dress, feed, warm and nurse them for the next three months, I dare say. Eighty beds are ready, and we were getting impatient for the men to come. Now you will begin to see hospital life in earnest, for you won't probably find time to sit down all day, and may think yourself fortunate if you get to bed by midnight. Come to me in the ball-room when you are ready; the worst cases are always carried there, and I shall need your help."

So saying, the energetic little woman twirled her hair into a button at the back of her head, in a "cleared for action" sort of style, and vanished, wrestling her way into a feminine kind of pea-jacket as she went.

I am free to confess that I had a realizing sense of the fact that my hospital bed was not a bed of roses just then, or the prospect before me one of unmingled rapture. My three days' experiences had begun with a death, and, owing to the defalcation of another nurse, a somewhat abrupt plunge into the superintendence of a ward containing forty beds, where I spent my shining hours washing faces, serving rations, giving medicine, and sitting in a very hard chair, with pneumonia on one side, diphtheria on the other, five typhoids on the opposite, and a dozen dilapidated patriots, hopping, lying, and lounging about, all staring more or less at the new "nuss," who suffered untold agonies, but concealed them under as matronly an aspect as a spinster could assume, and blundered through her trying labors with a Spartan firmness, which I hope they appreciated, but am afraid they didn't. Having a taste for "ghastliness," I had rather longed for the wounded to arrive, for rheumatism wasn't heroic, neither was liver complaint, or measles; even fever had lost its charms since "bathing burning brows" had been used up in romances, real and ideal; but when I peeped into the dusky street lined with what I at first had innocently called market carts, now unloading their sad freight at our door, I recalled sundry reminiscences I had heard from nurses of longer standing, my ardor experienced a sudden chill, and I indulged in a most unpatriotic wish that I was safe at home again, with a quiet day before me, and no necessity for being hustled up, as if I were a hen and had only to hop off my roost, give my plumage a peck, and be ready for action. A second bang at the door sent this recreant desire to the right about, as a little woolly head popped in, and Joey, (a six years' old contraband,) announced—

"Miss Blank is jes' wild fer ye, and says fly round right away. They's comin' in, I tell yer, heaps on 'em—one was took out dead, and I see him,—ky! warn't he a goner!"

With which cheerful intelligence the imp scuttled away, singing like a blackbird, and I followed, feeling that Richard was *not* himself again, and wouldn't be for a long time to come.

The first thing I met was a regiment of the vilest odors that ever assaulted the human nose, and took it by storm. Cologne, with its seven and seventy evil savors, was a posy-bed to it; and the worst of this affliction was, every one had assured me that it was a chronic weakness of all hospitals, and I must bear it. I did, armed with lavender water, with which I so besprinkled myself and premises, that, like my friend, Sairy, I was soon known among my patients as "the nurse with the bottle." Having been run over by three excited surgeons, bumped against by migratory coal-hods, water-pails, and small boys; nearly scalded by an avalanche of newly-filled tea-pots, and hopelessly entangled in a knot of colored sisters coming to wash, I progressed by slow stages up stairs and down, till the main hall was reached, and I paused to take breath and a survey. There they were! "our brave boys," as the papers justly call them, for cowards could hardly have been so riddled with shot and shell, so torn and shattered, nor have borne suffering for which we have no name, with an uncomplaining fortitude, which made one glad to cherish each as a brother. In they came, some on stretchers, some in men's arms, some feebly staggering along propped on rude crutches, and one lay stark and still with covered face, as a comrade gave his name to be recorded before they carried him away to the dead house. All was hurry and confusion; the hall was full of these wrecks of humanity, for the most exhausted could not reach a bed till duly ticketed and registered; the walls were lined with rows of such as could sit, the floor covered with the more disabled, the steps and doorways filled with helpers and lookers on; the sound of many feet and voices made that usually quiet hour as noisy as noon; and, in the midst of it all, the matron's motherly face brought more comfort to many a poor soul, than the cordial draughts she administered, or the cheery words that welcomed all, making of the hospital a home.

The sight of several stretchers, each with its legless, armless, or desperately wounded occupant, entering my ward, admonished me that

I was there to work, not to wonder or weep; so I corked up my feelings, and returned to the path of duty, which was rather "a hard road to travel" just then. The house had been a hotel before hospitals were needed, and many of the doors still bore their old names; some not so inappropriate as might be imagined, for my ward was in truth a *ball-room,* if gun-shot wounds could christen it. Forty beds were prepared, many already tenanted by tired men who fell down anywhere, and drowsed till the smell of food roused them. Round the great stove was gathered the dreariest group I ever saw—ragged, gaunt and pale, mud to the knees, with bloody bandages untouched since put on days before; many bundled up in blankets, coats being lost or useless; and all wearing that disheartened look which proclaimed defeat, more plainly than any telegram of the Burnside blunder. I pitied them so much, I dared not speak to them, though, remembering all they had been through since the route at Fredericksburg, I yearned to serve the dreariest of them all. Presently, Miss Blank tore me from my refuge behind piles of one-sleeved shirts, odd socks, bandages and lint; put basin, sponge, towels, and a block of brown soap into my hands, with these appalling directions:

"Come, my dear, begin to wash as fast as you can. Tell them to take off socks, coats and shirts, scrub them well, put on clean shirts, and the attendants will finish them off, and lay them in bed."

If she had requested me to shave them all, or dance a hornpipe on the stove funnel, I should have been less staggered; but to scrub some dozen lords of creation at a moment's notice, was really—really——. However, there was no time for nonsense, and, having resolved when I came to do everything I was bid, I drowned my scruples in my washbowl, clutched my soap manfully, and, assuming a businesslike air, made a dab at the first dirty specimen I saw, bent on performing my task *vi et armis* if necessary. I chanced to light on a withered old Irishman, wounded in the head, which caused that portion of his frame to be tastefully laid out like a garden, the bandages being the walks, his hair the shrubbery. He was so overpowered by the honor of having a lady wash him, as he expressed it, that he did nothing but roll up his eyes, and bless me, in an irresistible style which was too much for my sense of the ludicrous; so we laughed together, and when I knelt down to take off his shoes, he "flopped" also and wouldn't hear of my touching "them dirty craters. May your bed above be aisy darlin', for the day's work ye are doon!—Whoosh! there ye are, and bedad, it's hard tellin' which is the dirtiest, the fut or the shoe." It was; and if he hadn't been to the fore, I should have gone on pulling, under the impression that the "fut" was a boot, for trousers, socks, shoes and legs were a mass of mud. This comical tableau produced a general grin, at which propitious beginning I took heart and scrubbed away like any tidy parent on a Saturday night. Some of them took the performance like sleepy children, leaning their tired heads against me as I worked, others looked grimly scandalized, and several of the roughest colored like bashful girls. One wore a soiled little bag about his neck, and, as I moved it, to bathe his wounded breast, I said,

"Your talisman didn't save you, did it?"

"Well, I reckon it did, marm, for that shot would a gone a couple a inches deeper but for my old mammy's camphor bag," answered the cheerful philosopher.

Another, with a gun-shot wound through the cheek, asked for a looking-glass, and when I brought one, regarded his swollen face with a dolorous expression, as he muttered—

"I vow to gosh, that's too bad! I warn't a bad looking chap before, and now I'm done for; won't there be a thunderin' scar? and what on earth will Josephine Skinner say?"

He looked up at me with his one eye so appealingly, that I controlled my risibles, and assured him that if Josephine was a girl of sense, she would admire the honorable scar, as a lasting proof that he had faced the enemy, for all women thought a wound the best decoration a brave soldier could wear. I hope Miss Skinner verified the good opinion I so rashly expressed of her, but I shall never know.

The next scrubbee was a nice looking lad, with a curly brown mane, and a budding trace of gingerbread over the lip, which he called his beard, and defended stoutly, when the barber jocosely suggested its immolation. He lay on a bed, with one leg gone, and the right arm so shattered that it must evidently follow; yet the little Sergeant was as merry as if his afflictions were not worth lamenting over, and when a drop or two of salt water mingled with my suds at the sight of this strong young body, so marred and maimed, the boy looked up, with a brave smile, though there was a little quiver of the lips, as he said,

"Now don't you fret yourself about me, miss; I'm first rate here, for it's nuts to lie still on this bed, after knocking about in those confounded ambulances, that shake what there is left of a fellow to jelly. I never was in one of these places before, and think this cleaning up a jolly thing for us, though I'm afraid it isn't for you ladies."

"Is this your first battle, Sergeant?"

"No, miss; I've been in six scrimmages, and never got a scratch till this last one; but it's done the business pretty thoroughly for me, I should say. Lord! what a scramble there'll be for arms and legs, when we old boys come out of our graves, on the Judgment Day: wonder if we shall get our own again? If we do, my leg will have to tramp from Fredericksburg, my arm from here, I suppose, and meet my body, wherever it may be."

The fancy seemed to tickle him mightily, for he laughed blithely, and so did I; which, no doubt, caused the new nurse to be regarded as a light-minded sinner by the Chaplain, who roamed vaguely about, informing the men that they were all worms, corrupt of heart, with perishable bodies, and souls only to be saved by a diligent perusal of certain tracts, and other equally cheering bits of spiritual consolation, when spirituous ditto would have been preferred.

"I say, Mrs.!" called a voice behind me; and, turning, I saw a rough Michigander, with an arm blown off at the shoulder, and two or three bullets still in him—as he afterwards mentioned, as carelessly as if gentlemen were in the habit of carrying such trifles about with them. I went to him, and, while administering a dose of soap and water, he whispered, irefully:

"That red-headed devil, over yonder, is a reb, damn him! You'll agree to that, I'll bet? He's got shet of a foot, or he'd a cut like the rest of the lot. Don't you wash him, nor feed him, but jest let him holler till he's tired. It's a blasted shame to fetch them fellers in here, along side of us; and so I'll tell the chap that bosses this concern; cuss me if I don't."

I regret to say that I did not deliver a moral sermon upon the duty of forgiving our enemies, and the sin of profanity, then and there; but, being a red-hot Abolitionist, stared fixedly at the tall rebel, who was a copperhead, in every sense of the word, and privately resolved to put soap in his eyes, rub his nose the wrong way, and excoriate his cuticle generally, if I had the washing of him.

My amiable intentions however, were frustrated; for, when I approached, with as Christian an expression as my principles would allow, and asked the question—"Shall I try to make you more comfortable, sir?" all I got for my pains was a gruff—

"No; I'll do it myself."

"Here's your Southern chivalry, with a witness," thought I, dumping the basin down before him, thereby quenching a strong desire to give him a summary baptism, in return for his ungraciousness; for my angry passions rose, at this rebuff, in a way that would have scandalized good Dr. Watts. He was a disappointment in all respects, (the rebel, not the blessed Doctor,) for he was neither fiendish, romantic, pathetic, or anything interesting; but a long, fat man, with a head like a burning bush, and a perfectly expressionless face: so I could hate him without the slightest drawback, and ignored his existence from that day forth. One redeeming trait he certainly did possess, as the floor speedily testified; for his ablutions were so vigorously performed, that his bed soon stood like an isolated island, in a sea of soap-suds, and he resembled a dripping merman, suffering from the loss of a fin. If cleanliness is a near neighbor to godliness, then was the big rebel the godliest man in my ward that day.

Having done up our human wash, and laid it out to dry, the second syllable of our version of the word war-fare was enacted with much success. Great trays of bread, meat, soup and coffee appeared; and both nurses and attendants turned waiters, serving bountiful rations to all who could eat. I can call my pinafore to testify to my good will in the work, for in ten minutes it was reduced to a perambulating bill of fare, presenting samples of all the refreshments going or gone. It was a lively scene; the long room lined with rows of beds, each filled by an occupant, whom water, shears, and clean raiment, had transformed from a dismal ragamuffin into a recumbent hero, with a cropped head. To and fro rushed matrons, maids, and convalescent "boys," skirmishing with knives and forks; retreating with empty plates; marching and counter-marching, with unvaried success, while the clash of busy spoons made most inspiring music for the charge of our Light Brigade:

> *Beds to the front of them,*
> *Beds to the right of them,*
> *Beds to the left of them,*
> *Nobody blundered.*
> *Beamed at by hungry souls,*
> *Screamed at with brimming bowls,*
> *Steamed at by army rolls,*
> *Buttered and sundered.*
> *With coffee not cannon plied,*
> *Each must be satisfied,*
> *Whether they lived or died;*
> *All the men wondered.*

Very welcome seemed the generous meal, after a week of suffering, exposure, and short commons; soon the brown faces began to smile, as food, warmth, and rest, did their pleasant work; and the grateful "Thankee's" were followed by more graphic accounts of the battle and retreat, than any paid reporter could have given us. Curious contrasts of the tragic and comic met one everywhere; and some touching as well as ludicrous episodes, might have been recorded that day. A six foot New Hampshire man, with a leg broken and perforated by a piece of shell, so large that, had I not seen the wound, I should have regarded the story as a Munchausenism, beckoned me to come and help him, as he could not sit up, and both his bed and beard were getting plentifully anointed with soup. As I fed my big nestling with corresponding mouthfuls, I asked him how he felt during the battle.

"Well, 'twas my fust, you see, so I ain't ashamed to say I was a trifle flustered in the beginnin', there was such an allfired racket; for ef there's anything I do spleen agin, it's noise. But when my mate, Eph Sylvester, caved, with a bullet through his head, I got mad, and pitched in, licketty cut. Our part of the fight didn't last long; so a lot of us larked round Fredericksburg, and give some of them houses a pretty consid'able of a rummage, till we was ordered out of the mess. Some of our fellows cut like time; but I warn't a-goin to run for nobody; and, fust thing I knew, a shell bust, right in front of us, and I keeled over, feelin' as if I was blowed higher'n a kite. I sung out, and the boys come back for me, double quick; but the way they chucked me over them fences was a caution, I tell you. Next day I was most as black as that darkey yonder, lickin' plates on the sly. This is bully coffee, ain't it? Give us another pull at it, and I'll be obleeged to you."

I did; and, as the last gulp subsided, he said, with a rub of his old handkerchief over eyes as well as mouth:

"Look a here; I've got a pair a earbobs and a handkercher pin I'm a goin' to give you, if you'll have them; for you're the very moral o' Lizy Sylvester, poor Eph's wife: that's why I signalled you to come over here. They ain't much, I guess, but they'll do to memorize the rebs by."

Burrowing under his pillow, he produced a little bundle of what he called "truck," and gallantly presented me with a pair of earrings, each representing a cluster of corpulent grapes, and the pin a basket of astonishing fruit, the whole large and coppery enough for a small warming-pan. Feeling delicate about depriving him of such valuable relics, I accepted the earrings alone, and was obliged to depart, somewhat abruptly, when my friend stuck the warming-pan in the bosom of his night-gown, viewing it with much complacency, and, perhaps, some tender memory, in that rough heart of his, for the comrade he had lost.

Observing that the man next him had left his meal untouched, I offered the same service I had performed for his neighbor, but he shook his head.

"Thank you, ma'am; I don't think I'll ever eat again, for I'm shot in the stomach. But I'd like a drink of water, if you ain't too busy."

I rushed away, but the water-pails were gone to be refilled, and it was some time before they reappeared. I did not forget my patient patient, meanwhile, and, with the first mugful, hurried back to him. He seemed asleep; but something in the tired white face caused me to listen at his lips for a breath. None came. I touched his forehead; it was cold: and then I knew that, while he waited, a better nurse than I had given him a cooler draught, and healed him with a touch. I laid the sheet over the quiet sleeper, whom no noise could now disturb; and, half an hour later, the bed was empty. It seemed a poor requital for all he had sacrificed and suffered,—that hospital bed, lonely even in a crowd; for there was no familiar face for him to look his last upon; no friendly voice to say, Good bye; no hand to lead him gently down into the Valley of the Shadow; and he vanished, like a drop in that red sea upon whose shores so many women stand lamenting. For a moment I felt bitterly indignant at this seeming carelessness of the value of life, the sanctity of death; then consoled myself with the thought that, when the great muster roll was called, these nameless men might be promoted above many whose tall monuments record the barren honors they have won.

All having eaten, drank, and rested, the surgeons began their rounds; and I took my first lesson in the art of dressing wounds. It wasn't a festive scene, by any means; for Dr. P., whose Aid I constituted myself, fell to work with a vigor which soon convinced me that I was a weaker vessel, though nothing would have induced me to confess it then. He had served in the Crimea, and seemed to regard a dilapidated body very much as I should have regarded a damaged garment; and, turning up his cuffs, whipped out a very unpleasant looking housewife, cutting, sawing, patching and piecing, with the enthusiasm of an accomplished surgical seamstress; explaining the process, in scientific terms, to the patient, meantime; which, of course, was immensely cheering and comfortable. There was an uncanny sort of fascination in watching him, as he peered and probed into the mechanism of those wonderful bodies, whose mysteries he understood so well. The more intricate the wound, the better he liked it. A poor private, with both legs off, and shot through the lungs, possessed more attractions for him than a dozen generals, slightly scratched in some "masterly retreat"; and had any one appeared in small pieces, requesting to be put together again, he would have considered it a special dispensation.

The amputations were reserved till the morrow, and the merciful magic of ether was not thought necessary that day, so the poor souls had to bear their pains as best they might. It is all very well to talk of the patience of woman; and far be it from me to pluck that feather from her cap, for, heaven knows, she isn't allowed to wear many; but the patient endurance of these men, under trials of the flesh, was truly wonderful; their fortitude seemed contagious, and scarcely a cry escaped them, though I often longed to groan for them, when pride kept their white lips shut, while great drops stood upon their foreheads, and the bed shook with the irrepressible tremor of their tortured bodies. One or two Irishmen anathematized the doctors with the frankness of their nation, and ordered the Virgin to stand by them, as if she had been the wedded Biddy to whom they could administer the poker, if she didn't; but, as a general thing, the work went on in silence, broken only by some quiet request for roller, instruments, or plaster, a sigh from the patient, or a sympathizing murmur from the nurse.

It was long past noon before these repairs were even partially made; and, having got the bodies of my boys into something like order, the next task was to minister to their minds, by writing letters to the anxious souls at home; answering questions, reading papers, taking possession of money and valuables; for the eighth commandment was reduced to a very fragmentary condition, both by the blacks and whites, who ornamented our hospital with their presence. Pocket books, purses, miniatures, and watches, were sealed up, labelled, and handed over to the matron, till such times as the owners thereof were ready to depart homeward or campward again. The letters dictated to me, and revised by me, that afternoon, would have made an excellent chapter for some future history of the war; for, like that which Thackeray's "Ensign Spooney" wrote his mother just before Waterloo, they were "full of affection, pluck, and bad spelling"; nearly all giving lively accounts of the battle, and ending with a somewhat sudden plunge from patriotism to provender, desiring "Marm," "Mary Ann," or "Aunt Peters," to send along some pies, pickles, sweet stuff, and apples, "to yourn in haste," Joe, Sam, or Ned, as the case might be.

My little Sergeant insisted on trying to scribble something with his left hand, and patiently accomplished some half dozen lines of hieroglyphics, which he gave me to fold and direct, with a boyish blush, that rendered a glimpse of "My Dearest Jane," unnecessary, to assure me that the heroic lad had been more successful in the service of Commander-in-Chief Cupid than that of Gen. Mars; and a charming little romance blossomed instanter in Nurse Periwinkle's romantic fancy, though no further confidences were made that day, for Sergeant fell asleep, and, judging from his tranquil face, visited his absent sweetheart in the pleasant land of dreams.

At five o'clock a great bell rang, and the attendants flew, not to arms, but to their trays, to bring up supper, when a second uproar announced that it was ready. The new comers woke at the sound; and I presently discovered that it took a very bad wound to incapacitate the defenders of the faith for the consumption of their rations; the amount that some of them sequestered was amazing; but when I suggested the probability of a famine hereafter, to the matron, that motherly lady cried out: "Bless their hearts, why shouldn't they eat? It's their only amusement; so fill every one, and, if there's not enough ready to-night, I'll lend my share to the Lord by giving it to the boys." And, whipping up her coffee-pot and plate of toast, she gladdened the eyes and stomachs of two or three dissatisfied heroes, by serving them with a liberal hand; and I haven't the slightest doubt that, having cast her bread upon the waters, it came back buttered, as another large-hearted old lady was wont to say.

Then came the doctor's evening visit; the administration of medicines; washing feverish faces; smoothing tumbled beds; wetting wounds; singing lullabies; and preparations for the night. By eleven, the last labor of love was done; the last "good night" spoken; and, if any needed a reward for that day's work, they surely received it, in the silent eloquence of those long lines of faces, showing pale and peaceful in the shaded rooms, as we quitted them, followed by grateful glances that lighted us to bed, where rest, the sweetest, made our pillows soft, while Night and Nature took our places, filling that great house of pain with the healing miracles of Sleep, and his diviner brother, Death.

Chapter IV

A Night

BEING FOND OF THE NIGHT SIDE OF NATURE, I WAS SOON PRO-moted to the post of night nurse, with every facility for indulging in my favorite pastime of "owling." My colleague, a black-eyed widow, relieved me at dawn, we two taking care of the ward, between us, like the immortal Sairy and Betsey, "turn and turn about." I usually found my boys in the jolliest state of mind their condition allowed; for it was a known fact that Nurse Periwinkle objected to blue devils, and entertained a belief that he who laughed most was surest of recovery. At the beginning of my reign, dumps and dismals prevailed; the nurses looked anxious and tired, the men gloomy or sad; and a general "Hark!-from-the-tombs-a-doleful-sound" style of conversation seemed to be the fashion: a state of things which caused one coming from a merry, social New England town, to feel as if she had got into an exhausted receiver; and the instinct of self-preservation, to say nothing of a philanthropic desire to serve the race, caused a speedy change in Ward No. 1.

More flattering than the most gracefully turned compliment, more grateful than the most admiring glance, was the sight of those rows of faces, all strange to me a little while ago, now lighting up, with smiles of welcome, as I came among them, enjoying that moment heartily, with a womanly pride in their regard, a motherly affection for them all. The evenings were spent in reading aloud, writing letters, waiting on and amusing the men, going the rounds with Dr. P., as he made his second daily survey, dressing my dozen wounds afresh, giving last doses, and making them cozy for the long hours to come, till the nine o'clock bell rang, the gas was turned down, the day nurses went off duty, the night watch came on, and my nocturnal adventure began.

My ward was now divided into three rooms; and, under favor of the matron, I had managed to sort out the patients in such a way that I had what I called, "my duty room," my "pleasure room," and my "pathetic room," and worked for each in a different way. One, I visited, armed with a dressing tray, full of rollers, plasters, and pins; another, with books, flowers, games, and gossip; a third, with teapots, lullabies, consolation, and, sometimes, a shroud.

Wherever the sickest or most helpless man chanced to be, there I held my watch, often visiting the other rooms, to see that the general watchman of the ward did his duty by the fires and the wounds, the latter needing constant wetting. Not only on this account did I meander, but also to get fresher air than the close rooms afforded; for, owing to the stupidity of that mysterious "somebody" who does all the damage in the world, the windows had been carefully nailed down above, and the lower sashes could only be raised in the mildest weather, for the men lay just below. I had suggested a summary smashing of a few panes here and there, when frequent appeals to headquarters had proved unavailing, and daily orders to lazy attendants had come to nothing. No one seconded the motion, however, and the nails were far beyond my reach; for, though belonging to the sisterhood of "ministering angels," I had no wings, and might as well have asked for Jacob's ladder, as a pair of steps, in that charitable chaos.

One of the harmless ghosts who bore me company during the haunted hours, was Dan, the watchman, whom I regarded with a certain awe; for, though so much together, I never fairly saw his face, and, but for his legs, should never have recognized him, as we seldom met by day. These legs were remarkable, as was his whole figure, for his body was short, rotund, and done up in a big jacket, and muffler; his beard hid the lower part of his face, his hat-brim the upper; and all I ever discovered was a pair of sleepy eyes, and a very mild voice. But the legs!—very long, very thin, very crooked and feeble, looking like grey sausages in their tight coverings, without a ray of pegtopishness about them, and finished off with a pair of expansive, green cloth shoes, very like Chinese junks, with the sails down. This figure, gliding noiselessly about the dimly lighted rooms, was strongly suggestive of the spirit of a beer barrel mounted on cork-screws, haunting the old hotel in search of its lost mates, emptied and staved in long ago.

Another goblin who frequently appeared to me, was the attendant of the pathetic room, who, being a faithful soul, was often up to tend two or three men, weak and wandering as babies, after the fever had gone. The amiable creature beguiled the watches of the night by brewing jorums of a fearful beverage, which he called coffee, and insisted on sharing with me; coming in with a great bowl of something like mud soup, scalding hot, guiltless of cream, rich in an all-pervading flavor of molasses, scorch and tin pot. Such an amount of good will and neighborly kindness also went into the mess, that I never could find the heart to refuse, but always received it with thanks, sipped it with hypocritical relish while he remained, and whipped it into the slop-jar the instant he departed, thereby gratifying him, securing one rousing laugh in the doziest hour of the night, and no one was the worse for the transaction but the pigs. Whether they were "cut off untimely in their sins," or not, I carefully abstained from inquiring.

It was a strange life—asleep half the day, exploring Washington the other half, and all night hovering, like a massive cherubim, in a red rigolette, over the slumbering sons of man. I liked it, and found many things to amuse, instruct, and interest me. The snores alone were quite a study, varying from the mild sniff to the stentorian snort, which startled the echoes and hoisted the performer erect to accuse his neighbor of the deed, magnanimously forgive him, and, wrapping the drapery of his couch about him, lie down to vocal slumber. After listening for a week to this band of wind instruments, I indulged in the belief that I could recognize each by the snore alone, and was tempted to join the chorus by breaking out with John Brown's favorite hymn:

Blow ye the trumpet, blow!

I would have given much to have possessed the art of sketching, for many of the faces became wonderfully interesting when unconscious. Some grew stern and grim, the men evidently dreaming of war, as they gave orders, groaned over their wounds, or damned the rebels vigorously; some grew sad and infinitely pathetic, as if the pain borne silently all day, revenged itself by now betraying what the man's pride had concealed so well. Often the roughest grew young and pleasant when sleep smoothed the hard lines away, letting the real nature assert itself; many almost seemed to speak, and I learned to know these men better by night than through any intercourse by day. Sometimes they disappointed me, for faces that looked merry and good in the light, grew bad and sly when the shadows came; and though they made no confidences in words, I read their lives, leaving them to wonder at the change of manner this midnight magic wrought in their nurse. A few talked busily; one drummer boy sang sweetly, though no persuasions could win a note from him by day; and several depended on being told what they had talked of in the morning. Even my constitutionals in the chilly halls, possessed a certain charm, for the house was never still. Sentinels tramped round it all night long, their muskets glittering in the wintry moonlight as they walked, or stood before the doors, straight and silent, as figures of stone, causing one to conjure up romantic visions of guarded forts, sudden surprises, and daring deeds; for in these war times the hum drum life of Yankeedom has vanished, and the most prosaic feel some thrill of that excitement which stirs the nation's heart, and makes its capital a camp of hospitals. Wandering up and down these lower halls, I often heard cries from above, steps hurrying to and fro, saw surgeons passing up, or men coming down carrying a stretcher, where lay a long white figure, whose face was shrouded and whose fight was done. Sometimes I stopped to watch the passers in the street, the moonlight shining on the spire opposite, or the gleam of some vessel floating, like a white-winged sea-gull, down the broad Potomac, whose fullest flow can never wash away the red stain of the land.

The night whose events I have a fancy to record, opened with a little comedy, and closed with a great tragedy; for a virtuous and useful life untimely ended is always tragical to those who see not as God sees. My headquarters were beside the bed of a New Jersey boy, crazed by the horrors of that dreadful Saturday. A slight wound in the knee brought him there; but his mind had suffered more than his body; some string of that delicate machine was over strained, and, for days, he had been reliving, in imagination, the scenes he could not forget, till his distress broke out in incoherent ravings, pitiful to hear. As I sat by him, endeavoring to soothe his poor distracted brain by the constant touch of wet hands over his hot forehead, he lay cheering his comrades on, hurrying them back, then counting them as they fell around him, often clutching my arm, to drag me from the vicinity of a bursting shell, or covering up his head to screen himself from a shower of shot; his face brilliant with fever; his eyes restless; his head never still; every muscle strained and rigid; while an incessant stream of defiant shouts, whispered warnings, and broken laments, poured from his lips with that forceful bewilderment which makes such wanderings so hard to overhear.

It was past eleven, and my patient was slowly wearying himself into fitful intervals of quietude, when, in one of these pauses, a curious sound arrested my attention. Looking over my shoulder, I saw a one-legged phantom hopping nimbly down the room; and, going to meet it, recognized a certain Pennsylvania gentleman, whose wound-fever had taken a turn for the worse, and, depriving him of the few wits a drunken campaign had left him, set him literally tripping on the light, fantastic toe "toward home," as he blandly informed me, touching the military cap which formed a striking contrast to the severe simplicity of the rest of his decidedly *undress* uniform. When sane, the least movement produced a roar of pain or a volley of oaths; but the departure of reason seemed to have wrought an agreeable change, both in the man and his manners; for, balancing himself on one leg, like a meditative stork, he plunged into an animated discussion of the war, the President, lager beer, and Enfield rifles, regardless of any suggestions of mine as to the propriety of returning to bed, lest he be court-martialed for desertion.

Anything more supremely ridiculous can hardly be imagined than this figure, scantily draped in white, its one foot covered with a big blue sock, a dingy cap set rakingly askew on its shaven head, and placid satisfaction beaming in its broad red face, as it flourished a mug in one hand, an old boot in the other, calling them canteen and knap-sack, while it skipped and fluttered in the most unearthly fashion. What to do with the creature I didn't know; Dan was absent, and if I went to find him, the perambulator might festoon himself out of the window, set his toga on fire, or do some of his neighbors a mischief. The attendant of the room was sleeping like a near relative of the celebrated Seven, and nothing short of pins would rouse him; for he had been out that day, and whiskey asserted its supremacy in balmy whiffs. Still declaiming, in a fine flow of eloquence, the demented gentleman hopped on, blind and deaf to my graspings and entreaties;

and I was about to slam the door in his face, and run for help, when a second and saner phantom, "all in white," came to the rescue, in the likeness of a big Prussian, who spoke no English, but divined the crisis, and put an end to it, by bundling the lively monoped into his bed, like a baby, with an authoritative command to "stay put," which received added weight from being delivered in an odd conglomeration of French and German, accompanied by warning wags of a head decorated with a yellow cotton night cap, rendered most imposing by a tassel like a bell-pull. Rather exhausted by his excursion, the member from Pennsylvania subsided; and, after an irrepressible laugh together, my Prussian ally and myself were returning to our places, when the echo of a sob caused us to glance along the beds. It came from one in the corner—such a little bed!—and such a tearful little face looked up at us, as we stopped beside it! The twelve years old drummer boy was not singing now, but sobbing, with a manly effort all the while to stifle the distressful sounds that would break out.

"What is it, Teddy?" I asked, as he rubbed the tears away, and checked himself in the middle of a great sob to answer plaintively:

"I've got a chill, ma'am, but I ain't cryin' for that, 'cause I'm used to it. I dreamed Kit was here, and when I waked up he wasn't, and I couldn't help it, then."

The boy came in with the rest, and the man who was taken dead from the ambulance was the Kit he mourned. Well he might; for, when the wounded were brought from Fredericksburg, the child lay in one of the camps thereabout, and this good friend, though sorely hurt himself, would not leave him to the exposure and neglect of such a time and place; but, wrapping him in his own blanket, carried him in his arms to the transport, tended him during the passage, and only yielded up his charge when Death met him at the door of the hospital which promised care and comfort for the boy. For ten days, Teddy had shivered or burned with fever and ague, pining the while for Kit, and refusing to be comforted, because he had not been able to thank him for the generous protection, which, perhaps, had cost the giver's life. The vivid dream had wrung the childish heart with a fresh pang, and when I tried the solace fitted for his years, the remorseful fear that haunted him found vent in a fresh burst of tears, as he looked at the wasted hands I was endeavoring to warm:

"Oh! if I'd only been as thin when Kit carried me as I am now, maybe he wouldn't have died; but I was heavy, he was hurt worser than we knew, and so it killed him; and I didn't see him, to say good bye."

This thought had troubled him in secret; and my assurances that his friend would probably have died at all events, hardly assuaged the bitterness of his regretful grief.

At this juncture, the delirious man began to shout; the one-legged rose up in his bed, as if preparing for another dart; Teddy bewailed himself more piteously than before: and if ever a woman was at her wit's end, that distracted female was Nurse Periwinkle, during the space of two or three minutes, as she vibrated between the three beds, like an agitated pendulum. Like a most opportune reinforcement, Dan, the bandy, appeared, and devoted himself to the lively party, leaving me free to return to my post; for the Prussian, with a nod and a smile, took the lad away to his own bed, and lulled him to sleep with a soothing murmur, like a mammoth bumble bee. I liked that in Fritz, and if he ever wondered afterward at the dainties which sometimes found their way into his rations, or the extra comforts of his bed, he might have found a solution of the mystery in sundry persons' knowledge of the fatherly action of that night.

Hardly was I settled again, when the inevitable bowl appeared, and its bearer delivered a message I had expected, yet dreaded to receive:

"John is going, ma'am, and wants to see you, if you can come."

"The moment this boy is asleep; tell him so, and let me know if I am in danger of being too late."

My Ganymede departed, and while I quieted poor Shaw, I thought of John. He came in a day or two after the others; and, one evening, when I entered my "pathetic room," I found a lately emptied bed occupied by a large, fair man, with a fine face, and the serenest eyes I ever met. One of the earlier comers had often spoken of a friend, who had remained behind, that those apparently worse wounded than himself might reach a shelter first. It seemed a David and Jonathan sort of friendship. The man fretted for his mate, and was never tired of praising John—his courage, sobriety, self-denial, and unfailing kindliness of heart; always winding up with: "He's an out an' out fine feller, ma'am; you see if he ain't."

I had some curiosity to behold this piece of excellence, and when he came, watched him for a night or two, before I made friends with him; for, to tell the truth, I was a little afraid of the stately looking man, whose bed had to be lengthened to accommodate his commanding stature; who seldom spoke, uttered no complaint, asked no sympathy, but tranquilly observed what went on about him; and, as he lay high upon his pillows, no picture of dying statesman or warrior was ever fuller of real dignity than this Virginia blacksmith. A most attractive face he had, framed in brown hair and beard, comely featured and full of vigor, as yet unsubdued by pain; thoughtful and often beautifully mild while watching the afflictions of others, as if entirely forgetful of his own. His mouth was grave and firm, with plenty of will and courage in its lines, but a smile could make it as sweet as any woman's; and his eyes were child's eyes, looking one fairly in the face, with a clear, straightforward glance, which promised well for such as placed their faith in him. He seemed to cling to life, as if it were rich in duties and delights, and he had learned the secret of content. The only time I saw his composure disturbed, was when my surgeon brought another to examine John, who scrutinized their faces with an anxious look, asking of the elder: "Do you think I shall pull through, sir?" "I hope so, my man." And, as the two passed on, John's eye still followed them, with an intentness which would have won a clearer answer from them, had they seen it. A momentary shadow flitted over his face; then came the usual serenity, as if, in that brief eclipse, he had acknowledged the existence of some hard possibility, and, asking nothing yet hoping all things, left the issue in God's hands, with that submission which is true piety.

The next night, as I went my rounds with Dr. P., I happened to

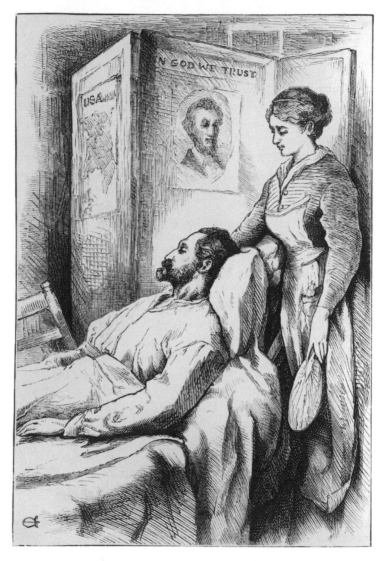

Nurse Tribulation Periwinkle watching over John, the mortally wounded Virginia blacksmith who "seemed to cling to life, as if it were rich in duties and delights, and he had learned the secret of content"—the frontispiece for Hospital Sketches *and* Camp and Fireside Stories *(1869).*

ask which man in the room probably suffered most; and, to my great surprise, he glanced at John:

"Every breath he draws is like a stab; for the ball pierced the left lung, broke a rib, and did no end of damage here and there; so the poor lad can find neither forgetfulness nor ease, because he must lie on his wounded back or suffocate. It will be a hard struggle, and a long one, for he possesses great vitality; but even his temperate life can't save him; I wish it could."

"You don't mean he must die, Doctor?"

"Bless you, there's not the slightest hope for him; and you'd better tell him so before long; women have a way of doing such things comfortably, so I leave it to you. He won't last more than a day or two, at furthest."

I could have sat down on the spot and cried heartily, if I had not learned the wisdom of bottling up one's tears for leisure moments. Such an end seemed very hard for such a man, when half a dozen worn out, worthless bodies round him, were gathering up the remnants of wasted lives, to linger on for years perhaps, burdens to others, daily reproaches to themselves. The army needed men like John, earnest, brave, and faithful; fighting for liberty and justice with both heart and hand, true soldiers of the Lord. I could not give him up so soon, or think with any patience of so excellent a nature robbed of its fulfill- ment, and blundered into eternity by the rashness or stupidity of those at whose hands so many lives may be required. It was an easy thing for Dr. P. to say: "Tell him he must die," but a cruelly hard thing to do, and by no means as "comfortable" as he politely suggested. I had not the heart to do it then, and privately indulged the hope that some change for the better might take place, in spite of gloomy prophesies; so, rendering my task unnecessary. A few minutes later, as I came in again, with fresh rollers, I saw John sitting erect, with no one to support him, while the surgeon dressed his back. I had never hitherto seen it done; for, having simpler wounds to attend to, and knowing the fidelity of the attendant, I had left John to him, thinking it might be more agreeable and safe; for both strength and experience were needed in his case. I had forgotten that the strong man might long for the gentler tendance of a woman's hands, the sympathetic magnetism of a woman's presence, as well as the feebler souls about him. The Doctor's words caused me to reproach myself with neglect, not of any real duty perhaps, but of those little cares and kindnesses that solace homesick spirits, and make the heavy hours pass easier. John looked lonely and forsaken just then, as he sat with bent head, hands folded on his knee, and no outward sign of suffering, till, looking nearer, I saw great tears roll down and drop upon the floor. It was a new sight there; for, though I had seen many suffer, some swore, some groaned, most endured silently, but none wept. Yet it did not seem weak, only very touching, and straightway my fear vanished, my heart opened wide and took him in, as, gathering the bent head in my arms, as freely as if he had been a little child, I said, "Let me help you bear it, John."

Never, on any human countenance, have I seen so swift and beautiful a look of gratitude, surprise and comfort, as that which answered me more eloquently than the whispered—

"Thank you, ma'am, this is right good! this is what I wanted!"

"Then why not ask for it before?"

"I didn't like to be a trouble; you seemed so busy, and I could manage to get on alone."

"You shall not want it any more, John."

Nor did he; for now I understood the wistful look that sometimes followed me, as I went out, after a brief pause beside his bed, or merely a passing nod, while busied with those who seemed to need me more than he, because more urgent in their demands; now I knew that to him, as to so many, I was the poor substitute for mother, wife, or sister, and in his eyes no stranger, but a friend who hitherto had seemed neglectful; for, in his modesty, he had never guessed the truth. This was changed now; and, through the tedious operation of probing, bathing, and dressing his wounds, he leaned against me, holding my hand fast, and, if pain wrung further tears from him, no one saw them fall but me. When he was laid down again, I hovered about him, in a remorseful state of mind that would not let me rest, till I had bathed his face, brushed his "bonny brown hair," set all things smooth about him, and laid a knot of heath and heliotrope on his clean pillow. While doing this, he watched me with the satisfied expression I so liked to see; and when I offered the little nosegay, held it carefully in his great hand, smoothed a ruffled leaf or two, surveyed and smelt it with an air of genuine delight, and lay contentedly regarding the glimmer of the sunshine on the green. Although the manliest man among my forty, he said, "Yes, ma'am," like a little boy; received suggestions for his comfort with the quick smile that brightened his whole face; and now and then, as I stood tidying the table by his bed, I felt him softly touch my gown, as if to assure himself that I was there. Anything more natural and frank I never saw, and found this brave John as bashful as brave, yet full of excellencies and fine aspirations, which, having no power to express themselves in words, seemed to have bloomed into his character and made him what he was.

After that night, an hour of each evening that remained to him was devoted to his ease or pleasure. He could not talk much, for breath was precious, and he spoke in whispers; but from occasional conversations, I gleaned scraps of private history which only added to the affection and respect I felt for him. Once he asked me to write a letter, and as I settled pen and paper, I said, with an irrepressible glimmer of feminine curiosity, "Shall it be addressed to wife, or mother, John?"

"Neither, ma'am; I've got no wife, and will write to mother myself when I get better. Did you think I was married because of this?" he asked, touching a plain ring he wore, and often turned thoughtfully on his finger when he lay alone.

"Partly that, but more from a settled sort of look you have, a look which young men seldom get until they marry."

"I don't know that; but I'm not so very young, ma'am, thirty in May, and have been what you might call settled this ten years; for mother's a widow, I'm the oldest child she has, and it wouldn't do for me to marry until Lizzy has a home of her own, and Laurie's learned his trade; for we're not rich, and I must be father to the children and husband to the dear old woman, if I can."

"No doubt but you are both, John; yet how came you to go to war, if you felt so? Wasn't enlisting as bad as marrying?"

"No, ma'am, not as I see it, for one is helping my neighbor, the other pleasing myself. I went because I couldn't help it. I didn't want the glory or the pay; I wanted the right thing done, and people kept saying the men who were in earnest ought to fight. I was in earnest, the Lord knows! but I held off as long as I could, not knowing which was my duty; mother saw the case, gave me her ring to keep me steady, and said 'Go': so I went."

A short story and a simple one, but the man and the mother were portrayed better than pages of fine writing could have done it.

"Do you ever regret that you came, when you lie here suffering so much?"

"Never, ma'am; I haven't helped a great deal, but I've shown I was willing to give my life, and perhaps I've got to; but I don't blame anybody, and if it was to do over again, I'd do it. I'm a little sorry I wasn't wounded in front; it looks cowardly to be hit in the back, but I obeyed orders, and it don't matter in the end, I know."

Poor John! it did not matter now, except that a shot in front might have spared the long agony in store for him. He seemed to read the thought that troubled me, as he spoke so hopefully when there was no hope, for he suddenly added:

"This is my first battle; do they think it's going to be my last?"

"I'm afraid they do, John."

It was the hardest question I had ever been called upon to answer; doubly hard with those clear eyes fixed on mine, forcing a truthful answer by their own truth. He seemed a little startled at first, pondered over the fateful fact a moment then shook his head, with a glance at the broad chest and muscular limbs stretched out before him:

"I'm not afraid, but it's difficult to believe all at once. I'm so strong it don't seem possible for such a little wound to kill me."

Merry Mercutio's dying words glanced through my memory as he spoke: " 'Tis not so deep as a well, nor so wide as a church door, but 'tis enough." And John would have said the same could he have seen the ominous black holes between his shoulders, he never had; and, seeing the ghastly sights about him, could not believe his own wound more fatal than these, for all the suffering it caused him.

"Shall I write to your mother, now?" I asked, thinking that these sudden tidings might change all plans and purposes; but they did not; for the man received the order of the Divine Commander to march with the same unquestioning obedience with which the soldier had received that of the human one, doubtless remembering that the first led him to life, and the last to death.

"No, ma'am; to Laurie just the same; he'll break it to her best, and I'll add a line to her myself when you get done."

So I wrote the letter which he dictated, finding it better than any I had sent; for, though here and there a little ungrammatical or inelegant, each sentence came to me briefly worded, but most expressive; full of excellent counsel to the boy, tenderly bequeathing "mother and Lizzie" to his care, and bidding him good bye in words the sadder for their simplicity. He added a few lines, with steady hand, and, as I sealed it, said, with a patient sort of sigh, "I hope the answer will come in time for me to see it"; then, turning away his face, laid the flowers against his lips, as if to hide some quiver of emotion at the thought of such a sudden sundering of all the dear home ties.

These things had happened two days before; now John was dying, and the letter had not come. I had been summoned to many death beds in my life, but to none that made my heart ache as it did then, since my mother called me to watch the departure of a spirit akin to this in its gentleness and patient strength. As I went in, John stretched out both hands:

"I knew you'd come! I guess I'm moving on, ma'am."

He was; and so rapidly that, even while he spoke, over his face I saw the grey veil falling that no human hand can lift. I sat down by him, wiped the drops from his forehead, stirred the air about him with the slow wave of a fan, and waited to help him die. He stood in sore need of help—and I could do so little; for, as the doctor had foretold, the strong body rebelled against death, and fought every inch of the way, forcing him to draw each breath with a spasm, and clench his hands with an imploring look, as if he asked, "How long must I endure this, and be still!" For hours he suffered dumbly, without a moment's respite, or a moment's murmuring; his limbs grew cold, his face damp, his lips white, and, again and again, he tore the covering off his breast, as if the lightest weight added to his agony; yet through it all, his eyes never lost their perfect serenity, and the man's soul seemed to sit therein, undaunted by the ills that vexed his flesh.

One by one, the men woke, and round the room appeared a circle of pale faces and watchful eyes, full of awe and pity; for, though a stranger, John was beloved by all. Each man there had wondered at his patience, respected his piety, admired his fortitude, and now lamented his hard death; for the influence of an upright nature had made itself deeply felt, even in one little week. Presently, the Jonathan who so loved this comely David, came creeping from his bed for a last look and word. The kind soul was full of trouble, as the choke in his voice, the grasp of his hand, betrayed; but there were no tears, and the farewell of the friends was the more touching for its brevity.

"Old boy, how are you?" faltered the one.

"Most through, thank heaven!" whispered the other.

"Can I say or do anything for you anywheres?"

"Take my things home, and tell them that I did my best."

"I will! I will!"

"Good bye, Ned."

"Good bye, John, good bye!"

They kissed each other, tenderly as women, and so parted, for poor Ned could not stay to see his comrade die. For a little while, there was no sound in the room but the drip of water, from a stump or two, and John's distressful gasps, as he slowly breathed his life away. I thought him nearly gone, and had just laid down the fan, believing its help to be no longer needed, when suddenly he rose up in his bed, and cried out with a bitter cry that broke the silence, sharply startling every one with its agonized appeal:

"For God's sake, give me air!"

It was the only cry pain or death had wrung from him, the only boon he had asked; and none of us could grant it, for all the airs that blew were useless now. Dan flung up the window. The first red streak of dawn was warming the grey east, a herald of the coming sun; John saw it, and with the love of light which lingers in us to the end, seemed to read in it a sign of hope of help, for, over his whole face there broke that mysterious expression, brighter than any smile, which often comes to eyes that look their last. He laid himself gently down; and, stretching out his strong right arm, as if to grasp and bring the blessed air to his lips in a fuller flow, lapsed into a merciful unconsciousness, which assured us that for him suffering was forever past. He died then; for, though the heavy breaths still tore their way up for a little longer, they were but the waves of an ebbing tide that beat unfelt against the wreck, which an immortal voyager had deserted with a smile. He never spoke again, but to the end held my hand close, so close that when he was asleep at last, I could not draw it away. Dan helped me, warning me as he did so that it was unsafe for dead and living flesh to lie so long together; but though my hand was strangely cold and stiff, and four white marks remained across its back, even when warmth and color had returned elsewhere, I could not but be glad that, through its touch, the presence of human sympathy, perhaps, had lightened that hard hour.

When they had made him ready for the grave, John lay in state for half an hour, a thing which seldom happened in that busy place; but a universal sentiment of reverence and affection seemed to fill the hearts of all who had known or heard of him; and when the rumor of his death went through the house, always astir, many came to see him, and I felt a tender sort of pride in my lost patient; for he looked a most heroic figure, lying there stately and still as the statue of some young knight asleep upon his tomb. The lovely expression which so often beautifies dead faces, soon replaced the marks of pain, and I longed for those who loved him best to see him when half an hour's acquaintance with Death had made them friends. As we stood looking at him, the ward master handed me a letter, saying it had been forgotten the night before. It was John's letter, come just an hour too late to gladden the eyes that had longed and looked for it so eagerly: yet he had it; for, after I had cut some brown locks for his mother, and taken off the ring to send her, telling how well the talisman had done its work, I kissed this good son for her sake, and laid the letter in his hand, still folded as when I drew my own away, feeling that its place was there, and making myself happy with the thought, that, even in his solitary place in the "Government Lot," he would not be without some token of the love which makes life beautiful and outlives death. Then I left him, glad to have known so genuine a man, and carrying with me an enduring memory of the brave Virginia blacksmith, as he lay serenely waiting for the dawn of that long day which knows no night.

Chapter V
Off Duty

"MY DEAR GIRL, WE SHALL HAVE YOU SICK IN YOUR BED, UNLESS you keep yourself warm and quiet for a few days. Widow Wadman can take care of the ward alone, now the men are so comfortable, and have her vacation when you are about again. Now do be prudent in time, and don't let me have to add a Periwinkle to my bouquet of patients."

This advice was delivered, in a paternal manner, by the youngest surgeon in the hospital, a kind-hearted little gentleman, who seemed to consider me a frail young blossom, that needed much cherishing, instead of a tough old spinster, who had been knocking about the world for thirty years. At the time I write of, he discovered me sitting on the stairs, with a nice cloud of unwholesome steam rising from the washroom; a party of January breezes disporting themselves in the halls; and perfumes, by no means from "Araby the blest," keeping them company; while I enjoyed a fit of coughing, which caused my head to spin in a way that made the application of a cool banister both necessary and agreeable, as I waited for the frolicsome wind to restore the breath I'd lost; cheering myself, meantime, with a secret conviction that pneumonia was waiting for me round the corner. This piece of advice had been offered by several persons for a week, and refused by me with the obstinacy with which my sex is so richly gifted. But the last few hours had developed several surprising internal and external phenomena, which impressed upon me the fact that if I didn't make a masterly retreat very soon, I should tumble down somewhere, and have to be borne ignominiously from the field. My head felt like a cannon ball; my feet had a tendency to cleave to the floor; the walls at times undulated in a most disagreeable manner; people looked unnaturally big; and the "very bottles on the mankle shelf" appeared to dance derisively before my eyes. Taking these things into consideration, while blinking stupidly at Dr. Z., I resolved to retire gracefully, if I must; so, with a valedictory to my boys, a private lecture to Mrs. Wadman, and a fervent wish that I could take off my body and work in my soul, I mournfully ascended to my apartment, and Nurse P. was reported off duty.

For the benefit of any ardent damsel whose patriotic fancy may have surrounded hospital life with a halo of charms, I will briefly describe the bower to which I retired, in a somewhat ruinous condition. It was well ventilated, for five panes of glass had suffered compound fractures, which all the surgeons and nurses had failed to heal; the two windows were draped with sheets, the church hospital opposite being a brick and mortar Argus, and the female mind cherishing a prejudice in favor of retiracy during the night-capped periods of existence. A bare floor supported two narrow iron beds, spread with thin mattresses like plasters, furnished with pillows in the last stages of consumption. In a fire place, guiltless of shovel, tongs, andirons, or grate, burned a log, inch by inch, being too long to go on all at once;

so, while the fire blazed away at one end, I did the same at the other, as I tripped over it a dozen times a day, and flew up to poke it a dozen times at night. A mirror (let us be elegant!) of the dimensions of a muffin, and about as reflective, hung over a tin basin, blue pitcher, and a brace of yellow mugs. Two invalid tables, ditto chairs, wandered here and there, and the closet contained a varied collection of bonnets, bottles, bags, boots, bread and butter, boxes and bugs. The closet was a regular Blue Beard cupboard to me; I always opened it with fear and trembling, owing to rats, and shut it in anguish of spirit; for time and space were not to be had, and chaos reigned along with the rats. Our chimney-piece was decorated with a flat-iron, a Bible, a candle minus stick, a lavender bottle, a new tin pan, so brilliant that it served nicely for a pier-glass, and such of the portly black bugs as preferred a warmer climate than the rubbish hole afforded. Two arks, commonly called trunks, lurked behind the door, containing the worldly goods of the twain who laughed and cried, slept and scrambled, in this refuge; while from the white-washed walls above either bed, looked down the pictured faces of those whose memory can make for us—

One little room an everywhere.

For a day or two I managed to appear at meals; for the human grub must eat till the butterfly is ready to break loose, and no one had time to come up two flights while it was possible for me to come down. Far be it from me to add another affliction or reproach to that enduring man, the steward; for, compared with his predecessor, he was a horn of plenty; but—I put it to any candid mind—is not the following bill of fare susceptible of improvement, without plunging the nation madly into debt? The three meals were "pretty much of a muchness," and consisted of beef, evidently put down for the men of '76; pork, just in from the street; army bread, composed of saw-dust and saleratus; butter, salt as if churned by Lot's wife; stewed blackberries, so much like preserved cockroaches, that only those devoid of imagination could partake thereof with relish; coffee, mild and muddy; tea, three dried huckleberry leaves to a quart of water—flavored with lime—also animated and unconscious of any approach to clearness. Variety being the spice of life, a small pinch of the article would have been appreciated by the hungry, hard-working sisterhood, one of whom, though accustomed to plain fare, soon found herself reduced to bread and water; having an inborn repugnance to the fat of the land, and the salt of the earth.

Another peculiarity of these hospital meals was the rapidity with which the edibles vanished, and the impossibility of getting a drop or crumb after the usual time. At the first ring of the bell, a general stampede took place; some twenty hungry souls rushed to the dining-room, swept over the table like a swarm of locusts, and left no fragment for any tardy creature who arrived fifteen minutes late. Thinking it of more importance that the patients should be well and comfortably fed, I took my time about my own meals for the first day or two after I came, but was speedily enlightened by Isaac, the black waiter, who bore with me a few times, and then informed me, looking as stern as fate:

"I say, mam, ef you comes so late you can't have no vittles,—'cause I'm 'bleeged fer ter git things ready fer de doctors 'mazin' spry arter you nusses and folks is done. De gen'lemen don't kere fer ter wait, no more does I; so you jes' please ter come at de time, and dere won't be no frettin' nowheres."

It was a new sensation to stand looking at a full table, painfully conscious of one of the vacuums which Nature abhors, and receive orders to right about face, without partaking of the nourishment which your inner woman clamorously demanded. The doctors always fared better than we; and for a moment a desperate impulse prompted me to give them a hint, by walking off with the mutton, or confiscating the pie. But Ike's eye was on me, and, to my shame be it spoken, I walked meekly away; went dinnerless that day, and that evening went to market, laying in a small stock of crackers, cheese and apples, that my boys might not be neglected, nor myself obliged to bolt solid and liquid dyspepsias, or starve. This plan would have succeeded admira-

bly had not the evil star under which I was born, been in the ascendant
during that month, and cast its malign influences even into my " 'um-
ble" larder; for the rats had their dessert off my cheese, the bugs set up
housekeeping in my cracker-bag, and the apples like all worldly riches,
took to themselves wings and flew away; whither no man could tell,
though certain black imps might have thrown light upon the matter,
had not the plaintiff in the case been loth to add another to the many
trials of long-suffering Africa. After this failure I resigned myself to
fate, and, remembering that bread was called the staff of life, leaned
pretty exclusively upon it; but it proved a broken reed, and I came to
the ground after a few weeks of prison fare, varied by an occasional
potato or surreptitious sip of milk.

Very soon after leaving the care of my ward, I discovered that I
had no appetite, and cut the bread and butter interests almost entirely,
trying the exercise and sun cure instead. Flattering myself that I had
plenty of time, and could see all that was to be seen, so far as a lone
lorn female could venture in a city, one-half of whose male population
seemed to be taking the other half to the guard-house,—every morning I took a brisk run in one direction or another; for the January days
were as mild as Spring. A rollicking north wind and occasional snow
storm would have been more to my taste, for the one would have
braced and refreshed tired body and soul, the other have purified the
air, and spread a clean coverlid over the bed, wherein the capital of
these United States appeared to be dozing pretty soundly just then.

One of these trips was to the Armory Hospital, the neatness, comfort, and convenience of which makes it an honor to its presiding
genius, and arouses all the covetous propensities of such nurses as
came from other hospitals to visit it.

The long, clean, warm, and airy wards, built barrack-fashion, with
the nurse's room at the end, were fully appreciated by Nurse Periwinkle, whose ward and private bower were cold, dirty, inconvenient, up
stairs and down stairs, and in everybody's chamber. At the Armory, in
ward K, I found a cheery, bright-eyed, white-aproned little lady, reading at her post near the stove; matting under her feet; a draft of fresh

air flowing in above her head; a table full of trays, glasses, and such matters, on one side, a large, well-stocked medicine chest on the other; and all her duty seemed to be going about now and then to give doses, issue orders, which well-trained attendants executed, and pet, advise, or comfort Tom, Dick, or Harry, as she found best. As I watched the proceedings, I recalled my own tribulations, and contrasted the two hospitals in a way that would have caused my summary dismissal, could it have been reported at headquarters. Here, order, method, common sense and liberality reigned and ruled, in a style that did one's heart good to see; at the Hurlyburly Hotel, disorder, discomfort, bad management, and no visible head, reduced things to a condition which I despair of describing. The circumlocution fashion prevailed, forms and fusses tormented our souls, and unnecessary strictness in one place was counterbalanced by unpardonable laxity in another. Here is a sample: I am dressing Sam Dammer's shoulder; and, having cleansed the wound look about for some strips of adhesive plaster to hold on the little square of wet linen which is to cover the gunshot wound; the case is not in the tray; Frank, the sleepy, half-sick attendant, knows nothing of it; we rummage high and low; Sam is tired, and fumes; Frank dawdles and yawns; the men advise and laugh at the flurry; I feel like a boiling tea-kettle, with the lid ready to fly off and damage somebody.

"Go and borrow some from the next ward, and spend the rest of the day in finding ours," I finally command. A pause; then Frank scuffles back with the message: "Miss Peppercorn ain't got none, and says you ain't no business to lose your own duds and go borrowin' other folkses." I say nothing, for fear of saying too much, but fly to the surgery. Mr. Toddypestle informs me that I can't have anything without an order from the surgeon of my ward. Great heavens! where is he? and away I rush, up and down, here and there, till at last I find him, in a state of bliss over a complicated amputation, in the fourth story. I make my demand; he answers: "In five minutes," and works away, with his head upside down, as he ties an artery, saws a bone, or does a little needle-work, with a visible relish and very sanguinary pair of hands. The five minutes grow to fifteen, and Frank appears, with the remark that, "Dammer wants to know what in thunder you are keeping him there with his finger on a wet rag for?" Dr. P. tears himself away long enough to scribble the order, with which I plunge downward to the surgery again, find the door locked, and, while hammering away on it, am told that two friends are waiting to see me in the hall. The matron being away, her parlor is locked, and there is no where to see my guests but in my own room, and no time to enjoy them till the plaster is found. I settle this matter, and circulate through the house to find Toddypestle, who has no right to leave the surgery till night. He is discovered in the dead house, smoking a cigar, and very much the worse for his researches among the spirituous preparations that fill the surgery shelves. He is inclined to be gallant, and puts the finishing blow to the fire of my wrath; for the tea-kettle lid flies off, and driving him before me to his post, I fling down the order, take what I choose; and, leaving the absurd incapable kissing his hand to me, depart, feeling as Grandma Riglesty is reported to have done, when she vainly sought for chips, in Bimleck Jackwood's "shifless paster."

I find Dammer a well acted charade of his own name, and, just as I get him done, struggling the while with a burning desire to clap an adhesive strip across his mouth, full of heaven-defying oaths, Frank takes up his boot to put it on, and exclaims:

"I'm blest ef here ain't that case now! I recollect seeing it pitch in this mornin', but forgot all about it, till my heel went smash inter it. Here, ma'am, ketch hold on it, and give the boys a sheet on't all round, 'gainst it tumbles inter t'other boot next time yer want it."

If a look could annihilate, Francis Saucebox would have ceased to exist, but it couldn't; therefore, he yet lives, to aggravate some unhappy woman's soul, and wax fat in some equally congenial situation.

Now, while I'm freeing my mind, I should like to enter my protest against employing convalescents as attendants, instead of strong, properly trained, and cheerful men. How it may be in other places I cannot say; but here it was a source of constant trouble and confusion, these feeble, ignorant men trying to sweep, scrub, lift, and wait upon their sicker comrades. One, with a diseased heart, was expected to run up and down stairs, carry heavy trays, and move helpless men; he tried it, and grew rapidly worse than when he first came: and, when he was ordered out to march away to the convalescent hospital, fell, in a sort of fit, before he turned the corner, and was brought back to die. Another, hurt by a fall from his horse, endeavored to do his duty, but failed entirely, and the wrath of the ward master fell upon the nurse, who must either scrub the rooms herself, or take the lecture; for the boy looked stout and well, and the master never happened to see him turn white with pain, or hear him groan in his sleep when an involuntary motion strained his poor back. Constant complaints were being made of incompetent attendants, and some dozen women did double duty, and then were blamed for breaking down. If any hospital director fancies this a good and economical arrangement, allow one used up nurse to tell him it isn't, and beg him to spare the sisterhood, who sometimes, in their sympathy, forget that they are mortal, and run the risk of being made immortal, sooner than is agreeable to their partial friends.

Another of my few rambles took me to the Senate Chamber, hoping to hear and see if this large machine was run any better than some small ones I knew of. I was too late, and found the Speaker's chair occupied by a colored gentleman of ten; while two others were "on their legs," having a hot debate on the cornball question, as they gathered the waste paper strewn about the floor into bags; and several white members played leap-frog over the desks, a much wholesomer relaxation than some of the older Senators indulge in, I fancy. Finding the coast clear, I likewise gambolled up and down, from gallery to gallery; sat in Sumner's chair, and cudgelled an imaginary Brooks within an inch of his life; examined Wilson's books in the coolest possible manner; warmed my feet at one of the national registers; read people's names on scattered envelopes, and pocketed a castaway autograph or two; watched the somewhat unparliamentary proceedings going on about me, and wondered who in the world all the sedate gentlemen were, who kept popping out of odd doors here and there, like respectable Jacks-in-the-box. Then I wandered over the "palatial residence" of Mrs. Columbia, and examined its many beauties, though I can't say I thought her a tidy housekeeper, and didn't admire her taste in pictures, for the eye of this humble individual soon wearied of expiring patriots, who all appeared to be quitting their earthly tabernacles in convulsions, ruffled shirts, and a whirl of torn banners, bomb shells, and buff and blue arms and legs. The statuary also was massive and concrete, but rather wearying to examine; for the colossal ladies and gentlemen, carried no cards of introduction in face or figure; so, whether the meditative party in a kilt, with well-developed legs, shoes like army slippers, and a ponderous nose, was Columbus, Cato, or Cockelorum Tibby, the tragedian, was more than I could tell. Several robust ladies attracted me, as I felt particularly "wimbly" myself, as old country women say: but which was America and which Pocahontas was a mystery, for all affected much looseness of costume, dishevelment of hair, swords, arrows, lances, scales, and other ornaments quite *passé* with damsels of our day, whose effigies should go down to posterity armed with fans, crochet needles, riding whips, and parasols, with here and there one holding pen or pencil, rolling-pin or broom. The statue of Liberty I recognized at once, for it had no pedestal as yet, but stood flat in the mud, with Young America most symbollically making dirt pies, and chip forts, in its shadow. But high above the squabbling little throng and their petty plans, the sun shone full on Liberty's broad forehead, and, in her hand, some summer bird had built its nest. I accepted the good omen then, and, on the first of January, the Emancipation Act gave the statue a nobler and more enduring pedestal than any marble or granite ever carved and quarried by human hands.

One trip to Georgetown Heights, where cedars sighed overhead, dead leaves rustled underfoot, pleasant paths led up and down, and a brook wound like a silver snake by the blackened ruins of some French Minister's house, through the poor gardens of the black washerwomen who congregated there, and, passing the cemetery with a murmurous lullaby, rolled away to pay its little tribute to the river. This breezy run was the last I took; for, on the morrow, came rain and wind: and confinement soon proved a powerful reinforcement to the enemy, who was quietly preparing to spring a mine, and blow me five hundred miles from the position I had taken in what I called my Chickahominy Swamp.

Shut up in my room, with no voice, spirits, or books, that week was not a holiday, by any means. Finding meals a humbug, I stopped away altogether, trusting that if this sparrow was of any worth, the Lord would not let it fall to the ground. Like a flock of friendly ravens, my sister nurses fed me, not only with food for the body, but kind words for the mind; and soon, from being half starved, I found myself so beteaed and betoasted, petted and served, that I was quite "in the lap of luxury," in spite of cough, headache, a painful consciousness of my pleura, and a realizing sense of bones in the human frame. From the pleasant house on the hill, the home in the heart of Washington, and the Willard caravansary, came friends new and old, with bottles, baskets, carriages and invitations for the invalid; and daily our Florence Nightingale climbed the steep stairs, stealing a moment from her busy life, to watch over the stranger, of whom she was as thoughtfully tender as any mother. Long may she wave! Whatever others may think or say, Nurse Periwinkle is forever grateful; and among her relics of that Washington defeat, none is more valued than the little book which appeared on her pillow, one dreary day; for the D. D. written in it means to her far more than Doctor of Divinity.

Being forbidden to meddle with fleshly arms and legs, I solaced myself by mending cotton ones, and, as I sat sewing at my window, watched the moving panorama that passed below; amusing myself with taking notes of the most striking figures in it. Long trains of army wagons kept up a perpetual rumble from morning till night; ambulances rattled to and fro with busy surgeons, nurses taking an airing, or convalescents going in parties to be fitted to artificial limbs. Strings of sorry looking horses passed, saying as plainly as dumb creatures could, "Why, in a city full of them, is there no *horse*pital for us?" Often a cart came by, with several rough coffins in it, and no mourners following;

barouches, with invalid officers, rolled round the corner, and carriage loads of pretty children, with black coachmen, footmen, and maids. The women who took their walks abroad, were so extinguished in three story bonnets, with overhanging balconies of flowers, that their charms were obscured; and all I can say of them is, that they dressed in the worst possible taste, and walked like ducks.

The men did the picturesque, and did it so well that Washington looked like a mammoth masquerade. Spanish hats, scarlet lined riding cloaks, swords and sashes, high boots and bright spurs, beards and mustaches, which made plain faces comely, and comely faces heroic; these vanities of the flesh transformed our butchers, bakers, and candlestick makers into gallant riders of gaily caparisoned horses, much handsomer than themselves; and dozens of such figures were constantly prancing by, with private prickings of spurs, for the benefit of the perambulating flower-bed. Some of these gentlemen affected painfully tight uniforms, and little caps, kept on by some new law of gravitation, as they covered only the bridge of the nose, yet never fell off; the men looked like stuffed fowls, and rode as if the safety of the nation depended on their speed alone. The fattest, greyest officers dressed most, and ambled statelily along, with orderlies behind, trying to look as if they didn't know the stout party in front, and doing much caracoling on their own account.

The mules were my especial delight; and an hour's study of a constant succession of them introduced me to many of their characteristics; for six of these odd little beasts drew each army wagon, and went hopping like frogs through the stream of mud that gently rolled along the street. The coquettish mule had small feet, a nicely trimmed tassel of a tail, perked up ears, and seemed much given to little tosses of the head, affected skips and prances; and, if he wore the bells, or were bedizzened with a bit of finery, put on as many airs as any belle. The moral mule was a stout, hard-working creature, always tugging with all his might; often pulling away after the rest had stopped, laboring under the conscientious delusion that food for the entire army depended upon his private exertions. I respected this style of mule;

and, had I possessed a juicy cabbage, would have pressed it upon him, with thanks for his excellent example. The historical mule was a melodramatic quadruped, prone to startling humanity by erratic leaps, and wild plunges, much shaking of his stubborn head, and lashing out of his vicious heels; now and then falling flat, and apparently dying *a la* Forrest: a gasp—a squirm—a flop, and so on, till the street was well blocked up, the drivers all swearing like demons in bad hats, and the chief actor's circulation decidedly quickened by every variety of kick, cuff, jerk and haul. When the last breath seemed to have left his body, and "Doctors were in vain," a sudden resurrection took place; and if ever a mule laughed with scornful triumph, that was the beast, as he leisurely rose, gave a comfortable shake; and, calmly regarding the excited crowd seemed to say—"A hit! a decided hit! for the stupidest of animals has bamboozled a dozen men. Now, then! what are *you* stopping the way for?" The pathetic mule was, perhaps, the most interesting of all; for, though he always seemed to be the smallest, thinnest, weakest of the six, the postillion, with big boots, long-tailed coat, and heavy whip, was sure to bestride this one, who struggled feebly along, head down, coat muddy and rough, eye spiritless and sad, his very tail a mortified stump, and the whole beast a picture of meek misery, fit to touch a heart of stone. The jovial mule was a roly poly, happy-go-lucky little piece of horse-flesh, taking everything easily, from cudgeling to caressing; strolling along with a roguish twinkle of the eye, and, if the thing were possible, would have had his hands in his pockets, and whistled as he went. If there ever chanced to be an apple core, a stray turnip, or wisp of hay, in the gutter, this Mark Tapley was sure to find it, and none of his mates seemed to begrudge him his bite. I suspected this fellow was the peacemaker, whereat the blood of two generations of abolitionists waxed hot in my veins, and, at the first opportunity, proclaimed itself, and asserted the right of free speech as doggedly as the irrepressible Folsom herself.

Happening to catch up a funny little black baby, who was toddling about the nurses' kitchen, one day, when I went down to make a mess for some of my men, a Virginia woman standing by elevated her most prominent features, with a sniff of disapprobation, exclaiming.

"Gracious, Miss P.! how can you? I've been here six months, and never so much as touched the little toad with a poker."

"More shame for you, ma'am," responded Miss P.; and, with the natural perversity of a Yankee, followed up the blow by kissing "the toad," with ardor. His face was providentially as clean and shiny as if his mamma had just polished it up with a corner of her apron and a drop from the tea-kettle spout, like old Aunt Chloe. This rash act, and the anti-slavery lecture that followed, while one hand stirred gruel for sick America, and the other hugged baby Africa, did not produce the cheering result which I fondly expected; for my comrade henceforth regarded me as a dangerous fanatic, and my protegé nearly came to his death by insisting on swarming up stairs to my room, on all occasions, and being walked on like a little black spider.

I waited for New Year's day with more eagerness than I had ever known before; and, though it brought me no gift, I felt rich in the act of justice so tardily performed toward some of those about me. As the bells rung midnight, I electrified my room-mate by dancing out of bed, throwing up the window, and flapping my handkerchief, with a feeble cheer, in answer to the shout of a group of colored men in the street below. All night they tooted and tramped, fired crackers, sung "Glory, Hallelujah," and took comfort, poor souls! in their own way. The sky was clear, the moon shone benignly, a mild wind blew across the river, and all good omens seemed to usher in the dawn of the day whose noontide cannot now be long in coming. If the colored people had taken hands and danced around the White House, with a few cheers for the much abused gentleman who has immortalized himself by one just act, no President could have had a finer levee, or one to be prouder of.

While these sights and sounds were going on without, curious scenes were passing within, and I was learning that one of the best methods of fitting oneself to be a nurse in a hospital, is to be a patient

"While one hand stirred gruel for sick America, and the other hugged baby Africa,"
Tribulation Periwinkle delivers an antislavery lecture in the nurses' kitchen—another
illustration from Hospital Sketches and Camp and Fireside Stories.

there; for then only can one wholly realize what the men suffer and sigh for; how acts of kindness touch and win; how much or little we are to those about us; and for the first time really see that in coming there we have taken our lives in our hands, and may have to pay dearly for a brief experience. Every one was very kind; the attendants of my ward often came up to report progress, to fill my woodbox, or bring messages and presents from my boys. The nurses took many steps with those tired feet of theirs, and several came each evening, to chat over my fire and make things cosy for the night. The doctors paid daily visits, tapped at my lungs to see if pneumonia was within, left doses without names, and went away, leaving me as ignorant, and much more uncomfortable than when they came. Hours began to get confused; people looked odd; queer faces haunted the room, and the nights were one long fight with weariness and pain. Letters from home grew anxious; the doctors lifted their eyebrows, and nodded ominously; friends said "Don't stay," and an internal rebellion seconded the advice; but the three months were not out, and the idea of giving up so soon was proclaiming a defeat before I was fairly routed; so to all "Don't stays" I opposed "I wills," till, one fine morning, a grey-headed gentleman rose like a welcome ghost on my hearth; and, at the sight of him, my resolution melted away, my heart turned traitor to my boys, and, when he said, "Come home," I answered, "Yes, father"; and so ended my career as an army nurse.

I never shall regret the going, though a sharp tussle with typhoid, ten dollars, and a wig, are all the visible results of the experiment; for one may live and learn much in a month. A good fit of illness proves the value of health; real danger tries one's mettle; and self-sacrifice sweetens character. Let no one who sincerely desires to help the work on in this way, delay going through any fear; for the worth of life lies in the experiences that fill it, and this is one which cannot be forgotten. All that is best and bravest in the hearts of men and women, comes out in scenes like these; and, though a hospital is a rough school, its lessons are both stern and salutary; and the humblest of pupils there, in proportion to his faithfulness, learns a deeper faith in God and in himself.

I, for one, would return tomorrow, on the "up-again,-and-take-an-other" principle, if I could; for the amount of pleasure and profit I got out of that month compensates for all after pangs; and, though a sadly womanish feeling, I take some satisfaction in the thought that, if I could not lay my head on the altar of my country, I have my hair; and that is more than handsome Helen did for her dead husband, when she sacrificed only the ends of her ringlets on his urn. Therefore, I close this little chapter of hospital experiences, with the regret that they were no better worth recording; and add the poetical gem with which I console myself for the untimely demise of "Nurse Periwinkle":

> *Oh, lay her in a little pit,*
> *With a marble stone to cover it;*
> *And carve thereon a gruel spoon,*
> *To show a "nuss" has died too soon.*

Chapter VI
A Postscript

M*Y DEAR S.:*—AS INQUIRIES LIKE YOUR OWN HAVE COME TO me from various friendly readers of the Sketches, I will answer them *en masse,* and in printed form, as a sort of postscript to what has gone before. One of these questions was, "Are there no services by hospital death-beds, or on Sundays?"

In most Hospitals I hope there are; in ours, the men died, and were carried away, with as little ceremony as on a battlefield. The first event of this kind which I witnessed was so very brief, and bare of anything like reverence, sorrow, or pious consolation, that I heartily agreed with the bluntly expressed opinion of a Maine man lying next his comrade, who died with no visible help near him, but a compassionate woman and a tender-hearted Irishman, who dropped upon his knees, and told his beads, with Catholic fervor, for the good of his Protestant brother's parting soul:

"If, after gettin' all the hard knocks, we are left to die this way, with nothing but a Paddy's prayers to help us, I guess Christians are rather scarce round Washington."

I thought so too; but though Miss Blank, one of my mates, anxious that souls should be ministered to, as well as bodies, spoke more than once to the Chaplain, nothing ever came of it. Unlike another Shepherd, whose earnest piety weekly purified the Senate Chamber, this man did not feed as well as fold his flock, nor make himself a human symbol of the Divine Samaritan, who never passes by on the other side.

I have since learned that our non-commital Chaplain had been a Professor, in some Southern College; and, though he maintained that he had no secesh proclivities, I can testify that he seceded from his ministerial duties, I may say, skedaddled; for, being one of his own words, it is as appropriate as inelegant. He read Emerson, quoted Carlyle, and tried to be a Chaplain; but, judging from his success, I am afraid he still hankered after the hominy pots of Rebeldom.

Occasionally, on a Sunday afternoon, such of the nurses, officers, attendants, and patients as could avail themselves of it, were gathered in the Ball Room, for an hour's service, of which the singing was the better part. To me it seemed that if ever strong, wise, and loving words were needed, it was then; if ever mortal man had living texts before his eyes to illustrate and illuminate his thought, it was there; and if ever hearts were prompted to devoutest self-abnegation, it was in the work which brought us to anything but a Chapel of Ease. But some spiritual paralysis seemed to have befallen our pastor; for, though many faces turned toward him, full of the dumb hunger that often comes to men when suffering or danger brings them nearer to the heart of things, they were offered the chaff of divinity, and its wheat was left for less needy gleaners, who knew where to look. Even the fine old Bible stories, which may be made as lifelike as any history of our day, by a vivid fancy and pictorial diction, were robbed of all their charms by dry explanations and literal applications, instead of being useful and pleasant lessons to those men, whom weakness had rendered as docile as children in a father's hands.

I watched the listless countenances all about me, while a mild Daniel was moralizing in a den of utterly uninteresting lions; while Shadrach, Meshech, and Abednego were leisurely passing through the fiery furnace, where, I sadly feared, some of us sincerely wished they had remained as permanencies; while the Temple of Solomon was laboriously erected, with minute descriptions of the process, and any quantity of bells and pomegranates on the raiment of the priests. List-less they were at the beginning, and listless at the end; but the instant some stirring old hymn was given out, sleepy eyes brightened, loung-ing figures sat erect, and many a poor lad rose up in his bed, or stretched an eager hand for the book, while all broke out with a heartiness that proved that somewhere at the core of even the most abandoned, there still glowed some remnant of the native piety that flows in music from the heart of every little child. Even the big rebel joined, and boomed away in a thunderous bass, singing—

"Salvation! let the echoes fly,"

as energetically as if he felt the need of a speedy execution of the command.

That was the pleasantest moment of the hour, for then it seemed a homelike and happy spot; the groups of men looking over one an-other's shoulders as they sang; the few silent figures in the beds; here and there a woman noiselessly performing some necessary duty, and singing as she worked; while in the arm chair standing in the midst, I placed, for my own satisfaction, the imaginary likeness of a certain faithful pastor, who took all outcasts by the hand, smote the devil in whatever guise he came, and comforted the indigent in spirit with the best wisdom of a great and tender heart, which still speaks to us from its Italian grave. With that addition, my picture was complete; and I often longed to take a veritable sketch of a Hospital Sunday, for, despite its drawbacks, consisting of continued labor, the want of proper books, the barren preaching that bore no fruit, this day was never like the other six.

True to their home training, our New England boys did their best to make it what it should be. With many, there was much reading of Testaments, humming over of favorite hymns, and looking at such books as I could cull from a miscellaneous library. Some lay idle, slept, or gossiped; yet, when I came to them for a quiet evening chat, they often talked freely and well of themselves; would blunder out some timid hope that their troubles might "do 'em good, and keep 'em stiddy"; would choke a little, as they said good night, and turned their faces to the wall to think of mother, wife, or home, these human ties seeming to be the most vital religion which they yet knew. I observed that some of them did not wear their caps on this day, though at other times they clung to them like Quakers; wearing them in bed, putting them on to read the paper, eat an apple, or write a letter, as if, like a new sort of Samson, their strength lay, not in their hair, but in their hats. Many read no novels, swore less, were more silent, orderly, and cheerful, as if the Lord were an invisible Wardmaster, who went his rounds but once a week, and must find all things at their best. I liked all this in the poor, rough boys, and could have found it in my heart to put down sponge and tea pot, and preach a little sermon then and there, while homesickness and pain had made these natures soft, that some good seed might be cast therein, to blossom and bear fruit here or hereafter.

Regarding the admission of friends to nurse their sick, I can only say, it was not allowed at Hurlyburly House; though one indomitable parent took my ward by storm, and held her position, in spite of doctors, matron, and Nurse Periwinkle. Though it was against the rules, though the culprit was an acid, frost-bitten female, though the young man would have done quite as well without her anxious fussiness, and the whole room-full been much more comfortable, there was something so irresistible in this persistent devotion, that no one had the heart to oust her from her post. She slept on the floor, without uttering a complaint; bore jokes somewhat of the rudest; fared scantily, though her basket was daily filled with luxuries for her boy; and tended that petulant personage with a never-failing patience beautiful to see.

I feel a glow of moral rectitude in saying this of her; for, though a perfect pelican to her young, she pecked and cackled (I don't know that pelicans usually express their emotions in that manner,) most obstreperously, when others invaded her premises; and led me a weary life, with "George's tea-rusks," "George's foot-bath," "George's measles," and "George's mother"; till, after a sharp passage of arms and tongues with the matron, she wrathfully packed up her rusks, her son, and herself, and departed, in an ambulance, scolding to the very last.

This is the comic side of the matter. The serious one is harder to describe; for the presence, however brief, of relations and friends by the bedsides of the dead or dying, is always a trial to the bystanders. They are not near enough to know how best to comfort, yet too near to turn their backs upon the sorrow that finds its only solace in listening to recitals of last words, breathed into nurse's ears, or receiving the tender legacies of love and longing bequeathed through them.

To me, the saddest sight I saw in that sad place, was the spectacle of a grey-haired father, sitting hour after hour by his son, dying from the poison of his wound. The old father, hale and hearty; the young son, past all help, though one could scarcely believe it; for the subtle fever, burning his strength away, flushed his cheeks with color, filled his eyes with lustre, and lent a mournful mockery of health to face and figure, making the poor lad comelier in death than in life. His bed was not in my ward; but I was often in and out, and, for a day or two, the pair were much together, saying little, but looking much. The old man tried to busy himself with book or pen, that his presence might not be a burden; and once, when he sat writing, to the anxious mother at home, doubtless, I saw the son's eyes fixed upon his face, with a look of mingled resignation and regret, as if endeavoring to teach himself to say cheerfully the long good bye. And again, when the son slept, the father watched him, as he had himself been watched; and though no feature of his grave countenance changed, the rough hand, smoothing the lock of hair upon the pillow, the bowed attitude of the grey head, were more pathetic than the loudest lamentations. The son died; and the father took home the pale relic of the life he gave, offering a little money to the nurse, as the only visible return it was in his power to make her; for, though very grateful, he was poor. Of course, she did not take it, but found a richer compensation in the old man's earnest declaration:

"My boy couldn't have been better cared for if he'd been at home; and God will reward you for it, though I can't."

My own experiences of this sort began when my first man died. He had scarcely been removed, when his wife came in. Her eye went straight to the well-known bed; it was empty; and feeling, yet not believing the hard truth, she cried out, with a look I never shall forget:

"Why, where's Emanuel?"

I had never seen her before, did not know her relationship to the man whom I had only nursed for a day, and was about to tell her he was gone, when McGee, the tender-hearted Irishman before mentioned, brushed by me with a cheerful—"It's shifted to a better bed he is, Mrs. Connel. Come out, dear, till I show ye"; and, taking her gently by the arm, he led her to the matron, who broke the heavy tidings to the wife, and comforted the widow.

Another day, running up to my room for a breath of fresh air and a five minutes' rest after a disagreeable task, I found a stout young woman sitting on my bed, wearing the miserable look which I had learned to know by that time. Seeing her, reminded me that I had heard of some one's dying in the night, and his sister's arriving in the morning. This must be she, I thought. I pitied her with all my heart. What could I say or do? Words always seem impertinent at such times; I did not know the man; the woman was neither interesting in herself nor graceful in her grief; yet, having known a sister's sorrow myself, I could not leave her alone with her trouble in that strange place, without a word. So, feeling heart-sick, home-sick, and not knowing what else to do, I just put my arms about her, and began to cry in a very helpless but hearty way; for, as I seldom indulge in this moist luxury, I like to enjoy it with all my might, when I do.

It so happened I could not have done a better thing; for, though not a word was spoken, each felt the other's sympathy; and, in the silence, our handkerchiefs were more eloquent than words. She soon sobbed herself quiet; and, leaving her on my bed, I went back to work, feeling much refreshed by the shower, though I'd forgotten to rest, and had washed my face instead of my hands. I mention this successful experiment as a receipt proved and approved, for the use of any nurse who may find herself called upon to minister to these wounds of the heart. They will find it more efficacious than cups of tea, smelling-bottles, psalms, or sermons; for a friendly touch and a companionable cry, unite the consolations of all the rest for womankind; and, if genuine, will be found a sovereign cure for the first sharp pang so many suffer in these heavy times.

I am gratified to find that my little Sergeant has found favor in several quarters, and gladly respond to sundry calls for news of him, though my personal knowledge ended five months ago. Next to my good John—I hope the grass is green above him, far away there in Virginia!—I placed the Sergeant on my list of worthy boys; and many a jovial chat have I enjoyed with the merry-hearted lad, who had a fancy for fun, when his poor arm was dressed. While Dr. P. poked and strapped, I brushed the remains of the Sergeant's brown mane—shorn sorely against his will—and gossiped with all my might, the boy making odd faces, exclamations, and appeals, when nerves got the better of nonsense, as they sometimes did:

"I'd rather laugh than cry, when I must sing out anyhow, so just say that bit from Dickens again, please, and I'll stand it like a man." He did; for "Mrs. Cluppins," "Chadband," and "Sam Weller," always helped him through; thereby causing me to lay another offering of love and admiration on the shrine of the god of my idolatry, though he does wear too much jewelry and talk slang.

The Sergeant also originated, I believe, the fashion of calling his neighbors by their afflictions instead of their names; and I was rather taken aback by hearing them bandy remarks of this sort, with perfect good humor and much enjoyment of the new game. "Hallo, old Fits is off again!" "How are you, Rheumatiz?" "Will you trade apples, Ribs?" "I say, Miss P., may I give Typus a drink of this?" "Look here, No Toes, lend us a stamp, there's a good feller," etc. He himself was christened "Baby B.," because he tended his arm on a little pillow, and called it his infant.

Very fussy about his grub was Sergeant B., and much trotting of attendants was necessary when he partook of nourishment. Anything more irresistably wheedlesome I never saw, and constantly found myself indulging him, like the most weak-minded parent, merely for the pleasure of seeing his brown eyes twinkle, his merry mouth break into a smile, and his one hand execute a jaunty little salute that was entirely captivating. I am afraid that Nurse P. damaged her dignity, frolicking with this persuasive young gentleman, though done for his well-being. But "boys will be boys," is perfectly applicable to the case; for, in spite of years, sex, and the "prunes-and-prisms" doctrine laid down for our use, I have a fellow feeling for lads, and always owed Fate a grudge because I wasn't a lord of creation instead of a lady.

Since I left, I have heard, from a reliable source, that my Sergeant has gone home; therefore, the small romance that budded the first day I saw him, has blossomed into its second chapter; and I now imagine "dearest Jane" filling my place, tending the wounds I tended, brushing the curly jungle I brushed, loving the excellent little youth I loved, and eventually walking altarward, with the Sergeant stumping gallantly at her side. If she doesn't do all this, and no end more, I'll never forgive her; and sincerely pray to the guardian saint of lovers, that "Baby B." may prosper in his wooing, and his name be long in the land.

One of the lively episodes of hospital life, is the frequent marching away of such as are well enough to rejoin their regiments, or betake themselves to some convalescent camp. The ward master comes to the door of each room that is to be thinned, reads off a list of names, bids

their owners look sharp and be ready when called for; and, as he
vanishes, the rooms fall into an indescribable state of topsy-turvyness,
as the boys begin to black their boots, brighten spurs, if they have
them, overhaul knapsacks, make presents; are fitted out with needfuls,
and—well, why not?—kissed sometimes, as they say, good by; for in
all human probability we shall never meet again, and a woman's heart
yearns over anything that has clung to her for help and comfort. I
never liked these breakings-up of my little household; though my short
stay showed me but three. I was immensely gratified by the hand
shakes I got, for their somewhat painful cordiality assured me that I
had not tried in vain. The big Prussian rumbled out his unintelligible
adieux, with a grateful face and a premonitory smooth of his yellow
moustache, but got no farther, for some one else stepped up, with a
large brown hand extended, and this recommendation of our very
faulty establishment:

"We're off, ma'am, and I'm powerful sorry, for I'd no idea a
'orspittle was such a jolly place. Hope I'll git another ball somewheres
easy, so I'll come back, and be took care on again. Mean, ain't it?"

I didn't think so, but the doctrine of inglorious ease was not the
right one to preach up, so I tried to look shocked, failed signally, and
consoled myself by giving him the fat pincushion he had admired as
the "cutest little machine agoin." Then they fell into line in front of
the house, looking rather wan and feeble, some of them, but trying to
step out smartly and march in good order, though half the knapsacks
were carried by the guard, and several leaned on sticks instead of
shouldering guns. All looked up and smiled, or waved their hands and
touched their caps, as they passed under our windows down the long
street, and so away, some to their homes in this world, and some to
that in the next; and, for the rest of the day, I felt like Rachel mourning for her children, when I saw the empty beds and missed the
familiar faces.

You ask if nurses are obliged to witness amputations and such
matters, as a part of their duty? I think not, unless they wish; for the
patient is under the effects of ether, and needs no care but such as the

surgeons can best give. Our work begins afterward, when the poor soul comes to himself, sick, faint, and wandering; full of strange pains and confused visions, of disagreeable sensations and sights. Then we must sooth and sustain, tend and watch; preaching and practicing patience, till sleep and time have restored courage and self-control.

I witnessed several operations; for the height of my ambition was to go to the front after a battle, and feeling that the sooner I inured myself to trying sights, the more useful I should be. Several of my mates shrunk from such things; for though the spirit was wholly willing, the flesh was inconveniently weak. One funereal lady came to try her powers as a nurse; but, a brief conversation eliciting the facts that she fainted at the sight of blood, was afraid to watch alone, couldn't possibly take care of delirious persons, was nervous about infections, and unable to bear much fatigue, she was mildly dismissed. I hope she found her sphere, but fancy a comfortable bandbox on a high shelf would best meet the requirements of her case.

Dr. Z. suggested that I should witness a dissection; but I never accepted his invitations, thinking that my nerves belonged to the living, not to the dead, and I had better finish my education as a nurse before I began that of a surgeon. But I never met the little man skipping through the hall, with oddly shaped cases in his hand, and an absorbed expression of countenance, without being sure that a select party of surgeons were at work in the dead house, which idea was a rather trying one, when I knew the subject was some person whom I had nursed and cared for.

But this must not lead any one to suppose that the surgeons were willfully hard or cruel, though one of them remorsefully confided to me that he feared his profession blunted his sensibilities, and, perhaps, rendered him indifferent to the sight of pain.

I am inclined to think that in some cases it does; for, though a capital surgeon and a kindly man, Dr. P., through long acquaintance with many of the ills flesh is heir to, had acquired a somewhat trying habit of regarding a man and his wound as separate institutions, and seemed rather annoyed that the former should express any opinion upon the latter, or claim any right in it, while under his care. He had a way of twitching off a bandage, and giving a limb a comprehensive sort of clutch, which, though no doubt entirely scientific, was rather startling than soothing, and highly objectionable as a means of preparing nerves for any fresh trial. He also expected the patient to assist in small operations, as he considered them, and to restrain all demonstrations during the process.

"Here, my man, just hold it this way, while I look into it a bit," he said one day to Fitz G., putting a wounded arm into the keeping of a sound one, and proceeding to poke about among bits of bone and visible muscles, in a red and black chasm made by some infernal machine of the shot or shell description. Poor Fitz held on like grim Death, ashamed to show fear before a woman, till it grew more than he could bear in silence; and, after a few smothered groans, he looked at me imploringly, as if he said, "I wouldn't, ma'am, if I could help it," and fainted quietly away.

Dr. P. looked up, gave a compassionate sort of cluck, and poked away more busily than ever, with a nod at me and a brief—"Never mind; be so good as to hold this till I finish."

I obeyed, cherishing the while a strong desire to insinuate a few of his own disagreeable knives and scissors into him, and see how he liked it. A very disrespectful and ridiculous fancy, of course; for he was doing all that could be done, and the arm prospered finely in his hands. But the human mind is prone to prejudice; and, though a personable man, speaking French like a born "Parley voo," and whipping off legs like an animated guillotine, I must confess to a sense of relief when he was ordered elsewhere; and suspect that several of the men would have faced a rebel battery with less trepidation than they did Dr. P., when he came briskly in on his morning round.

As if to give us the pleasures of contrast, Dr. Z. succeeded him, who, I think, suffered more in giving pain than did his patients in enduring it; for he often paused to ask: "Do I hurt you?" and, seeing his solicitude, the boys invariably answered: "Not much; go ahead, Doctor," though the lips that uttered this amiable fib might be white with pain as they spoke. Over the dressing of some of the wounds, we used to carry on conversations upon subjects foreign to the work in hand, that the patient might forget himself in the charms of our dis course. Christmas eve was spent in this way; the Doctor strapping the little Sergeant's arm, I holding the lamp, while all three laughed and talked, as if anywhere but in a hospital ward; except when the chat was broken by a long-drawn "Oh!" from "Baby B.," an abrupt request from the Doctor to "Hold the lamp a little higher, please," or an encouraging, "Most through, Sergeant," from Nurse P.

The chief Surgeon, Dr. O., I was told, refused the higher salary, greater honor, and less labor, of an appointment to the Officer's Hospital, round the corner, that he might serve the poor fellows at Hurlyburly House, or go to the front, working there day and night, among the horrors that succeed the glories of a battle. I liked that so much, that the quiet, brown-eyed Doctor was my especial admiration; and when my own turn came, had more faith in him than in all the rest put together, although he did advise me to go home, and authorize the consumption of blue pills.

Speaking of the surgeons reminds me that, having found all manner of fault, it becomes me to celebrate the redeeming feature of Hurlyburly House. I had been prepared by the accounts of others, to expect much humiliation of spirit from the surgeons, and to be treated by them like a door-mat, a worm, or any other meek and lowly article, whose mission it is to be put down and walked upon; nurses being considered as mere servants, receiving the lowest pay, and, it's my private opinion, doing the hardest work of any part of the army, except the mules. Great, therefore, was my surprise, when I found myself treated with the utmost courtesy and kindness. Very soon my carefully prepared meekness was laid upon the shelf; and, going from one extreme to the other, I more than once expressed a difference of opinion regarding sundry messes it was my painful duty to administer.

As eight of us nurses chanced to be off duty at once, we had an excellent opportunity of trying the virtues of these gentlemen; and I am bound to say they stood the test admirably, as far as my personal

observation went. Dr. O.'s stethescope was unremitting in its attentions; Dr. S. brought his buttons into my room twice a day, with the
regularity of a medical clock; while Dr. Z. filled my table with neat
little bottles, which I never emptied, prescribed Browning, bedewed
me with Cologne, and kept my fire going, as if, like the candles in St.
Peter's, it must never be permitted to die out. Waking, one cold night,
with the certainty that my last spark had pined away and died, and
consequently hours of coughing were in store for me, I was much
amazed to see a ruddy light dancing on the wall, a jolly blaze roaring
up the chimney, and, down upon his knees before it, Dr. Z., whittling
shavings. I ought to have risen up and thanked him on the spot; but,
knowing that he was one of those who like to do good by stealth, I
only peeped at him as if he were a friendly ghost; till, having made
things as cosy as the most motherly of nurses could have done, he
crept away, leaving me to feel, as somebody says, "as if angels were a
watching of me in my sleep"; though that species of wild fowl do not
usually descend in broadcloth and glasses. I afterwards discovered that
he split the wood himself on that cool January midnight, and went
about making or mending fires for the poor old ladies in their dismal
dens; thus causing himself to be felt—a bright and shining light in
more ways than one. I never thanked him as I ought; therefore, I
publicly make a note of it, and further aggravate that modest M. D. by
saying that if this was not being the best of doctors and the gentlest of
gentlemen, I shall be happy to see any improvement upon it.

To such as wish to know where these scenes took place, I must
respectfully decline to answer; for Hurlyburly House has ceased to
exist as a hospital; so let it rest, with all its sins upon its head,—
perhaps I should say chimney top. When the nurses felt ill, the doctors
departed, and the patients got well, I believe the concern gently faded
from existence, or was merged into some other and better establishment, where I hope the washing of three hundred sick people is done
out of the house, the food is eatable, and mortal women are not
expected to possess an angelic exemption from all wants, and the
endurance of truck horses.

Since the appearance of these hasty Sketches, I have heard from several of my comrades at the Hospital; and their approval assures me that I have not let sympathy and fancy run away with me, as that lively team is apt to do when harnessed to a pen. As no two persons see the same thing with the same eyes, my view of hospital life must be taken through my glass, and held for what it is worth. Certainly, nothing was set down in malice, and to the serious-minded party who objected to a tone of levity in some portions of the Sketches, I can only say that it is a part of my religion to look well after the cheerfulnesses of life, and let the dismals shift for themselves; believing, with good Sir Thomas More, that it is wise to "be merrie in God."

The next hospital I enter will, I hope, be one for the colored regiments, as they seem to be proving their right to the admiration and kind offices of their white relations, who owe them so large a debt, a little part of which I shall be so proud to pay.

> Yours,
> With a firm faith
> In the good time coming,
> TRIBULATION PERIWINKLE.

PART II

THE HEART OF
LOUISA MAY ALCOTT:

Selections from Her Letters, Poems, and Journals

A SELECTION OF LETTERS

To Amos Bronson Alcott

Boston, Nov. 29, 1856

Dearest Father,—Your little parcel was very welcome to me as I sat alone in my room, with snow falling fast outside, and a few tears in (for birthdays are dismal times to me); and the fine letter, the pretty gift, and, most of all, the loving thought so kindly taken for your old absent daughter, made the cold, dark day as warm and bright as summer to me.

And now, with the birthday pin upon my bosom, many thanks on my lips, and a whole heart full of love for its giver, I will tell you a little about my doings, stupid as they will seem after your own grand proceedings. How I wish I could be with you, enjoying what I have always longed for,—fine people, fine amusements, and fine books. But as I can't, I am glad you are; for I love to see your name first among the lecturers, to hear it kindly spoken of in papers and inquired about by good people here,—to say nothing of the delight and pride I take in seeing you at last filling the place you are so fitted for, and which you have waited for so long and patiently. If the New Yorkers raise a statue

to the modern Plato, it will be a wise and highly creditable action . . .

I am very well and very happy. Things go smoothly, and I think I
shall come out right, and prove that though an *Alcott* I *can* support
myself. I like the independent feeling; and though not an easy life, it is
a free one, and I enjoy it. I can't do much with my hands; so I will
make a battering-ram of my head and make a way through this rough-
and-tumble world. I have very pleasant lectures to amuse my evenings,—Professor Gajani on "Italian Reformers," the Mercantile Library course, Whipple, Beecher, and others, and, best of all, a free pass
at the Boston Theatre. I saw Mr. Barry, and he gave it to me with
many kind speeches, and promises to bring out the play very soon. I
hope he will.

My farce is in the hands of Mrs. W. H. Smith, who acts at Laura
Keene's theatre in New York. She took it, saying she would bring it
out there. If you see or hear anything about it, let me know. I want
something doing. My mornings are spent in writing. C. takes me one a
month, and I am to see Mr. B., who may take some of my wares.

In the afternoons I walk and visit my hundred relations, who are all
kind and friendly, and seem interested in our various successes.

Sunday evenings I go to Parker's parlor, and there meet Phillips,
Garrison, Scherb, Sanborn, and many other pleasant people. All talk,
and I sit in a corner listening, and wishing a certain placid gray-haired
gentleman was there talking too. Mrs. Parker calls on me, reads my
stories, and is very good to me. Theodore asks Louisa "how her
worthy parents do," and is otherwise very friendly to the large, bashful
girl who adorns his parlor steadily.

Abby is preparing for a busy and, I hope, a profitable winter. She
has music lessons already, French and drawing in store, and, if her
eyes hold out, will keep her word and become what none of us can be,
"an accomplished Alcott." Now, dear Father, I shall hope to hear from
you occasionally, and will gladly answer all epistles from the Plato
whose parlor parish is becoming quite famous. I got the "Tribune,"

but not the letter, and shall look it up. I have been meaning to write, but did not know where you were.

Good bye, and a happy birthday from your ever loving child,

LOUISA.

To Adeline May

[July? 1860?]

Dear Ade:

I should have answered your note before . . . We are all blooming and just now full of the Hawthornes whose arrival gives us new neighbors and something to talk about besides Parker, Sumner and Sanborn. Mr. H. is as queer as ever and we catch glimpses of a dark mysterious looking man in a big hat and red slippers darting over the hills or skimming by as if he expected the house of Alcott were about to rush out and clutch him. Mrs. H. is as sentimental and muffing as of old, wears crimson silk jackets, a rosary from Jerusalem, fire-flies in her hair and dirty white skirts with the sacred mud of London still extant thereon.

Una is a stout English looking sixteen year older with the most ardent hair and eyebrows, Monte Bene airs and graces and no accomplishments but riding which was put an end to this morning by a somerset from her horse in the grand square of this vast town. She was not hurt but her Byronic papa forbid her to distinguish herself in any manner again and she is in a high state of wrath and woe.

Julian is a worthy boy full of pictures, fishing rods and fun and Rose a little bud of a child with scarlet hair and no particular raiment, which is cool and artistic but somewhat startling to the common herd.

Annie is making us a visit and is as blithe a bride as one need wish to see. The world is composed of John and John is composed of all the virtues ever known, which amiable delusion I admire and wonder at from the darkness of my benighted spinsterhood. Abby lives for her

May Alcott's drawing of The Wayside, the home of Nathaniel Hawthorne and his family, which directly adjoined the Alcotts' Orchard House. Though the two homesteads were separated only by a gate and shaded avenue, the famous novelist remained an enigma. "By what stratagem he got into his own house or left it, was a marvel," the relentlessly affable Bronson was forced to concede. "There he was in the twilight, there he stayed."

crayons and dancing, Father for his garden, Mother for the world in general and I for my pens and ink, and there you have a brief account of the "pathetic family" for the time being.

Love to your circle all around . . . This note is written with a room full of people all in full gab and with a pen inflicted with the rickets so you will doubtless be able to join your father in his opinion regarding the handwriting . . . I should love to go to Leicester but have a glimmering hope of Conway [New Hampshire] and am waiting.

To Sophia Foord

Concord May 11th [1862]

Dear Miss Foord

As I promised to write you when Henry died I send these few lines to fulfil that promise through I suppose you have seen notices of the event in the papers.

Father saw him the day before he died lying patiently & cheerfully on the bed he would never leave again alive. He was very weak but suffered nothing & talked in his old pleasant way saying "it took Nature a long time to do her work but he was most out of the world." On Tuesday at eight in the morning he asked to be lifted, tried to help do it but was too weak & lying down again passed quietly & painlessly out of the old world into the new.

On Friday at Mr. Emerson's desire he was publicly buried from the church, a thing Henry would not have liked but Emerson said his sorrow was so great he wanted all the world to mourn with him. Many friends came from Boston & Worcester, Emerson read an address good in itself but not appropriate to the time or place, the last few sentences were these & very true.

"In the Tyrol there grows a flower on the most inaccessible peaks of the mountains, called 'Adelvezia' or 'noble purity,' it is so much loved by the maidens that their lovers risk their lives in seeking it & are often found dead at the foot of the precipices with the flower in

Dear Miss Foord,

I wish I had something better to give in return for all you have done for me, but as you expressed a wish to see some of my nonsense I here present you with a good dose, Now I hope you appreciate the great sacrifice I am making in thus allowing you to see this choice collection of poems, which being no exceedingly brilliant will cause to lift your hands in admiration and thus let them tumble into the fire, so that no one may suffer the mortification of not being able to write as finely

as your ever loving nonsensical.

Louy.

The dedicatory page to a small manuscript notebook of her poems that Alcott presented to Sophia Foord sometime after 1850. Miss Foord had first arrived in Concord in the summer of 1845, planning to assist Bronson in one of his new educational ventures. When that project fell through, she stayed on to teach the Alcott girls, all the while nurturing a violent and completely unrequited passion for Henry David Thoreau, who was moved to declare, "I really had anticipated no such foe in my career."

their hands. I think our friend's life was a search for this rare flower, & I know that could we see him now we should find him adorned with profuse garlands of it for none could more fittly wear them."

Mr. Channing wrote the Stanzas & they were very sweetly sung, Father read selections from Henry's own books, for many people said he was an infidel & as he never went to church when living he ought not to be carried there dead. If ever a man was a real Christian it was Henry, & I think his own wise & pious thoughts read by one who loved him & whose own life was a beautiful example of religious faith, convinced many & touched the hearts of all.

It was a lovely day, clear, & calm, & spring like, & as we all walked after Henry's coffin with its fall of flowers, carried by six of his townsmen who had grown up with him, it seemed as if Nature wore her most benignant aspect to welcome her dutiful & loving son to his long sleep in her arms. As we entered the church yard birds were singing, early violets blooming in the grass & the pines singing their softest lullaby, & there between his father & his brother we left him, feeling that though his life seemed too short, it would blossom & bear fruit for as long after he was gone, & that perhaps we should know a closer friendship now than even while he lived.

I never can mourn for such men because they never seem lost to me but nearer & dearer for the solemn change. I hope you have this consolation, & if these few words of mine can give you anything you have not already learned I am very glad, & can only add much love from us all & a heart full from your

Lou.

Come & see us when you can, after this week we shall be clean & in order, & always ready.

I enclose a little sprig of "andromeda" his favorite plant a wreath of which *we* put on his coffin.

To Moncure Daniel Conway

My Dear Mr. Conway,

Mr. Sanborn offers me a place in his parcel & I want to do myself the pleasure of sending you a copy of my little book because you were so kindly interested in the other one.

"Moods" is not what I meant to have it, for I followed bad advice & took out many things which explained my idea & made the characters more natural & consistent. I see my mistake now for I find myself accused of Spiritualism, Free Love, Affinities & all sorts of horrors that I know very little about & don't believe in.

Perhaps I was over bold to try the experiment of treating an old theme in a new way. But out of my own observation & experience I ventured to say what I thought to the young people whom I see so often making blunders that mar their whole lives, & then blaming God or fate, & becoming dismal martyrs when they should be cheerful workers.

Self abnegation is a noble thing but I think there is a limit to it; & though in a few rare cases it may work well yet half the misery of the world seems to come from unmated pairs trying to live their lie decorously to the end, & bringing children into the world to inherit the unhappiness & discord out of which they were born. There is discipline enough in the most perfect marriage & I dont agree to the doctrine of "marry in haste & repent at leisure" which seems to prevail. I honor it too much not to want to see it all it should be & to try to help others to prepare for it that they may find it life's best lesson not its heaviest burden.

The book has been sharply criticized & I am glad of it, though I wish I had done better justice to my own idea. I heartily believe it, am willing to be blamed for it, & am not sorry I wrote it, for it has not only cleared & fixed many things in my own mind, but brought me thanks & good wishes from many whom I find I have served better than I knew.

Pardon my egotistical note, but I did want to set myself right before you if I could, as it is too late to do it here before others, & with all its imperfections "Moods" is an honest, well meaning, little book.

Please remember me to Mrs. Conway, & with affectionate regards from us all believe me

Very truly yours
L. M. ALCOTT.

Concord Feb. 18 / 65.

To Abigail May Alcott(?)

Dinan, Sunday, 17th April [1870]

Here we are all settled at our first neat stopping place and are in clover as you will see when I tell you how plummy and lovely it is.

We left Morlaix Friday at 8 a.m. and were so amazed at the small bill presented us that we couldn't praise the town enough. You can judge of the cheapness of things when I say that my share of the expenses from Brest here, including two days at a hotel, car, 'bus, and diligence fare, fees and every thing, was $8.00. The day was divine, and we had a fine little journey to Lamballe where the fun began; for instead of a big diligence, we found only a queer ramshackle thing, like an insane carry all, with a wooden boot and queer perch for the driver. Our four trunks were piled on behind and tied on with old ropes, our bags stowed in a wooden box on top, and ourselves inside with a fat Frenchman. The humpbacked driver "ya hooped" to the horses, and away we clattered at a wild pace, all feeling dead sure that something would happen, for the old thing bounced and swayed awfully, the trunks were in danger of tumbling off, and to our dismay we soon discovered that the big Frenchman was tipsy. He gabbled to Alice as only a tipsy Frenchman could, quoted poetry, said he was Victor Hugo's best friend, and a child of nature, that English ladies were all divine, but too cold, for when he pressed Alice's hand, she told him it was not allowed in England, and he was overwhelmed with remorse, bowed, sighed, rolled his eyes, and told her that he drank much ale, because it flew to his head and gave him "commercial ideas." I never saw any thing so perfectly absurd, as it was, and after we got used to it we laughed ourselves sick over the lark. You ought to have seen us and our turnout, tearing over the road at a break-neck pace, pitching, creaking, and rattling. The funny driver, hooting at the horses, who had their tails done up in chignons, blue harness and strings of bells. The drunken man warbling, exhorting, and languishing at us all by turns, while Alice headed him off with great skill. I sat a mass of English dignity and coolness suffering alternate agonies of anxiety and amusement, and May, who tied her head up in a bundle, and looked like a wooden image. It was rich, and when we took up, first a peasant woman in wooden shoes and a fly-away cap, and then a red-nosed priest smoking a long pipe, we were a supurb spectacle. In this style, we banged into Dinan, stopped at the gate, and were dumped, bag and baggage, in the Square. Finding Madame Coste's man was not for us we hired a man to bring our trunks up for us. To our great amazement an oldish woman, who was greasing the wheels of a diligence, came, and catching up our big trunks, whisked them into two broad carts, and taking one trotted down the street at a fine pace followed by the man with the other. That was the finishing touch, and we went laughing after them through the great arched gate into the quaintest, prettiest, most romantic town I ever saw. Narrow streets with overhanging gables, distracting roofs, windows and porches, carved beams, and every sort of richness. The strong old lady beat the man, and finally landed us close by another old gate at a charming house fronting the south, overlooking a lovely green valley, full of gardens, blooming plum and peach trees, windmills, and a ruined castle, at sight of which we all skipped. Madame Coste received us with rapture, for Alice brought a letter from Mrs. Lodge who stayed here, and was the joy of the old lady's soul. We were in great luck, for being early in the season, she had three rooms left, and we nabbed them at once. A salon with old oak walls and wardrobes, blue damask furniture, a fireplace, sunny windows and quaint furniture. A little room out of it for Alice, and upstairs a larger room for May and me, with two beds draped in green chintz, and carved big wardrobe &c. and best of all, a sunny window toward the valley. For these rooms and our board we each pay $1.00 a day, and I call that cheap. It would be worth that to get the sun and air alone, for it is like June, and we sit about with open windows, flowers in the fields, birds singing, and every thing lovely and spring like.

We took possession at once and dressed for dinner at six. We were then presented to our fellow boarders, Madame Forney, a buxom widow, her son Gaston, a handsome Frenchy youth of 23, and her daughter, a homely girl of 20, who is to be married here on the 3rd May. After a great bowing and scraping, we had a funny fish dinner, it being Good Friday. When they found we didn't speak French, they were "desolated," and begged us to learn at once, which we solemnly vowed to do. Gaston knew English, so May at once began to teach him more, and the ice being broken we got gay and friendly at once. I could understand them pretty well, but can't talk, and Alice told them that I was forbidden to say much on account of my throat. This will give me a chance to get a fair start. May pegs away at her grammar, and with that and the elegant Gaston, she will soon begin to "parley-voo."

After dinner, we were borne to the great salon, where a fire, lights and a piano appeared. Every one sat round and gabbled except the Alcotts, who looked and laughed. Madamoiselle Forney played, and then May convulsed them by singing some "Chants Amérique" which they thought very lively and droll. They were all attention and devotion to Madame Coste, a tall old lady with whiskers, [who] kept embracing Alice and beaming at us in her great content at being friends of "Chère Madame Lodge." Alice told them that I was a celebrated authoress, and May a very fine artist, and we were beamed at more than ever.—Being tired, we turned in early, after a jolly time in our own little salon, eating chocolate and laying plans.

Saturday, we had coffee in bed at 8, walked on the ramparts and in the Park under the old tavern till 10 when we had breakfast; then till dinner at 6, we rampaged about having raptures about every thing. I can't tell you how lovely it is! The climate *must* cure me, for they say throat and lung invalids always get well here. The air is dry and soft, the town lies high, and we are in the sunny country part. Shall live cheaply, learn French, enjoy my life, and grow fat and strong. D. V.
Private

I think this is to be one of our lucky years, and this trip a success if things go on as well as they have begun, for not a single hitch have we had from the time we left Boston. It don't seem possible that a fortnight could do so much, and put us in such an entirely new scene.

May is in a state of unutterable like bliss, and keeps flying out with her big sketch book, and coming back in despair, for every thing is so picturesque she don't know where to begin. This is a good chance for her in every way. No one speaks English in the house but Alice, and she threatens to talk only French to us, which will be awful but useful. Two pleasant half English ladies live near, and I shall rush to them when I'm exhausted by "the baby talk," as I call French.

Our house is on the walk close to the great tower of Anne of Brittany, and the public walk which is made on what used to be the moat. Ask some one to lend you a "Murry's Guide" and you can read all about the place. There are a good many English here, and we shall come to know some of them, I don't doubt, which will complete our task and give a relish. Tomorrow Gaston is to escort us to the mineral waters on donkeys, and we shall be an imposing sight as you may suppose.

Direct your letters to me, "Care of Mademoiselle Coste, place St. Louis, Dinan," for the present. It will save a postage, and we shall stay a month at least.

Good bye, God bless you all, May sends lots of love, and so does

Your Lu.

To Abigail Williams May

Boston Sept. 25th [1874]
15 Joy St.

Dear Abby

I address you on the subject of boots & beer or legs & lager if you prefer it, or gas & gaiters. I have been told that you, in memory of my honored grand pa I suppose, wear the latter articles upon your aristocratic legs. I would fain do likewise as one [of] my highly connected limbs is afflicted with—let us say gout as rheumatism is a vulgar malady—so much so—referring now to the leg not the gout, that I cannot wear a boot with any comfort. Therefore the question arises, Where does A. W. M. get her noble gaiters? I have asked here & there at stores & the men look as scandalized as if I had demanded the ballot. I mean to have both ballot & gaiters however, & beginning with the smaller desire of my soul ask you, man to man, "Who makes em for you?"

Likewise having been ordered to drink lager that the intense brilliancy & activity of my brain may be somewhat quenched & a pleasing doziness produced so I can sleep & rest my colossal mind, therefore, dearly beloved, I ask you, Where does your venerable parent procure *her* lager? I know this was a deep & awful family-secret till Leicester burglars revealed it to an astonished world. But I will keep it & no one can think ill of aged ladies who need a drop of comfort as we do.

As you are *not* a busy woman I don't expect a speedy reply—any time before frost sets in will do. *Then* my legs are nipped & perish like other morning glories.

Yrs truly L. M. A.

As I have no idea in what part of the world you are I cast my note upon the tender mercies of the P. O. trusting that you may get it in the fulness of time. Love to Aunt. L.

To Miss Churchill

Xmas Day [1878?]

My Dear Miss Churchill,

I can only say to you as I do to the many young writers who ask for advice—There is no *easy* road to successful authorship; it has to be earned by long & patient labor, many disappointments, uncertainties & trials. Success is often a lucky accident, coming to those who may not deserve it, while others who do have to wait & hope till they have *earned* it. That is the best sort & the most enduring.

I worked for twenty years poorly paid, little known, & quite without any ambition but to eke out a living, as I chose to support myself & began to do it at sixteen. This long drill was of use, & when I wrote "Hospital Sketches" by the beds of my soldier boys in the shape of letters home I had no idea that I was taking the first step toward what is called fame. It nearly cost my life but I discovered the secret of winning the ear & touching the heart of the public by simply telling the comic & pathetic incidents of life.

"Little Women" was written when I was ill, & to prove that I could *not* write books for girls. The publisher thought it *flat,* so did I, & neither hoped much for or from it. We found out our mistake, & since then, though I do not enjoy writing "moral tales" for the young, I do it because it pays well.

But the success I value most was making my dear mother happy in her last years & taking care of my family. The rest soon grows wearisome & seems very poor beside the comfort of being an earthly Providence to those we love.

I hope you will win this joy at least, & think you *will,* for you seem to have got on well so far, & the stories are better than many sent me. I like the short one best. Lively tales of home-life or children go well, & the "Youth's Companion" is a good paying paper. I do not like Loring as he is neither honest nor polite. I have had dealings with him

Abigail May Alcott in the study at Orchard House. In Little Women, *she is immortalized as Mrs. March ("Marmee" to her loving daughters). "The Marches are all well," Louisa informed an admirer in the spring of 1874, when her mother was seventy-three. "Marmee sits in her easy arm-chair and makes sunshine for her family."*

& know. Try Roberts Brothers, 299 Washington St. They are very kind & just & if the book suits will give it a fair chance. With best wishes for a prosperous & happy New Year I am your friend

L. M. A.

To Maggie Lukens

Feb. 5th [1884]

My Dear Maggie,

I hope I never shall be too busy or too old to answer letters like yours as far as I can, for to all of us comes this desire for something to hold by, look up to, & believe in. I will tell you my experience & as it has stood the test of youth & age, health & sickness, joy & sorrow, poverty & wealth I feel that it is genuine, & seem to get more light, warmth & help as I go on learning more of it year by year.

My parents never bound us to any church but taught us that the love of goodness was the love of God, the cheerful doing of duty made life happy, & that the love of one's neighbor in its widest sense was the best help for oneself. Their lives showed us how lovely this simple faith was, how much honor, gratitude & affection it brought them, & what a sweet memory they left behind for, though father still lives his life is over as far as thought or usefulness are possible.

Theodore Parker & R. W. Emerson did much to help me to see that one can shape life best by trying to build up a strong & noble character through good books, wise people's society, an interest in all reforms that help the world, & a cheerful acceptance of whatever is inevitable. Seeing a beautiful compensation in what often seems a great sacrifice, sorrow or loss, & believing always that a wise, loving & just Father cares for us, sees our weakness & is near to help if we call. Have you read Emerson? He is called a Pantheist or believer in Nature instead of God. He was truly *Christian* & saw God *in* Nature, finding strength & comfort in the sane, sweet influences of the great Mother as well as the Father of all. I too believe this, & when tired, sad, or tempted find my best comfort in the woods, the sky, the healing solitude that lets my poor, weary soul find the rest, the fresh hope, or the patience which only God can give us.

People used to tell me that when sorrow came I should find my faith faulty because it had no name, but they were wrong, for when the heavy loss of my dear, gifted sister found me too feeble to do anything but suffer passively, I still had the sustaining sense of a love that never failed even when I could not see why this lovely life should end when it was happiest.

As a poor, proud, struggling girl I held to the belief that if I *deserved* success it would surely come so long as my ambition was not for selfish ends but for my dear family, & it did come, far more fully than I ever hoped or dreamed tho youth, health & many hopes went to earn it. Now when I might enjoy rest, pleasure & travel I am still tied by new duties to my baby, & give up my dreams sure that something better will be given me in time.

Freedom was always my longing, but I have never had it, so I am still trying to feel that this is the discipline I need & when I am ready the liberty will come.

I think you need not worry about any name for your faith but simply try to be & do good, to love virtue in others & study the lives of those who are truely worthy of imitation. Women need a religion of their own, for they are called upon to lead a quiet self sacrificing life with peculiar trials, needs, & joys, & it seems to me that a very simple one is fitted to us whose hearts are usually more alive than heads, & whose hands are tied in many ways.

Health of body helps health of soul, cheerful views of all things keep up the courage & brace the nerves. Work for the mind *must* be had, or daily duty becomes drudgery & the power to enjoy higher things is lost. Change of scene is sometimes salvation for girls or women who out grow the place they are born in, & it is their duty to go away even if it is to harder work, for hungry minds prey on themselves & ladies suffer for escape from a too pale or narrow life.

I have felt this, & often gone away from Concord to teach, (which I never liked) because there was no food for my mind in that small conservative town, especially since Mr. Emerson died.

Food, fire & shelter are not *all* that women need, & the noble discontent that asks for more should not be condemned but helped if possible.

At 21 I took my little earnings ($20) & a few clothes, & went to seek my fortune tho I might have sat still & been supported by rich friends. All those hard years were teaching me what I afterward put into the books, & so I made my fortune out of my seeming *mis* fortunes; I speak of myself because what one has *lived* one really knows & so can speak honestly. I wish I had my own house (as I still hope to have) so that I might ask the young women who often write to me as you do, to come & see me, & look about & find what they need, & see the world of wise, good people to whom I could introduce them as others did me thirty years ago. I hope to have it soon, & then you must come & have our talk, & see if any change can be made without neglecting duty.

When one cannot go away one can travel in spirit by means of books. Tell me what you read & like, & perhaps I can send you a key that will at least open a window through which your eyes can wander while the faithful hands & feet are tied by duty at home.

Write freely to me, dear girl, & if I can help in any way be sure I gladly will. A great sorrow often softens & prepares the heart for a new harvest of good seed, & the sowers God sends are often very humble ones, used only as instruments by him because being very human they come naturally & by every day ways to the help of those who are passing through trials like their own.

I find one of the compensations for age in the fact that it seems to bring young people nearer to me, & that the experiences so hard to live through now help me to understand others. So I am always glad to

do what I can, remembering how I wrote to my father for just such help as you ask, & how he answered as I have tried to answer you.
Let me know if it does comfort you any.
With love to my other girls

I am always your friend

L. M. A.

The simple Buddha religion is very attractive to me, & I believe in it. God is enough for me, & all the prophets are only stepping stones to him. Christ is a great reformer to me not God.

To Maggie Lukens

Feb. 14th [1884]

Dear Maggie,

I am glad that my letter pleased you, & though always busy I at once answer your last because if by word or act one can help a fellow creature in the care or conduct of a soul that is one's first duty.

About the great Hereafter I can only give you my own feeling & belief, for we can *know* nothing, & must wait hopefully & patiently to learn the secret.

Death never seemed terrible to me, the fact I mean, though the ways of going & the sad blow of a sudden end are of course hard to bear & understand.

I feel that in this life we are learning to enjoy a higher, & fitting ourselves to take our place there. If we use well our talents, opportunities, trials & joys here when we pass on it is to the society of nobler souls, as in this world we find our level inevitably.

I think immortality is the passing of a soul thro many lives or experiences, & such as are *truly* lived, used & learned help on to the next, each growing richer, higher, happier, carr[y]ing with it only the real memories of what has gone before. If in my present life I love one person truly, no matter who it is, I believe that we meet somewhere again, though where or how I don't know or care, for genuine love is immortal. So is real wisdom, virtue, heroism &c. & these noble attributes lift humble lives into the next experience, & prepare them to go on with greater power & happiness.

I seem to remember former states before this, & feel that in them I have learned some of the lessons that have never been mine here, & in my next step I hope to leave behind many of the trials that I have struggled to bear here & begin to find lightened as I go on.

This accounts for the genius & the great virtue some show here. They have done well in many phases of this great school & bring into our class the virtue or the gifts that make them great & good.

We don't remember the lesser things, they slip away as childish trifles, & we carry on only the real experiences. Some are born sad, some bad, some feeble, mentally & morally I mean, & all their life here is an effort to get rid of this shadow of grief, sin, weakness in the life before. Others come as Shakespeare, Milton, Emerson &c. bringing their lovely reward with them & pass on leaving us the better for their lives.

This is my idea of immortality. An endless life of helpful change, with the instinct, the longing to rise, to learn, to love, to get nearer the source of all good, & go on from the lowest plane to the highest, rejoicing more & more as we climb into the clearer light, the purer air, the happier life which must exist, for, as Plato said, "The soul cannot imagine what does not exist because it is the shadow of God who knows & creates all things."

I don't believe in spiritualism as commonly presented. I don't want to see or feel or hear dead friends except in my own sense of nearness, & as my love & memory paint them. I do believe that they remember us, are with us in a spiritual sense when we need them, & we feel their presence with joy & comfort, not with fear or curiosity.

My mother is near me sometimes I am sure, for help comes of the sort she alone gave me, & May is about her baby I feel, for out of the innocent blue eyes sometimes come looks so like her mother's that I am startled, for I tended May as a child as I now tend Lulu. This slight tie is enough to hold us still tenderly together, though death drops a veil between us, & I look without doubt or fear toward the time when in some way we shall meet again.

About books. Yes, I've read "Mr. Isaacs" & "Dr. C." & like them both. The other, "To Leeward," is not so good. "Little Pilgrim" was pretty, but why try to paint Heaven? Let it alone, & prepare for it whatever it is, sure that God knows what we need & deserve.

I will send you Emerson's "Essays." Read those marked & see what you think of them. They did much for me, & if you like them you shall have more. Ever yr. friend L. M. A.

Love to the girls & respects to Papa.

FIVE POEMS

The Hawthorne

The Hawthorne is a gracious tree
    From latest twig to parent root,
For when all others leafless stand
    It gaily blossoms & bears fruit.
On certain days a friendly wind
    Wafts from its spreading boughs a store
Of canny gifts that flutter in
    Like snowflakes at a neighbor's door.

The spinster who has just been blest,
    Finds solemn thirty much improved
By proofs that such a crabbed soul,
    Is still remembered & beloved.
Kind wishes "ancient Lu" has stored
    In the "best chamber" of her heart,
And every gift on Fancy's stage
    Already plays its little part.

When through the Washingtonian mud,
    (Fit symbol of the moral slough

When in the dawn she getteth up
  With weary bones & sleepy eyes,
And searching for the woman's friend
  "My kingdom for a pin!" she cries,
Then joyfully recalls the rose
  That one day bore a scarlet flower.
She plucks a thorn with much content
  And takes her place at the given hour.

———

Long may it stand the friendly tree
  That blooms in Autumn as in Spring,
Beneath whose shade the humblest line
  May safely sit, may gratefully sing.
Time will give it an evergreen name,
  Axe cannot harm it, frost cannot kill,
With Emerson's pine & Thoreau's oak
  Will the Hawthorne be loved & honored still.

——//——

With thanks from neighbor Lu.

The third and last page of the autograph manuscript of "The Hawthorne," Alcott's
witty verse tribute to Nathaniel Hawthorne and his family. Alcott celebrated her
thirtieth birthday on November 29, 1862, and as this affectionate poem attests,
"ancient Lu" was deeply touched that her neighbors at The Wayside had not
forgotten the occasion.

In which the land like Bunyan's man,
    Laments & fights & fusses now)
Nurse Gamp undauntedly doth walk
    With graceful elephantine pace,
She kilts her drapery Diana-wise
    To show her ankelets of lace.

When gallant Neds or Wilkies come
    From tented fields to beds of pain,
The housewife sews their bandages,
    And soon the legs are well again.
If Captain Hamlet should perchance
    The fever or the ague take,
In holding skeins like blesséd Bags
    He might his heart's "quietus make."

When Mrs G perplexed & soured
    Despairing seeks her "Nurse's Guide,"
Blithe memories of a jovial LU
    Across the page will seem to glide,
And the book illuminated lie
    By the well painted prophesy,
Like a gilded rainbow setting forth
    Not what she is but may yet be.

When in the dawn she getteth up
    With weary bones & sleepy eyes,
And searching for the woman's friend
    "My Kingdom for a pin!" she cries,
Then joyfully recalls the Rose
    That one day bore a scarlet flower,
She plucks a thorn with much content
    And takes her place at the given hour.

Long may it stand the friendly tree
   That blooms in Autumn as in Spring,
Beneath whose shade the humblest hind
   May safely sit, may gratefully sing.
Time will give it an ever green name,
   Ice cannot harm it, frost cannot kill,
With Emerson's pine & Thoreau's oak
   Will the Hawthorne be loved & honored still.

Thoreau's Flute

We, sighing, said, "Our Pan is dead;
   His pipe hangs mute beside the river;—
   Around it wistful sunbeams quiver,
But Music's airy voice is fled.
Spring mourns as for untimely frost;
   The bluebird chants a requiem;
   The willow-blossom waits for him;—
The Genius of the wood is lost."

Then from the flute, untouched by hands,
   There came a low, harmonious breath:
   "For such as he there is no death;—
His life the eternal life commands;
Above man's aims his nature rose:
   The wisdom of a just content
   Made one small spot a continent,
And turned to poetry Life's prose.

"Haunting the hills, the stream, the wild,
    Swallow and aster, lake and pine,
    To him grew human or divine,—
Fit mates for this large-hearted child.
Such homage Nature ne'er forgets,
    And yearly on the coverlid
    'Neath which her darling lieth hid
Will write his name in violets.

"To him no vain regrets belong,
    Whose soul, that finer instrument,
    Gave to the world no poor lament,
But wood-notes ever sweet and strong.

*A daguerreotype of Henry David Thoreau, taken in 1856, when he was thirty-nine.
In her novel* Moods, *Louisa caught something of Thoreau's strange power in her
portrait of Adam Warwick, whose "Master's eye saw the grand lines that were to
serve as models for the perfect man."*

O lonely friend! he still will be
  A potent presence, though unseen,—
  Steadfast, sagacious, and serene:
Seek not for him,—he is with thee."

Anonymous.

Transfiguration

IN MEMORIAM

Mysterious Death! who in a single hour
  Life's gold can so refine;
  And by thy art divine
Change mortal weakness to immortal power!

Bending beneath the weight of eighty years,
  Spent with the noble strife
  Of a victorious life,
We watched her fading heavenward, through our tears.

But, ere the sense of loss our hearts had wrung,
  A miracle was wrought,
  And swift as happy thought
She lived again, brave, beautiful, and young.

Age, Pain, and Sorrow dropped the veils they wore,
  And showed the tender eyes
  Of angels in disguise,
Whose discipline so patiently she bore.

The past years brought their harvests rich and fair,
   While Memory and Love
   Together fondly wove
A golden garland for the silver hair.

How could we mourn like those who are bereft,
   When every pang of grief
   Found balm for its relief
In counting up the treasure she had left?

Faith that withstood the shocks of toil and time,
   Hope that defied despair,
   Patience that conquered care,
And loyalty whose courage was sublime.

The great, deep heart that was a home for all;
   Just, eloquent and strong,
   In protest against wrong;
Wide charity that knew no sin, no fall.

The Spartan spirit that made life so grand,
   Mating poor daily needs
   With high, heroic deeds,
That wrested happiness from Fate's hard hand.

We thought to weep, but sing for joy instead,
   Full of the grateful peace
   That followed her release;
For nothing but the weary dust lies dead.

Oh noble woman! never more a queen
   Than in the laying down
   Of sceptre and of crown,
To win a greater kingdom yet unseen:

Teaching us how to seek the highest goal;
  To earn the true success;
  To live, to love, to bless,
And make death proud to take a royal soul.

Our Madonna

A child, her wayward pencil drew
  On margins of her book
Garlands of flowers, dancing elves,
  Bird, butterfly and brook.
Lessons undone, and play forgot
  Seeking with hand and heart
The teacher whom she learned to love
  Before she knew 't was Art.

A maiden, full of lofty dreams,
  Slender and fair and tall
As were the goddesses she traced
  Upon her chamber wall.
Still laboring with brush and tool,
  Still seeking everywhere
Ideal beauty, grace and strength
  In the "divine despair."

A woman, sailing forth alone,
  Ambitious, brave, elate,
To mould life with a dauntless will,
  To seek and conquer fate.
Rich colors on her palette glowed

Patience bloomed into power;
Endeavor earned its just reward,
Art had its happy hour.

A wife, low sitting at his feet
To paint with tender skill
The hero of her early dreams,
Artist, but woman still.
Glad now to shut the world away,
Forgetting even Rome;
Content to be the household saint
Shrined in a peaceful home.

A mother, folding in her arms
The sweet, supreme success;
Giving a life to win a life,
Dying that she might bless.
Grateful for joy unspeakable,
In that brief, blissful past;
The picture of a baby face
Her loveliest and last.

Death the stern sculptor, with a touch
No earthly power can stay,
Changes to marble in an hour
The beautiful, pale clay.
But Love the mighty master comes
Mixing his tints with tears,
Paints an immortal form to shine
Undimmed by coming years.

A fair Madonna, golden-haired,
Whose soft eyes seem to brood
Upon the child whose little hand

Alcott long delighted friends and family with her occasional and nonsense verses, but the purpose of this little poetic note to Mr. Whittlesbury of Elmira, New York, remains obscure.

> *Most women do whatever they can,*
> *Often bearing the burdens of man,*
> *A few earn fortune & win fame,*
> *And such are proud of their own name.*

Crowns her with motherhood.
Sainted by death, yet bound to earth
    By its most tender ties,
For life has yielded up to her
    Its sacred mysteries.

So live, dear soul, serene and safe,
    Throned as in Raphael's skies,
Type of the love, the faith, the grief
    Whose pathos never dies.
Divine or human still the same
    To touch and lift the heart:
Earth's sacrifice to Heaven's fame
    And Nature truest Art.

A Wail Uttered in the Woman's Club

God bless you, merry ladies,
    May nothing you dismay,
As you sit here at ease and hark
    Unto my dismal lay.

Get out your pocket-handkerchiefs,
    Give o'er your jokes and songs,
Forget awhile your Woman's Rights,
    And pity author's wrongs.

There is a town of high repute,
    Where saints and sages dwell,
Who in these latter days are forced

A view of the North Bridge in Concord, with Daniel Chester French's famous bronze minuteman just visible in the distance. A sacred spot for the "little battalions of late Victorian highbrows," as Julian Hawthorne labeled them, who trekked to Concord. Here one could well tune in both revolutionary vibrations (from the town's patriot ancestors) and "celestial cogitations" (from her more recent transcendental residents).

To bid sweet peace farewell;
For all their men are demigods,—
    So rumor doth declare,—
And all the women are De Staëls,
    And genius fills the air.

So eager pilgrims penetrate
    To their most private nooks,
Storm their back doors in search of news
    And interview their cooks,
Worship at every victim's shrine,
    See halos round their hats,
Embalm the chickweed from their yards,
    And photograph their cats.

There's Emerson, the poet wise,
    That much-enduring man,
Sees Jenkinses from every clime,
    But dodges when he can.
Chaos and Cosmos down below
    Their waves of trouble roll,
While safely in his attic locked,
    He woos the Oversoul.

And Hawthorne, shy as any maid,
    From these invaders fled
Out of the window like a wraith,
    Or to his tower sped—
Till vanishing from this rude world,
    He left behind no clue,
Except along the hillside path
    The violet's tender blue.
 Channing scarce dares at eventide

To leave his lonely lair;
Reporters lurk on every side
 And hunt him like a bear.
Quaint Thoreau sought the wilderness,
 But callers by the score
Scared the poor hermit from his cell,
 The woodchuck from his door.

There's Alcott, the philosopher,
 Who labored long and well
Plato's Republic to restore,
 Now keeps a free hotel;
Whole boarding-schools of gushing girls
 That hapless mansion throng,
And Young Men's Christian U-ni-ons,
 Full five-and-seventy strong.

Alas! what can the poor souls do?
 Their homes are homes no more;
No washing-day is sacred now;
 Spring cleaning's never o'er.
Their doorsteps are the stranger's camp,
 Their trees bear many a name,
Artists their very nightcaps sketch;
 And this—and this is fame!

Deluded world! your Mecca is
 A sand-bank glorified;
The river that you see and sing
 Has "skeeters," but no tide.
The gods raise "garden-sarse" and milk
 And in these classic shades

Dwell nineteen chronic invalids
  And forty-two old maids.

Some April shall the world behold
  Embattled authors stand,
With steel pens of the sharpest tip
  In every inky hand.
Their bridge shall be a bridge of sighs,
  Their motto, "Privacy";
Their bullets like that Luther flung
  When bidding Satan flee.

Their monuments of ruined books,
  Of precious wasted days,
Of tempers tried, distracted brains,
  That might have won fresh bays.
And round this sad memorial,
  Oh, chant for requiem:
Here lie our murdered geniuses;
  Concord has conquered them.

SELECTIONS FROM THE JOURNALS

1846

Hillside

MARCH, 1846.—I have at last got the little room I have wanted so long, and am very happy about it. It does me good to be alone, and Mother has made it very pretty and neat for me. My work-basket and desk are by the window, and my closet is full of dried herbs that smell very nice. The door that opens into the garden will be very pretty in summer, and I can run off to the woods when I like.

I have made a plan for my life, as I am in my teens, and no more a child. I am old for my age, and don't care much for girls' things. People think I'm wild and queer; but Mother understands and helps me. I have not told any one about my plan; but I'm going to *be* good. I've made so many resolutions, and written sad notes, and cried over my sins, and it doesn't seem to do any good! Now I'm going to *work really,* for I feel a true desire to improve, and be a help and comfort, not a care and sorrow, to my dear mother.

1850

Boston, MAY, 1850.—So long a time has passed since I kept a journal that I hardly know how to begin. Since coming to the city I don't seem to have thought much, for the bustle and dirt and change send all lovely images and restful feelings away. Among my hills and woods I had fine free times alone, and though my thoughts were silly, I dare-say, they helped to keep me happy and good. I see now what Nature did for me, and my "romantic tastes," as people called that love of solitude and out-of-door life, taught me much . . .

In looking over our journals, Father says, "Anna's is about other people, Louisa's about herself." That is true, for I don't *talk* about myself; yet must always think of the willful, moody girl I try to manage, and in my journal I write of her to see how she gets on. Anna is so good she need not take care of herself, and can enjoy other people. If I look in my glass, I try to keep down vanity about my long hair, my well-shaped head, and my good nose. In the street I try not to covet fine things. My quick tongue is always getting me into trouble, and my moodiness makes it hard to be cheerful when I think how poor we are, how much worry it is to live, and how many things I long to do I never can.

So every day is a battle, and I'm so tired I don't want to live; only it's cowardly to die till you have done something.

1854

1854.—*Pinckney Street* [Boston]. I have neglected my journal for months, so must write it up. School for me month after month. Mother busy with boarders and sewing. Father doing as well as a philosopher can in a money-loving world. Anna at S[yracuse].

I earned a good deal by sewing in the evening when my day's work was done.

In February Father came home. Paid his way, but no more. A dramatic scene when he arrived in the night. We were waked by hearing the bell. Mother flew down, crying, "My husband!" We rushed after, and five white figures embraced the half-frozen wanderer who came in hungry, tired, cold, and disappointed, but smiling bravely and

LOUISA M. ALCOTT'S FAMOUS BOOKS.

Jo in a Vortex. — Every few weeks she would shut herself up in her room, put on her scribbling suit, and "fall into a vortex," as she expressed it. — Page 44.

LITTLE WOMEN; or, Meg, Jo, Beth, and Amy. Parts First and Second. Price of each, $1.50.

ROBERTS BROTHERS, *Publishers, Boston.*

"*I am 'Jo' in the principal characteristics, not the good ones,*" *Alcott once explained to a fan. In this advertisement, Jo is portrayed in Chapter 27 of* Little Women: "*Every few weeks she would shut herself up in her room, put on her scribbling suit, and 'fall into a vortex,' as she expressed it, writing away at her novel with all her heart and soul, for till that was finished she could find no peace.*"

as serene as ever. We fed and warmed and brooded over him, longing to ask if he had made any money, but no one did till little May said, after he had told all the pleasant things, "Well, did people pay you?" Then, with a queer look, he opened his pocket-book and showed one dollar, saying with a smile that made our eyes fill, "Only that! My overcoat was stolen, and I had to buy a shawl. Many promises were not kept, and travelling is costly; but I have opened the way, and another year shall do better."

I shall never forget how beautifully Mother answered him, though the dear, hopeful soul had built much on his success; but with a beaming face she kissed him, saying, "I call that doing *very well*. Since you are safely home, dear, we don't ask anything more."

Anna and I choked down our tears, and took a little lesson in real love which we never forgot, nor the look that the tired man and the tender woman gave one another. It was half tragic and comic, for Father was very dirty and sleepy, and Mother in a big nightcap and funny old jacket.

"I began," Alcott commented years later about the above passage, "to see the strong contrasts and the fun and follies in every-day life about this time."

1855

APRIL, 1855.—I am in the garret with my papers round me, and a pile of apples to eat while I write my journal, plan stories, and enjoy the patter of rain on the roof, in peace and quiet.

Being behindhand, as usual, I'll make note of the main events up to date, for I don't waste ink in poetry and pages of rubbish now. I've begun to *live,* and have no time for sentimental musing.

In October I began my school; Father talked, Mother looked after her boarders, and tried to help everybody. Anna was in Syracuse teaching . . .

My book [*Flower Fables*] came out; and people began to think that topsy-turvey Louisa would amount to something after all, since she could do so well as housemaid, teacher, seamstress, and story-teller. Perhaps she may . . .

A busy and a pleasant winter, because, though hard at times, I do seem to be getting on a little; and that encourages me.

Have heard [James Russell] Lowell . . . lecture, acted in plays, and thanks to our rag-money and good cousin H[amilton Willis], have been to the theatre several times,—always my great joy.

Summer plans are yet unsettled. Father wants to go to England: not a wise idea, I think. We shall probably stay here, and A[nna] and I go into the country as governesses. It's a queer way to live, but dramatic, and I rather like it; for we never know what is to come next. We are real "Micawbers," and always "ready for a spring."

1857

JUNE.—All happy together. My dear Nan was with me, and we had good times. Betty was feeble, but seemed to cheer up for a time. The long, cold, lonely winter has been to hard for the frail creature, and we are all anxious about her. I fear she may slip away; for she never seemed to care much for this world beyond home.

Read Charlotte Brönte's life. A very interesting, but sad one. So full of talent; and after working long, just as success, love, and happiness come, she dies.

Wonder if I shall ever be famous enough for people to care to read my story and my struggles. I can't be a C. B., but I may do a little something yet.

NOVEMBER.—

. . . Twenty-five this month. I feel my quarter of a century rather heavy on my shoulders just now. I lead two lives. One seems gay with plays, etc., the other very sad,—in Betty's room; for though she wishes us to act, and loves to see us get ready, the shadow is there, and Mother and I see it. Betty loves to have me with her; and I am with her at night, for Mother needs rest. Betty says she feels "strong" when I am near. So glad to be of use.

1858

MARCH 14TH.—My dear Beth died at three this morning, after two years of patient pain. Last week she put her work away, saying the needle was "too heavy," and having given us her few possessions, made ready for the parting in her own simple, quiet way. For two days she suffered much, begging for ether, though its effect was gone. Tuesday she lay in Father's arms, and called us round her, smiling contentedly as she said, "All here!" I think she bid us good bye then, as she held our hands and kissed us tenderly. Saturday she slept, and at midnight became unconscious, quietly breathing her life away till three; then, with one last look of the beautiful eyes, she was gone.

A curious thing happened, and I will tell it here, for Dr. G[eist] said it was a fact. A few moments after the last breath came, as Mother and I sat silently watching the shadow fall on the dear little face, I saw a light mist rise from the body, and float up and vanish in the air. Mother's eyes followed mine, and when I said, "What did you see?" she described the same light mist. Dr. G. said it was the life departing visibly.

For the last time we dressed her in her usual cap and gown, and laid her on her bed,—at rest at last. What she had suffered was seen in the face; for at twenty-three she looked like a woman of forty, so worn was she, and all her pretty hair gone.

On Monday Dr. Huntington read the Chapel service, and we sang her favorite hymn. Mr. Emerson, Henry Thoreau, [F. B.] Sanborn, and John Pratt, carried her out of the old home to the new one at Sleepy Hollow chosen by herself. So the first break comes, and I know what death means,—a liberator for her, a teacher for us.

1859

NOVEMBER.—Hurrah! My story ["Love and Self-Love"] was accepted; and [James Russell] Lowell asked if it was not a translation from the German, it was so unlike most tales. I felt much set up, and my fifty dollars will be very happy money. People seem to think it a great thing to get into the "Atlantic"; but I've not been pegging away all these years in vain, and may yet have books and publishers and a fortune of my own. Success has gone to my head, and I wander a little. Twenty-seven years old, and very happy.

The Harpers Ferry tragedy makes this a memorable month. Glad I have lived to see the Antislavery movement and this last heroic act in it. Wish I could do my part in it.

DECEMBER, 1859.—The execution of Saint John the Just [abolitionist John Brown] took place on the second. A meeting at the hall, and all Concord was there. Emerson, Thoreau, Father, and Sanborn spoke, and all were full of reverence and admiration for the martyr.

1862

NOVEMBER.—Thirty years old. Decided to go to Washington as a nurse if I could find a place. Help needed, and I love nursing, and *must* let out my pent-up energy in some new way. Winter is always a hard and a dull time, and if I am away there is one less to feed and warm and worry over.

I want new experiences, and am sure to get 'em if I go. So I've sent in my name, and bide my time writing tales, to leave all snug behind me, and mending up my old clothes,—for nurses don't need nice things, thank Heaven!

THE UNITED STATES GENERAL HOSPITAL AT GEORGETOWN, D. C., FORMERLY THE UNION HOTEL—VOLUNTEER NURSES ATTENDING THE SICK AND WOUNDED.—FROM A SKETCH BY OUR SPECIAL ARTIST IN WASHINGTON, D. C.—SEE PAGE 119.

The Union Hotel Hospital in Georgetown, where Alcott reported for duty in December 1862, full of zeal to begin her mission as a "nuss" (as she called herself). She was shocked by what she found there: "A more perfect pestilence-box than this house I never saw . . ."

1863

JANUARY, 1863. Union Hotel Hospital, Georgetown, D.C.—
. . . Ordered to keep [to] my room being threatened with pneumonia. Sharp pain in the side, cough, fever & dizziness. A pleasant prospect for a lonely soul five hundred miles from home! Sit & sew on the boys' clothes, write letters, sleep & read; try to talk & keep merry but fail decidedly as day after day goes & I feel no better. Dream awfully, & wake unrefreshed, think of home & wonder if I am to die here as Mrs. Ropes the matron is likely to do. Feel too miserable to care much what becomes of me. Dr. Smith creaks up twice a day to feel my pulse, give me doses, & ask if I am at all consumptive, or some other cheering question. Dr. Otman examines my lungs & looks sober. Dr. John haunts the room coming by day & night with wood, cologne, books & messes like a motherly little man as he is. Nurses fussy & anxious, matron dying, & every thing very gloomy. They want me to go home but I *won't* yet . . .

On the 21st I suddenly decided to go home, feeling very strangely & dreading to be worse . . .

Had a strange excited journey of a day & night, half asleep, half wandering, just conscious that I was going home . . . Just remember seeing May's shocked face at the Depot, mother's bewildered one at home, & getting to bed in the firm belief that the house was roofless & no one wanted to see me.

As I never shall forget the strange fancies that haunted me I shall amuse myself with recording some of them. The most vivid & enduring was a conviction that I had married a stout, handsome Spaniard, dressed in black velvet with very soft hands & a voice that was continually saying, "Lie still, my dear." This was Mother, I suspect, but with all the comfort I often found in her presence there was blended an awful fear of the Spanish spouse who was always coming after me, appearing out of closets, in at windows, or threatening me dreadfully all night long. I appealed to the Pope & really got up & made a touching plea in something meant for Latin they tell me. Once I went to heaven & found it a twilight place with people darting thro the air in a queer way. All very busy & dismal & ordinary. Miss Dix, W. H. Channi[n]g & other people were there but I thought it dark & "slow" & wished I hadn't come. A mob at Baltimore breaking down the door to get me; being hung for a witch, burned, stoned & otherwise maltreated were some of my fancies. Also being tempted to join Dr. W. & two of the nurses in worshipping the Devil. Also tending millions of sick men who never died or got well.

FEBRUARY.—Recovered my senses after 3 weeks of delirium, & was told I had had a very bad typhoid fever, had nearly died & was still very sick. All of which seemed rather curious for I remembered nothing of it. Found a queer, thin, big-eyed face when I looked in the glass; didn't know myself at all, & when I tried to walk discovered that I couldn't, & cried because "my legs wouldn't go."

Never having been sick before it was all new & very interesting when I got quiet enough to understand matters. Such long, long nights—such feeble, idle days, dozing, fretting about nothing, longing to eat & no mouth to do it with, mine being so sore & full of all manner of queer sensations it was nothing but a plague. The old fancies still lingered, seeming so real I believed in them & deluded Mother & May with the most absurd stories, so soberly told that they thought them true.

Dr. Bartlett came every day & was very kind. Father & Mother were with me night & day, & May sung "Birks of Sherfeldie" or read to me to wile away the tiresome hours. People sent letters, money, kind inquiries & goodies for the old "Nuss" . . . Tried to sew; read & write & found I had to begin all over again. Received $10 for my labors in Washington. Had all my hair 1$\frac{1}{2}$ yards long cut off & went into caps like a grandma. Felt badly about losing my one beauty. Never mind, it might have been my head & a wig outside is better than a loss of wits inside.

In May/June, Alcott's Hospital Sketches *were serialized, to great acclaim, in the* Boston Commonwealth; *in the fall, Alcott worked on her "Transcendental" novel,* Moods, *the first draft of which she had written four years before.*

OCTOBER, 1863.—. . . Father spoke of "Moods" & the great [Henry] James [Sr.] desired to see it. So I fell to work & finished it off, thinking the world must be coming to an end & all my dreams getting fulfilled in a most amazing way. If ever there was an astonished young woman it is myself, for things have gone on so swimmingly of late I don't know who I am. A year ago I had no publisher & went begging with my wares; now *three* have asked me for something, several papers are ready to print my contributions & F. B. S[anborn] says "any publisher this side of Baltimore would be glad to get a book." There is a sudden hoist for a meek & lowly scribbler who was told to "stick to her teaching," & never had a literary friend to lend a helping hand! Fifteen years of hard grubbing may be coming to something after all, & I may yet "pay all the debts, fix the house, send May to Italy & keep the old folks cosy," as I've said I would so long yet so hopelessly.

1865

APRIL.—Richmond taken on the 2nd! Hurrah! Went to Boston & enjoyed the grand jollification. Saw [Edwin] Booth again in "Hamlet" & thought him finer than ever . . .

On the 15th in the midst of the rejoicing came the sad news of the President's assassination & the city went into mourning. I am glad to have seen such a strange & sudden change in a nation's feelings. Saw the great procession, & though colored men were in it one was walking arm in arm with a white gentleman & I exulted thereat.

1867

JANUARY.—Sick from too hard work. Did nothing all the month but sit in a dark room & ache. Head & eyes full of neuralgia.

FEBRUARY.—Ditto ditto. Mother rheumatic fever had bad time with her eyes.

MARCH.—Ditto ditto. Got a little better at one time but tried to work & down I went again worse than ever.

APRIL.—Slowing mending . . .

MAY.—Still gaining, but all feeble. Mother half blind, Father lame & I weak, nervous & used up generally. Cold, wet weather & dull times for every one.

SEPTEMBER.—[Thomas] Niles, partner of Roberts [Bros.], asked me to write a girls' book. Said I'd try.

[Horace B.] Fuller asked me to be the Editor of "Merry's Museum." Said I'd try. Began at once on both new jobs, but didn't like either.

1868

MAY, 1868.—Father saw Mr. Niles about a fairy book. Mr. N. wants a *girls' story*, and I begin "Little Women." Marmee, Anna, and May all approve my plan. So I plod away, though I don't enjoy this sort of thing. Never liked girls or knew many, except my sisters; but our queer plays and experiences may prove interesting, though I doubt it.

1872

JANUARY, 1872.—Roberts Brothers paid $4,400 as six months' receipts for the books. A fine New Year's gift. S. E. S[ewall] invested $3,000, and the rest I put in the bank for family needs. Paid for the furnace and all the bills. What bliss it is to be able to do that and ask no help!

APRIL and MAY.—Wrote another sketch for the "Independent," . . . and the events of my travels paid my winter expenses. All is fish that comes to the literary net. Goethe puts his joys and sorrows into poems; I turn my adventures into bread and butter.

JUNE, 1872.—Home, and begin a new task. Twenty years ago I resolved to make the family independent if I could. At forty that is done. Debts all paid, even the outlawed ones, and we have enough to be comfortable. It has cost me my health, perhaps; but as I still live, there is more for me to do, I suppose.

JULY, 1872.—May makes a lovely hostess, and I fly round behind the scenes, or skip out of the back window when ordered out for inspection by the inquisitive public. Hard work to keep things running smoothly, for this sight-seeing fiend is a new torment to us.

AUGUST.—May goes to Clark's Island for rest, having kept hotel long enough. I say "No," and shut the door. People *must* learn that authors have some rights; I can't entertain a dozen a day, and write the tales they demand also. I'm but a human worm, and when walked on must turn in self-defence.

Reporters sit on the wall and take notes; artists sketch me as I pick pears in the garden; and strange women interview Johnny [Alcott's nephew] as he plays in the orchard.

It looks like impertinent curiosity to me; but it is called "fame," and considered a blessing to be grateful for, I find. Let 'em try it.

1874

JANUARY, 1874.—Mother quite ill this month. Dr. Wesselhoeft does his best for the poor old body, now such a burden to her. The slow decline has begun, and she knows it, having nursed her mother to the same end.

Father disappointed and rather sad, to be left out of so much that he would enjoy and should be asked to help and adorn. A little more money, a pleasant house and time to attend to it, and I'd bring all the best people to see and entertain *him* . . .

When I had the youth I had no money; now I have the money I have no time; and when I get the time, if I ever do, I shall have no health to enjoy life. I suppose it's the discipline I need; but it's rather hard to love the things I do and see them go by because duty chains me to my galley. If I come into port at last with all sail set that will be reward perhaps.

Life always was a puzzle to me, and gets more mysterious as I go on. I shall find it out by and by and see that it's all right, if I can only keep brave and patient to the end.

May still in London painting Turners, and doing pretty panels as "potboilers." They sell well, and she is a thrifty child. Good luck to our mid-summer girl.

1875

JANUARY, 1875.— . . . Father flourishing about the Western cities, "riding in Louisa's chariot, and adored as the grandfather of 'Little Women,'" he says.

FEBRUARY.—Finish my little tale and go to Vassar College on a visit . . . talk with four hundred girls, write in stacks of albums and schoolbooks, and kiss every one who asks me. Go to New York; am rather lionized, and run away; but things look rather jolly, and I may try a winter there some time, as I need a change and new ideas.

SEPTEMBER and OCTOBER, 1875.—I go to Woman's Congress in Syracuse, and see Niagara. Funny time with the girls.

Write loads of autographs, dodge at the theatre, and am kissed to death by gushing damsels. One energetic lady grasped my hand in the crowd, exclaiming, "If you ever come to Oshkosh, your feet will not be allowed to touch the ground: you will be borne in the arms of the people! Will you come?" "Never," responded Miss A., trying to look affable, and dying to laugh as the good soul worked my arm like a pump-handle, and from the gallery generations of girls were looking on. "This, this, is fame!"

1878

MARCH, 1878.—A happy event,—May's marriage to Ernest Nieriker . . . He is a Swiss, handsome, cultivated, and good . . . Send her $1,000 as a gift, and all good wishes for the new life.

APRIL.—Happy letters from May, who is enjoying life as one can but once. E[rnest] writes finely to Father, and is a son to welcome I am sure. May sketches and E. attends to his business by day, and both revel in music in the evening, as E. is a fine violin player.

How different our lives are just now!—I so lonely, sad, and sick; she so happy, well, and blest. She always had the cream of things, and deserved it. My time is yet to come somewhere else, when I am ready for it.

1879

JULY.— . . . On the 15th the School of Philosophy began in the study at Orchard House. Thirty students, Father the Dean. He has *his* dream realized at last, & is in glory with plenty of talk to swim in. People laugh but will enjoy some thing new in this dull old town, & the fresh Westerners will show them that all the culture of the world is not in Concord . . .

AUGUST.— . . . The town swarms with budding philosophers, & they roost on our step like hens, waiting for corn. Father revels in it, so we keep the hotel going & try to look as if we like it. If they were philanthropists I *should* enjoy it, but speculation seems a waste of time

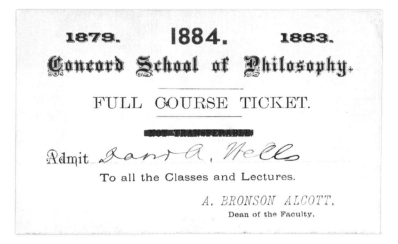

The Concord School of Philosophy, with Bronson Alcott as its revered Dean, was a sort of metaphysical watering hole for the high-minded from all corners of America, who gathered there each summer to attend lectures by such distinguished parties as Emerson, Julia Ward Howe, Ednah D. Cheney, and, of course, the Dean himself.

when there is so much real work crying to be done. Why discuss the Unknowable till our poor are fed & the wicked saved?

OCTOBER 8th.—Dear Marmee's birthday. Never forgotten. Lovely day. Go to Sleepy Hollow with flowers. Her grave is green, black berry vines with red leaves trail over it. A little white stone with her initials is at the head, & among the tall grass over her breast a little bird had made a nest. Empty now, but a pretty symbol of the refuge that tender bosom always was for all feeble & sweet things. Her favorite asters bloomed all about, & the pines sang overhead. So she & dear Beth lie quietly asleep in God's Acre, & we remember them more tenderly with each year that brings us nearer them & home . . .

I mourn much because all say I must not go to May. Not safe & I cannot add to Mamma Nieriker's cares at this time by another invalid, as the voyage would upset me I am so sea sick.

Give up my hope & long cherished plan with grief. May sadly disappointed. I know I shall wish I had gone. It is my luck!

NOVEMBER 8th.—Little *Louisa May* Nieriker ["Lulu"] arrived in Paris at 9 p.m. after a short journey. All doing well. Much rejoicing. Nice little lass & May very happy. Ah, if I had only been there! Too much happiness for me.

DECEMBER.—May not doing well. The weight on my heart is not all imagination. She was too happy to have it last, & I fear the end is coming. Hope it is my nerves, but this peculiar feeling has never misled me before.

WED. 31ST.—A dark day for us. A telegram from Ern[e]st [Nieriker] to Mr. Emerson tells us "May is dead." Anna was gone to B[oston]. Father to the P.O. anxious for letters, the last being overdue, I was alone when Mr. E[merson] came. E[rnest] sent to him knowing I was feeble & hoping Mr. E[merson] would soften the blow. I found him looking at May's portrait, pale & tearful with the paper in his hand.

"My child, I *wish* I could prepare you, but alas, alas!" there his voice failed & he gave me the telegram.

I was not surprised & read the hard words as if I knew it all before. "I *am* prepared," I said & thanked him. He was much moved & very tender. I shall remember gratefully the look, the grasp, the tears he gave me, & I am sure that hard moment was made bearable by the presence of this our best & tenderest friend. He went to find Father but missed him, & I had to tell both him & Anna when they came. A very bitter sorrow for all.

I never shall forgive myself for not going even if it put me back. If I had lived to see her & help her die, or save her, I should have been content.

The dear baby may comfort E[rnest] but what can comfort us?

It is the distance that is so hard, & the thought of so much happiness ended so soon. "Two years of perfect happiness," May called those married years, & said, "If I die when baby comes don't mourn for I have had as much happiness in this short time as many in twenty years."

She wished me to have her baby & her pictures. A very precious legacy! All she had to leave. Rich payment for the little I could do for her.

I see now why I lived. To care for May's child & not leave Annie all alone.

1880

SEPTEMBER

Put papers in order, & arrange[d] things generally to be in order when our Lulu comes. Make a cosy nursery for the darling, & say my prayers over the little white crib that waits for her if she ever comes. God watch over her!

Paid my first poll tax. As my head is my most valuable piece of

A portrait of the youngest Alcott daughter, Abby May. Gifted with pen and brush, she was, like Amy in Little Women, *so graceful and ingratiating that "less fortunate souls" were tempted to believe she had been "born under a lucky star."*

property I thought $2.00 a cheap tax on it. Saw my townswomen about voting &c. Hard work to stir them up. Cake & servants more interesting.

18th in Boston waiting for the steamer that brings my treasure. The ocean seems very wide & terrible when I think of the motherless little creature coming so far to us.

19th . . . As I waited on the wharf while the people came off the ship I saw several babies & wondered each time if that was mine. At last the Captain appeared, & in his arms a little yellow haired thing in white, with its hat off as it looked about with lively blue eyes & hobbled prettily . . .

I held out my arms to Lulu only being able to say her name. She looked at me for a moment, then came to me saying "Marmar?" in a wistful way & nestling close as if she had found her own people & home at last, as she had, thank Heaven!

I could only listen while I held her & the others told their tale. Then we got home as soon as we could, & dear Baby behaved very well though hungry & tired.

The little Princess was received with tears & smiles, & being washed & fed went quietly to sleep in her new bed, while we brooded over her & were never tired of looking at the little face of "May's baby."

She is a very active, bright child, not pretty yet, being browned by sea air & having only a yellow down on her head & pug nose. Her little body is beautifully formed, broad shoulders, fine chest, & lovely arms. A happy thing, laughing & waving her hands, confiding & bold, with a keen look in the eyes so like May, who hated shams & saw through them at once. She always comes to me, & seems to have decided that I am really "Marmar." My heart is full of pride & joy, & the touch of the dear little hands seems to take away the bitterness of grief. I often go at night to see if she is *really* here, & the sight of the little yellow head is like sunshine to me.

Father adores her, & she loves to sit in his strong arms. They make a pretty picture as he walks in the garden with her to "see birdies."

Anna tends her as she did May, who was her baby once, being ten years younger, & we all find life easier to like now the Baby has come . . .

OCTOBER

. . . Lulu is rosy & fair now, & grows pretty in her native air. A merry little lass who seems to feel at home & blooms in an atmosphere of adoration. People come to see "Miss Alcott's baby," & strangers way-lay her little carriage in the street to look at her, but she does not allow herself to be kissed.

As Father wants to go West I decide to hire Cousin L[izzie] W[ells]'s house furnished for the winter . . .

Get settled, & find things in a bad state, though told that "all would be in order." A hard mixed up family to run, but if Lulu is well we won't mind rats & drains, & dirt & cold & broken promises.

NOVEMBER (48 ON THE 29TH)

. . . 8th. Lulu's birthday. One year old. Her gifts were set out on a table for her to see when she came down in the a.m. A little cake with *one* candle, a rose crown for the queen, a silver mug, dolly, picture books, gay ball, toys, flowers & many kisses.

She sat smiling at her treasures just under her mother's picture. Suddenly, attracted by the sunshine on the face of the portrait which she knows is "Marmar" she held up a white rose to it calling "Mum! Mum!" & smiling at it in a way that made us all cry.

A happy day for her, a sad one for us.

1883

MAY

Take care of Lulu, as we can find no good woman to walk & dress & play with her. The ladies are incapable or proud, the girls vulgar or rough, so my poor baby has a bad time with her little tempers & active mind & body. Could do it myself if I had the nerves & strength, but am needed else where & must leave the child to some one. Long to go away with her & do as I like. Shall never lead my own life.

JUNE

Get J. H. a nice little person for Lulu, & we get on very well.

Mrs. F. the nurse got tipsey & had to go. A sad pity as she is a good nurse & does very well with Father who is hard to take care of being unreasonable, fretful & weak.

JULY

Go to Nonquitt [Mass.] with Miss H. & Lulu for the summer. A quiet, healthy place with pleasant people & fine air. Turn Lulu loose with H. to run after her, & try to rest.

Lulu takes her first bath in the sea. Very bold, walks off toward Europe up to her neck & is much afflicted that I wont let her go to the bottom & see the "little trabs." Makes a Cupid of herself & is very pretty & gay.

1884

JANUARY

New Year's day is made memorable by my solemnly *spanking* my child. Miss C[assall] & others assure me it is the only way to cure her wilfulness. I doubt it, but proving that mothers are usually too tender & blind I correct my dear in the old fashioned way.

She proudly says, "Do it, do it!" & when it is done is heart broken at the idea of Aunt Wee Wee's giving her pain. Her bewilderment was pathetic, & the effect, as I expected, a failure. Love is better, but also endless patience.

APRIL

Miss C[assall] goes. No love in her. Cold & tired & careless. Get old Maria for a time & Lu & I are happy. We understand one another, & with her I can be as much of a child as she. Dr. D. found me on the floor playing lion, hair down, roaring & romping to L.'s great delight. C. thought it undignified to play as children play.

DECEMBER.—Began again on "Jo's Boys" as T. N[iles] wants a new book very much & I am tired of being idle. Wrote two hours for three days, then had a violent attack of vertigo & was ill for a week. Head won't bear work yet. Put away papers & tried to dawdle & go about as other people do.

Pleasant Xmas with Lulu & Nan & poor father who loves to see us about him. A narrow world now but a happy one for him.

Last day of the year. All well at home except myself. Body feeble but soul improving.

1885

JANUARY 1st, 1885.—

. . . Tried the Mind Cure with Mrs. Newman. Agreeable at first. Blue clouds & sunshine in my head. Mesmerism, though Mrs. N. said is was *not*. Breath short, heart fluttered, seemed to float away. Could not move. Very quiet after it. Queer times. Will try the experiment & gratefully accept any miracle that can be wrought for me.

FEBRUARY.—My Mind Cure not a success. First I am told to be "passive." So I do, say & think nothing. No effect. Then I am not "positive" enough, must exert my mind. Do so & try to grasp the mystery. Then I am *"too* positive" & must not try to *understand* anything. Inconsistency & too much hurry. God & Nature can't be hustled about every ten minutes to cure a dozen different ails. Too much money made & too much delusion all round.

Mrs. Burnett is trying it. Says it quiets her mind but doesn't help her body. Too much is claimed for it.

Read Geo. Eliot's Life. Glad it is not gossipy. No one's business what she thought & did. Dr. Munroe with good plain massage does me more good than Mrs. N[ewman] & "letting divine strength flow in."

MARCH.—Mrs. N[ewman] says "you've got it!" but she deceives herself for I have lost my faith & never feel any better after a séance. Try Miss Adams as Mrs. N. says she herself is "too powerful" for me. Mrs. N. made no more impression on me than a moonbeam. After 30 trials I give it up. No miracle for me. My ills are not imaginary, so are hard to cure.

AUGUST 8th.— . . . Sorted old letters & burned many. Not wise to keep for curious eyes to read, & gossip-lovers to print by & by. Lived in the past for days, & felt very old recalling all I have been through.

Experiences go deep with me, & I begin to think it might be well to keep some record of my life if it will help others to read it when I'm gone. People seem to think our lives interesting & peculiar.

Life rather a burden.

OCTOBER

To B[oston] . . . to open our new house. Hard week. Things left dirty & in disorder. Shiftless cook & careless man in charge. General rummage & settling.

Family came later. Father drove down very nicely. Pleased with his new room. Lulu charmed with her big, sunny nursery & the play house left for her. Boys in clover, & Nan ready for the new sort of housekeeping.

I shall miss my quiet, care free life in B[oston] but it is best for all so I shall try to bear the friction & the worry many persons always bring me.

1886

FEBRUARY.—Try massage & feel better, thank God! It is tiresome to be always aching. Why can't people use their brains without breaking down?

MARCH 27TH.—Another attack of vertigo. Ill for a week. Sleepless nights. Head worked like a steam engine & would not stop. Planned "Jo's Boys" to the end & longed to get up & write it. Told Dr. W[esselhoeft] that he had better let me get the ideas *out* then I could rest. He very wisely agreed & said, "As soon as you can write half an hour a day & see if it does you good. Rebellious brains must be attended to or trouble comes." So I began as soon as able, & was satisfied that we were right for my head felt better very soon, & with much care about not over doing I had some pleasant hours when I forgot my body & lived in my mind.

1887

JANUARY 1.—A sad & lonely day. Feeble & sick, away from home & worn out with the long struggle for health. Have had many hard days but few harder than this. Say my prayers & try to see many mercies. Fred [Alcott's nephew] & his happy love, A[nna] & her pride in her good boys, Lulu well & good and happy. Father comfortable, & plenty to make all safe & easy. More courage & patience are all *I* ask.

DECEMBER 31.—Dr. G[reen] All well. Lulu nicely & I all right. Thank the Lord for all his mercies. A hard year, but over now. Please God the next be happier for us all. Wrote letters. Good bye 1887!

1888

JANUARY 1.—A happy day & great contrast to Jan. 1st of last year. Then I was ill & hopeless & sad. Now though still alone & absent from home I am on the road to health at last & feel hopeful after much tribulation & pain for two years. Very grateful for my many mercies, & better for my trials I trust. Read & wrote letters. L[ulu] brought a box of gifts from home & I have not seen any one but Lulu for 8 weeks . . . Rain outside but peace within.

JANUARY 12.—Cold & Fine. Dr. G[reen]. Gave me an Inhaler. Said I could drive in tomorrow & see Father who is feeble. Glad! Can't have callers yet, nor eat. Must wait. No freedom yet. (Had drive out & play all I can to keep jolly.)

FEBRUARY 5.—Go in to see Father who fails fast. Say good bye as he seems nearly gone. In a stupor half the time. Opened his eyes & smiled at me. No pain but so weak . . . A sad p.m. Lay still & Dr. read Coleridge, Wordsworth to me so I should not think of sad things. Slept well. Made a poem.

MARCH 1.—Fine. In to see Papa. Very sweet & feeble. Kissed me & said, "Come soon." Smelt my flowers & asked me to write him a letter. Nearly gone. A[nna] very dear . . .

At about 11 o'clock in the morning on March 4, Amos Bronson Alcott died at the family's home on Louisburg Square in Boston. Two days later, early in the morning, Louisa May Alcott died at Dr. Rhoda Lawrence's rest home in Roxbury, but a few hours before her father's funeral was to take place at Louisburg Square.

PART III

FROM THE MAGIC INKSTAND:

Four Stories

PAULINE'S PASSION AND PUNISHMENT

Chapter I

To and fro, like a wild creature in its cage, paced that handsome woman, with bent head, locked hands, and restless steps. Some mental storm, swift and sudden as a tempest of the tropics, had swept over her and left its marks behind. As if in anger at the beauty now proved powerless, all ornaments had been flung away, yet still it shone undimmed, and filled her with a passionate regret. A jewel glittered at her feet, leaving the lace rent to shreds on the indignant bosom that had worn it; the wreaths of hair that had crowned her with a woman's most womanly adornment fell disordered upon shoulders that gleamed the fairer for the scarlet of the pomegranate flowers clinging to the bright meshes that had imprisoned them an hour ago; and over the face, once so affluent in youthful bloom, a stern pallor had fallen like a blight, for pride was slowly conquering passion, and despair had murdered hope.

Pausing in her troubled march, she swept away the curtain swaying in the wind and looked out, as if imploring help from Nature, the great mother of us all. A summer moon rode high in a cloudless heaven, and far as eye could reach stretched the green wilderness of a Cuban *cafetal*. No forest, but a tropical orchard, rich in lime, banana, plantain, palm, and orange trees, under whose protective shade grew the ever-

PAULINE'S PASSION

AND

PUNISHMENT.

CHAPTER I.

O and fro, like a wild creature in its cage, paced that handsome woman, with bent head, locked hands and restless steps. Some mental storm, swift and sudden as a tempest of the tropics, had swept over her and left its marks behind. As if in anger at the beauty now proved powerless, all ornaments had been flung away, yet still it shone undimmed, and filled her with a passionate regret. A jewel glittered at her feet, leaving the lace rent to shreds on the indignant bosom that had worn it; the wreaths of hair that had crowned her with a woman's most womanly adornment fell disordered upon shoulders that gleamed the fairer for the

Alcott was an actress born, and adored the flamboyance and flair of melodrama. That love is zestily on display in "Pauline's Passion and Punishment." Here Alcott tells an old, old story, and tells it exceedingly well.

green coffee plant, whose dark-red berries are the fortune of their possessor, and the luxury of one-half the world. Wide avenues diverging from the mansion, with its belt of brilliant shrubs and flowers, formed shadowy vistas, along which, on the wings of the wind, came a breath of far-off music, like a wooing voice; for the magic of night and distance lulled the cadence of a Spanish *contradanza* to a trance of sound, soft, subdued, and infinitely sweet. It was a southern scene, but not a southern face that looked out upon it with such unerring glance; there was no southern languor in the figure, stately and erect; no southern swarthiness on fairest cheek and arm; no southern darkness in the shadowy gold of the neglected hair; the light frost of northern snows lurked in the features, delicately cut, yet vividly alive, betraying a temperament ardent, dominant, and subtle. For passion burned in the deep eyes, changing their violet to black. Pride sat on the forehead, with its dark brows; all a woman's sweetest spells touched the lips, whose shape was a smile; and in the spirited carriage of the head appeared the freedom of an intellect ripened under colder skies, the energy of a nature that could wring strength from suffering, and dare to act where feebler souls would only dare desire.

Standing thus, conscious only of the wound that bled in that high heart of hers, and the longing that gradually took shape and deepened to a purpose, an alien presence changed the tragic atmosphere of that still room and woke her from her dangerous mood. A wonderfully winning guise this apparition wore, for youth, hope, and love endowed it with the charm that gives beauty to the plainest, while their reign endures. A boy in any other climate, in this his nineteen years had given him the stature of a man; and Spain, the land of romance, seemed embodied in this figure, full of the lithe slenderness of the whispering palms overhead, the warm coloring of the deep-toned flowers sleeping in the room, the native grace of the tame antelope lifting its human eyes to his as he lingered on the threshold in an attitude eager yet timid, watching that other figure as it looked into the night and found no solace there.

"Pauline!"

She turned as if her thought had taken voice and answered her, regarded him a moment, as if hesitating to receive the granted wish, then beckoned with the one word.

"Come!"

Instantly the fear vanished, the ardor deepened, and with an imperious "Lie down!" to his docile attendant, the young man obeyed with equal docility, looking as wistfully toward his mistress as the brute toward her master, while he waited proudly humble for her commands.

"Manuel, why are you here?"

"Forgive me! I saw Dolores bring a letter; you vanished, an hour passed, I could wait no longer, and I came."

"I am glad, I needed my one friend. Read that."

She offered a letter, and with her steady eyes upon him, her purpose strengthening as she looked, stood watching the changes of that expressive countenance. This was the letter:

Pauline—

Six months ago I left you, promising to return and take you home my wife; I loved you, but I deceived you; for though my heart was wholly yours, my hand was not mine to give. This it was that haunted me through all that blissful summer, this that marred my happiness when you owned you loved me, and this drove me from you, hoping I could break the tie with which I had rashly bound myself. I could not, I am married, and there all ends. Hate me, forget me, solace your pride with the memory that none knew your wrong, assure your peace with the knowledge that mine is destroyed forever, and leave my punishment to remorse and time.

Gilbert

With a gesture of wrathful contempt, Manuel flung the paper from him as he flashed a look at his companion, muttering through his teeth, "Traitor! Shall I kill him?"

Pauline laughed low to herself, a dreary sound, but answered with a slow darkening of the face that gave her words an ominous significance. "Why should you? Such revenge is brief and paltry, fit only for mock tragedies or poor souls who have neither the will to devise nor the will to execute a better. There are fates more terrible than death; weapons more keen than poniards, more noiseless than pistols. Women use such, and work out a subtler vengeance than men can conceive. Leave Gilbert to remorse—and me."

She paused an instant, and by some strong effort banished the black frown from her brow, quenched the baleful fire of her eyes, and left nothing visible but the pale determination that made her beautiful face more eloquent than her words.

"Manuel, in a week I leave the island."

"Alone, Pauline?"

"No, not alone."

A moment they looked into each other's eyes, each endeavoring to read the other. Manuel saw some indomitable purpose, bent on conquering all obstacles. Pauline saw doubt, desire, and hope; knew that a word would bring the ally she needed; and, with a courage as native to her as her pride, resolved to utter it.

Seating herself, she beckoned her companion to assume the place beside her, but for the first time he hesitated. Something in the unnatural calmness of her manner troubled him, for his southern temperament was alive to influences whose presence would have been unfelt by one less sensitive. He took the cushion at her feet, saying, half tenderly, half reproachfully, "Let me keep my old place till I know in what character I am to fill the new. The man you trusted has deserted you; the boy you pitied will prove loyal. Try him, Pauline."

"I will."

And with the bitter smile unchanged upon her lips, the low voice unshaken in its tones, the deep eyes unwavering in their gaze, Pauline went on:

"You know my past, happy as a dream till eighteen. Then all was swept away, home, fortune, friends, and I was left, like an unfledged bird, without even the shelter of a cage. For five years I have made my life what I could, humble, honest, but never happy, till I came here, for here I saw Gilbert. In the poor companion of your guardian's daughter he seemed to see the heiress I had been, and treated me as such. This flattered my pride and touched my heart. He was kind, I grateful; then he loved me, and God knows how utterly I loved him! A few months of happiness the purest, then he went to make home ready for me, and I believed him; for where I wholly love I wholly trust. While my own peace was undisturbed, I learned to read the language of your eyes, Manuel, to find the boy grown into the man, the friend warmed into a lover. Your youth had kept me blind too long. Your society had grown dear to me, and I loved you like a sister for your unvarying kindness to the solitary woman who earned her bread and found it bitter. I told you my secret to prevent the utterance of your own. You remember the promise you made me then, keep it still, and bury the knowledge of my lost happiness deep in your pitying heart, as I shall in my proud one. Now the storm is over, and I am ready for my work again, but it must be a new task in a new scene. I hate this house, this room, the faces I must meet, the duties I must perform, for the memory of that traitor haunts them all. I see a future full of interest, a stage whereon I could play a stirring part. I long for it intensely, yet cannot make it mine alone. Manuel, do you love me still?"

Bending suddenly, she brushed back the dark hair that streaked his forehead and searched the face that in an instant answered her. Like a swift rising light, the eloquent blood rushed over swarthy cheek and brow, the slumberous softness of the eyes kindled with a flash, and the lips, sensitive as any woman's, trembled yet broke into a rapturous smile as he cried, with fervent brevity, "I would die for you!"

A look of triumph swept across her face, for with this boy, as chivalrous as ardent, she knew that words were not mere breath. Still, with her stern purpose uppermost, she changed the bitter smile into one half-timid, half-tender, as she bent still nearer, "Manuel, in a week I leave the island. Shall I go alone?"

"No, Pauline."

He understood her now. She saw it in the sudden paleness that fell on him, heard it in the rapid beating of his heart, felt it in the strong grasp that fastened on her hand, and knew that the first step was won. A regretful pang smote her, but the dark mood which had taken possession of her stifled the generous warnings of her better self and drove her on.

"Listen, Manuel. A strange spirit rules me tonight, but I will have no reserves from you, all shall be told; then, if you will come, be it so; if not, I shall go my way as solitary as I came. If you think that this loss has broken my heart, undeceive yourself, for such as I live years in an hour and show no sign. I have shed no tears, uttered no cry, asked no comfort; yet, since I read that letter, I have suffered more than many suffer in a lifetime. I am not one to lament long over any hopeless sorrow. A single paroxysm, sharp and short, and it is over. Contempt has killed my love, I have buried it, and no power can make it live again, except as a pale ghost that will not rest till Gilbert shall pass through an hour as bitter as the last."

"Is that the task you give yourself, Pauline?"

The savage element that lurks in southern blood leaped up in the boy's heart as he listened, glittered in his eye, and involuntarily found expression in the nervous grip of the hands that folded a fairer one between them. Alas for Pauline that she had roused the sleeping devil, and was glad to see it!

"Yes, it is weak, wicked, and unwomanly; yet I persist as relentlessly as any Indian on a war trail. See me as I am, not the gay girl you have known, but a revengeful woman with but one tender spot now left in her heart, the place you fill. I have been wronged, and I long to right myself at once. Time is too slow; I cannot wait, for that man must be taught that two can play at the game of hearts, taught soon and sharply. I can do this, can wound as I have been wounded, can sting him with contempt, and prove that I too can forget."

"Go on, Pauline. Show me how I am to help you."

"Manuel, I want fortune, rank, splendor, and power; you can give me all these, and a faithful friend beside. I desire to show Gilbert the creature he deserted no longer poor, unknown, unloved, but lifted higher than himself, cherished, honored, applauded, her life one of royal pleasure, herself a happy queen. Beauty, grace, and talent you tell me I possess; wealth gives them luster, rank exalts them, power makes them irresistible. Place these worldly gifts in my hand and that hand is yours. See, I offer it."

She did so, but it was not taken. Manuel had left his seat and now stood before her, awed by the undertone of strong emotion in her calmly spoken words, bewildered by the proposal so abruptly made, longing to ask the natural question hovering on his lips, yet too generous to utter it. Pauline read his thought, and answered it with no touch of pain or pride in the magical voice that seldom spoke in vain.

"I know your wish; it is as just as your silence is generous, and I reply to it in all sincerity. You would ask, 'When I have given all that I possess, what do I receive in return?' This—a wife whose friendship is as warm as many a woman's love; a wife who will give you all the heart still left her, and cherish the hope that time may bring a harvest of real affection to repay you for the faithfulness of years; who, though she takes the retribution of a wrong into her hands and executes it in the face of heaven, never will forget the honorable name you give into her keeping or blemish it by any act of hers. I can promise no more. Will this content you, Manuel?"

Before she ended his face was hidden in his hands, and tears streamed through them as he listened, for like a true child of the south each emotion found free vent and spent itself as swiftly as it rose. The reaction was more than he could bear, for in a moment his life was changed, months of hopeless longing were banished with a word, a blissful yes canceled the hard no that had been accepted as inexorable, and Happiness, lifting her full cup to his lips, bade him drink. A moment he yielded to the natural relief, then dashed his tears away and threw himself at Pauline's feet in that attitude fit only for a race as graceful as impassioned.

"Forgive me! Take all I have—fortune, name, and my poor self; use us as you will, we are proud and happy to be spent for you! No service will be too hard, no trial too long if in the end you learn to love me with one tithe of the affection I have made my life. Do you mean it? Am I to go with you? To be near you always, to call you wife, and know we are each other's until death? What have I ever done to earn a fate like this?"

Fast and fervently he spoke, and very winsome was the glad abandonment of this young lover, half boy, half man, possessing the simplicity of the one, the fervor of the other. Pauline looked and listened with a soothing sense of consolation in the knowledge that this loyal heart was all her own, a sweet foretaste of the devotion which henceforth was to shelter her from poverty, neglect, and wrong, and turn life's sunniest side to one who had so long seen only its most bleak and barren. Still at her feet, his arms about her waist, his face flushed and proud, lifted to hers, Manuel saw the cold mask soften, the stern eyes melt with a sudden dew as Pauline watched him, saying, "Dear Manuel, love me less; I am not worth such ardent and entire faith. Pause and reflect before you take this step. I will not bind you to my fate too soon lest you repent too late. We both stand alone in the world, free to make or mar our future as we will. I have chosen my lot. Recall all it may cost you to share it and be sure the price is not too high a one. Remember I am poor, you the possessor of one princely fortune, the sole heir to another."

"The knowledge of this burdened me before; now I glory in it because I have the more for you."

"Remember, I am older than yourself, and may early lose the beauty you love so well, leaving an old wife to burden your youth."

"What are a few years to me? Women like you grow lovelier with age, and you shall have a strong young husband to lean on all your life."

"Remember, I am not of your faith, and the priests will shut me out from your heaven."

"Let them prate as they will. Where you go I will go; Santa Paula shall be my madonna!"

"Remember, I am a deserted woman, and in the world we are going to my name may become the sport of that man's cruel tongue. Could you bear that patiently, and curb your fiery pride if I desired it?"

"Anything for you, Pauline!"

"One thing more. I give you my liberty; for a time give me forbearance in return, and though wed in haste woo me slowly, lest this sore heart of mine find even your light yoke heavy. Can you promise this, and wait till time has healed my wound, and taught me to be meek?"

"I swear to obey you in all things; make me what you will, for soul and body I am wholly yours henceforth."

"Faithful and true! I knew you would not fail me. Now go, Manuel. Tomorrow do your part resolutely as I shall do mine, and in a week we will begin the new life together. Ours is a strange betrothal, but it shall not lack some touch of tenderness from me. Love, good night."

Pauline bent till her bright hair mingled with the dark, kissed the boy on lips and forehead as a fond sister might have done, then put him gently from her; and like one in a blessed dream he went away to pace all night beneath her window, longing for the day.

As the echo of his steps died along the corridor, Pauline's eye fell on the paper lying where her lover flung it. At this sight all the softness vanished, the stern woman reappeared, and, crushing it in her hand with slow significance, she said low to herself, "This is an old, old story, but it shall have a new ending."

Chapter II

"What jewels will the señora wear tonight?"

"None, Dolores. Manuel has gone for flowers—he likes them best. You may go."

"But the señora's toilette is not finished; the sandals, the gloves, the garland yet remain."

"Leave them all; I shall not go down. I am tired of this endless folly. Give me that book and go."

The pretty Creole obeyed; and careless of Dolores' work, Pauline sank into the deep chair with a listless mien, turned the pages for a little, then lost herself in thoughts that seemed to bring no rest.

Silently the young husband entered and, pausing, regarded his wife with mingled pain and pleasure—pain to see her so spiritless, pleasure to see her so fair. She seemed unconscious of his presence till the fragrance of his floral burden betrayed him, and looking up to smile a welcome she met a glance that changed the sad dreamer into an excited actor, for it told her that the object of her search was found. Springing erect, she asked eagerly, "Manuel, is he here?"

"Yes."

"Alone?"

"His wife is with him."

"Is she beautiful?"

"Pretty, petite, and petulant."

"And he?"

"Unchanged: the same imposing figure and treacherous face, the same restless eye and satanic mouth. Pauline, let me insult him!"

"Not yet. Were they together?"

"Yes. He seemed anxious to leave her, but she called him back imperiously, and he came like one who dared not disobey."

"Did he see you?"

"The crowd was too dense, and I kept in the shadow."

"The wife's name? Did you learn it?"

"Barbara St. Just."

"Ah! I knew her once and will again. Manuel, am I beautiful tonight?"

"How can you be otherwise to me?"

"That is not enough. I must look my fairest to others, brilliant and blithe, a happy-hearted bride whose honeymoon is not yet over."

"For his sake, Pauline?"

"For yours. I want him to envy you your youth, your comeliness, your content; to see the man he once sneered at the husband of the woman he once loved; to recall impotent regret. I know his nature, and can stir him to his heart's core with a look, revenge myself with a word, and read the secrets of his life with a skill he cannot fathom."

"And when you have done all this, shall you be happier, Pauline?"

"Infinitely; our three weeks' search is ended, and the real interest of the plot begins. I have played the lover for your sake, now play the man of the world for mine. This is the moment we have waited for. Help me to make it successful. Come! Crown me with your garland, give me the bracelets that were your wedding gift—none can be too brilliant for tonight. Now the gloves and fan. Stay, my sandals—you shall play Dolores and tie them on."

With an air of smiling coquetry he had never seen before, Pauline stretched out a truly Spanish foot and offered him its dainty covering. Won by the animation of her manner, Manuel forgot his misgivings and played his part with boyish spirit, hovering about his stately wife as no assiduous maid had ever done; for every flower was fastened with a word sweeter than itself, the white arms kissed as the ornaments went on, and when the silken knots were deftly accomplished, the lighthearted bridegroom performed a little dance of triumph about his idol, till she arrested him, beckoning as she spoke.

"Manuel, I am waiting to assume the last best ornament you have given me, my handsome husband." Then, as he came to her laughing with frank pleasure at her praise, she added, "You, too, must look your best and bravest now, and remember you must enact the man tonight. Before Gilbert wear your stateliest aspect, your tenderest to me, your courtliest to his wife. You possess dramatic skill. Use it for my sake, and come for your reward when this night's work is done."

The great hotel was swarming with life, ablaze with light, resonant with the tread of feet, the hum of voices, the musical din of the band, and full of the sights and sounds which fill such human hives at a fashionable watering place in the height of the season. As Manuel led his wife along the grand hall thronged with promenaders, his quick ear caught the whispered comments of the passers-by, and the fragmentary rumors concerning themselves amused him infinitely.

"Mon ami! There are five bridal couples here tonight, and there is the handsomest, richest, and most enchanting of them all. The groom is not yet twenty, they tell me, and the bride still younger. Behold them!"

Manuel looked down at Pauline with a mirthful glance, but she had not heard.

"See, Belle! Cubans; own half the island between them. Splendid, aren't they? Look at the diamonds on her lovely arms, and his ravishing moustache. Isn't he your ideal of Prince Djalma, in *The Wandering Jew?*"

A pretty girl, forgetting propriety in interest, pointed as they passed. Manuel half-bowed to the audible compliment, and the blushing damsel vanished, but Pauline had not seen.

"Jack, there's the owner of the black span you fell into raptures over. My lord and lady look as highbred as their stud. We'll patronize them!"

Manuel muttered a disdainful *"Impertinente!"* between his teeth as he surveyed a brace of dandies with an air that augured ill for the patronage of Young America, but Pauline was unconscious of both criticism and reproof. A countercurrent held them stationary for a moment, and close behind them sounded a voice saying, confidentially, to some silent listener, "The Redmonds are here tonight, and I am curious to see how he bears his disappointment. You know he married for money, and was outwitted in the bargain; for his wife's fortune not only proves to be much less than he was led to believe, but is so tied up that he is entirely dependent upon her, and the bachelor debts he sold himself to liquidate still harass him, with a wife's reproaches to augment the affliction. To be ruled by a spoiled child's whims is a fit punishment for a man whom neither pride nor principle could curb before. Let us go and look at the unfortunate."

Pauline heard now. Manuel felt her start, saw her flush and pale, then her eye lit, and the dark expression he dreaded to see settled on her face as she whispered, like a satanic echo, "Let us also go and look at this unfortunate."

A jealous pang smote the young man's heart as he recalled the past. "You pity him, Pauline, and pity is akin to love."

"I only pity what I respect. Rest content, my husband."

Steadily her eyes met his, and the hand whose only ornament was a wedding ring went to meet the one folded on his arm with a confiding gesture that made the action a caress.

"I will try to be, yet mine is a hard part," Manuel answered with a sigh, then silently they both paced on.

Gilbert Redmond lounged behind his wife's chair, looking intensely bored.

"Have you had enough of this folly, Babie?"

"No, we have but just come. Let us dance."

"Too late; they have begun."

"Then go about with me. It's very tiresome sitting here."

"It is too warm to walk in all that crowd, child."

"You are so indolent! Tell me who people are as they pass. I know no one here."

"Nor I."

But his act belied the words, for as they passed his lips he rose erect, with a smothered exclamation and startled face, as if a ghost had suddenly confronted him. The throng had thinned, and as his wife followed the direction of his glance, she saw no uncanny apparition to cause such evident dismay, but a woman fair-haired, violet-eyed, blooming and serene, sweeping down the long hall with noiseless grace. An air of sumptuous life pervaded her, the shimmer of bridal snow surrounded her, bridal gifts shone on neck and arms, and bridal happiness seemed to touch her with its tender charm as she looked up at her companion, as if there were but one human being in the world to her. This companion, a man slender and tall, with a face delicately dark as a fine bronze, looked back at her with eyes as eloquent as her own, while both spoke rapidly and low in the melodious language which seems made for lover's lips.

"Gilbert, who are they?"

There was no answer, and before she could repeat the question the approaching pair paused before her, and the beautiful woman offered her hand, saying, with inquiring smiles, "Barbara, have you forgotten your early friend, Pauline?"

Recognition came with the familiar name, and Mrs. Redmond welcomed the newcomer with a delight as unrestrained as if she were still the schoolgirl, Babie. Then, recovering herself, she said, with a pretty attempt at dignity, "Let me present my husband. Gilbert, come and welcome my friend Pauline Valary."

Scarlet with shame, dumb with conflicting emotions, and utterly deserted by self-possession, Redmond stood with downcast eyes and agitated mien, suffering a year's remorse condensed into a moment. A mute gesture was all the greeting he could offer. Pauline slightly bent her haughty head as she answered, in a voice frostily sweet, "Your wife mistakes. Pauline Valary died three weeks ago, and Pauline Laroche rose from her ashes. Manuel, my schoolmate, Mrs. Redmond; Gilbert you already know."

With the manly presence he could easily assume and which was henceforth to be his role in public, Manuel bowed courteously to the lady, coldly to the gentleman, and looked only at his wife. Mrs. Redmond, though childish, was observant; she glanced from face to face, divined a mystery, and spoke out at once.

"Then you have met before? Gilbert, you have never told me this."

"It was long ago—in Cuba. I believed they had forgotten me."

"I never forget." And Pauline's eye turned on him with a look he dared not meet.

Unsilenced by her husband's frown, Mrs. Redmond, intent on pleasing herself, drew her friend to the seat beside her as she said petulantly, "Gilbert tells me nothing, and I am constantly discovering things which might have given me pleasure had he only chosen to be frank. I've spoken of you often, yet he never betrayed the least knowledge of you, and I take it very ill of him, because I am sure he has not forgotten you. Sit here, Pauline, and let me tease you with questions, as I used to do so long ago. You were always patient with me, and though far more beautiful, your face is still the same kind one that comforted the little child at school. Gilbert, enjoy your friend, and leave us to ourselves until the dance is over."

Pauline obeyed; but as she chatted, skillfully leading the young wife's conversation to her own affairs, she listened to the two voices behind her, watched the two figures reflected in the mirror before her, and felt a secret pride in Manuel's address, for it was evident that the former positions were renewed.

The timid boy who had feared the sarcastic tongue of his guardian's guest, and shrunk from his presence to conceal the jealousy that was his jest, now stood beside his formal rival, serene and self-possessed, by far the manliest man of the two, for no shame daunted him, no fear oppressed him, no dishonorable deed left him at the mercy of another's tongue.

Gilbert Redmond felt this keenly, and cursed the falsehood which had placed him in such an unenviable position. It was vain to assume the old superiority that was forfeited; but too much a man of the world to be long discomforted by any contretemps like this, he rapidly regained his habitual ease of manner, and avoiding the perilous past clung to the safer present, hoping, by some unguarded look or word, to fathom the purpose of his adversary, for such he knew the husband of Pauline must be at heart. But Manuel schooled his features, curbed his tongue, and when his hot blood tempted him to point his smooth speech with a taunt, or offer a silent insult with the eye, he remembered Pauline, looked down on the graceful head below, and forgot all other passions in that of love.

"Gilbert, my shawl. The sea air chills me."

"I forgot it, Babie."

"Allow me to supply the want."

Mindful of his wife's commands, Manuel seized this opportunity to win a glance of commendation from her. And taking the downy mantle that hung upon his arm, he wrapped the frail girl in it with a care that made the act as cordial as courteous. Mrs. Redmond felt the charm of his manner with the quickness of a woman, and sent a reproachful glance at Gilbert as she said plaintively, "Ah! It is evident that my honeymoon is over, and the assiduous lover replaced by the negligent husband. Enjoy your midsummer night's dream while you may, Pauline, and be ready for the awakening that must come."

"Not to her, Madame, for our honeymoon shall last till the golden wedding day comes round. Shall it not, *cariña?*"

"There is no sign of waning yet, Manuel," and Pauline looked up into her husband's face with a genuine affection which made her own more beautiful and filled his with a visible content. Gilbert read the glance, and in that instant suffered the first pang of regret that Pauline had foretold. He spoke abruptly, longing to be away.

"Babie, we may dance now, if you will."

"I am going, but not with you—so give me my fan, and entertain Pauline till my return."

He unclosed his hand, but the delicately carved fan fell at his feet in a shower of ivory shreds—he had crushed it as he watched his first love with the bitter thought "It might have been!"

"Forgive me, Babie, it was too frail for use; you should choose a stronger."

"I will next time, and a gentler hand to hold it. Now, Monsieur Laroche, I am ready."

Mrs. Redmond rose in a small bustle of satisfaction, shook out her flounces, glanced at the mirror, then Manuel led her away; and the other pair were left alone. Both felt a secret agitation quicken their breath and thrill along their nerves, but the woman concealed it best. Gilbert's eye wandered restlessly to and fro, while Pauline fixed her own on his as quietly as if he were the statue in the niche behind him. For a moment he tried to seem unconscious of it, then essayed to meet and conquer it, but failed signally and, driven to his last resources by that steady gaze, resolved to speak out and have all over before his wife's return. Assuming the seat beside her, he said, impetuously, "Pauline, take off your mask as I do mine—we are alone now, and may see each other as we are."

Leaning deep into the crimson curve of the couch, with the indolent grace habitual to her, yet in strong contrast to the vigilant gleam

One of the illustrations that graced "Pauline's Passion and Punishment" when it made its debut in the January 3, 1863, issue of Frank Leslie's Illustrated Newspaper.

of her eye, she swept her hand across her face as if obeying him, yet no change followed, as she said with a cold smile, "It is off; what next?"

"Let me understand you. Did my letter reach your hands?"

"A week before my marriage."

He drew a long breath of relief, yet a frown gathered as he asked, like one loath and eager to be satisfied, "Your love died a natural death, then, and its murder does not lie at my door?"

Pointing to the shattered toy upon the ground, she only echoed his own words. "It was too frail for use—I chose a stronger."

It wounded, as she meant it should; and the evil spirit to whose guidance she had yielded herself exulted to see his self-love bleed, and pride vainly struggle to conceal the stab. He caught the expression in her averted glance, bent suddenly a fixed and scrutinizing gaze upon her, asking, below his breath, "Then why are you here to tempt me with the face that tempted me a year ago?"

"I came to see the woman to whom you sold yourself. I have seen her, and am satisfied."

Such quiet contempt iced her tones, such pitiless satisfaction shone through the long lashes that swept slowly down, after her eye had met and caused his own to fall again, that Gilbert's cheek burned as if the words had been a blow, and mingled shame and anger trembled in his voice.

"Ah, you are quick to read our secret, for you possess the key. Have you no fear that I may read your own, and tell the world you sold your beauty for a name and fortune? Your bargain is a better one than mine, but I know you too well, though your fetters are diamonds and your master a fond boy."

She had been prepared for this, and knew she had a shield in the real regard she bore her husband, for though sisterly, it was sincere. She felt its value now, for it gave her courage to confront the spirit of retaliation she had roused, and calmness to answer the whispered taunt with an unruffled mien, as lifting her white arm she let its single decoration drop glittering to her lap.

"You see my 'fetters' are as loose as they are light, and nothing binds me but my will. Read my heart, if you can. You will find there contempt for a love so poor that it feared poverty; pity for a man who dared not face the world and conquer it, as a girl had done before him, and gratitude that I have found my 'master' in a true-hearted boy, not a falsehearted man. If I am a slave, I never know it. Can you say as much?"

Her woman's tongue avenged her, and Gilbert owned his defeat. Pain quenched the ire of his glance, remorse subdued his pride, self-condemnation compelled him to ask, imploringly, "Pauline, when may I hope for pardon?"

"Never."

The stern utterance of the word dismayed him, and, like one shut out from hope, he rose, as if to leave her, but paused irresolutely, looked back, then sank down again, as if constrained against his will by a longing past control. If she had doubted her power this action set the doubt at rest, as the haughtiest nature she had known confessed it by a bittersweet complaint. Eyeing her wistfully, tenderly, Gilbert murmured, in the voice of long ago, "Why do I stay to wound and to be wounded by the hand that once caressed me? Why do I find more pleasure in your contempt than in another woman's praise, and feel myself transported into the delights of that irrecoverable past, now grown the sweetest, saddest memory of my life? Send me away, Pauline, before the old charm asserts its power, and I forget that I am not the happy lover of a year ago."

"Leave me then, Gilbert. Good night."

Half unconsciously, the former softness stole into her voice as it lingered on his name. The familiar gesture accompanied the words, the old charm did assert itself, and for an instant changed the cold woman into the ardent girl again. Gilbert did not go but, with a hasty glance down the deserted hall behind him, captured and kissed the hand he had lost, passionately whispering, "Pauline, I love you still, and that look assures me that you have forgiven, forgotten, and kept a place for me in that deep heart of yours. It is too late to deny it. I have seen the tender eyes again, and the sight has made me the proudest, happiest man that walks the world tonight, slave though I am."

Over cheek and forehead rushed the treacherous blood as the violet eyes filled and fell before his own, and in the glow of mingled pain and fear that stirred her blood, Pauline, for the first time, owned the peril of the task she had set herself, saw the dangerous power she possessed, and felt the buried passion faintly moving in its grave. Indignant at her own weakness, she took refuge in the memory of her wrong, controlled the rebel color, steeled the front she showed him, and with feminine skill mutely conveyed the rebuke she would not trust herself to utter, by stripping the glove from the hand he had touched and dropping it disdainfully as if unworthy of its place. Gilbert had not looked for such an answer, and while it baffled him it excited his man's spirit to rebel against her silent denial. With a bitter laugh he snatched up the glove.

"I read a defiance in your eye as you flung this down. I accept the challenge, and will keep gage until I prove myself the victor. I have asked for pardon. You refuse it. I have confessed my love. You scorn it. I have possessed myself of your secret, yet you deny it. Now we will try our strength together, and leave those children to their play."

"We are the children, and we play with edge tools. There has been enough of this, there must be no more." Pauline rose with her haughtiest mien, and the brief command, "Take me to Manuel."

Silently Gilbert offered his arm, and silently she rejected it.

"Will you accept nothing from me?"

"Nothing."

Side by side they passed through the returning throng till Mrs. Redmond joined them, looking blithe and bland with the exhilaration of gallantry and motion. Manuel's first glance was at Pauline, his second at her companion; there was a shadow upon the face of each, which seemed instantly to fall upon his own as he claimed his wife with a masterful satisfaction as novel as becoming, and which prompted her to whisper, "You enact your role to the life, and shall enjoy a foretaste of your reward at once. I want excitement; let us show these graceless, frozen people the true art of dancing, and electrify them with the life and fire of a Cuban valse."

Manuel kindled at once, and Pauline smiled stealthily as she glanced over her shoulder from the threshold of the dancing hall, for her slightest act, look, and word had their part to play in that night's drama.

"Gilbert, if you are tired I will go now."

"Thank you, I begin to find it interesting. Let us watch the dancers."

Mrs. Redmond accepted the tardy favor, wondering at his unwonted animation, for never had she seen such eagerness in his countenance, such energy in his manner as he pressed through the crowd and won a place where they could freely witness one of those exhibitions of fashionable figurante which are nightly to be seen at such resorts. Many couples were whirling around the white hall, but among them one pair circled with slowly increasing speed, in perfect time to the inspiring melody of trumpet, flute, and horn, that seemed to sound for them alone. Many paused to watch them, for they gave to the graceful pastime the enchantment which few have skill enough to lend it, and made it a spectacle of life-enjoying youth, to be remembered long after the music ceased and the agile feet were still.

Gilbert's arm was about his little wife to shield her from the pressure of the crowd, and as they stood his hold unconsciously tightened, till, marveling at this unwonted care, she looked up to thank him with a happy glance and discovered that his eye rested on a single pair, kindling as they approached, keenly scanning every gesture as they floated by, following them with untiring vigilance through the many-colored mazes they threaded with such winged steps, while his breath quickened, his hand kept time, and every sense seemed to own the intoxication of the scene. Sorrowfully she too watched this pair, saw their grace, admired their beauty, envied their happiness; for, short as her wedded life had been, the thorns already pierced her through the roses, and with each airy revolution of those figures, dark and bright, her discontent increased, her wonder deepened, her scrutiny grew keener, for she knew no common interest held her husband there, fascinated, flushed, and excited as if his heart beat responsive to the rhythmic rise and fall of that booted foot and satin slipper. The music ended with a crash, the crowd surged across the floor, and the spell was broken. Like one but half disenchanted, Gilbert stood a moment, then remembered his wife, and looking down met brown eyes, full of tears, fastened on his face.

"Tired so soon, Babie? Or in a pet because I cannot change myself into a thistledown and float about with you, like Manuel and Pauline?"

"Neither; I was only wishing that you loved me as he loves her, and hoping he would never tire of her, they are so fond and charming now. How long have you known them—and where?"

"I shall have no peace until I tell you. I passed a single summer with them in a tropical paradise, where we swung half the day in hammocks, under tamarind and almond trees; danced half the night to music, of which this seems but a faint echo; and led a life of luxurious delight in an enchanted climate, where all is so beautiful and brilliant that its memory haunts a life as pressed flowers sweeten the leaves of a dull book."

"Why did you leave it then?"

"To marry you, child."

"That was a regretful sigh, as if I were not worth the sacrifice. Let us go back and enjoy it together."

"If you were dying for it, I would not take you to Cuba. It would be purgatory, not paradise, now."

"How stern you look, how strangely you speak. Would you not go to save your own life, Gilbert?"

"I would not cross the room to do that much, less the sea."

"Why do you both love and dread it? Don't frown, but tell me. I have a right to know."

"Because the bitterest blunder of my life was committed there—a blunder that I never can repair in this world, and may be damned for

in the next. Rest satisfied with this, Babie, lest you prove like Blue-
beard's wife, and make another skeleton in my closet, which has
enough already."

Strange regret was in his voice, strange gloom fell upon his face;
but though rendered doubly curious by the change, Mrs. Redmond
dared not question further and, standing silent, furtively scanned the
troubled countenance beside her. Gilbert spoke first, waking out of his
sorrowful reverie with a start.

"Pauline is coming. Say adieu, not au revoir, for tomorrow we
must leave this place."

His words were a command, his aspect one of stern resolve, though
the intensest longing mingled with the dark look he cast on the approaching pair. The tone, the glance displeased his willful wife, who
loved to use her power and exact obedience where she had failed to
win affection, often ruling imperiously when a tender word would
have made her happy to submit.

"Gilbert, you take no thought for my pleasures though you pursue
your own at my expense. Your neglect forces me to find solace and
satisfaction where I can, and you have forfeited your right to command
or complain. I love Pauline, I am happy with her, therefore I shall stay
until we tire of one another. I am a burden to you; go if you will."

"You know I cannot without you, Babie. I ask it as a favor. For my
sake, for your own, I implore you to come away."

"Gilbert, do you love her?"

She seized his arm and forced an answer by the energy of her
sharply whispered question. He saw that it was vain to dissemble, yet
replied with averted head, "I did and still remember it."

"And she? Did she return your love?"

"I believed so; but she forgot me when I went. She married Manuel
and is happy. Babie, let me go!"

"No! you shall stay and feel a little of the pain I feel when I look
into your heart and find I have no place there. It is this which has
stood between us and made all my efforts vain. I see it now and
despise you for the falsehood you have shown me, vowing you loved

no one but me until I married you, then letting me so soon discover that I was only an encumbrance to your enjoyment of the fortune I possessed. You treat me like a child, but I suffer like a woman, and you shall share my suffering, because you might have spared me, and you did not. Gilbert, you shall stay."

"Be it so, but remember I have warned you."

An exultant expression broke through the gloom of her husband's face as he answered with the grim satisfaction of one who gave restraint to the mind, and stood ready to follow whatever impulse should sway him next. His wife trembled inwardly at what she had done, but was too proud to recall her words and felt a certain bitter pleasure in the excitement of the new position she had taken, the new interest given to her listless life.

Pauline and Manuel found them standing silently together, for a moment had done the work of years and raised a barrier between them never to be swept away.

Mrs. Redmond spoke first, and with an air half resentful, half triumphant:

"Pauline, this morose husband of mine says we must leave tomorrow. But in some things I rule; this is one of them. Therefore we remain and go with you to the mountains when we are tired of the gay life here. So smile and submit, Gilbert, else these friends will count your society no favor. Would you not fancy, from the aspect he thinks proper to assume, that I had sentenced him to a punishment, not a pleasure?"

"Perhaps you have unwittingly, Babie. Marriage is said to cancel the follies of the past, but not those of the future, I believe; and, as there are many temptations to an idle man in a place like this, doubtless your husband is wise enough to own that he dares not stay but finds discretion the better part of valor."

Nothing could be softer than the tone in which these words were uttered, nothing sharper than the hidden taunt conveyed, but Gilbert only laughed a scornful laugh as he fixed his keen eyes full upon her and took her bouquet with the air of one assuming former rights.

"My dear Pauline, discretion is the last virtue I should expect to be accused of by you; but if valor consists in daring all things, I may lay claim to it without its 'better part,' for temptation is my delight—the stronger the better. Have no fears for me, my friend. I gladly accept Babie's decree and, ignoring the last ten years, intend to begin life anew, having discovered a *sauce piquante* which will give the stalest pleasures a redoubled zest. I am unfortunate tonight, and here is a second wreck; this I can rebuild happily. Allow me to do so, for I remember you once praised my skill in floral architecture."

With an air of eager gallantry in strange contrast to the malign expression of his countenance, Gilbert knelt to regather the flowers which a careless gesture of his own had scattered from their jeweled holder. His wife turned to speak to Manuel, and, yielding to the unconquerable anxiety his reckless manner awoke, Pauline whispered below her breath as she bent as if to watch the work, "Gilbert, follow your first impulse, and go tomorrow."

"Nothing shall induce me to."

"I warn you harm will come of it."

"Let it come; I am past fear now."

"Shun me for Babie's sake, if not for your own."

"Too late for that; she is headstrong—let her suffer."

"Have you no power, Gilbert?"

"None over her, much over you."

"We will prove that!"

"We will!"

Rapidly as words could shape them, these questions and answers fell, and with their utterance the last generous feeling died in Pauline's breast; for as she received the flowers, now changed from a love token to a battle gage, she saw the torn glove still crushed in Gilbert's hand, and silently accepted his challenge to the tournament so often held between man and woman—a tournament where the keen tongue is the lance, pride the shield, passion the fiery steed, and the hardest heart the winner of the prize, which seldom fails to prove a barren honor, ending in remorse.

Chapter III

FOR SEVERAL DAYS the Cubans were almost invisible, appearing only for a daily drive, a twilight saunter on the beach, or a brief visit to the ballroom, there to enjoy the excitement of the pastime in which they both excelled. Their apartments were in the quietest wing of the hotel, and from the moment of their occupancy seemed to acquire all the charms of home. The few guests admitted felt the atmosphere of poetry and peace that pervaded the nest which Love, the worker of miracles, had built himself even under that tumultuous roof. Strollers in the halls or along the breezy verandas often paused to listen to the music of instrument or voice which came floating out from these sequestered rooms. Frequent laughter and the murmur of conversation proved that ennui was unknown, and a touch of romance inevitably enhanced the interest wakened by the beautiful young pair, always together, always happy, never weary of the *dolce far niente* of this summer life.

In a balcony like a hanging garden, sheltered from the sun by blossoming shrubs and vines that curtained the green nook with odorous shade, Pauline lay indolently swinging in a gaily fringed hammock as she had been wont to do in Cuba, then finding only pleasure in the luxury of motion which now failed to quiet her unrest. Manuel had put down the book to which she no longer listened and, leaning his head upon his hand, sat watching her as she swayed to and fro with thoughtful eyes intent upon the sea, whose murmurous voice possessed a charm more powerful than his own. Suddenly he spoke:

"Pauline, I cannot understand you! For three weeks we hurried east and west to find this man, yet when found you shun him and seem content to make my life a heaven upon earth. I sometimes fancy that you have resolved to let the past sleep, but the hope dies as soon as born, for in moments like this I see that, though you devote yourself to me, the old purpose is unchanged, and I marvel why you pause."

Her eyes came back from their long gaze and settled on him full of an intelligence which deepened his perplexity. "You have not learned to know me yet; death is not more inexorable or time more tireless than I. This week has seemed one of indolent delight to you. To me it has been one of constant vigilance and labor, for scarcely a look, act, or word of mine has been without effect. At first I secluded myself that Gilbert might contrast our life with his and, believing us all and all to one another, find impotent regret his daily portion. Three days ago accident placed an unexpected weapon in my hand which I have used in silence, lest in spite of promises you should rebel and end his trial too soon. Have you no suspicion of my meaning?"

"None. You are more mysterious than ever, and I shall, in truth, believe you are the enchantress I have so often called you if your spells work invisibly."

"They do not, and I use no supernatural arts, as I will prove to you. Take my lorgnette that lies behind you, part the leaves where the green grapes hang thickest, look up at the little window in the shadowy angle of the low roof opposite, and tell me what you see."

"Nothing but a half-drawn curtain."

"Ah! I must try the ruse that first convinced me. Do not show yourself, but watch, and if you speak, let it be in Spanish."

Leaving her airy cradle, Pauline bent over the balcony as if to gather the climbing roses that waved their ruddy clusters in the wind. Before the third stem was broken Manuel whispered, "I see the curtain move; now comes the outline of a head, and now a hand, with some bright object in it. Santo Pablo! It is a man staring at you as coolly as if you were a lady in a balcony. What prying rascal is it?"

"Gilbert."

"Impossible! He is a gentleman."

"If gentlemen play the traitor and the spy, then he is one. I am not mistaken; for since the glitter of his glass first arrested me I have watched covertly, and several trials as successful as the present have confirmed the suspicion which Babie's innocent complaints of his long absences aroused. Now do you comprehend why I remained in these rooms with the curtains seldom drawn? Why I swung the hammock here and let you sing and read to me while I played with your hair or leaned upon your shoulder? Why I have been all devotion and made this balcony a little stage for the performance of our version of the honeymoon for one spectator?"

Still mindful of the eager eyes upon her, Pauline had been fastening the roses in her bosom as she spoke, and ended with a silvery laugh that made the silence musical with its heartsome sound. As she paused, Manuel flung down the lorgnette and was striding past her with ireful impetuosity, but the white arms took him captive, adding another figure to the picture framed by the green arch as she whispered decisively, "No farther! There must be no violence. You promised obedience and I exact it. Do you think detection to a man so lost to honor would wound as deeply as the sights which make his daily watch a torment? Or that a blow would be as hard to bear as the knowledge that his own act has placed you where you are and made him what he is? Silent contempt is the law now, so let this insult pass, unclench your hand and turn that defiant face to me, while I console you for submission with a kiss."

He yielded to the command enforced by the caress but drew her jealously from sight, and still glanced rebelliously through the leaves, asking with a frown, "Why show me this if I may not resent it? How long must I bear with this man? Tell me your design, else I shall mar it in some moment when hatred of him conquers love of you."

"I will, for it is time, because though I have taken the first step you must take the second. I showed you this that you might find action pleasanter than rest, and you must bear with this man a little longer for my sake, but I will give you an amusement to beguile the time. Long ago you told me that Gilbert was a gambler. I would not believe it then, now I can believe anything, and you can convince the world of this vice of his as speedily as you will."

"Do you wish me to become a gambler that I may prove him one? I also told you that he was suspected of dishonorable play—shall I load the dice and mark the cards to catch him in his own snares?"

Manuel spoke bitterly, for his high spirit chafed at the task assigned him; womanly wiles seemed more degrading than the masculine method of retaliation, in which strength replaces subtlety and speedier vengeance brings speedier satisfaction. But Pauline, fast learning to play upon that mysterious instrument, the human heart, knew when to stimulate and when to soothe.

"Do not reproach me that I point out a safer mode of operation than your own. You would go to Gilbert and by a hot word, a rash act, put your life and my happiness into his hands, for though dueling is forbidden here, he would not hesitate to break all laws, human or divine, if by so doing he could separate us. What would you gain by it? If you kill him he is beyond our reach forever, and a crime remains to be atoned for. If he kill you your blood will be upon my head, and where should I find consolation for the loss of the one heart always true and tender?"

With the inexplicable prescience which sometimes foreshadows coming ills, she clung to him as if a vision of the future dimly swept before her, but he only saw the solicitude it was a sweet surprise to find he had awakened, and in present pleasure forgot past pain.

"You shall not suffer from this man any grief that I can shield you from, rest assured of that, my heart. I will be patient, though your ways are not mine, for the wrong was yours, and the retribution shall be such as you decree."

"Then hear your task and see the shape into which circumstances have molded my design. I would have you exercise a self-restraint that shall leave Gilbert no hold upon you, accept all invitations like that which you refused when we passed him on the threshold of the billiard room an hour ago, and seem to find in such amusements the same fascination as himself. Your skill in games of chance excels his, as you proved at home where these pastimes lose their disreputable aspect by being openly enjoyed. Therefore I would have you whet this appetite of his by losing freely at first—he will take a grim delight in lessening the fortune he covets—then exert all your skill till he is deeply in your debt. He has nothing but what is doled out to him by Babie's father, I find; he dare not ask help there for such a purpose; other resources have failed else he would not have married; and if the sum be large enough, it lays him under an obligation which will be a thorn in his flesh, the sharper for your knowledge of his impotence to draw it out. When this is done, or even while it is in progress, I would have you add the pain of a new jealousy to the old. He neglects this young wife of his, and she is eager to recover the affections she believes she once possessed. Help her, and teach Gilbert the value of what he now despises. You are young, comely, accomplished, and possessed of many graces more attractive than you are conscious of; your southern birth and breeding gift you with a winning warmth of manners in strong contrast to the colder natures around you; and your love for me lends an almost tender deference to your intercourse with all woman-kind. Amuse, console this poor girl, and show her husband what he should be; I have no fear of losing your heart nor need you fear for hers; she is one of those spaniel-like creatures who love the hand that strikes them and fawn upon the foot that spurns them."

"Am I to be the sole actor in the drama of deceit? While I woo Babie, what will you do, Pauline?"

"Let Gilbert woo me—have patience till you understand my mean-ing; he still loves me and believes I still return that love. I shall not undeceive him yet, but let silence seem to confess what I do not own in words. He fed me with false promises, let me build my life's happiness on baseless hopes, and rudely woke me when he could delude no longer, leaving me to find I had pursued a shadow. I will do the same. He shall follow me undaunted, undeterred by all obstacles, all ties; shall stake his last throw and lose it, for when the crowning moment comes I shall show him that through me he is made bankrupt in love, honor, liberty, and hope, tell him I am yours entirely and forever, then vanish like an *ignis-fatuus*, leaving him to the darkness of despair and defeat. Is not this a better retribution than the bullet that would give him peace at once?"

Boy, lover, husband though he was, Manuel saw and stood aghast at the baleful spirit which had enslaved this woman, crushing all generous impulses, withering all gentle charities, and making her the saddest spectacle this world can show—one human soul rebelling against Providence, to become the nemesis of another. Involuntarily he recoiled from her, exclaiming, "Pauline! Are you possessed of a devil?"

"Yes! One that will not be cast out till every sin, shame, and sorrow mental ingenuity can conceive and inflict has been heaped on that man's head. I thought I should be satisfied with one accusing look, one bitter word; I am not, for the evil genii once let loose cannot be recaptured. Once I ruled it, now it rules me, and there is no turning back. I have come under the law of fate, and henceforth the powers I possess will ban, not bless, for I am driven to whet and wield them as weapons which may win me success at the price of my salvation. It is not yet too late for you to shun the spiritual contagion I bear about me. Choose now, and abide by that choice without a shadow of turning, as I abide by mine. Take me as I am; help me willingly and unwillingly; and in the end receive the promised gift—years like the days you have called heaven upon earth. Or retract the vows you plighted, receive again the heart and name you gave me, and live unvexed by the stormy nature time alone can tame. Here is the ring. Shall I restore or keep it, Manuel?"

Never had she looked more beautiful as she stood there, an image of will, daring, defiant, and indomitable, with eyes darkened by intensity of emotion, voice half sad, half stern, and outstretched hand on which the wedding ring no longer shone. She felt her power, yet was wary enough to assure it by one bold appeal to the strongest element of her husband's character: passions, not principles, were the allies she desired, and before the answer came she knew that she had gained them at the cost of innocence and self-respect.

As Manuel listened, an expression like a dark reflection of her own settled on his face; a year of youth seemed to drop away; and with the air of one who puts fear behind him, he took the hand, replaced the ring, resolutely accepted the hard conditions, and gave all to love, only saying as he had said before, "Soul and body, I belong to you; do with me as you will."

A fortnight later Pauline sat alone, waiting for her husband. Under the pretext of visiting a friend, she had absented herself a week, that Manuel might give himself entirely to the distasteful task she set him. He submitted to the separation, wrote daily, but sent no tidings of his progress, told her nothing when they met that night, and had left her an hour before asking her to have patience till he could show his finished work. Now, with her eye upon the door, her ear alert to catch the coming step, her mind disturbed by contending hopes and fears, she sat waiting with the vigilant immobility of an Indian on the watch. She had not long to look and listen. Manuel entered hastily, locked the door, closed the windows, dropped the curtains, then paused in the middle of the room and broke into a low, triumphant laugh as he eyed his wife with an expression she had never seen in those dear eyes before. It startled her, and, scarcely knowing what to desire or dread, she asked eagerly, "You are come to tell me you have prospered."

"Beyond your hopes, for the powers of darkness seem to help us, and lead the man to his destruction faster than any wiles of ours can do. I am tired, let me lie here and rest. I have earned it, so when I have told all say, 'Love, you have done well,' and I am satisfied."

He threw himself along the couch where she still sat and laid his head in her silken lap, her cool hand on his hot forehead, and continued in a muffled voice.

"You know how eagerly Gilbert took advantage of my willingness to play, and soon how recklessly he pursued it, seeming to find the satisfaction you foretold, till, obeying your commands, I ceased losing and won sums which surprised me. Then you went, but I was not idle, and in the effort to extricate himself, Gilbert plunged deeper into debt; for my desire to please you seemed to gift me with redoubled skill. Two days ago I refused to continue the unequal conflict, telling him to give himself no uneasiness, for I could wait. You were right in thinking it would oppress him to be under any obligation to me, but wrong in believing he would endure, and will hardly be prepared for the desperate step he took to free himself. That night he played falsely, was detected, and though his opponent generously promised silence for

Babie's sake, the affair stole out—he is shunned and this resource has failed. I thought he had no other, but yesterday he came to me with a strange expression of relief, discharged the debt to the last farthing, then hinted that my friendship with his wife was not approved by him and must cease. This proves that I have obeyed you in all things, though the comforting of Babie was an easy task, for, both loving you, our bond of sympathy and constant theme has been Pauline and her perfections."

"Hush! No praise—it is a mockery. I am what one man's perfidy has made; I may yet learn to be worthy of another man's devotion. What more, Manuel?"

"I thought I should have only a defeat to show you, but today has given me a strange success. At noon a gentleman arrived and asked for Gilbert. He was absent, but upon offering information relative to the time of his return, which proved my intimacy with him, this Seguin entered into conversation with me. His evident desire to avoid Mrs. Redmond and waylay her husband interested me, and when he questioned me somewhat closely concerning Gilbert's habits and movements of late, my suspicions were roused; and on mentioning the debt so promptly discharged, I received a confidence that startled me. In a moment of despair Gilbert had forged the name of his former friend, whom he believed abroad, had drawn the money and freed himself from my power, but not for long. The good fortune which has led him safely through many crooked ways seems to have deserted him in this strait. For the forgery was badly executed, inspection raised doubts, and Seguin, just returned, was at his banker's an hour after Gilbert, to prove the fraud; he came hither at once to accuse him of it and made me his confidant. What would you have had me do, Pauline? Time was short, and I could not wait for you."

"How can I tell at once? Why pause to ask? What did you do?"

"Took a leaf from your book and kept accusation, punishment, and power in my own hands, to be used in your behalf. I returned the money, secured the forged check, and prevailed on Seguin to leave the matter in my hands, while he departed as quietly as he had come. Babie's presence when we met tonight prevented my taking you into my counsels. I had prepared this surprise for you and felt a secret pride in working it out alone. An hour ago I went to watch for Gilbert. He came, I took him to his rooms, told him what I had done, added that compassion for his wife had actuated me. I left him saying the possession of the check was a full equivalent for the money, which I now declined to receive from such dishonorable hands. Are you satisfied, Pauline?"

With countenance and gestures full of exultation she sprang up to pace the room, exclaiming, as she seized the forged paper, "Yes, that stroke was superb! How strangely the plot thickens. Surely the powers of darkness are working with us and have put this weapon in our hands when that I forged proved useless. By means of this we have a hold upon him which nothing can destroy unless he escape by death. Will he, Manuel?"

"No; there was more wrath than shame in his demeanor when I accused him. He hates me too much to die yet, and had I been the only possessor of this fatal fact, I fancy it might have gone hard with me; for if ever there was murder in a man's heart it was in his when I showed him that paper and then replaced it next the little poniard you smile at me for wearing. This is over. What next, my queen?"

There was energy in the speaker's tone but none in attitude or aspect, as, still lying where she had left him, he pillowed his head upon his arm and turned toward her a face already worn and haggard with the feverish weariness that had usurped the blithe serenity which had been his chiefest charm a month ago. Pausing in her rapid walk, as if arrested by the change that seemed to strike her suddenly, she recalled her thoughts from the dominant idea of her life and, remembering the youth she was robbing of its innocent delights, answered the wistful look which betrayed the hunger of a heart she had never truly fed, as she knelt beside her husband and, laying her soft cheek to his, whispered in her tenderest accents, "I am not wholly selfish or ungrateful,

Manuel. You shall rest now while I sing to you, and tomorrow we will go away among the hills and leave behind us for a time the dark temptation which harms you through me."

"No! Finish what you have begun. I will have all or nothing, for if we pause now you will bring me a divided mind, and I shall possess only the shadow of a wife. Take Gilbert and Babie with us, and end this devil's work without delay. Hark! What is that?"

Steps came flying down the long hall, a hand tried the lock, then beat impetuously upon the door, and a low voice whispered with shrill importunity, "Let me in! Oh, let me in!"

Manuel obeyed the urgent summons, and Mrs. Redmond, half dressed, with streaming hair and terror-stricken face, fled into Pauline's arms, crying incoherently, "Save me! Keep me! I never can go back to him; he said I was a burden and a curse, and wished I never had been born!"

"What has happened, Babie? We are your friends. Tell us, and let us comfort and protect you if we can."

But for a time speech was impossible, and the poor girl wept with a despairing vehemence sad to see, till their gentle efforts soothed her; and, sitting by Pauline, she told her trouble, looking oftenest at Manuel, who stood before them, as if sure of redress from him.

"When I left here an hour or more ago I found my rooms still empty, and, though I had not seen my husband since morning, I knew he would be displeased to find me waiting, so I cried myself to sleep and dreamed of the happy time when he was kind, till the sound of voices woke me. I heard Gilbert say, 'Babie is with your wife, her maid tells me; therefore we are alone here. What is this mysterious affair, Laroche?' That tempted me to listen, and then, Manuel, I learned all the shame and misery you so generously tried to spare me. How can I ever repay you, ever love and honor you enough for such care of one so helpless and forlorn as I?"

"I am repaid already. Let that pass, and tell what brings you here with such an air of fright and fear?"

"When you were gone he came straight to the inner room in search of something, saw me, and knew I must have heard all he had concealed from me so carefully. If you have ever seen him when that fierce temper of his grows ungovernable, you can guess what I endured. He said such cruel things I could not bear it, and cried out that I would come to you, for I was quite wild with terror, grief, and shame, that seemed like oil to fire. He swore I should not, and oh, Pauline, he struck me! See, if I do not tell the living truth!"

Trembling with excitement, Mrs. Redmond pushed back the wide sleeve of her wrapper and showed the red outline of a heavy hand. Manuel set his teeth and stamped his foot into the carpet with an indignant exclamation and the brief question, "Then you left him, Babie?"

"Yes, although he locked me in my room, saying the law gave him the right to teach obedience. I flung on these clothes, crept noiselessly along the balcony till the hall window let me in, and then I ran to you. He will come for me. Can he take me away? Must I go back to suffer any more?"

In the very act of uttering the words, Mrs. Redmond clung to Manuel with a cry of fear, for on the threshold stood her husband. A comprehensive glance seemed to stimulate his wrath and lend the hardihood wherewith to confront the three, saying sternly as he beckoned, "Babie, I am waiting for you."

She did not speak, but still clung to Manuel as if he were her only hope. A glance from Pauline checked the fiery words trembling on his lips, and he too stood silent while she answered with a calmness that amazed him:

"Your wife has chosen us her guardians, and I think you will scarcely venture to use force again with two such witnesses as these to prove that you have forfeited your right to her obedience and justify the step she has taken."

With one hand she uncovered the discolored arm, with the other held the forgery before him. For a moment Gilbert stood daunted by these mute accusations, but just then his ire burned hottest against Manuel; and believing that he could deal a double blow by wounding

Pauline through her husband, he ignored her presence and, turning to the young man, asked significantly, "Am I to understand that you refuse me my wife, and prefer to abide by the consequences of such an act?"

Calmed by Pauline's calmness, Manuel only drew the trembling creature closer, and answered with his haughtiest mien, "I do; spare yourself the labor of insulting me, for having placed yourself beyond the reach of a gentleman's weapon, I shall accept no challenge from a—"

A soft hand at his lips checked the opprobrious word, as Babie, true woman through it all, whispered with a broken sob, "Spare him, for I loved him once."

Gilbert Redmond had a heart, and, sinful though it was, this generous forbearance wrung it with a momentary pang of genuine remorse, too swiftly followed by a selfish hope that all was not lost if through his wife he could retain a hold upon the pair which now possessed for him the strong attraction of both love and hate. In that brief pause this thought came, was accepted and obeyed, for, as if yielding to an uncontrollable impulse of penitent despair, he stretched his arms to his wife, saying humbly, imploringly, "Babie, come back to me, and teach me how I may retrieve the past. I freely confess I bitterly repent my manifold transgressions, and submit to your decree alone; but in executing justice, oh, remember mercy! Remember that I was too early left fatherless, motherless, and went astray for want of some kind heart to guide and cherish me. There is still time. Be compassionate and save me from myself. Am I not punished enough? Must death be my only comforter? Babie, when all others cast me off, will you too forsake me?"

"No, I will not! Only love me, and I can forgive, forget, and still be happy!"

Pauline was right. The spaniel-like nature still loved the hand that struck it, and Mrs. Redmond joyfully returned to the arms from which she had so lately fled. The tenderest welcome she had ever received from him welcomed the loving soul whose faith was not yet dead, for

Gilbert felt the value this once neglected possession had suddenly acquired, and he held it close; yet as he soothed with gentle touch and tone, could not forbear a glance of triumph at the spectators of the scene.

Pauline met it with that inscrutable smile of hers, and a look of intelligence toward her husband, as she said, "Did I not prophesy truly, Manuel? Be kind to her, Gilbert, and when next we meet show us a happier wife than the one now sobbing on your shoulder. Babie, good night and farewell, for we are off to the mountains in the morning."

"Oh, let us go with you as you promised! You know our secret, you pity me and will help Gilbert to be what he should. I cannot live at home, and places like this will seem so desolate when you and Manuel are gone. May we, can we be with you a little longer?"

"If Gilbert wishes it and Manuel consents, we will bear and forbear much for your sake, my poor child."

Pauline's eye said, "Dare you go?" and Gilbert's answered, "Yes," as the two met with a somber fire in each; but his lips replied, "Anywhere with you, Babie," and Manuel took Mrs. Redmond's hand with a graceful warmth that touched her deeper than his words.

"Your example teaches me the beauty of compassion, and Pauline's friends are mine."

"Always so kind to me! Dear Manuel, I never can forget it, though I have nothing to return but this," and, like a grateful child, she lifted up her innocent face so wistfully he could only bend his tall head to receive the kiss she offered.

Gilbert's black brows lowered ominously at the sight, but he never spoke; and, when her good-nights were over, bowed silently and carried his little wife away, nestling to him as if all griefs and pains were banished by returning love.

"Poor little heart! She should have a smoother path to tread. Heaven grant she may hereafter; and this sudden penitence prove no sham." Manuel paused suddenly, for as if obeying an unconquerable impulse, Pauline laid a hand on either shoulder and searched his face with an expression which baffled his comprehension, though he bore it steadily till her eyes fell before his own, when he asked smilingly:

"Is the doubt destroyed, *cariña?*"

"No; it is laid asleep."

Then as he drew her nearer, as if to make his peace for his un-known offense, she turned her cheek away and left him silently. Did she fear to find Babie's kiss upon his lips?

Chapter IV

THE WORK OF WEEKS is soon recorded, and when another month was gone these were the changes it had wrought. The four so strangely bound together by ties of suffering and sin went on their way, to the world's eye, blessed with every gracious gift, but below the tranquil surface rolled that undercurrent whose mysterious tides ebb and flow in human hearts unfettered by race or rank or time. Gilbert was a good actor, but, though he curbed his fitful temper, smoothed his mien, and sweetened his manner, his wife soon felt the vanity of hoping to recover that which never had been hers. Silently she accepted the fact and, uttering no complaint, turned to others for the fostering warmth without which she could not live. Conscious of a hunger like her own, Manuel could offer her sincerest sympathy, and soon learned to find a troubled pleasure in the knowledge that she loved him and her hus-band knew it, for his life of the emotions was rapidly maturing the boy into the man, as the fierce ardors of his native skies quicken the growth of wondrous plants that blossom in a night. Mrs. Redmond, as young in character as in years, felt the attraction of a nature generous and sweet, and yielded to it as involuntarily as an unsupported vine yields to the wind that blows it to the strong arms of a tree, still unconscious that a warmer sentiment than gratitude made his companionship the sunshine of her life. Pauline saw this, and sometimes owned within herself that she had evoked spirits which she could not rule, but her purpose drove her on, and in it she found a charm more perilously potent than before. Gilbert watched the three with a smile darker than a frown, yet no reproach warned his wife of the danger which she did not see; no jealous demonstration roused Manuel to rebel against the oppression of a presence so distasteful to him; no rash act or word gave Pauline power to banish him, though the one desire of his soul became the discovery of the key to the inscrutable expression of her eyes as they followed the young pair, whose growing friendship left their mates alone. Slowly her manner softened toward him, pity seemed to bridge across the gulf that lay between them, and in rare moments time appeared to have retraced its steps, leaving the tender woman of a year ago. Nourished by such unexpected hope, the early passion throve and strengthened until it became the mastering ambition of his life, and, only pausing to make assurance doubly sure, he waited the advent of the hour when he could "put his fortune to the touch and win or lose it all."

"MANUEL, ARE YOU COMING?"

He was lying on the sward at Mrs. Redmond's feet, and, waking from the reverie that held him, while his companion sang the love lay he was teaching her, he looked up to see his wife standing on the green slope before him. A black lace scarf lay over her blonde hair as Spanish women wear their veils, below it the violet eyes shone clear, the cheek glowed with the color fresh winds had blown upon their paleness, the lips parted with a wistful smile, and a knot of bright-hued leaves upon her bosom made a mingling of snow and fire in the dress, whose white folds swept the grass. Against a background of hoary cliffs and somber pines, this figure stood out like a picture of blooming womanhood, but Manuel saw three blemishes upon it—Gilbert had sketched her with that shadowy veil upon her head, Gilbert had swung himself across a precipice to reach the scarlet nosegay for her breast, Gilbert stood beside her with her hand upon his arm; and troubled by the fear that often haunted him since Pauline's manner to himself had grown so shy and sad, Manuel leaned and looked forgetful of reply, but Mrs. Redmond answered blithely:

"He is coming, but with me. You are too grave for us, so go your ways, talking wisely of heaven and earth, while we come after, enjoying both as we gather lichens, chase the goats, and meet you at the waterfall. Now Señor, put away guitar and book, for I have learned my lesson; so help me with this unruly hair of mine and leave the Spanish for today."

They looked a pair of lovers as Manuel held back the long locks blowing in the wind, while Babie tied her hat, still chanting the burthen of the tender song she had caught so soon. A voiceless sigh stirred the ruddy leaves on Pauline's bosom as she turned away, but Gilbert embodied it in words, "They are happier without us. Let us go."

Neither spoke till they reached the appointed tryst. The others were not there, and, waiting for them, Pauline sat on a mossy stone, Gilbert leaned against the granite boulder beside her, and both silently surveyed a scene that made the heart glow, the eye kindle with delight as it swept down from that airy height, across valleys dappled with shadow and dark with untrodden forests, up ranges of majestic mountains, through gap after gap, each hazier than the last, far out into that sea of blue which rolls around all the world. Behind them roared the waterfall swollen with autumn rains and hurrying to pour itself into the rocky basin that lay boiling below, there to leave its legacy of shattered trees, then to dash itself into a deeper chasm, soon to be haunted by a tragic legend and go glittering away through forest, field, and intervale to join the river rolling slowly to the sea. Won by the beauty and the grandeur of the scene, Pauline forgot she was not alone, till turning, she suddenly became aware that while she scanned the face of nature her companion had been scanning hers. What he saw there she could not tell, but all restraint had vanished from his manner, all reticence from his speech, for with the old ardor in his eye, the old impetuosity in his voice, he said, leaning down as if to read her heart, "This is the moment I have waited for so long. For now you see what I see, that both have made a bitter blunder, and may yet repair it. Those children love each other; let them love, youth mates them, fortune makes them equals, fate brings them together that we may be free. Accept this freedom as I do, and come out into the world with me to lead the life you were born to enjoy.''

With the first words he uttered Pauline felt that the time had come, and in the drawing of a breath was ready for it, with every sense alert, every power under full control, every feature obedient to the art which had become a second nature. Gilbert had seized her hand, and she did not draw it back; the sudden advent of the instant which must end her work sent an unwonted color to her cheek, and she did avert it; the exultation which flashed into her eyes made it unsafe to meet his own, and they drooped before him as if in shame or fear, her whole face woke and brightened with the excitement that stirred her blood. She did not seek to conceal it, but let him cheat himself with the belief that love touched it with such light and warmth, as she softly answered in a voice whose accents seemed to assure his hope.

"You ask me to relinquish much. What do you offer in return, Gilbert, that I may not for a second time find love's labor lost?''

It was a wily speech, though sweetly spoken, for it reminded him how much he had thrown away, how little now remained to give, but her mien inspired him, and nothing daunted, he replied more ardently than ever:

"I can offer you a heart always faithful in truth though not in seeming, for I never loved that child. I would give years of happy life to undo that act and be again the man you trusted. I can offer you a name which shall yet be an honorable one, despite the stain an hour's madness cast upon it. You once taunted me with cowardice because I dared not face the world and conquer it. I dare do that now; I long to escape from this disgraceful servitude, to throw myself into the press, to struggle and achieve for your dear sake. I can offer you strength, energy, devotion—three gifts worthy any woman's acceptance who possesses power to direct, reward, and enjoy them as you do, Pauline. Because with your presence for my inspiration, I feel that I can retrieve my faultful past, and with time become God's noblest work—an honest man. Babie never could exert this influence over me. You can, you will, for now my earthly hope is in your hands, my soul's salvation in your love."

If that love had not died a sudden death, it would have risen up to answer him as the one sincere desire of an erring life cried out to her for help, and this man, as proud as sinful, knelt down before her with a passionate humility never paid at any other shrine, human or divine. It seemed to melt and win her, for he saw the color ebb and flow, heard the rapid beating of her heart, felt the hand tremble in his own, and received no denial but a lingering doubt, whose removal was a keen satisfaction to himself.

"Tell me, before I answer, are you sure that Manuel loves Babie?"

"I am; for every day convinces me that he has outlived the brief delusion, and longs for liberty, but dares not ask it. Ah! that pricks pride! But it is so. I have watched with jealous vigilance and let no sign escape me; because in his infidelity to you lay my chief hope. Has he not grown melancholy, cold, and silent? Does he not seek Babie and, of late, shun you? Will he not always yield his place to me without a token of displeasure or regret? Has he ever uttered reproach, warning, or command to you, although he knows I was and am your lover? Can you deny these proofs, or pause to ask if he will refuse to break the tie that binds him to a woman, whose superiority in all things keeps him a subject where he would be a king? You do not know the heart of man if you believe he will not bless you for his freedom."

Like the cloud which just then swept across the valley, blotting out its sunshine with a gloomy shadow, a troubled look flitted over Pauline's face. But if the words woke any sleeping fear she cherished, it was peremptorily banished, for scarcely had the watcher seen it than it was gone. Her eyes still shone upon the ground, and still she prolonged the bittersweet delight at seeing this humiliation of both soul and body by asking the one question whose reply would complete her sad success.

"Gilbert, do you believe I love you still?"

"I know it! Can I not read the signs that proved it to me once? Can

I forget that, though you followed me to pity and despise, you have remained to pardon and befriend? Am I not sure that no other power could work the change you have wrought in me? I was learning to be content with slavery, and slowly sinking into that indolence of will which makes submission easy. I was learning to forget you, and be resigned to hold the shadow when the substance was gone, but you came, and with a look undid my work, with a word destroyed my hard-won peace, with a touch roused the passion which was not dead but sleeping, and have made this month of growing certainty to be the sweetest in my life—for I believed all lost, and you showed me that all was won. Surely that smile is propitious! and I may hope to hear the happy confirmation of my faith from lips that were formed to say 'I love!' "

She looked up then, and her eyes burned on him, with an expression which made his heart leap with expectant joy, as over cheek and forehead spread a glow of womanly emotion too genuine to be feigned, and her voice thrilled with the fervor of that sentiment which blesses life and outlives death.

"Yes, I love; not as of old, with a girl's blind infatuation, but with the warmth and wisdom of heart, mind, and soul—love made up of honor, penitence and trust, nourished in secret by the better self which lingers in the most tried and tempted of us, and now ready to blossom and bear fruit, if God so wills. I have been once deceived, but faith still endures, and I believe that I may yet earn this crowning gift of a woman's life for the man who shall make my happiness as I make his—who shall find me the prouder for past coldness, the humbler for past pride—whose life shall pass serenely loving. And that beloved is—my husband."

If she had lifted her white hand and stabbed him, with that smile upon her face, it would not have shocked him with a more pale dismay than did those two words as Pauline shook him off and rose up, beautiful and stern as an avenging angel. Dumb with an amazement too fathomless for words, he knelt there motionless and aghast. She did not speak. And, passing his hand across his eyes as if he felt himself the prey to some delusion, he rose slowly, asking, half incredulously, half imploringly, "Pauline, this is a jest?"

"To me it is; to you—a bitter earnest."

A dim foreboding of the truth fell on him then, and with it a strange sense of fear; for in this apparition of human judgment he seemed to receive a premonition of the divine. With a sudden gesture of something like entreaty, he cried out, as if his fate lay in her hands, "How will it end? how will it end?"

"As it began—in sorrow, shame and loss."

Then, in words that fell hot and heavy on the sore heart made desolate, she poured out the dark history of the wrong and the atonement wrung from him with such pitiless patience and inexorable will. No hard fact remained unrecorded, no subtle act unveiled, no hint of her bright future unspared to deepen the gloom of his. And when the final word of doom died upon the lips that should have awarded pardon, not punishment, Pauline tore away the last gift he had given, and dropping it to the rocky path, set her foot upon it, as if it were the scarlet badge of her subjection to the evil spirit which had haunted her so long, now cast out and crushed forever.

Gilbert had listened with a slowly gathering despair, which deepened to the blind recklessness that comes to those whose passions are their masters, when some blow smites but cannot subdue. Pale to his very lips, with the still white wrath, so much more terrible to witness than the fiercest ebullition of the ire that flames and feeds like a sudden fire, he waited till she ended, then used the one retaliation she had left him. His hand went to his breast, a tattered glove flashed white against the cliff as he held it up before her, saying, in a voice that rose gradually till the last words sounded clear above the waterfall's wild song:

"It was well and womanly done, Pauline, and I could wish Manuel a happy life with such a tender, frank, and noble wife; but the future which you paint so well never shall be his. For, by the Lord that hears me! I swear I will end this jest of yours in a more bitter earnest than you prophesied. Look; I have worn this since the night you began the conflict, which has ended in defeat to me, as it shall to you. I do not war with women, but you shall have one man's blood upon your soul, for I will goad that tame boy to rebellion by flinging this in his face and taunting him with a perfidy blacker than my own. Will that rouse him to forget your commands and answer like a man?"

"Yes!"

The word rang through the air sharp and short as a pistol shot, a slender brown hand wrenched the glove away, and Manuel came between them. Wild with fear, Mrs. Redmond clung to him. Pauline sprang before him, and for a moment the two faced each other, with a year's smoldering jealousy and hate blazing in fiery eyes, trembling in clenched hands, and surging through set teeth in defiant speech.

"This is the gentleman who gambles his friend to desperation, and skulks behind a woman, like the coward he is," sneered Gilbert.

"Traitor and swindler, you lie!" shouted Manuel, and, flinging his wife behind him, he sent the glove, with a stinging blow, full in his opponent's face.

Then the wild beast that lurks in every strong man's blood leaped up in Gilbert Redmond's, as, with a single gesture of his sinewy right arm he swept Manuel to the verge of the narrow ledge, saw him hang poised there one awful instant, struggling to save the living weight that weighed him down, heard a heavy plunge into the black pool below, and felt that thrill of horrible delight which comes to murderers alone.

So swift and sure had been the act it left no time for help. A rush, a plunge, a pause, and then two figures stood where four had been—a man and woman staring dumbly at each other, appalled at the dread silence that made high noon more ghostly than the deepest night. And with that moment of impotent horror, remorse, and woe, Pauline's long punishment began.

MY CONTRABAND; OR,
THE BROTHERS

DOCTOR FRANCK CAME IN AS I SAT SEWING UP THE RENTS IN AN old shirt, that Tom might go tidily to his grave. New shirts were needed for the living, and there was not wife or mother to "dress him handsome when he went to meet the Lord," as one woman said, describing the fine funeral she had pinched herself to give her son.

"Miss Dane, I'm in a quandary," began the Doctor, with that expression of countenance which says as plainly as words, "I want to ask a favor, but I wish you'd save me the trouble."

"Can I help you out of it?"

"Faith! I don't like to propose it, but you certainly can, if you please."

"Then give it a name, I beg."

"You see a Reb has just been brought in crazy with typhoid; a bad case every way; a drunken, rascally little captain somebody took the trouble to capture, but whom nobody wants to take the trouble to cure. The wards are full, the ladies worked to death, and willing to be for our own boys, but rather slow to risk their lives for a Reb. Now you've had the fever, you like queer patients, your mate will see to your ward for a while, and I will find you a good attendant. The fellow won't last long, I fancy; but he can't die without some sort of care, you know.

I've put him in the fourth story of the west wing, away from the rest. It is airy, quiet, and comfortable there. I'm on that ward, and will do my best for you in every way. Now, then, will you go?"

"Of course I will, out of perversity, if not common charity; for some of these people think that because I'm an abolitionist I am also a heathen, and I should rather like to show them that, though I cannot quite love my enemies, I am willing to take care of them."

"Very good; I thought you'd go; and speaking of abolition reminds me that you can have a contraband for servant, if you like. It is that fine mulatto fellow who was found burying his Rebel master after the fight, and, being badly cut over the head, our boys brought him along. Will you have him?"

"By all means—for I'll stand to my guns on that point, as on the other; these black boys are far more faithful and handy than some of the white scamps given me to serve, instead of being served by. But is this man well enough?"

"Yes, for that sort of work, and I think you'll like him. He must have been a handsome fellow before he got his face slashed; not much darker than myself; his master's son, I dare say, and the white blood makes him rather high and haughty about some things. He was in a bad way when he came in, but vowed he'd die in the street rather than turn in with the black fellows below; so I put him up in the west wing, to be out of the way, and he's seen to the captain all the morning. When can you go up?"

"As soon as Tom is laid out, Skinner moved, Haywood washed, Marble dressed, Charley rubbed, Downs taken up, Upham laid down, and the whole forty fed."

We both laughed, though the Doctor was on his way to the deadhouse and I held a shroud on my lap. But in a hospital one learns that cheerfulness is one's salvation; for, in an atmosphere of suffering and death, heaviness of heart would soon paralyze usefulness of hand, if the blessed gift of smiles had been denied us.

In an hour I took possession of my new charge, finding a dissipated-looking boy of nineteen or twenty raving in the solitary little room, with no one near him but the contraband in the room adjoining. Feeling decidedly more interest in the black man than in the white, yet remembering the Doctor's hint of his being "high and haughty," I glanced furtively at him as I scattered chloride of lime about the room to purify the air, and settled matters to suit myself. I had seen many contrabands, but never one so attractive as this. All colored men are called "boys," even if their heads are white; this boy was five-and-twenty at least, strong-limbed and manly, and had the look of one who never had been cowed by abuse or worn with oppressive labor. He sat on his bed doing nothing; no book, no pipe, no pen or paper anywhere appeared, yet anything less indolent or listless than his attitude and expression I never saw. Erect he sat, with a hand on either knee, and eyes fixed on the bare wall opposite, so rapt in some absorbing thought as to be unconscious of my presence, though the door stood wide open and my movements were by no means noiseless. His face was half averted, but I instantly approved the Doctor's taste, for the profile which I saw possessed all the attributes of comeliness belonging to his mixed race. He was more quadroon than mulatto, with Saxon features, Spanish complexion, darkened by exposure, color in lips and cheek, waving hair, and an eye full of the passionate melancholy which in such men always seems to utter a mute protest against the broken law that doomed them at their birth. What could he be thinking of? The sick boy cursed and raved, I rustled to and fro, steps passed the door, bells rang, and the steady rumble of army-wagons came up from the street, still he never stirred. I had seen colored people in what they call "the black sulks," when for days, they neither smiled nor spoke, and scarcely ate. But this was something more than that; for the man was not dully brooding over some small grievance; he seemed to see an all-absorbing fact or fancy recorded on the wall, which was a blank to me. I wondered if it were some deep wrong or sorrow, kept alive by memory and impotent regret; if he mourned for the dead master to whom he had been faithful to the end; or if the liberty now his were robbed of half its sweetness by the knowledge that someone near and dear to him still languished in the hell from which he had escaped. My heart warmed to him at that idea; I wanted to know and comfort him; and, following the impulse of the moment, I went in and touched him on the shoulder.

In an instant the man vanished and the slave appeared. Freedom was too new a boon to have wrought its blessed changes yet, and as he started up, with his hand at his temple and an obsequious "Yes, Ma'am," any romance that had gathered round him fled away, leaving the saddest of all sad facts in living guise before me. Not only did the manhood seem to die out of him, but the comeliness that first attracted me; for, as he turned, I saw the ghastly wound that had laid open cheek and forehead. Being partly healed, it was no longer bandaged, but held together with strips of that transparent plaster which I never see without a shiver and swift recollections of the scenes with which it is associated in my mind. Part of his black hair had been shorn away, and one eye was nearly closed; pain so distorted, and the cruel sabre-cut so marred that portion of his face, that, when I saw it, I felt as if a fine medal had been suddenly reversed, showing me a far more striking type of human suffering and wrong than Michel Angelo's bronze prisoner. By one of those inexplicable processes that often teach us how little we understand ourselves, my purpose was suddenly changed, and though I went in to offer comfort as a friend, I merely gave an order as a mistress.

"Will you open these windows? This man needs more air."

He obeyed at once, and, as he slowly urged up the unruly sash, the handsome profile was again turned toward me, and again I was possessed by my first impression so strongly that I involuntarily said,

"Thank you, Sir."

Perhaps it was fancy, but I thought that in the look of mingled surprise and something like reproach which he gave me there was also a trace of grateful pleasure. But he said, in that tone of spiritless humility these poor souls learn so soon,

"I a'n't a white man, Ma'am, I'm a contraband."

"Yes, I know it; but a contraband is a free man, and I heartily congratulate you."

He liked that; his face shone, he squared his shoulders, lifted his head, and looked me full in the eye with a brisk

"Thank ye, Ma'am; anything more to do fer yer?"

"Doctor Franck thought you would help me with this man, as there are many patients and few nurses or attendants. Have you had the fever?"

"No, Ma'am."

"They should have thought of that when they put him here; wounds and fevers should not be together. I'll try to get you moved."

He laughed a sudden laugh—if he had been a white man, I should have called it scornful; as he was a few shades darker than myself, I suppose it must be considered an insolent, or at least an unmannerly one.

"It don't matter, Ma'am. I'd rather be up here with the fever than down with those niggers; and there a'n't no other place fer me."

Poor fellow! that was true. No ward in all the hospital would take him in to lie side by side with the most miserable white wreck there. Like the bat in Aesop's fable, he belonged to neither race; and the pride of one, the helplessness of the other, kept him hovering alone in the twilight a great sin has brought to overshadow the whole land.

"You shall stay, then; for I would far rather have you than my lazy Jack. But are you well and strong enough?"

"I guess I'll do, Ma'am."

He spoke with a passive sort of acquiescence—as if it did not much matter, if he were not able, and no one would particularly rejoice, if he were.

"Yes, I think you will. By what name shall I call you?"

"Bob, Ma'am."

Every woman has her pet whim; one of mine was to teach the men self-respect by treating them respectfully. Tom, Dick and Harry would pass, when lads rejoiced in those familiar abbreviations; but to address men often old enough to be my father in that style did not suit my old-fashioned ideas of propriety. This "Bob" would never do; I should have found it as easy to call the chaplain "Gus" as my tragical-looking contraband by a title so strongly associated with the tail of a kite.

"What is your other name?" I asked. "I like to call my attendants by their last names rather than by their first."

"I've got no other, Ma'am; we have our masters' names, or do without. Mine's dead, and I won't have anything of his about me."

"Well, I'll call you Robert, then, and you may fill this pitcher for me, if you will be so kind."

He went; but, through all the tame obedience years of servitude had taught him, I could see that the proud spirit his father gave him was not yet subdued, for the look and gesture with which he repudiated his master's name were a more effective declaration of independence than any Fourth-of-July orator could have prepared.

We spent a curious week together. Robert seldom left his room, except upon my errands; and I was a prisoner all day, often all night, by the bedside of the Rebel. The fever burned itself rapidly away, for there seemed little vitality to feed it in the feeble frame of this old young man, whose life had been none of the most righteous, judging from the revelations made by his unconscious lips; since more than once Robert authoritatively silenced him, when my gentler hushings were of no avail, and blasphemous wanderings or ribald camp-songs made my cheeks burn and Robert's face assume an aspect of disgust. The captain was a gentleman in the world's eye, but the contraband was the gentleman in mine; I was a fanatic, and that accounts for such depravity of taste, I hope. I never asked Robert of himself, feeling that somewhere there was a spot still too sore to bear the lightest touch; but, from his language, manner, and intelligence, I inferred that his color had procured for him the few advantages within the reach of a quick-witted, kindly treated slave. Silent, grave, and thoughtful, but most serviceable, was my contraband; glad of the books I brought him, faithful in the performance of the duties I assigned to him, grateful for the friendliness I could not but feel and show toward him. Often I longed to ask what purpose was so visibly altering his aspect with such daily deepening gloom. But I never dared, and no one else had either time or desire to pry into the past of this specimen of one branch of the chivalrous "F.F.Vs."

On the seventh night, Dr. Franck suggested that it would be well for some one, besides the general watchman of the ward, to be with the captain, as it might be his last. Although the greater part of the two preceding nights had been spent there, of course I offered to remain—for there is a strange fascination in these scenes, which renders one careless of fatigue and unconscious of fear until the crisis is passed.

"Give him water as long as he can drink, and if he drops into a natural sleep, it may save him. I'll look in at midnight, when some change will probably take place. Nothing but sleep or a miracle will keep him now. Good night."

Away went the Doctor; and, devouring a whole mouthful of gapes, I lowered the lamp, wet the captain's head, and sat down on a hard stool to begin my watch. The captain lay with his hot, haggard face turned toward me, filling the air with his poisonous breath, and feebly muttering, with lips and tongue so parched that the sanest speech would have been difficult to understand. Robert was stretched on his bed in the inner room, the door of which stood ajar, that a fresh draught from his open window might carry the fever-fumes away through mine. I could just see a long, dark figure, with the lighter outline of a face, and, having little else to do just then I fell to thinking of this curious contraband, who evidently prized his freedom highly, yet seemed in no haste to enjoy it. Doctor Franck had offered to send him on to safer quarters, but he had said, "No, thank yer, Sir, not yet," and then had gone away to fall into one of those black moods of his, which began to disturb me, because I had no power to lighten them. As I sat listening to the clocks from the steeples all about us, I amused myself with planning Robert's future, as I often did my own, and had dealt out to him a generous hand of trumps wherewith to play this game of life which hitherto had gone so cruelly against him, when a harsh, choked voice called,

"Lucy!"

It was the captain, and some new terror seemed to have gifted him with momentary strength.

"Yes, here's Lucy," I answered, hoping that by following the fancy I might quiet him—for his face was damp with the clammy moisture, and his frame shaken with the nervous tremor that so often precedes death. His dull eye fixed upon me, dilating with a bewildered look of incredulity and wrath, till he broke out fiercely,

"That's a lie! she's dead—and so's Bob, damn him!"

Finding speech a failure, I began to sing the quiet tune that had often soothed delirium like this; but hardly had the line,

"See gentle patience smile on pain,"

passed my lips, when he clutched me by the wrist, whispering like one in mortal fear,

"Hush! she used to sing that way to Bob, but she never would to me. I swore I'd whip the Devil out of her, and I did; but you know before she cut her throat she said she'd haunt me, and there she is!"

He pointed behind me with an aspect of such pale dismay, that I involuntarily glanced over my shoulder and started as if I had seen a veritable ghost; for, peering from the gloom of that inner room, I saw a shadowy face, with dark hair all about it, and a glimpse of scarlet at the throat. An instant showed me that it was only Robert leaning from his bed's-foot, wrapped in a gray army-blanket, with his red shirt just visible above it, and his long hair disordered by sleep. But what a strange expression was on his face! The unmarred side was toward me, fixed and motionless as when I first observed it—less absorbed now, but more intent. His eye glittered, his lips were apart like one who listened with every sense, and his whole aspect reminded me of a hound to which some wind had brought the scent of unsuspected prey.

"Do you know him, Robert? Does he mean you?"

"Lord, no, Ma'am; they all own half a dozen Bobs: but hearin' my name woke me; that's all."

He spoke quite naturally, and lay down again, while I returned to my charge, thinking that this paroxysm was probably his last. But by another hour I perceived a hopeful change, for the tremor had subsided, the cold dew was gone, his breathing was more regular, and Sleep, the healer, had descended to save or take him gently away. Doctor Franck looked in at midnight, bade me keep all cool and quiet, and not fail to administer a certain draught as soon as the captain woke. Very much relieved, I laid my head on my arms, uncomfortably folded on the little table, and fancied I was about to perform one of the feats which practice renders possible—"sleeping with one eye open," as we say: a half-and-half doze, for all senses sleep but that of hearing; the faintest murmur, sigh, or motion will break it, and give one back one's wits much brightened by the brief permission to "stand at ease." On this night, the experiment was a failure, for previous vigils, confinement, and much care had rendered naps a dangerous indulgence. Having roused half a dozen times in an hour to find all quiet, I dropped my heavy head on my arms, and, drowsily resolving to look up again in fifteen minutes, fell fast asleep.

The striking of a deep-voiced clock woke me with a start. "That is one," thought I, but, to my dismay, two more strokes followed; and in remorseful haste I sprang up to see what harm my long oblivion had done. A strong hand put me back into my seat, and held me there. It was Robert. The instant my eye met his my heart began to beat, and all along my nerves tingled that electric flash which foretells a danger that we cannot see. He was very pale, his mouth grim, and both eyes full of sombre fire—for even the wounded one was open now, all the more sinister for the deep scar above and below. But his touch was steady, his voice quiet, as he said,

"Sit still, Ma'am; I won't hurt yer, nor even scare yer, if I can help it, but yer waked too soon."

"Let me go, Robert—the captain is stirring—I must give him something."

"No, Ma'am, yer can't stir an inch. Look here!"

Holding me with one hand, with the other he took up the glass in which I had left the draught, and showed me it was empty.

"Hao he taken it?" I asked, more and more bewildered.

"I flung it out o'winder, Ma'am; he'll have to do without."

"But why, Robert? why did you do it?"

"Because I hate him!"

Impossible to doubt the truth of that; his whole face showed it, as he spoke through his set teeth, and launched a fiery glance at the unconscious captain. I could only hold my breath and stare blankly at him, wondering what mad act was coming next. I suppose I shook and turned white, as women have a foolish habit of doing when sudden danger daunts them; for Robert released my arm, sat down upon the bedside just in front of me, and said, with the ominous quietude that made me cold to see and hear,

"Don't yer be frightened, Ma'am; don't try to run away, fer the door's locked an' the key in my pocket; don't yer cry out, fer yer'd have to scream a long while, with my hand on yer mouth, before yer was heard. Be still, an' I'll tell yer what I'm goin' to do."

"Lord help us! he has taken the fever in some sudden, violent way, and is out of his head. I must humor him till someone comes"; in pursuance of which swift determination, I tried to say, quite composedly,

"I will be still and hear you; but open the window. Why did you shut it?"

"I'm sorry I can't do it, Ma'am; but yer'd jump out, or call, if I did, an' I'm not ready yet. I shut it to make yer sleep, an' heat would do it quicker 'n anything else I could do."

The captain moved, and feebly muttered, "Water!" Instinctively I rose to give it to him, but the heavy hand came down upon my shoulder, and in the same decided tone Robert said,

"The water went with the physic; let him call."

"Do let me go to him! he'll die without care!"

"I mean he shall; don't yer interfere, if yer please, Ma'am."

In spite of his quiet tone and respectful manner, I saw murder in his eyes, and turned faint with fear; yet the fear excited me, and, hardly knowing what I did, I seized the hands that had seized me, crying,

"No, no, you shall not kill him! it is base to hurt a helpless man. Why do you hate him? He is not your master?"

"He's my brother."

I felt that answer from head to foot, and seemed to fathom what was coming, with a prescience vague, but unmistakable. One appeal was left to me, and I made it.

"Robert, tell me what it means? Do not commit a crime and make me accessory to it. There is a better way of righting wrong than by violence; let me help you find it."

My voice trembled as I spoke, and I heard the frightened flutter of my heart; so did he, and if any little act of mine had ever won affection or respect from him, the memory of it served me then. He looked down, and seemed to put some question to himself; whatever it was, the answer was in my favor, for when his eyes rose again, they were gloomy, but not desperate.

"I will tell you, Ma'am; but mind, this makes no difference; the boy is mine. I'll give the Lord a chance to take him fust; if He don't, I shall."

"Oh, no! remember, he is your brother."

An unwise speech; I felt it as it passed my lips, for a black frown gathered on Robert's face, and his strong hands closed with an ugly sort of grip. But he did not touch the poor soul gasping there behind him, and seemed content to let the slow suffocation of that stifling room end his frail life.

"I'm not like to forget that, Ma'am, when I've been thinkin' of it all this week. I knew him when they fetched him in, an' would 'a' done it long 'fore this, but I wanted to ask where Lucy was; he knows—he told to-night—an' now he's done for."

"Who is Lucy?" I asked hurriedly, intent on keeping his mind busy with any thought but murder.

With one of the swift transitions of a mixed temperament like this, at my question Robert's deep eyes filled, the clenched hands were spread before his face, and all I heard were the broken words,

"My wife—he took her."

In that instant every thought of fear was swallowed up in burning indignation for the wrong, and a perfect passion of pity for the desperate man so tempted to avenge an injury for which there seemed no redress but this. He was no longer slave or contraband, no drop of black blood marred him in my sight, but an infinite compassion yearned to save, to help, to comfort him. Words seemed so powerless I offered none, only put my hand on his poor head, wounded, homeless, bowed down with grief for which I had no cure, and softly smoothed the long neglected hair pitifully wondering the while where was the wife who must have loved this tender-hearted man so well.

The captain moaned again, and faintly whispered, "Air!" but I never stirred. God forgive me! just then I hated him as only a woman thinking of a sister woman's wrong could hate. Robert looked up; his eyes were dry again, his mouth grim. I saw that, said, "Tell me more," and he did—for sympathy is a gift the poorest may give, the proudest stoop to receive.

"Yer see, Ma'am, his father—I might say ours, if I warn't ashamed of both of 'em—his father died two years ago, an' left us all to Marster Ned—that's him here, eighteen then. He always hated me, I looked so like old Marster: he don't—only the light skin an' hair. Old Marster was kind to all of us, me 'specially, an' bought Lucy off the next plantation down there in South Car'lina, when he found I liked her. I married her, all I could, Ma'am; it warn't much, but we was true to one another till Marster Ned come home a year after an' made hell fer both of us. He sent my old mother to be used up in his rice-swamp in Georgy; he found me with my pretty Lucy, an' though young Miss cried, an' I prayed to him on my knees, an' Lucy run away, he wouldn't have no mercy; he brought her back, an'—took her, Ma'am."

"Oh! what did you do?" I cried, hot with helpless pain and passion. How the man's outraged heart sent the blood flaming up into his face and deepened the tones of his impetuous voice, as he stretched his arm across the bed, saying with a terribly expressive gesture,

"I half murdered him, an' to-night I'll finish."

"Yes, yes—but go on now; what came next?"

He gave me a look that showed no white man could have felt a deeper degradation in remembering and confessing these last acts of brotherly oppression.

"They whipped me till I couldn't stand, an' then they sold me further South. Yer thought I was a white man once; look here!"

With a sudden wrench he tore the shirt from neck to waist, and on his strong brown shoulders showed me furrows deeply ploughed, wounds which, though healed, were ghastlier to me than any in that house. I could not speak to him, and, with the pathetic dignity a great grief lends the humblest sufferer, he ended his brief tragedy by simply saying,

"That's all, Ma'am. I've never seen her since, an' now I never shall in this world—maybe not in t'other."

"But, Robert, why think her dead? The captain was wandering when he said those sad things; perhaps he will retract them when he is sane. Don't despair; don't give up yet."

"No, Ma'am, I guess he's right; she was too proud to bear that long. It's like her to kill herself. I told her to, if there was no other way; an' she always minded me, Lucy did. My poor girl! Oh, it warn't right! No, by God, it warn't!"

As the memory of this bitter wrong, this double bereavement, burned in his sore heart, the devil that lurks in every strong man's blood leaped up; he put his hand upon his brother's throat, and, watching the white face before him, muttered low between his teeth,

"I'm lettin' him go too easy; there's no pain in this; we a'n't even yet. I wish he knew me. Marster Ned! it's Bob; where's Lucy?"

From the captain's lips there came a long faint sigh, and nothing but a flutter of the eyelids showed that he still lived. A strange stillness filled the room as the elder brother held the younger's life suspended in his hand, while wavering between a dim hope and a deadly hate.

In the whirl of thoughts that went on in my brain, only one was clear enough to act upon. I must prevent murder, if I could—but how? What could I do up there alone, locked in with a dying man and a lunatic?—for any mind yielded utterly to any unrighteous impulse is mad while the impulse rules it. Strength I had not, nor much courage, neither time nor wit for stratagem, and chance only could bring me help before it was too late. But one weapon I possessed—a tongue— often a woman's best defense; and sympathy, stronger than fear, gave me power to use it. What I said Heaven only knows, but surely Heaven helped me; words burned on my lips, tears streamed from my eyes, and some good angel prompted me to use the one name that had power to arrest my hearer's hand and touch his heart. For at that moment I heartily believed that Lucy lived, and this earnest faith roused in him a like belief.

He listened with the lowering look of one in whom brute instinct was sovereign for the time—a look that makes the noblest countenance base. He was but a man—a poor, untaught, outcast, outraged man. Life had few joys for him; the world offered him no honors, no success, no home, no love. What future would this crime mar? and why should he deny himself that sweet, yet bitter morsel called revenge? How many white men, with all New England's freedom, culture, Christianity, would not have felt as he felt then? Should I have reproached him for a human anguish, a human longing for redress, all now left him from the ruin of his few poor hopes? Who had taught him that self-control, self-sacrifice, are attributes that make men masters of the earth and lift them nearer heaven? Should I have urged the beauty of forgiveness, the duty of devout submission? He had no religion, for he was no saintly "Uncle Tom," and Slavery's black shadow seemed to darken all the world to him and shut out God. Should I have warned him of penalties, of judgments, and the potency of law? What did he know of justice, or the mercy that should temper that stern virtue, when every law, human and divine, had been broken on his hearthstone? Should I have tried to touch him by appeals to filial duty, to brotherly love? How had his appeals been answered?

What memories had father and brother stored up in his heart to plead for either now? No—all these influences, these associations, would have proved worse than useless, had I been calm enough to try them. I was not; but instinct, subtler than reason, showed me the one safe clue by which to lead this troubled soul from the labyrinth in which it groped and nearly fell. When I paused, breathless, Robert turned to me, asking, as if human assurances could strengthen his faith in Divine Omnipotence,

"Do you believe, if I let Marster Ned live, the Lord will give me back my Lucy?"

"As surely as there is a Lord, you will find her here or in the beautiful hereafter, where there is no black or white, no master and no slave."

He took his hand from his brother's throat, lifted his eyes from my face to the wintry sky beyond, as if searching for that blessed country, happier even than the happy North. Alas, it was the darkest hour before the dawn!—there was no star above, no light below but the pale glimmer of the lamp that showed the brother who had made him desolate. Like a blind man who believes there is a sun, yet cannot see it, he shook his head, let his arms drop nervelessly upon his knees, and sat there dumbly asking that question which many a soul whose faith is firmer fixed than his had asked in hours less dark than this, "Where is God?" I saw the tide had turned, and strenuously tried to keep this rudderless life-boat from slipping back into the whirlpool wherein it had been so nearly lost.

"I have listened to you, Robert; now hear me, and heed what I say, because my heart is full of pity for you, full of hope for your future, and a desire to help you now. I want you to go away from here, from the temptation of this place, and the sad thoughts that haunt it. You have conquered yourself once, and I honor you for it, because the harder the battle, the more glorious the victory; but it is safer to put a greater distance between you and this man. I will write you letters, give you money, and send you to good old Massachusetts to begin your new life a freeman—yes, and a happy man; for when the captain is himself again, I will learn where Lucy is, and move heaven and earth to find and give her back to you. Will you do this, Robert?"

Slowly, very slowly, the answer came; for the purpose of a week, perhaps a year, was hard to relinquish in an hour.

"Yes, Ma'am, I will."

"Good! Now you are the man I thought you, and I'll work for you with all my heart. You need sleep, my poor fellow; go, and try to forget. The captain is still alive, and as yet you are spared that sin. No, don't look there; I'll care for him. Come, Robert, for Lucy's sake."

Thank Heaven for the immortality of love! for when all other means of salvation failed, a spark of this vital fire softened the man's iron will until a woman's hand could bend it. He let me take from him the key, let me draw him gently away and lead him to the solitude which now was the most healing balm I could bestow. Once in his little room, he fell down on his bed and lay there as if spent with the sharpest conflict of his life. I slipped the bolt across his door, and unlocked my own, flung up the window, steadied myself with a breath of air, then rushed to Doctor Franck. He came; and till dawn we worked together, saving one brother's life, and taking earnest thought how best to secure the other's liberty. When the sun came up as blithely as if it shone only upon happy homes, the Doctor went to Robert. For an hour I heard the murmur of their voices; once I caught the sound of heavy sobs, and for a time reverent hush, as if in the silence that good man were ministering to soul as well as sense. When he departed he took Robert with him, pausing to tell me he should get him off as soon as possible, but not before we met again.

Nothing more was seen of them all day; another surgeon came to see the captain, and another attendant came to fill the empty place. I tried to rest, but could not, with the thought of poor Lucy tugging at my heart, and was soon back at my post again, anxiously hoping that my contraband had not been too hastily spirited away. Just as night fell there came a tap, and, opening, I saw Robert literally "clothed and in his right mind." The Doctor had replaced the ragged suit with tidy garments, and no trace of that tempestuous night remained but deeper lines upon the forehead and the docile look of a repentant child. He did not cross the threshold, did not offer me his hand—only took off his cap, saying with a traitorous falter in his voice,

"God bless you, Ma'am! I'm goin'."

I put out both my hands, and held his fast.

"Good bye, Robert! Keep up good heart, and when I come home to Massachusetts we'll meet in a happier place than this. Are you quite ready, quite comfortable for your journey?"

"Yes, Ma'am, yes; the Doctor's fixed everything; I'm goin' with a friend of his; my papers are all right, an' I'm as happy as I can be till I find—"

He stopped there; then went on, with a glance into the room,

"I'm glad I didn't do it, an' I thank yer, Ma'am, fer hinderin' me—thank yer hearty; but I'm afraid I hate him jest the same."

Of course he did; and so did I; for these faulty hearts of ours cannot turn perfect in a night, but need frost and fire, wind and rain, to ripen and make them ready for the great harvest-home. Wishing to divert his mind, I put my poor mite into his hand, and, remembering the magic of a certain little book, I gave him mine, on whose dark cover whitely shone the Virgin Mother and the Child, the grand history of whose life the book contained. The money went into Robert's pocket with a grateful murmur, the book into his bosom with a long look and a tremulous

"I never saw *my* baby, Ma'am."

I broke down then; and though my eyes were too dim to see, I felt the touch of lips upon my hands, heard the sound of departing feet, and knew my contraband was gone.

When one feels an intense dislike, the less one says about the subject of it the better; therefore I shall merely record that the captain lived—in time was exchanged; and that, whoever the other party was, I am convinced the Government got the best of the bargain. But long before this occurred, I had fulfilled my promise to Robert; for as soon as my patient recovered strength of memory enough to make his answer trustworthy, I asked, without any circumlocution,

"Captain Fairfax, where is Lucy?"

And too feeble to be angry, surprised or insincere, he straightway answered,

"Dead, Miss Dane."

"And she killed herself, when you sold Bob?"

"How the Devil did you know that?" he muttered, with an expression half-remorseful, half-amazed; but I was satisfied, and said no more.

Of course, this went to Robert, waiting far away there in a lonely home—waiting, working, hoping for his Lucy. It almost broke my heart to do it; but delay was weak, deceit was wicked; so I sent the heavy tidings, and very soon the answer came—only three lines; but I felt that the sustaining power of the man's life was gone.

"I thought I'd never see her any more; I'm glad to know she's out of trouble. I thank yer, Ma'am; an' if they let us, I'll fight fer yer till I'm killed, which I hope will be 'fore long."

Six months later he had his wish, and kept his word.

Every one knows the story of the attack on Fort Wagner; but we should not tire yet of recalling how our Fifty-Fourth, spent with three sleepless nights, a day's fast, and a march under the July sun, stormed the fort as night fell, facing death in many shapes, following their brave leaders through a fiery rain of shot and shell, fighting valiantly for "God and Governor Andrew"—how the regiment that went into action seven hundred strong came out having had nearly half its number captured, killed, or wounded, leaving their young commander to be buried, like a chief of earlier times, with his body-guard around him, faithful to the death. Surely, the insult turns to honor, and the wide grave needs no monument but the heroism that consecrates it in our sight; surely, the hearts that held him nearest see through their tears a noble victory in the seeming sad defeat; and surely, God's benediction was bestowed, when this loyal soul answered, as Death called the roll, "Lord, here am I, with the brothers Thou has given me!"

The future must show how well that fight was fought; for though

Fort Wagner still defies us, public prejudice is down; and through the cannon-smoke of that black night the manhood of the colored race shines before many eyes that would not see, rings in many ears that would not hear, wins many hearts that would not hitherto believe.

When the news came that we were needed, there was none so glad as I to leave teaching contrabands, the new work I had taken up, and go to nurse "our boys," as my dusky flock so proudly called the wounded of the Fifty-Fourth. Feeling more satisfaction, as I assumed my big apron and turned up my cuffs, than if dressing for the President's levee, I fell to work on board the hospital-ship in Hilton-Head harbor. The scene was most familiar, and yet strange; for only dark faces looked up at me from the pallets so thickly laid along the floor, and I missed the sharp accent of my Yankee boys in the slower, softer voices calling cheerily to one another, or answering my questions with a stout, "We'll never give it up, Ma'am, till the last Reb's dead," or, "If our people's free, we can afford to die."

Passing from bed to bed, intent on making one pair of hands do the work of three, at least, I gradually washed, fed, and bandaged my way down the long line of sable heroes, and coming to the very last, found that he was my contraband. So old, so worn, so deathly weak and wan, I never should have known him but for the deep scar on his cheek. That side lay uppermost, and caught my eye at once; but even then I doubted, such an awful change had come upon him, when, turning to the ticket just above his head, I saw the name, "Robert Dane."

That both assured and touched me, for, remembering that he had no name, I knew that he had taken mine. I longed for him to speak to me, to tell how he had fared since I lost sight of him, and let me perform some little service for him in return for many he had done for me; but he seemed asleep; and as I stood reliving that strange night again, a bright lad, who lay next him softly waving an old fan across both beds, looked up and said,

"I guess you know him, Ma'am?"

"You are right. Do you?"

"As much as any one was able to, Ma'am."

"Why do you say 'was,' as if the man were dead and gone?"

"I s'pose because I know he'll have to go. He's got a bad jab in the breast an' is bleedin' inside, the Doctor says. He don't suffer any, only gets weaker 'n' weaker every minute. I've been fannin' him this long while, an' he's talked a little; but he don't know me now, so he's most gone, I guess."

There was so much sorrow and affection in the boy's face, that I remembered something, and asked, with redoubled interest,

"Are you the one that brought him off? I was told about a boy who nearly lost his life in saving that of his mate."

I dare say the young fellow blushed, as any modest lad might have done; I could not see it, but I heard the chuckle of satisfaction that escaped him, as he glanced from his shattered arm and bandaged side to the pale figure opposite.

"Lord, Ma'am, tha's nothin'; we boys always stan' by one another, an' I warn't goin' to leave him to be tormented any more by them cussed Rebs. He's been a slave once, though he don't look half so much like it as me, an' I was born in Boston."

He did not; for the speaker was as black as the ace of spades—being a sturdy specimen, the knave of clubs would perhaps be a fitter representative—but the dark freeman looked at the white slave with the pitiful, yet puzzled expression I have so often seen on the faces of our wisest men, when this tangled question of Slavery presents itself, asking to be cut or patiently undone.

"Tell me what you know of this man; for, even if he were awake, he is too weak to talk."

"I never saw him till I joined the regiment, an' no one 'peared to have got much out of him. He was a shut-up sort of feller, an' didn't seem to care for anything but gettin' at the Rebs. Some say he was the fust man of us that enlisted; I know he fretted till we were off, an' when we pitched into old Wagner, he fought like the Devil.

"Were you with him when he was wounded? How was it?"

"Yes, Ma'am. There was somethin' queer about it; for he 'peared to know the chap that killed him, an' the chap knew him. I don't dare to

ask, but I rather guess one owned the other some time—for, when
they clinched, the chap sung out, 'Bob!' an' Dane, 'Marster Ned!'—
then they went at it."

I sat down suddenly, for the old anger and compassion struggled in
my heart, and I both longed and feared to hear what was to follow.

"You see, when the Colonel—Lord keep an' send him back to
us!—it a'n't certain yet, you know, Ma'am, though it's two days ago
we lost him—well, when the Colonel shouted, 'Rush on, boys, rush
on!' Dane tore away as if he was goin' to take the fort alone; I was next
him, an' kept close as we went through the ditch an' up the wall. Hi!
warn't that a rusher!" and the boy flung up his well arm with a whoop,
as if the mere memory of that stirring moment came over him in a gust
of irrepressible excitement.

"Were you afraid?" I said—asking the question women often put,
and receiving the answer they seldom fail to get.

"No, Ma'am!"—emphasis on the "Ma'am"—"I never thought of
anything but the damn' Rebs, that scalp, slash, an' cut our ears off,
when they git us. I was bound to let daylight into one of 'em at least,
an' I did. Hope he liked it!"

"It is evident that you did, and I don't blame you in the least. Now
go on about Robert, for I should be at work."

"He was one of the fust up; I was just behind, an' though the
whole thing happened in a minute, I remember how it was, for all I
was yellin' an' knockin' round like mad. Just where we were, some sort
of an officer was wavin' his sword an' cheerin' on his men; Dane saw
him by a big flash that come by; he flung away his gun, give a leap, an'
went at that feller as if he was Jeff, Beauregard, an' Lee, all in one. I
scrabbled after as quick as I could, but was only up in time to see him
git the sword straight through him an' drop into the ditch. You needn't
ask what I did next, Ma'am, for I don't quite know myself; all I'm clear
about is, that I managed somehow to pitch that Reb into the fort as
dead as Moses, git hold of Dane, an' bring him off. Poor old feller! we
said we went in to live or die; he said he went in to die, an' he's done
it."

I had been intently watching the excited speaker; but as he regretfully added those last words I turned again, and Robert's eyes met mine—those melancholy eyes, so full of an intelligence that proved he had heard, remembered, and reflected with that preternatural power which often outlives all other faculties. He knew me, yet gave no greeting; was glad to see a woman's face, yet had no smile wherewith to welcome it; felt that he was dying, yet uttered no farewell. He was too far across the river to return or linger now; departing thought, strength, breath, were spent in one grateful look, one murmur of submission to the last pang he could ever feel. His lips moved, and, bending to them, a whisper chilled my cheek, as it shaped the broken words—

"I would have done it—but it's better so—I'm satisfied."

Ah! well he might be—for, as he turned his face from the shadow of the life that was, the sunshine of the life to be touched it with a beautiful content, and in the drawing of a breath my contraband found wife and home, eternal liberty and God.

DEBBY'S DEBUT

O N A CHEERY JUNE DAY MRS. PENELOPE CARROLL AND HER niece Debby Wilder were whizzing along on their way to a certain gay watering-place, both in the best of humors with each other and all the world beside. Aunt Pen was concocting sundry mild romances, and laying harmless plots for the pursuance of her favorite pastime, match-making; for she had invited her pretty relative to join her summer jaunt, ostensibly that the girl might see a little of fashionable life, but the good lady secretly proposed to herself to take her to the beach and get her a rich husband, very much as she would have proposed to take her to Broadway and get her a new bonnet, for both articles she considered necessary, but somewhat difficult for a poor girl to obtain.

Debby was slowly getting her poise, after the excitement of a first visit to New York; for ten days of bustle had introduced the young philosopher to a new existence, and the working-day world seemed to have vanished when she made her last pat of butter in the dairy at home. For an hour she sat thinking over the good-fortune which had befallen her, and the comforts of this life which she had suddenly acquired. Debby was a true girl—with all a girl's love of ease and pleasure; and it must not be set down against her that she surveyed her pretty travelling-suit with much complacency, rejoicing inwardly that she could use her hands without exposing fractured gloves, that her bonnet was of the newest mode, needing no veil to hide a faded ribbon or a last year's shape, that her dress swept the ground with fashionable untidiness, and her boots were guiltless of a patch—that she was the possessor of a mine of wealth in two of the eight trunks belonging to her aunt, that she was travelling like any lady of the land with man- and maid-servant at her command, and that she was leaving work and care behind her for a month or two of novelty and rest.

When these agreeable facts were fully realized, and Aunt Pen had fallen asleep behind her veil, Debby took out a book, and indulged in her favorite luxury, soon forgetting past, present, and future in the inimitable history of Martin Chuzzlewit. The sun blazed, the cars rattled, children cried, ladies nodded, gentlemen longed for the solace of prohibited cigars, and newspapers were converted into sun-shades, nightcaps, and fans; but Debby read on, unconscious of all about her, even of the pair of eyes that watched her from the opposite corner of the car. A gentleman with a frank, strong-featured face sat therein, and amused himself by scanning with thoughtful gaze the countenances of his fellow-travellers. Stout Aunt Pen, dignified even in her sleep, was a "model of deportment" to the rising generation; but the student of human nature found a more attractive subject in her companion, the girl with an apple-blossom face and merry brown eyes, who sat smiling into her book, never heeding that her bonnet was awry, and the wind taking unwarrantable liberties with her ribbons and her hair.

Innocent Debby turned her pages, unaware that her fate sat opposite in the likeness of a serious, black-bearded gentleman, who watched the smiles rippling from her lips to her eyes with an interest that deepened as the minutes passed. If his paper had been full of anything but "Bronchial Troches" and "Spalding's Prepared Glue," he would have found more profitable employment; but it wasn't, and with the usual readiness of idle souls he fell into evil ways, and permitted curiosity, that feminine sin, to enter in and take possession of his manly mind. A great desire seized him to discover what book so interested his pretty neighbor; but a cover hid the name, and he was too distant to catch it on the fluttering leaves. Presently a stout Emerald-Islander, with her wardrobe oozing out of sundry paper parcels, vacated the seat behind the two ladies; and it was soon quietly occupied by the individual for whom Satan was finding such indecorous employment. Peeping round the little gray bonnet, past a brown braid and a fresh cheek, the young man's eye fell upon the words the girl was reading, and forgot to look away again. Books were the desire of his life; but an honorable purpose and an indomitable will kept him steady at his ledgers till he could feel that he had earned the right to read. Like wine to many another was an open page to him; he read a line, and, longing for more, took a hasty sip from his neighbor's cup, forgetting that it was a stranger's also.

Down the page went the two pairs of eyes, and the merriment from Debby's seemed to light up the sombre ones behind her with a sudden shine that softened the whole face and made it very winning. No wonder they twinkled, for Elijah Pogram spoke, and "Mrs. Hominy, the mother of the modern Gracchi, in the classical blue cap and the red cotton picket-handkerchief, came down the room in a procession of one." A low laugh startled Debby, though it was smothered like the babes in the Tower; and, turning, she beheld the trespasser scarlet with confusion, and sobered with a tardy sense of his transgression. Debby was not a starched young lady of the "prune and prism" school, but a frank, free-hearted little body, quick to read the sincerity of others, and to take looks and words at their real value. Dickens was her idol; and for his sake she could have forgiven a greater offense than this. The stranger's contrite countenance and respectful apology won her good-will at once; and with a finer courtesy than any Aunt Pen would have taught, she smilingly bowed her pardon, and taking another book from her basket, opened it, saying, pleasantly,

"Here is the first volume, if you like it, Sir. I can recommend it as an invaluable consolation for the discomforts of a summer day's journey, and it is heartily at your service."

As much surprised as gratified, the gentleman accepted the book,

Oyez! Oyez! — this is to declare that these forty col.?
designs to "Martin Chuzzlewit" were made
by me for F. W. Cosens Esq.e — & that there are
no more others. —
Sept. 1866.   *Hablot K. Browne*

Alcott adored the works of Charles Dickens and did a brilliant impersonation of Mrs.
Sairey Gamp, the bibulous and incompetent nurse immortalized in Martin
Chuzzlewit. *Sairey was clearly a favorite, for she pops up everywhere in Alcott's life*
and art (even in "Debby's Debut"), everlasting umbrella in tow. Here, in a drawing
by "Phiz," Mrs. Gamp pops in on the—very startled—artist himself.

and retired behind it with the sudden discovery that wrong-doing has its compensation in the pleasurable sensation of being forgiven. Stolen delights are well known to be specially saccharine; and much as this pardoned sinner loved books, it seemed to him that the interest of the story flagged, and that the enjoyment of reading was much enhanced by the proximity of a gray bonnet and a girlish profile. But Dickens soon proved more powerful than Debby, and she was forgotten, till, pausing to turn a leaf, the young man met her shy glance, as she asked, with the pleased expression of a child who has shared an apple with a playmate,

"Is it good?"

"Oh, very!"—and the man looked as honestly grateful for the book as the boy would have done for the apple.

Only five words in the conversation, but Aunt Pen woke, as if the watchful spirit of propriety had roused her to pluck her charge from the precipice on which she stood.

"Dora, I'm astonished at you! Speaking to strangers in that free manner is a most unladylike thing. How came you to forget what I have told you over and over again about a proper reserve?"

The energetic whisper reached the gentleman's ear, and he expected to be annihilated with a look when his offense was revealed; but he was spared that ordeal, for the young voice answered, softly,

"Don't faint, Aunt Pen; I only did as I'd be done by; for I had two books, and the poor man looked so hungry for something to read that I couldn't resist sharing my 'goodies.' He will see that I'm a countrified little thing in spite of my fine feathers, and won't be shocked at my want of rigidity and frigidity; so don't look dismal, and I'll be prim and proper all the rest of the way—if I don't forget it."

"I wonder who he is; may belong to some of our first families, and in that case it might be worth while to exert ourselves, you know. Did you learn his name, Dora?" whispered the elder lady.

Debby shook her head, and murmured, "Hush!"—but Aunt Pen had heard of matches being made in cars as well as in heaven; and as an experienced general, it became her to reconnoitre, when one of the enemy approached her camp. Slightly altering her position, she darted an all-comprehensive glance at the invader, who seemed entirely absorbed, for not an eyelash stirred during the scrutiny. It lasted but an instant, yet in that instant he was weighed and found wanting; for that experienced eye detected that his cravat was two inches wider than fashion ordained, that his coat was not of the latest style, that his gloves were mended, and his handkerchief neither cambric nor silk. That was enough, and sentence was passed forthwith—"Some respectable clerk, good-looking, but poor, and not at all the thing for Dora"; and Aunt Pen turned to adjust a voluminous green veil over her niece's bonnet, "To shield it from the dust, dear," which process also shielded the face within from the eye of man.

A curious smile, half mirthful, half melancholy, passed over their neighbor's lips; but his peace of mind seemed undisturbed, and he remained buried in his book till they reached ———, at dusk. As he returned it, he offered his services in procuring a carriage or attending to luggage; but Mrs. Carroll, with much dignity of aspect, informed him that her servants would attend to those matters, and, bowing gravely, he vanished into the night.

As they rolled away to the hotel, Debby was wild to run down to the beach whence came the solemn music of the sea, making the twilight beautiful. But Aunt Pen was too tired to do anything but sup in her own apartment and go early to bed; and Debby might as soon have proposed to walk up the Great Pyramid as to make her first appearance without that sage matron to mount guard over her; so she resigned herself to pie and patience, and fell asleep, wishing it were tomorrow.

At five A.M., a nightcapped head appeared at one of the myriad windows of the ——— Hotel, and remained there as if fascinated by the miracle of sunrise over the sea. Under her simplicity of character and girlish merriment Debby possessed a devout spirit and a nature full of the real poetry of life, two gifts that gave her dawning womanhood its sweetest charm, and made her what she was. As she looked out that summer dawn upon the royal marriage of the ocean and the sun, all petty hopes and longings faded out of sight, and her young face grew luminous with thoughts too deep for words. Her day was happier for that silent hour, her life richer for the aspirations that uplifted her like beautiful strong angels, and left a blessing when they went. The smile of the June sky touched her lips, the morning red seemed to linger on her cheek, and in her eye arose a light kindled by the shimmer of that broad sea of gold; for Nature rewarded her young votary well, and gave her beauty, when she offered love. How long she leaned there Debby did not know; steps from below roused her from her reverie, and led her back into the world again. Smiling at herself, she stole to bed, and lay wrapped in waking dreams as changeful as the shadows dancing on her chamber-wall.

The advent of her aunt's maid, Victorine, some two hours later, was the signal to be "up and doing"; and she meekly resigned herself into the hands of that functionary, who appeared to regard her in the light of an animated pin-cushion, as she performed the toilet-ceremonies with an absorbed aspect, which impressed her subject with a sense of the solemnity of the occasion.

"Now, Mademoiselle, regard yourself, and pronounce that you are ravishing," Victorine said at length, folding her hands with a sigh of satisfaction, as she fell back in an attitude of serene triumph.

Debby obeyed, and inspected herself with great interest and some astonishment; for there was a sweeping amplitude of array about the young lady whom she beheld in the much-befrilled gown and embroidered skirts, which somewhat alarmed her as to the navigation of a vessel "with such a spread of sail," while a curious sensation of being somebody else pervaded her from the crown of her head, with its shining coils of hair, to the soles of the French slippers, whose energies seemed to have been devoted to the production of marvellous rosettes.

"Yes, I look very nice, thank you; and yet I feel like a doll, helpless and fine, and fancy I was more of a woman in my fresh gingham, with a knot of clovers in my hair, than I am now. Aunt Pen was very kind to get me all these pretty things; but I'm afraid my mother would look horrified to see me in such a high state of flounce externally and so little room to breathe internally."

"Your mamma would not flatter me, Mademoiselle; but come now to Madame; she is waiting to behold you, and I have yet her toilet to make"; and, with a pitying shrug, Victorine followed Debby to her aunt's room.

"Charming! really elegant!" cried that lady, emerging from her towel with a rubicund visage. "Drop that braid half an inch lower, and pull the worked end of her handkerchief out of the right-hand pocket, Vic. There! Now, Dora, don't run about and get rumpled, but sit quietly down and practice repose till I am ready."

Debby obeyed, and sat mute, with the air of a child in its Sunday-best on a week-day, pleased with the novelty, but somewhat oppressed with the responsibility of such unaccustomed splendor, and utterly unable to connect any ideas of repose with tight shoes and skirts in a rampant state of starch.

"Well, you see, I bet on Lady Gay against Cockadoodle, and if you'll believe me— Hullo! there's Mrs. Carroll, and deuce take me if she hasn't got a girl with her! Look, Seguin!"—and Joe Leavenworth, a "man of the world," aged twenty, paused in his account of an exciting race to make the announcement.

Mr. Seguin, his friend and Mentor, as much his senior in worldly wickedness as in years, tore himself from his breakfast long enough to survey the newcomers, and then returned to it, saying, briefly,

"The old lady is worth cultivating—gives good suppers, and thanks you for eating them. The girl is well got up, but has no style, and blushes like a milkmaid. Better fight shy of her, Joe."

"Do you think so? Well, now I rather fancy that kind of thing. She's new, you see, and I get on with that sort of girl the best, for the old ones are so deuced knowing that a fellow has no chance of a— By the Lord Harry, she's eating bread and milk!"

Young Leavenworth whisked his glass into his eye, and Mr. Seguin put down his roll to behold the phenomenon. Poor Debby! her first step had been a wrong one.

All great minds have their weak points. Aunt Pen's was her breakfast, and the peace of her entire day depended upon the success of that
meal. Therefore being down rather late, the worthy lady concentrated
her energies upon the achievement of a copious repast, and, trusting to
former lessons, left Debby to her own resources for a few fatal moments. After the flutter occasioned by being scooped into her seat by a
severe-nosed waiter, Debby had only courage enough left to refuse tea
and coffee and accept milk. That being done, she took the first familiar
viand that appeared, and congratulated herself upon being able to get
her usual breakfast. With returning composure, she looked about her
and began to enjoy the buzz of voices, the clatter of knives and forks,
and the long lines of faces all intent upon the business of the hour; but
her peace was of short duration. Pausing for a fresh relay of toast,
Aunt Pen glanced toward her niece with the comfortable conviction
that her appearance was highly creditable; and her dismay can be
imagined, when she beheld that young lady placidly devouring a great
cup of brown-bread and milk before the eyes of the assembled multitude. The poor lady choked in her coffee, and between her gasps
whispered irefully behind her napkin,

"For Heaven's sake, Dora put away that mess! The Ellenboroughs
are directly opposite, watching everything you do. Eat that omelet, or
anything respectable, unless you want me to die of mortification."

Debby dropped her spoon, and, hastily helping herself from the
dish her aunt pushed toward her, consumed the leathery compound
with as much grace as she could assume, though unable to repress a
laugh at Aunt Pen's disturbed countenance. There was a slight lull in
the clatter, and the blithe sound caused several heads to turn toward
the quarter whence it came, for it was as unexpected and pleasant a
sound as a bobolink's song in a cage of shrill-voiced canaries.

"She's a jolly little thing and powerful pretty, so deuce take me if I
don't make up to the old lady and find out who the girl is. I've been
introduced to Mrs. Carroll at our house; but I suppose she won't
remember me till I remind her."

The "deuce" declining to accept of his repeated offers (probably because there was still too much honor and honesty in the boy), young Leavenworth sought out Mrs. Carroll on the piazza, as she and Debby were strolling there an hour later.

"Joe Leavenworth, my dear, from one of our first families—very wealthy—fine match—pray, be civil—smooth your hair, hold back your shoulders, and put down your parasol," murmured Aunt Pen, as the gentleman approached with as much pleasure in his countenance as it was consistent with manly dignity to express upon meeting two of the inferior race.

"My niece, Miss Dora Wilder. This is her first season at the beach, and we must endeavor to make it pleasant for her, or she will be getting homesick and running away to mamma," said Aunt Pen, in her society-tone, after she had returned his greeting, and perpetrated a polite fiction, by declaring that she remembered him perfectly, for he was the image of his father.

Mr. Leavenworth brought the heels of his varnished boots together with a click, and executed the latest bow imported, then stuck his glass in his eye and stared till it fell out (the glass, not the eye), upon which he fell into step with them, remarking,

"I shall be most happy to show the lions: they are deuced tame ones, so you needn't be alarmed, Miss Wilder."

Debby was good-natured enough to laugh; and, elated with that success, he proceeded to pour forth his stores of wit and learning in true collegian style, quite unconscious that the "jolly little thing" was looking him through and through with the smiling eyes that were producing such pleasurable sensations under the mosaic studs. They strolled toward the beach, and, meeting an old acquaintance, Aunt Pen fell behind, and beamed upon the young pair as if her prophetic eye even at this early stage beheld them walking altarward in a proper state of blond white vest and bridal awkwardness.

"Can you skip a stone, Mr. Leavenworth?" asked Debby, possessed with a mischievous desire to shock the piece of elegance at her side.

"Eh? what's that?" he inquired, with his head on one side, like an inquisitive robin.

Debby repeated her question, and illustrated it by sending a stone skimming over the water in the most scientific manner. Mr. Joe was painfully aware that this was not at all "the thing," that his sisters never did so, and that Seguin would laugh confoundedly, if he caught him at it; but Debby looked so irresistibly fresh and pretty under her rose-lined parasol that he was moved to confess that he had done such a thing, and to sacrifice his gloves by poking in the sand, that he might indulge in a like unfashionable pastime.

"You'll be at the hop to-night, I hope, Miss Wilder," he observed, introducing a topic suited to a young lady's mental capacity.

"Yes, indeed; for dancing is one of the joys of my life, next to husking and making hay"; and Debby polked a few steps along the beach, much to the edification of a pair of old gentlemen, serenely taking their first "constitutional."

"Making what?" cried Mr. Joe, polking after her.

"Hay; ah, that is the pleasantest fun in the world—and better exercise, my mother says, for soul and body, than dancing till dawn in crowded rooms, with everything in a state of unnatural excitement. If one wants real merriment, let him go into a new-mown field, where all the air is full of summer odors, where wild-flowers nod along the walls, where blackbirds make finer music than any band, and sun and wind and cheery voices do their part, while windrows rise, and great loads go rumbling through the lanes with merry brown faces atop. Yes, much as I like dancing, it is not to be compared with that; for in the one case we shut out the lovely world, and in the other we become a part of it, till by its magic labor turns to poetry, and we harvest something better than dried buttercups and grass."

As she spoke, Debby looked up, expecting to meet a glance of disapproval; but something in the simple earnestness of her manner had recalled certain boyish pleasures as innocent as they were hearty, which now contrasted very favorably with the later pastimes in which fast horses, and that lower class of animals, fast men, bore so large a part. Mr. Joe thoughtfully punched five holes in the sand, and for a moment Debby liked the expression of his face; then the old listless-ness returned, and, looking up, he said, with an air of ennui that was half sad, half ludicrous, in one so young and so generously endowed with youth, health, and the good gifts of this life,

"I used to fancy that sort of thing years ago, but I'm afraid I should find it a little slow now, though you describe it in such an inviting manner that I should be tempted to try it, if a hay-cock came in my way; for, upon my life, it's deuced heavy work loafing about at these watering-places all summer. Between ourselves, there's a deal of humbug about this kind of life, as you will find, when you've tried it as long as I have."

"Yes, I begin to think so already; but perhaps you can give me a few friendly words of warning from the stores of your experience, that I may be spared the pain of saying what so many look—'Grandma, the world is hollow; my doll is stuffed with sawdust; and I should like to go into a convent, if you please.' "

Debby's eyes were dancing with merriment; but they were demurely downcast, and her voice was perfectly serious.

The milk of human kindness had been slightly curdled for Mr. Joe by sundry College-tribulations; and having been "suspended," he very naturally vibrated between the inborn jollity of his temperament and the bitterness occasioned by his wrongs. He had lost at billiards the night before, had been hurried at breakfast, had mislaid his cigar-case, and splashed his boots; consequently the darker mood prevailed that morning, and when his counsel was asked, he gave it like one who had known the heaviest trials of this "Piljin Projiss of a wale."

"There's no justice in the world, no chance for us young people to enjoy ourselves, without some penalty to pay, some drawback to worry us like these confounded 'all-rounders.' Even here, where all seems free and easy, there's no end of gossips and spies who tattle and watch till you feel as if you lived in a lantern. 'Every one for himself, and the Devil take the hindmost': that's the principle they go on, and you have to keep your wits about you in the most exhausting manner, or you are done for before you know it. I've seen a good deal of this sort of thing, and hope you'll get on better than some do, when it's known that you are the rich Mrs. Carroll's niece; though you don't need that fact to enhance your charms—upon my life, you don't."

Debby laughed behind her parasol at this burst of candor; but her independent nature prompted her to make a fair beginning, in spite of Aunt Pen's polite fictions and well-meant plans.

"Thank you for your warning, but I don't apprehend much annoyance of that kind," she said, demurely. "Do you know, I think, if young ladies were truthfully labelled when they went into society, it would be a charming fashion and save a world of trouble? Something in this style: 'Arabella Marabout, aged nineteen, fortune $100,000, temper warranted'; 'Laura Eau-de-Cologne, aged twenty-eight, fortune $30,000, temper slightly damaged'; 'Deborah Wilder, aged eighteen, fortune, one pair of hands, one head, indifferently well filled, one heart, (not in the market), temper decided, and no expectations.' There, you see, that would do away with much of the humbug you lament, and we poor souls would know at once whether we were sought for our fortunes or ourselves, and that would be so comfortable!"

Mr. Leavenworth turned away, with a convicted sort of expression, as she spoke, and, making a spyglass of his hand, seemed to be watching something out at sea with absorbing interest. He had been guilty of a strong desire to discover whether Debby was an heiress, but had not expected to be so entirely satisfied on that important subject, and was dimly conscious that a keen eye had seen his anxiety, and a quick wit devised a means of setting it at rest forever. Somewhat disconcerted, he suddenly changed the conversation, and, like many another distressed creature, took to the water, saying briskly,

"By-the-by, Miss Wilder, as I've engaged to do the honors, shall I have the pleasure of bathing with you when the fun begins? As you are fond of hay-making, I suppose you intend to pay your respects to the old gentleman with the three-pronged pitchfork?"

"Yes, Aunt Pen means to put me through a course of salt water, and any instructions in the art of navigation will be gratefully received; for I never saw the ocean before, and labor under a firm conviction, that, once in, I never shall come out again till I am brought, like Mr. Mantilini, a 'damp, moist, unpleasant body.' "

As Debby spoke, Mrs. Carroll hove in sight, coming down before the wind with all sails set, and signals of distress visible long before she dropped anchor and came along-side. The devoted woman had been strolling slowly for the girl's sake, though oppressed with a mournful certainty that her most prominent feature was fast becoming a fine copper-color; yet she had sustained herself like a Spartan matron, till it suddenly occurred to her that her charge might be suffering a like

> Sea-change
> Into something rich and strange.

Her fears, however, were groundless, for Debby met her without a freckle, looking all the better for her walk; and though her feet were wet with chasing the waves, and her pretty gown the worse for salt water, Aunt Pen never chid her for the destruction of her raiment, nor uttered a warning word against an unladylike exuberance of spirits, but replied to her inquiry most graciously,

"Certainly, my love, we shall bathe at eleven, and there will be just time to get Victorine and our dresses; so run on to the house, and I will join you as soon as I have finished what I am saying to Mrs. Earle"—then added, in a stage-aside, as she put a fallen lock off the girl's forehead, "You are doing beautifully! He is evidently struck; make yourself interesting, and don't burn your nose, I beg of you."

Debby's bright face clouded over, and she walked on with so much stateliness that her escort wondered "what the deuce the old lady had done to her," and exerted himself to the utmost to recall her merry mood, but with indifferent success.

"Now I begin to feel more like myself, for this is getting back to first principles, though I fancy I look like the little old woman who fell asleep on the king's highway and woke up with abbreviated drapery; and you look funnier still, Aunt Pen," said Debby, as she tied on her pagoda-hat, and followed Mrs. Carroll, who walked out of her dressing-room an animated bale of blue cloth surmounted by a gigantic sun-bonnet.

Mr. Leavenworth was in waiting, and so like a blond-headed lobster in his scarlet suit that Debby could hardly keep her countenance as they joined the groups of bathers gathering along the breezy shore.

For an hour each day the actors and actresses who played their different roles at the ———— Hotel with such precision and success put off their masks and dared to be themselves. The ocean wrought the change, for it took old and young into its arms, and for a little while they played like children in their mother's lap. No falsehood could withstand its rough sincerity; for the waves washed paint and powder from worn faces, and left a fresh bloom there. No ailment could entirely resist its vigorous cure; for every wind brought healing on its wings, endowing many a meagre life with another year of health. No gloomy spirit could refuse to listen to its lullaby, and the spray baptized it with the subtile benediction of a cheerier mood. No rank held place there; for the democratic sea toppled down the greatest statesman in the land, and dashed over the bald pate of a millionaire with the same white-crested wave that stranded a poor parson on the beach and filled a fierce reformer's mouth with brine. No fashion ruled, but that which is as old as Eden—the beautiful fashion of simplicity. Belles dropped their affectations with their hoops, and ran about the shore blithe-hearted girls again. Young men forgot their vices and their follies, and were not ashamed of the real courage, strength, and skill they had tried to leave behind them with their boyish plays. Old men gathered shells with the little Cupids dancing on the sand, and were better for that innocent companionship; and young mothers never looked so beautiful as when they rocked their babies on the bosom of the sea.

Debby vaguely felt this charm, and, yielding to it, splashed and sang like any beach-bird, while Aunt Pen bobbed placidly up and down in a retired corner, and Mr. Leavenworth swam to and fro, expressing

his firm belief in mermaids, sirens, and the rest of the aquatic sisterhood, whose warbling no manly ear can resist.

"Miss Wilder, you must learn to swim. I've taught quantities of
young ladies, and shall be delighted to launch the 'Dora,' if you'll
accept me as a pilot. Stop a bit; I'll get a life-preserver"; and leaving
Debby to flirt with the waves, the scarlet youth departed like a flame of
fire.

A dismal shriek interrupted his pupil's play, and looking up, she
saw her aunt beckoning wildly with one hand, while she was groping
in the water with the other. Debby ran to her, alarmed at her tragic
expression, and Mrs. Carroll, drawing the girl's face into the privacy of
her big bonnet, whispered one awful word, adding, distractedly,

"Dive for them! oh, dive for them! I shall be perfectly helpless, if
they are lost!"

"I can't dive, Aunt Pen; but there is a man, let us ask him," said
Debby, as a black head appeared to windward.

But Mrs. Carroll's "nerves" had received a shock, and gathering up
her dripping garments, she fled precipitately along the shore and vanished into her dressing-room.

Debby's keen sense of the ludicrous got the better of her respect,
and peal after peal of laughter broke from her lips, till a splash behind
her put an end to her merriment, and, turning, she found that this
friend in need was her acquaintance of the day before. The gentleman
seemed pausing for permission to approach, with much the appearance
of a sagacious Newfoundland, wistful and wet.

"Oh, I'm very glad it's you, Sir!" was Debby's cordial greeting, as
she shook a drop off the end of her nose, and nodded, smiling.

The new comer immediately beamed upon her like an amiable
Triton, saying as they turned shoreward,

"Our first interview opened with a laugh on my side, and our
second with one on yours. I accept the fact as a good omen. Your
friend seemed in trouble; allow me to atone for my past misdemeanors
by offering my services now. But first let me introduce myself; and as I

believe in the fitness of things, let me present you with an appropriate card"; and, stooping, the young man wrote "Frank Evan" on the hard sand at Debby's feet.

The girl liked his manner, and, entering into the spirit of the thing, swept as grand a curtsy as her limited drapery would allow, saying, merrily,

"I am Debby Wilder, or Dora, as aunt prefers to call me; and instead of laughing, I ought be four feet under water, looking for something we have lost; but I can't dive, and my distress is dreadful as you see."

"What have you lost? I will look for it, and bring it back in spite of the kelpies, if it is a human possibility," replied Mr. Evan, pushing his wet locks out of his eyes, and regarding the ocean with a determined aspect.

Debby leaned toward him, whispering with solemn countenance,

"It is a set of teeth, Sir."

Mr. Evan was more a man of deeds than words, therefore he disappeared at once with a mighty splash, and after repeated divings and much laughter appeared bearing the chief ornament of Mrs. Penelope Carroll's comely countenance. Debby looked very pretty and grateful as she returned her thanks, and Mr. Evan was guilty of a secret wish that all the worthy lady's features were at the bottom of the sea, that he might have the satisfaction of restoring them to her attractive niece; but curbing this unnatural desire, he bowed, saying, gravely,

"Tell your aunt, if you please, that this little accident will remain a dead secret, so far as I am concerned, and I am very glad to have been of service at such a critical moment."

Whereupon Mr. Evan marched again into the briny deep, and Debby trotted away to her aunt, whom she found a clammy heap of blue flannel and despair. Mrs. Carroll's temper was ruffled, and though she joyfully rattled in her teeth, she said, somewhat testily, when Debby's story was done,

"Now that man will have a sort of claim on us, and we must be civil, whoever he is. Dear! dear! I wish it had been Joe Leavenworth instead. Evan—I don't remember any of our first families with connections of that name, and I dislike to be under obligations to a person of that sort, for there's no knowing how far he may presume; so, pray, be careful, Dora."

"I think you are very ungrateful, Aunt Pen; and if Mr. Evan should happen to be poor, it does not become me to turn up my nose at him, for I'm nothing but a make-believe myself just now. I don't wish to go down upon my knees to him, but I do intend to be as kind to him as I should to that conceited Leavenworth boy; yes, kinder even; for poor people value such things more, as I know very well."

Mrs. Carroll instantly recovered her temper, changed the subject, and privately resolved to confine her prejudices to her own bosom, as they seemed to have an aggravating effect upon the youthful person whom she had set her heart on disposing of to the best advantage.

Debby took her swimming-lesson with much success, and would have achieved her dinner with composure, if white-aproned gentlemen had not effectually taken away her appetite by whisking bills-of-fare into her hands, and awaiting her orders with a fatherly interest, which induced them to congregate mysterious dishes before her, and blandly rectify her frequent mistakes. She survived the ordeal, however, and at four P.M. went to drive with "that Leavenworth boy" in the finest turnout ——— could produce. Aunt Pen then came off guard, and with a sigh of satisfaction subsided into a peaceful doze, still murmuring, even in her sleep,

"Propinquity, my love, propinquity works wonders."

"Aunt Pen, are you a modest woman?" asked the young crusader against established absurdities, as she came into the presence-chamber that evening ready for the hop.

"Bless the child, what does she mean?" cried Mrs. Carroll, with a start that twitched her back hair out of Victorine's hands.

"Would you like to have a daughter of yours go to a party looking as I look?" continued her niece, spreading her airy dress, and standing very erect before her astonished relative.

"Why, of course I should, and be proud to own such a charming creature," regarding the slender white shape with much approbation— adding, with a smile, as she met the girl's eye,

"Ah, I see the difficulty, now; you are disturbed because there is not a bit of lace over these pretty shoulders of yours. Now don't be absurd, Dora; the dress is perfectly proper, or Madam Tiphany never would have sent it home. It is the fashion, child; and many a girl with such a figure would go twice as decolletee, and think nothing of it, I assure you."

Debby shook her head with an energy that set the pink heather- bells a-tremble in her hair, and her color deepened beautifully as she said, with reproachful eyes,

"Aunt Pen, I think there is a better fashion in every young girls' heart than any Madame Tiphany can teach. I am very grateful for all you have done for me, but I cannot go into public in such an undress as this; my mother would never allow it, and father never forgive it. Please don't ask me to, for indeed I cannot do it even for you."

Debby looked so pathetic that both mistress and maid broke into a laugh which somewhat reassured the young lady, who allowed her determined features to relax into a smile, as she said,

"Now, Aunt Pen, you want me to look pretty and be a credit to you; but how would you like to see my face the color of those gerani- ums all evening?"

"Why, Dora, you are out of your mind to ask such a thing, when you know it's the desire of my life to keep your color down and make you look more delicate," said her aunt, alarmed at the fearful prospect of a peony-faced protégée.

"Well, I should be anything but that, if I wore this gown in its present waistless condition; so here is a remedy which will prevent such a calamity and ease my mind."

As she spoke, Debby tied on her little blonde fichu with a gesture which left nothing more to be said.

Victorine scolded, and clasped her hands; but Mrs. Carroll, fearing to push her authority too far, made a virtue of necessity, saying, resignedly,

"Have your own way, Dora, but in return oblige me by being agreeable to such persons as I may introduce to you; and some day, when I ask a favor remember how much I hope to do for you, and grant it cheerfully."

"Indeed I will, Aunt Pen, if it is anything I can do without disobeying mother's 'notions,' as you call them. Ask me to wear an orange-colored gown, or dance with the plainest, poorest man in the room, and I'll do it; for there never was a kinder aunt than mine in all the world," cried Debby, eager to atone for her seeming wilfulness, and really grateful for her escape from what seemed to her benighted mind a very imminent peril.

Like a clover-blossom in a vase of camellias little Debby looked that night among the dashing or languid women who surrounded her; for she possessed the charm they had lost—the freshness of her youth. Innocent gayety sat smiling in her eyes, healthful roses bloomed upon her cheek, and maiden modesty crowned her like a garland. She was the creature that she seemed, and, yielding to the influence of the hour, danced to the music of her own blithe heart. Many felt the spell whose secret they had lost the power to divine, and watched the girlish figure as if it were symbol of their early aspirations dawning freshly from the dimness of their past. More than one old man thought again of some little maid whose love made his boyish days a pleasant memory to him now. More than one smiling fop felt the emptiness of his smooth speech, when the truthful eyes looked up into his own; and more than one pale woman sighed regretfully within herself, "I, too, was a happy-hearted creature once!"

"That Mr. Evan does not seem very anxious to claim our acquaintance, after all, and I think better of him on that account. Has he spoken to you to-night, Dora?" asked Mrs. Carroll, as Debby dropped down beside her after a "splendid polka."

"No, Ma'am, he only bowed. You see some people are not so

presuming as other people thought they were; for we are not the most attractive beings on the planet; therefore a gentleman can be polite and then forget us without breaking any of the Ten Commandments. Don't be offended with him yet, for he may prove to be some great creature with a finer pedigree than any of 'our first families.' Mr. Leavenworth, as you know everybody, perhaps you can relieve Aunt Pen's mind, by telling her something about the tall, brown man standing behind the lady with salmon-colored hair."

Mr. Joe, who was fanning the top of Debby's head with the best intentions in life, took a survey, and answered readily,

"Why, that's Frank Evan. I know him, and a deuced good fellow he is—though he don't belong to our set, you know."

"Indeed! pray, tell us something about him, Mr. Leavenworth. We met in the cars, and he did us a favor or two. Who and what is the man?" asked Mrs. Carroll, relenting at once toward a person who was favorably spoken of by one who did belong to her "set."

"Well, let me see," began Mr. Joe, whose narrative powers were not great. "He is a book-keeper in my Uncle Josh Loring's importing concern, and a powerful smart man, they say. There's some kind of clever story about his father's leaving a load of debts, and Frank's working a deuced number of years till they were paid. Good of him, wasn't it? Then, just as he was going to take things easier and enjoy life a bit, his mother died, and that rather knocked him up, you see. He fell sick, and came to grief generally, Uncle Josh said; so he was ordered off to get righted, and here he is, looking like a tombstone. I've a regard for Frank, for he took care of me through the smallpox a year ago, and I don't forget things of that sort; so, if you wish to be introduced, Mrs. Carroll, I'll trot him out with pleasure, and make a proud man of him."

Mrs. Carroll glanced at Debby, and as that young lady was regarding Mr. Joe with a friendly aspect, owing to the warmth of his words, she graciously assented, and the youth departed on his errand. Mr. Evan went through the ceremony with a calmness wonderful to behold, considering the position of one lady and the charms of the other, and soon glided into the conversation with the ease of a more accomplished courtier.

"Now I must tear myself away, for I'm engaged to that stout Miss Bandoline for this dance. She's a friend of my sister's, and I must do the civil, you know; powerful slow work it is, too, but I pity the poor soul upon my life, I do"; and Mr. Joe assumed the air of a martyr.

Debby looked up with a wicked smile in her eyes, as she said,

"Ah, that sounds very amiable here; but in five minutes you'll be murmuring in Miss Bandoline's ear, 'I've been pining to come to you this half hour, but I was obliged to take out that Miss Wilder, you see—countrified little thing enough, but not bad-looking, and has a rich aunt; so I've done my duty to her, but deuce take me if I can stand it any longer.' "

Mr. Evan joined in Debby's merriment; but Mr. Joe was so appalled at the sudden attack that he could only stammer a remonstrance and beat a hasty retreat, wondering how on earth she came to know that his favorite style of making himself agreeable to one young lady was by decrying another.

"Dora, my love, that is very rude, and 'Deuce' is not a proper expression for a woman's lips. Pray, restrain your lively tongue, for strangers may not understand that it is nothing but the sprightliness of your disposition which sometimes runs away with you."

"It was only a quotation, and I thought you would admire anything Mr. Leavenworth said, Aunt Pen," replied Debby, demurely.

Mrs. Carroll trod on her foot, and abruptly changed the conversation, by saying, with an appearance of deep interest,

"Mr. Evan, you are doubtless connected with the Malcoms of Georgia; for they, I believe, are descended from the ancient Evans of Scotland. They are a very wealthy and aristocratic family, and I remember seeing their coat-of-arms once: three bannocks and thistle."

Mr. Evan had been standing before them with a composure which impressed Mrs. Carroll with a belief in his gentle blood, for she remembered her own fussy, plebeian husband, whose fortune had never been able to purchase him the manners of a gentleman. Mr. Evan only grew a little more erect, as he replied, with an untroubled mien,

"I cannot claim relationship with the Malcoms of Georgia or the Evans of Scotland, I believe, Madam. My father was a farmer, my grandfather a blacksmith, and beyond that my ancestors may have been street-sweepers, for anything I know; but whatever they were, I fancy they were honest men, for that has always been our boast, though, like President Jackson's, our coat-of-arms is nothing but 'a pair of shirt-sleeves.' "

From Debby's eyes there shot a bright glance of admiration for the young man who could look two comely women in the face and serenely own that he was poor. Mrs. Carroll tried to appear at ease, and gliding out of personalities, expatiated on the comfort of "living in a land where fame and fortune were attainable by all who chose to earn them," and the contempt she felt for those "who had no sympathy with the humbler classes, no interest in the welfare of the race," and many more moral reflections as new and original as the Multiplication-Table or the Westminster Catechism. To all of which Mr. Evan listened with polite deference, though there was something in the keen intelligence of his eye that made Debby blush for shallow Aunt Pen, and rejoice when the good lady got out of her depth and seized upon a new subject as a drowning mariner would a hen-coop.

"Dora, Mr. Ellenborough is coming this way; you have danced with him but once, and he is a very desirable partner; so, pray, accept, if he asks you," said Mrs. Carroll, watching a far-off individual who seemed steering his zigzag course toward them.

"I never intend to dance with Mr. Ellenborough again, so please don't urge me, Aunt Pen"; and Debby knit her brows with a somewhat irate expression.

"My love, you astonish me! He is a most agreeable and accomplished young man—spent three years in Paris, moves in the first circles, and is considered an ornament to fashionable society. What can be your objection, Dora?" cried Mrs. Carroll, looking as alarmed as if her niece had suddenly announced her belief in the Koran.

"One of his accomplishments consists in drinking Champagne till he is not a 'desirable partner' for any young lady with a prejudice in favor of decency. His moving in 'circles' is just what I complain of; and if he is an ornament, I prefer my society undecorated. Aunt Pen, I cannot make the nice distinctions you would have me, and a sot in broadcloth is as odious as one in rags. Forgive me, but I cannot dance with that silver-labelled decanter again."

Debby was a genuine little piece of womanhood; and though she tried to speak lightly, her color deepened, as she remembered looks that had wounded her like insults, and her indignant eyes silenced the excuses rising to her aunt's lips. Mrs. Carroll began to rue the hour that she ever undertook the guidance of Sister Deborah's headstrong child, and for an instant heartily wished she had left her to bloom unseen in the shadow of the parsonage; but she concealed her annoyance, still hoping to overcome the girl's absurd resolve, by saying, mildly,

"As you please, dear; but if you refuse Mr. Ellenborough, you will be obliged to sit through the dance, which is your favorite, you know."

Debby's countenance fell, for she had forgotten that, and the Lancers was to her the crowning rapture of the night. She paused a moment, and Aunt Pen brightened; but Debby made her little sacrifice to principle as heroically as many a greater one had been made, and, with a wistful look down the long room, answered steadily, though her foot kept time to the first strains as she spoke,

"Then I will sit, Aunt Pen; for that is preferable to staggering about the room with a partner who has no idea of the laws of gravitation."

"Shall I have the honor of averting either calamity?" said Mr. Evan, coming to the rescue with a devotion beautiful to see; for dancing was nearly a lost art with him, and the Lancers to a novice is equal to a second Labyrinth of Crete.

"Oh, thank you!" cried Debby, tumbling fan, bouquet, and handkerchief into Mrs. Carroll's lap, with a look of relief that repaid him fourfold for the trials he was about to undergo. They went merrily away together, leaving Aunt Pen to wish that it was according to the laws of etiquette to rap officious gentlemen over the knuckles, when they introduce their fingers into private pies without permission from the chief cook. How the dance went Debby hardly knew, for the conversation fell upon books, and in the interest of her favorite theme she found even the "grand square" an impertinent interruption, while her own deficiencies became almost as great as her partner's; yet, when the music ended with a flourish, and her last curtsy was successfully achieved, she longed to begin all over again, and secretly regretted that she was engaged four deep.

"How do you like our new acquaintance, Dora?" asked Aunt Pen, following Joe Leavenworth with her eye, as the "yellow-haired laddie" whirled by with the ponderous Miss Flora. "Very much; and I'm glad we met as we did, for it makes things free and easy, and that is so agreeable in this ceremonious place," replied Debby, looking in quite an opposite direction.

"Well, I'm delighted to hear you say so, dear, for I was afraid you had taken a dislike to him, and he is really a very charming young man, just the sort of person to make a pleasant companion for a few weeks. These little friendships are part of the summer's amusement, and do no harm; so smile away, Dora, and enjoy yourself while you may."

"Yes, Aunt, I certainly will, and all the more because I have found a sensible soul to talk to. Do you know, he is very witty and well informed though he says he never had much time for self-cultivation? But I think trouble makes people wise, and he seems to have had a good deal, though he leaves it for others to tell of. I am glad you are willing I should know him, for I shall enjoy talking about my pet heroes with him as a relief from the silly chatter I must keep up most of the time."

Mrs. Carroll was a woman of one idea; and though a slightly

puzzled expression appeared in her face, she listened approvingly, and answered, with a gracious smile—

"Of course, I should not object to your knowing such a person, my love; but I'd no idea Joe Leavenworth was a literary man, or had known much trouble, except his father's death and his sister Clementina's runaway-marriage with her drawing-master."

Debby opened her brown eyes very wide, and hastily picked at the down on her fan, but had no time to correct her aunt's mistake, for the real subject of her commendations appeared at that moment, and Mrs. Carroll was immediately absorbed in the consumption of a large pink ice.

"THAT GIRL IS WHAT I call a surprise-party, now," remarked Mr. Joe confidentially to his cigar, as he pulled off his coat and stuck his feet up in the privacy of his own apartment. "She looks as mild as strawberries and cream till you come to the complimentary, then she turns on a fellow with that deuced satirical look of hers, and makes him feel like a fool. I'll try the moral dodge to-morrow, and see what effect that will have; for she is mighty taking, and I must amuse myself somehow, you know."

"HOW MANY YEARS will it take to change that fresh-hearted little girl into a fashionable belle, I wonder?" thought Frank Evan, as he climbed the four flights that led to his "sky-parlor."

"WHAT A CURIOUS world this is!" mused Debby, with her nightcap in her hand. "The right seems odd and rude, and the wrong respectable and easy, and this sort of life a merry-go-round, with no higher aim than pleasure. Well, I have made my Declaration of Independence, and Aunt Pen must be ready for a Revolution, if she taxes me too heavily."

As she leaned her hot cheek on her arm, Debby's eye fell on the quaint little cap made by the motherly hands that never were tired of working for her. She touched it tenderly, and love's simple magic swept the gathering shadows from her face, and left it clear again, as her thoughts flew home like birds into the shelter of their nest.

"Good night, mother! I'll face temptation steadily. I'll try to take life cheerily, and do nothing that shall make your dear face a reproach, when it looks into my own again."

Then Debby said her prayers like any pious child, and lay down to dream of pulling buttercups with Baby Bess, and singing in the twilight on her father's knee.

THE HISTORY OF Debby's first day might serve as a sample of most that followed, as week after week went by with varying pleasures and increasing interest to more than one young debutante. Mrs. Carroll did her best, but Debby was too simple for a belle, too honest for a flirt, too independent for a fine lady; she would be nothing but her sturdy little self, open as daylight, gay as a lark, and blunt as any Puritan. Poor Aunt Pen was in despair, till she observed that the girl often "took" with the very peculiarities which she was lamenting; this somewhat consoled her, and she tried to make the best of the pretty bit of homespun which would not and could not become velvet or brocade. Seguin, Ellenborough, & Co. looked with lordly scorn upon her, as a worm blind to their attractions. Miss MacFlimsy and her "set" quizzed her unmercifully behind her back, after being worsted in several passages of arms; and more than one successful mamma condoled with Aunt Pen upon the terribly defective education of her charge, till that stout matron could have found it in her heart to tweak off their caps and walk on them, like the irascible Betsey Trotwood.

But Debby had a circle of admirers who loved her with a sincerity few summer queens could boast; for they were real friends, won by gentle arts, and retained by the gracious sweetness of her nature. Moon-faced babies crowed and clapped their chubby hands when she passed by their wicker thrones; story-loving children clustered round her knee, and never were denied; pale invalids found wild-flowers on their pillows; and forlorn papas forgot the state of the money-market when she sang for them the homely airs their daughters had no time to learn. Certain plain young ladies poured their woes into her friendly ear, and were comforted; several smart Sophomores fell into a state of chronic stammer, blush, and adoration, when she took a motherly interest in their affairs; and a melancholy old Frenchman blessed her with the enthusiasm of his nation, because she put a posy in the button-hole of his rusty coat, and never failed to smile and bow as he passed by. Yet Debby was no Edgeworth heroine, preternaturally prudent, wise, and untemptable, she had a fine crop of piques, vanities, and dislikes growing up under this new style of cultivation. She loved admiration, enjoyed her purple and fine linen, hid new-born envy, disappointed hope, and wounded pride behind a smiling face, and often thought with a sigh of the humdrum duties that awaited her at home. But under the airs and graces Aunt Pen cherished with such sedulous care under the flounces and furbelows Victorine daily adjusted with groans, under the polish which she acquired with feminine ease, the girl's heart still beat steadfast and strong, and conscience kept watch and ward that no traitor should enter in to surprise the citadel which mother-love had tried to garrison so well.

In pursuance of his sage resolve, Mr. Joe tried the "moral dodge," as he elegantly expressed it, and, failing in that, followed it up with the tragic, religious, negligent, and devoted ditto; but acting was not his forte, so Debby routed him in all; and at last, when he was at his wit's end for an idea, she suggested one, and completed her victory by saying pleasantly,

"You took me behind the curtain too soon, and now the paste-diamonds and cotton-velvet don't impose upon me a bit. Just be your natural self, and we shall get on nicely, Mr. Leavenworth."

The novelty of the proposal struck his fancy, and after a few relapses it was carried into effect, and thenceforth, with Debby, he became the simple, good-humored lad Nature designed him to be, and, as a proof of it, soon fell very sincerely in love.

Frank Evan, seated in the parquet of society, surveyed the dress-circle with much the same expression that Debby had seen during Aunt Pen's oration; but he soon neglected that amusement to watch several actors in the drama going on before his eyes, while a strong desire to perform a part therein slowly took possession of his mind. Debby always had a look of welcome when he came, always treated him with the kindness of a generous woman who has had an opportunity to forgive, and always watched the serious, solitary man with a great compassion for his loss, a growing admiration for his upright life. More than once the beach-birds saw two figures pacing the sands at sunrise with the peace of early day upon their faces and the light of a kindred mood shining in their eyes. More than once the friendly ocean made a third in the pleasant conversation, and its low undertone came and went between the mellow bass and the silvery treble of the human voices with a melody that lent another charm to interviews which soon grew wondrous sweet to man and maid. Aunt Pen seldom saw the twain together, seldom spoke of Evan; and Debby held her peace, for, when she planned to make her innocent confessions, she found that what seemed much to her was nothing to another ear and scarcely worth the telling; so, unconscious as yet whither the green path led, she went on her way, leading two lives, one rich and earnest, hoarded deep within herself, the other frivolous and gay for all the world to criticize. But those venerable spinsters, the Fates, took the matter into their own hands, and soon got the better of those short-sighted matrons, Mesdames Grundy and Carroll; for, long before they knew it, Frank and Debby had begun to read together a book greater than Dickens ever wrote, and when they had come to the fairest part of the sweet story Adam first told Eve, they looked for the name upon the title-page, and found that it was "Love."

Eight weeks came and went—eight wonderfully happy weeks to Debby and her friend; for "propinquity" had worked more wonders than poor Mrs. Carroll knew, as the only one she saw or guessed was the utter captivation of Joe Leavenworth. He had become "himself" to such an extent that a change of identity would have been a relief; for the object of his adoration showed no signs of relenting, and he began to fear, that, as Debby said, her heart was "not in the market." She was always friendly, but never made those interesting betrayals of regard which are so encouraging to youthful gentlemen "who fain would climb, yet fear to fall." She never blushed when he pressed her hand, never fainted or grew pale when he appeared with a smashed trotting-wagon and a black eye, and actually slept through a serenade that would have won any other woman's soul out of her body with its despairing quavers. Matters were getting desperate; for horses lost their charms, "flowing bowls" palled upon his lips, ruffled shirt-bosoms no longer delighted him, and hops possessed no soothing power to allay the anguish of his mind. Mr. Seguin, after unavailing ridicule and pity, took compassion on him, and from his large experience suggested a remedy, just as he was departing for a more congenial sphere.

"Now don't be an idiot, Joe, but, if you want to keep your hand in and go through a regular chapter of flirtation, just right about face, and devote yourself to some one else. Nothing like jealousy to teach womankind their own minds, and a touch of it will bring little Wilder round in a jiffy. Try it, my boy, and good luck to you!"—with which Christian advice Mr. Seguin slapped his pupil on the shoulder, and disappeared, like a modern Mephistopheles, in a cloud of cigar-smoke.

"I'm glad he's gone, for in my present state of mind he's not up to my mark at all. I'll try his plan, though, and flirt with Clara West; she's engaged, so it won't damage her affections; her lover isn't here, so it won't disturb his; and, by Jove! I must do something, for I can't stand this suspense."

Debby was infinitely relieved by this new move, and infinitely amused as she guessed the motive that prompted it; but the more contented she seemed, the more violently Mr. Joe flirted with her rival, till at last weak-minded Miss Clara began to think her absent George the most undesirable of lovers, and to mourn that she ever said "Yes" to a merchant's clerk, when she might have said it to a merchant's son. Aunt Pen watched and approved this stratagem, hoped for the best results, and believed the day won when Debby grew pale and silent, and followed with her eyes the young couple who were playing battledoor and shuttlecock with each other's hearts, as if she took some interest in the game. But Aunt Pen clashed her cymbals too soon; for Debby's trouble had a better source than jealousy, and in the silence of the sleepless nights that stole her bloom she was taking counsel of her own full heart, and resolving to serve another woman as she would herself be served in a like peril, though etiquette was outraged and the customs of polite society turned upside down.

"Look, Aunt Pen! what lovely shells and moss I've got! Such a splendid scramble over the rocks as I've had with Mrs. Duncan's boys! It seemed so like home to run and sing with a troop of topsy-turvy children that it did me good; and I wish you had all been there to see," cried Debby, running into the drawing room, one day, where Mrs. Carroll and a circle of ladies sat enjoying a dish of highly flavored scandal, as they exercised their eyesight over fancy-work.

"My dear Dora, spare my nerves; and if you have any regard for the proprieties of life, don't go romping in the sun with a parcel of noisy boys. If you could see what an object you are, I think you would try to imitate Miss Clara, who is always a model of elegant repose."

Miss West primmed up her lips, and settled a fold in her ninth flounce, as Mrs. Carroll spoke, while the whole group fixed their eyes with dignified disapproval on the invader of their refined society. Debby had come like a fresh wind into a sultry room; but no one welcomed the healthful visitant, no one saw a pleasant picture in the bright-faced girl with wind-tossed hair and rustic hat heaped with moss and many-tinted shells; they only saw that her gown was wet, her gloves forgotten, and her scarf trailing at her waist in a manner no well-bred lady could approve. The sunshine faded out of Debby's face, and there was a touch of bitterness in her tone, as she glanced at the circle of fashion-plates, saying with an earnestness which caused Miss West to open her pale eyes to their widest extent,

"Aunt Pen, don't freeze me yet—don't take away my faith in simple things, but let me be a child a little longer—let me play and sing and keep my spirit blithe among the dandelions and the robins while I can; for trouble comes soon enough, and all my life will be the richer and the better for a happy youth.

Mrs. Carroll had nothing at hand to offer in reply to this appeal, and four ladies dropped their work to stare; but Frank Evan looked in from the piazza, saying, as he beckoned like a boy,

"I'll play with you, Miss Dora; come and make sand pies upon the shore. Please let her, Mrs. Carroll; we'll be very good, and not wet our pinafores or feet."

Without waiting for permission, Debby poured her treasures in the lap of a certain lame Freddy, and went away to a kind of play she had never known before. Quiet as a chidden child, she walked beside her companion, who looked down at the little figure, longing to take it on his knee and call the sunshine back again. That he dared not do; but accident, the lover's friend, performed the work, and did him a good turn beside. The old Frenchman was slowly approaching, when a frolicsome wind whisked off his hat and sent it skimming along the beach. In spite of her late lecture, away went Debby, and caught the truant chapeau just as a wave was hurrying up to claim it. This restored her cheerfulness, and when she returned, she was herself again.

"A thousand thanks; but does Mademoiselle remember the forfeit I might demand to add to the favor she has already done me?" asked the gallant old gentleman, as Debby took the hat off her own head, and presented it with a martial salute.

"Ah, I had forgotten that; but you may claim it, Sir—indeed, you may; I only wish I could do something more to give you pleasure"; and Debby looked up into the withered face which had grown familiar to her, with kind eyes, full of pity and respect.

Her manner touched the old man very much; he bent his gray head before her, saying, gratefully,

"My child, I am not good enough to salute these blooming cheeks; but I shall pray the Virgin to reward you for the compassion you bestow on the poor exile, and I shall keep your memory very green through all my life."

He kissed her hand, as if it were a queen's, and went on his way, thinking of the little daughter whose death left him childless in a foreign land.

Debby softly began to sing, "Oh, come unto the yellow sands!" but stopped in the middle of a line, to say,

"Shall I tell you why I did what Aunt Pen would call a very unladylike and improper thing, Mr. Evan?"

"If you will be so kind"; and her companion looked delighted at the confidence about to be reposed in him.

"Somewhere across this great wide sea I hope I have a brother," Debby said, with softened voice and a wistful look into the dim horizon. "Five years ago he left us, and we have never heard from him since, except to know that he landed safely in Australia. People tell us he is dead; but I believe he will yet come home; and so I love to help and pity any man who needs it, rich or poor, young or old, hoping that as I do by them some tender-hearted woman far away will do by Brother Will."

As Debby spoke, across Frank Evan's face there passed the look that seldom comes but once to any young man's countenance; for suddenly the moment dawned when love asserted its supremacy, and putting pride, doubt, and fear underneath its feet, ruled the strong heart royally and bent it to its will. Debby's thoughts had floated across the sea; but they came swiftly back when her companion spoke again, steadily and slow, but with a subtle change in tone and manner which arrested them at once.

"Miss Dora, if you should meet a man who had known a laborious youth, a solitary manhood, who had no sweet domestic ties to make home beautiful and keep his nature warm, who longed most ardently to be so blessed, and made it the aim of his life to grow more worthy the good gift, should it ever come—if you should learn that you possessed the power to make this fellow-creature's happiness, could you find it in your gentle heart to take compassion on him for the love of 'Brother Will'?"

Debby was silent, wondering why heart and nerves and brain were stirred by such a sudden thrill, why she dared not look up, and why, when she desired so much to speak, she could only answer, in a voice that sounded strange to her own ears,

"I cannot tell."

Still, steadily and slow, with strong emotion deepening and soften-ing his voice, the lover at her side went on—

"Will you ask yourself this question in some quiet hour? For such a man has lived in the sunshine of your presence for eight happy weeks, and now, when his holiday is done, he finds that the old solitude will be more sorrowful than ever, unless he can discover whether his sum-mer dream will change into a beautiful reality. Miss Dora, I have very little to offer you; a faithful heart to cherish you, a strong arm to work for you, an honest name to give into your keeping—these are all; but if they have any worth in your eyes, they are most truly yours forever."

Debby was steadying her voice to reply, when a troop of bathers came shouting down the bank, and she took flight into her dressing-room, there to sit staring at the wall, till the advent of Aunt Pen forced her to resume the business of the hour by assuming her aquatic attire and stealing shyly down into the surf.

Frank Evan, still pacing in the footprints they had lately made, watched the lithe figure tripping to and fro, and, as he looked, mur-mured to himself the last line of a ballad Debby sometimes sang,

"Dance light! for my heart it lies under your feet, love!"

Presently a great wave swept Debby up, and stranded her very near him, much to her confusion and his satisfaction. Shaking the spray out her eyes, she was hurrying away, when Frank said,

"You will trip, Miss Dora; let me tie these strings for you"; and, suiting the action to the word, he knelt down and began to fasten the cords of her bathing shoe.

Debby stood looking down at the tall head bent before her, with a curious sense of wonder that a look from her could make a strong man flush and pale, as he had done and she was trying to concoct some friendly speech, when Frank, still fumbling at the knots, said very earnestly and low,

"Forgive me, if I am selfish in pressing for an answer; but I must go tomorrow, and a single word will change my whole future for the better or the worse. Won't you speak it, Dora?"

If they had been alone, Debby would have put her arms about his neck, and said it with all her heart; but she had a presentiment that she should cry, if her love found vent; and here forty pairs of eyes were on them, and salt water seemed superfluous. Besides, Debby had not breathed the air of coquetry so long without a touch of the infection; and the love of power, that lies dormant in the meekest woman's breast, suddenly awoke and tempted her.

"If you catch me before I reach that rock, perhaps I will say 'Yes,'" was her unexpected answer; and before her lover caught her meaning, she was floating leisurely away.

Frank was not in bathing-costume, and Debby never dreamed that he would take her at her word; but she did not know the man she had to deal with; for, taking no second thought, he flung hat and coat away, and dashed into the sea. This gave a serious aspect to Debby's foolish jest. A feeling of dismay seized her, when she saw a resolute face dividing the waves behind her, and thought of the rash challenge she had given; but she had a spirit of her own, and had profited well by Mr. Joe's instructions; so she drew a long breath, and swam as if for life, instead of love. Evan was incumbered by his clothing, and Debby had much the start of him; but, like a second Leander, he hoped to win his Hero, and, lending every muscle to the work, gained rapidly upon the little hat which was his beacon through the foam. Debby heard the deep breathing drawing nearer and nearer, as her pursuer's strong arms cleft the water and sent it rippling past her lips. Something like terror took possession of her for the strength seemed going out of her limbs, and the rock appeared to recede before her; but the unconquerable blood of the Pilgrims was in her veins and "Nil desperandum" her motto; so, setting her teeth, she muttered, defiantly,

"I'll not be beaten, if I go to the bottom!"

A great splashing arose, and when Evan recovered the use of his eyes, the pagoda-hat had taken a sudden turn, and seemed making for the farthest point of the goal. "I am sure of her now," thought Frank; and, like a gallant sea-god, he bore down upon his prize, clutching it with a shout of triumph. But the hat was empty, and like a mocking echo came Debby's laugh, as she climbed, exhausted, to a cranny in the rock.

"A very neat thing, by Jove! Deuce take me if you a'n't 'an honor to your teacher, and terror to the foe,' Miss Wilder," cried Mr. Joe, as he came up from a solitary cruise and dropped anchor at her side. "Here, bring along the hat, Evan; I'm going to crown the victor with appropriate what-d'-ye-call-'ems," he continued, pulling a handful of sea-weed that looked like well-boiled greens.

Frank came up, smiling; but his lips were white, and in his eye a look Debby could not meet; so, being full of remorse, she naturally assumed an air of gayety, and began to sing the merriest air she knew, merely because she longed to throw herself upon the stones and cry violently.

"It was 'most as exciting as a regatta, and you pulled well, Evan; but you had too much ballast aboard, and Miss Wilder ran up false colors just in time to save her ship. What was the wager?" asked the lively Joseph complacently surveying his marine millinery, which would have scandalized a fashionable mermaid.

"Only a trifle," answered Debby, knotting up her braids with a revengeful jerk.

"It's taken the wind out of your sails, I fancy, Evan, for you look immensely Byronic with the starch minus in your collar and your hair in a poetic toss. Come, I'll try a race with you; and Miss Wilder will dance all the evening with the winner. Bless the man, what's he doing down there? Burying sunfish, hey?"

Frank had been sitting below them on a narrow strip of sand, absently piling up a little mound that bore some likeness to a grave. As his companion spoke, he looked at it, and a sudden flush of feeling swept across his face, as he replied,

"No, only a dead hope."

"Deuce take it, yes, a good many of that sort of craft founder in these waters as I know to my sorrow"; and, sighing tragically, Mr. Joe turned to help Debby from her perch, but she had glided silently into the sea and was gone.

For the next four hours the poor girl suffered the sharpest pain she had ever known; for now she clearly saw the strait her folly had betrayed her into. Frank Evan was a proud man, and would not ask her love again, believing she had tacitly refused it; and how could she tell him that she had trifled with the heart she wholly loved and longed to make her own? She could not confide in Aunt Pen, for that worldly lady would have no sympathy to bestow. She longed for her mother; but there was no time to write, for Frank was going on the morrow— might even then be gone; and as this fear came over her, she covered up her face and wished that she were dead. Poor Debby! her last mistake was sadder than her first, and she was reaping a bitter harvest from her summer's sowing. She sat and thought till her cheeks burned and her temples throbbed; but she dared not ease her pain with tears. The gong sounded like a Judgment-Day trump of doom, and she trembled at the idea of confronting many eyes with such a telltale face; but she could not stay behind, for Aunt Pen must know the cause. She tried to play her hard part well; but wherever she looked, some fresh anxiety appeared, as if every fault and folly of those months had blossomed suddenly within the hour. She saw Frank Evan more sombre and more solitary than when she met him first, and cried regretfully within herself, "How could I so forget the truth I owed him?" She saw Clara West watching with eager eyes for the coming of young Leavenworth, and sighed, "This is the fruit of my wicked vanity!" She saw Aunt Pen regarding her with an anxious face, and longed to say, "Forgive me, for I have not been sincere!" At last, as her trouble grew, she resolved to go away and have a quiet "think"—a remedy which had served her in many a lesser perplexity; so, stealing out, she went to a grove of cedars usually deserted at that hour. But in ten minutes Joe Leavenworth appeared at the door of the summer-house, and, looking in, said, with a well-acted start of pleasure and surprise,

"Beg pardon, I thought there was no one here. My dear Miss Wilder, you look contemplative; but I fancy it wouldn't do to ask the subject of your meditations, would it?"

He paused with such an evident intention of remaining that Debby resolved to make use of the moment, and ease her conscience of one care that burdened it; therefore she answered his questions with her usual directness,

"My meditations were partly about you."

Mr. Joe was guilty of the weakness of blushing violently and looking immensely gratified; but his rapture was of short duration, for Debby went on very earnestly,

"I believe I am going to do what you may consider a very impertinent thing; but I would rather be unmannerly than unjust to others or untrue to my own sense of right. Mr. Leavenworth, if you were an older man, I should not dare to say this to you; but I have brothers of my own, and, remembering how many unkind things they do for want of thought, I venture to remind you that a woman's heart is a perilous plaything, and too tender to be used for a selfish purpose or an hour's pleasure. I know this kind of amusement is not considered wrong; but it is wrong, and I cannot shut my eyes to the fact, or sit silent while another woman is allowed to deceive herself and wound the heart that trusts her. Oh if you love your own sisters, be generous, be just, and do not destroy that poor girl's happiness, but go away before your sport becomes a bitter pain to her!"

Joe Leavenworth had stood staring at Debby with a troubled countenance, feeling as if all the misdemeanors of his life were about to be paraded before him; but, as he listened to her plea, the womanly spirit that prompted it appealed more loudly than her words, and in his really generous heart he felt regret for what had never seemed a fault before. Shallow as he was, nature was stronger than education, and he admired and accepted what many a wiser, worldlier man would have resented with anger or contempt. He loved Debby with all his little might; he meant to tell her so, and graciously present his fortune and himself for her acceptance; but now, when the moment came, the well-turned speech he had prepared vanished from his memory, and with the better eloquence of feeling he blundered out his passion like a very boy.

"Miss Dora, I never meant to make trouble between Clara and her lover; upon my soul I didn't, and wish Seguin had not put the notion into my head, since it has given you pain. I only tried to pique you into showing some regret when I neglected you; but you didn't and then I got desperate and didn't care what became of any one. Oh, Dora, if you knew how much I loved you, I am sure you'd forgive it, and let me prove my repentance by giving up everything that you dislike. I mean what I say; upon my life I do; and I'll keep my word, if you will only let me hope."

If Debby had wanted a proof of her love for Frank Evan, she might have found it in the fact that she had words enough at her command now, and no difficulty in being sisterly pitiful toward her second suitor.

"Please get up," she said; for Mr. Joe, feeling very humble and very earnest, had gone down upon his knees, and sat there entirely regardless of his personal appearance.

He obeyed; and Debby stood looking up at him with her kindest aspect, as she said, more tenderly than she had ever spoken to him before,

"Thank you for the affection you offer me, but I cannot accept it, for I have nothing to give you in return but the friendliest regard, the most sincere good-will. I know you will forgive me, and do for your own sake the good things you would have done for mine, that I may add to my esteem a real respect for one who has been very kind to me."

"I'll try—indeed, I will, Miss Dora, though it will be powerful hard without yourself for a help and a reward."

Poor Joe choked a little, but called up an unexpected manliness, and added, stoutly,

"Don't think I shall be offended at your speaking so, or saying 'No' to me—not a bit; it's all right, and I'm much obliged to you. I might have known you couldn't care for such a fellow as I am, and don't blame you, for nobody in the world is good enough for you. I'll go away at once, I'll try to keep my promise, and I hope you'll be very happy all your life."

He shook Debby's hands heartily, and hurried down the steps, but at the bottom paused and looked back. Debby stood upon the threshold with sunshine dancing on her winsome face, and kind words trembling on her lips; for the moment it seemed impossible to part, and, with an impetuous gesture, he cried to her,

"Oh, Dora, let me stay and try to win you! for everything is possible to love, and I never knew how dear you were to me till now!"

There were sudden tears in the young man's eyes, the flush of a genuine emotion on his cheek, the tremor of an ardent longing in his voice, and, for the first time, a very true affection strengthened his whole countenance. Debby's heart was full of penitence; she had given so much pain to more than one that she longed to atone for it—longed to do some very friendly thing, and soothe some trouble such as she herself had known. She looked into the eager face uplifted to her own and thought of Will, then stooped and touched her lover's forehead with the lips that softly whispered, "No."

If she had cared for him, she never would have done it; poor Joe knew that, and murmuring an incoherent "Thank you!" he rushed away, feeling very much as he remembered to have felt when his baby sister died and he wept his grief away upon his mother's neck. He began his preparations for departure at once, in a burst of virtuous energy quite refreshing to behold, thinking within himself, as he flung his cigar-case into the grate, kicked a billiard-ball into a corner, and suppressed his favorite allusion to the Devil,

"This is a new sort of thing to me, but I can bear it, and upon my life I think I feel the better for it already."

And so he did; for though he was no Augustine to turn in an hour from worldly hopes and climb to sainthood through long years of inward strife, yet in aftertimes no one knew how many false steps had been saved, how many small sins repented of, through the power of the memory that far away a generous woman waited to respect him, and in his secret soul he owned that one of the best moments of his life was that in which little Debby Wilder whispered "No," and kissed him.

As he passed from sight, the girl leaned her head upon her hand, thinking sorrowfully to herself,

"What right had I to censure him, when my own actions are so far from true? I have done a wicked thing, and as an honest girl I should undo it, if I can. I have broken through the rules of a false propriety for Clara's sake; can I not do as much for Frank's? I will. I'll find him, if I search the house—and tell him all, though I never dare to look him in the face again, and Aunt Pen sends me home to-morrow."

Full of zeal and courage, Debby caught up her hat and ran down the steps, but, as she saw Frank Evan coming up the path, a sudden panic fell upon her, and she could only stand mutely waiting his approach.

It is asserted that Love is blind; and on the strength of that popular delusion novel heroes and heroines go blundering through three volumes of despair with the plain truth directly under their absurd noses: but in real life this theory is not supported; for to a living man the countenance of a loving woman is more eloquent than any language, more trustworthy than a world of proverbs, more beautiful than the sweetest love-lay ever sung.

Frank looked at Debby, and "all her heart stood up in her eyes," as she stretched her hands to him, though her lips only whispered very low,

"Forgive me, and let me say the 'Yes' I should have said so long ago."

Had she required any assurance of her lover's truth, or any reward for her own, she would have found it in the change that dawned so swiftly in his face, smoothing the lines upon his forehead, lighting the gloom of his eye, stirring his firm lips with a sudden tremor and making his touch as soft as it was strong. For a moment both stood very still, while Debby's tears streamed down like summer rain; then Frank drew her into the green shadow of the grove, and its peace soothed her like a mother's voice, till she looked up smiling with a shy delight her glance had never known before. The slant sunbeams dropped a benediction on their heads, the robins peeped, and the cedars whispered, but no rumor of what further passed ever went beyond the precincts of the wood; for such hours are sacred, and

Nature guards the first blossoms of a human love as tenderly as she nurses May-flowers underneath the leaves.

Mrs. Carroll had retired to her bed with a nervous headache, leaving Debby to the watch and ward of friendly Mrs. Earle, who performed her office finely by letting her charge entirely alone. In her dreams Aunt Pen was just imbibing a copious draught of Champagne at the wedding-breakfast of her niece, "Mrs. Joseph Leavenworth," when she was roused by the bride elect, who passed through the room with a lamp and a shawl in her hand.

"What time is it, and where are you going, dear?" she asked, dozily wondering if the carriage for the wedding-tour was at the door so soon.

"It's only nine, and I am going for a sail, Aunt Pen."

As Debby spoke, the light flashed full into her face, and a sudden thought into Mrs. Carroll's mind. She rose up from her pillow, looking as stately in her nightcap as Maria Theresa is said to have done in like unassuming head-gear.

"Something has happened, Dora! What have you done? What have you said? I insist upon knowing immediately," she demanded, with somewhat startling brevity.

"I have said 'No' to Mr. Leavenworth and 'Yes' to Mr. Evan; and I should like to go home to-morrow, if you please," was the equally concise reply.

Mrs. Carroll fell flat in her bed, and lay there stiff and rigid as Morlena Kenwigs. Debby gently drew the curtains, and stole away, leaving Aunt Pen's wrath to effervesce before morning.

The moon was hanging luminous and large on the horizon's edge, sending shafts of light before her till the melancholy ocean seemed to smile, and along that shining pathway happy Debby and her lover floated into that new world where all things seem divine.

PERILOUS PLAY

"I F SOMEONE DOES NOT PROPOSE A NEW AND INTERESTING AMUSE-ment, I shall die of ennui!" said pretty Belle Daventry, in a tone of despair. "I have read all my books, used up all my Berlin wools, and it's too warm to go to town for more. No one can go sailing yet, as the tide is out; we are all nearly tired to death of cards, croquet, and gossip, so what shall we do to while away this endless afternoon? Dr. Meredith, I command you to invent and propose a new game in five minutes."

"To hear is to obey," replied the young man, who lay in the grass at her feet, as he submissively slapped his forehead, and fell a-thinking with all his might.

Holding up her finger to preserve silence, Belle pulled out her watch and waited with an expectant smile. The rest of the young party, who were indolently scattered about under the elms, drew nearer, and brightened visibly, for Dr. Meredith's inventive powers were well-known, and something refreshingly novel might be expected from him. One gentleman did not stir, but then he lay within earshot, and merely turned his fine eyes from the sea to the group before him. His glance rested a moment on Belle's piquant figure, for she looked very pretty with her bright hair blowing in the wind, one plump white arm extended to keep order, and one little foot, in a distracting slipper, just visible below the voluminous folds of her dress. Then the glance passed to another figure, sitting somewhat apart in a cloud of white muslin, for an airy burnoose floated from head and shoulders, showing only a singularly charming face. Pale and yet brilliant, for the Southern eyes were magnificent, the clear olive cheeks contrasted well with darkest hair; lips like a pomegranate flower, and delicate, straight brows, as mobile as the lips. A cluster of crimson flowers, half falling from the loose black braids, and a golden bracelet of Arabian coins on the slender wrist were the only ornaments she wore, and became her better than the fashionable frippery of her companions. A book lay on her lap, but her eyes, full of a passionate melancholy, were fixed on the sea, which glittered round an island green and flowery as a summer paradise. Rose St. Just was as beautiful as her Spanish mother, but had inherited the pride and reserve of her English father; and this pride was the thorn which repelled lovers from the human flower. Mark Done sighed as he looked, and as if the sigh, low as it was, roused her from her reverie, Rose flashed a quick glance at him, took up her book, and went on reading the legend of "The Lotus Eaters."

"Time is up now, Doctor," cried Belle, pocketing her watch with a flourish.

"Ready to report," answered Meredith, sitting up and producing a little box of tortoiseshell and gold.

"How mysterious! What is it? Let me see, first!" And Belle removed the cover, looking like an inquisitive child. "Only bonbons; how stupid! That won't do, sir. We don't want to be fed with sugarplums. We demand to be amused."

"Eat six of these despised bonbons, and you *will* be amused in a new, delicious, and wonderful manner," said the young doctor, laying half a dozen on a green leaf and offering them to her.

"Why, what are they?" she asked, looking at him askance.

"Hashish; did you never hear of it?"

"Oh, yes; it's that Indian stuff which brings one fantastic visions, isn't it? I've always wanted to see and taste it, and now I will," cried Belle, nibbling at one of the bean-shaped comfits with its green heart.

"I advise you not to try it. People do all sorts of queer things when they take it. I wouldn't for the world," said a prudent young lady warningly, as all examined the box and its contents.

"Six can do no harm, I give you my word. I take twenty before I can enjoy myself, and some people even more. I've tried many experiments, both on the sick and the well, and nothing ever happened amiss, though the demonstrations were immensely interesting," said Meredith, eating his sugarplums with a tranquil air, which was very convincing to others.

"How shall I feel?" asked Belle, beginning on her second comfit.

"A heavenly dreaminess comes over one, in which they move as if on air. Everything is calm and lovely to them: no pain, no care, no fear of anything, and while it lasts one feels like an angel half asleep."

"But if one takes too much, how then?" said a deep voice behind the doctor.

"Hum! Well, that's not so pleasant, unless one likes phantoms, frenzies, and a touch of nightmare, which seems to last a thousand years. Ever try it, Done?" replied Meredith, turning toward the speaker, who was now leaning on his arm and looking interested.

"Never. I'm not a good subject for experiments. Too nervous a temperament to play pranks with."

"I should say ten would be about your number. Less than that seldom affects men. Ladies go off sooner, and don't need so many. Miss St. Just, may I offer you a taste of Elysium? I owe my success to you," said the doctor, approaching her deferentially.

"To me! And how?" she asked, lifting her large eyes with a slight smile.

"I was in the depths of despair when my eye caught the title of your book, and I was saved. For I remembered that I had hashish in my pocket."

"Are you a lotus-eater?" she said, permitting him to lay the six charmed bonbons on the page.

"My faith, no! I use it for my patients. It is very efficacious in nervous disorders, and is getting to be quite a pet remedy with us."

"I do not want to forget the past, but to read the future. Will hashish help me to do that?" asked Rose with an eager look, which made the young man flush, wondering if he bore any part in her hopes of that veiled future.

"Alas, no. I wish it could, for I, too, long to know my fate," he answered, very low, as he looked into the lovely face before him.

The soft glance changed to one of cool indifference and Rose gently brushed the hashish off her book, saying, with a little gesture of dismissal, "Then I have no desire to taste Elysium."

The white morsels dropped into the grass at her feet; but Dr. Meredith let them lie, and turning sharply, went back to sun himself in Belle's smiles.

"I've eaten all mine, and so has Evelyn. Mr. Norton will see goblins, I know, for he has taken quantities. I'm glad of it, for he don't believe in it, and I want to have him convinced by making a spectacle of himself for our amusement," said Belle, in great spirits at the new plan.

"When does the trance come on?" asked Evelyn, a shy girl, already rather alarmed at what she had done.

"About three hours after you take your dose, though the time varies with different people. Your pulse will rise, heart beat quickly, eyes darken and dilate, and an uplifted sensation will pervade you generally. Then these symptoms change, and the bliss begins. I've seen people sit or lie in one position for hours, rapt in a delicious dream, and wake from it as tranquil as if they had not a nerve in their bodies."

"How charming! I'll take some every time I'm worried. Let me see. It's now four, so our trances will come about seven, and we will devote the evening to manifestations," said Belle.

"Come, Done, try it. We are all going in for the fun. Here's your dose," and Meredith tossed him a dozen bonbons, twisted up in a bit of paper.

"No, thank you; I know myself too well to risk it. If you are all going to turn hashish-eaters, you'll need someone to take care of you, so I'll keep sober," tossing the little parcel back.

It fell short, and the doctor, too lazy to pick it up, let it lie, merely saying, with a laugh, "Well, I advise any bashful man to take hashish when he wants to offer his heart to any fair lady, for it will give him the courage of a hero, the eloquence of a poet, and the ardor of an Italian. Remember that, gentlemen, and come to me when the crisis approaches."

"Does it conquer the pride, rouse the pity, and soften the hard hearts of the fair sex?" asked Done.

"I dare say now is your time to settle the fact, for here are two ladies who have imbibed, and in three hours will be in such a seraphic state of mind that 'No' will be an impossibility to them."

"Oh, mercy on us; what *have* we done? If that's the case, I shall shut myself up till my foolish fit is over. Rose, you haven't taken any; I beg you to mount guard over me, and see that I don't disgrace myself by any nonsense. Promise me you will," cried Belle, in half-real, half-feigned alarm at the consequences of her prank.

"I promise," said Rose, and floated down the green path as noiselessly as a white cloud, with a curious smile on her lips.

"Don't tell any of the rest what we have done, but after tea let us go into the grove and compare notes," said Norton, as Done strolled away to the beach, and the voices of approaching friends broke the summer quiet.

At tea, the initiated glanced covertly at one another, and saw, or fancied they saw, the effects of the hashish, in a certain suppressed excitement of manner, and unusually brilliant eyes. Belle laughed often, a silvery ringing laugh, pleasant to hear; but when complimented on her good spirits, she looked distressed, and said she could not help her merriment; Meredith was quite calm, but rather dreamy; Evelyn was pale, and her next neighbor heard her heart beat; Norton talked incessantly, but as he talked uncommonly well, no one suspected anything. Done and Miss St. Just watched the others with interest, and were very quiet, especially Rose, who scarcely spoke, but smiled her sweetest, and looked very lovely.

The moon rose early, and the experimenters slipped away to the grove, leaving the outsiders on the lawn as usual. Some bold spirit asked Rose to sing, and she at once complied, pouring out Spanish airs in a voice that melted the hearts of her audience, so full of fiery sweetness or tragic pathos was it. Done seemed quite carried away, and lay with his face in the grass, to hide the tears that would come; till, afraid of openly disgracing himself, he started up and hurried down to the little wharf, where he sat alone, listening to the music with a countenance which plainly revealed to the stars the passion which possessed him. The sound of loud laughter from the grove, followed by entire silence, caused him to wonder what demonstrations were taking place, and half resolve to go and see. But that enchanting voice held him captive, even when a boat put off mysteriously from a point nearby, and sailed away like a phantom through the twilight.

Half an hour afterward, a white figure came down the path, and Rose's voice broke in on his midsummer night's dream. The moon shone clearly now, and showed him the anxiety in her face as she said hurriedly, "Where is Belle?"

"Gone sailing, I believe."

"How could you let her go? She was not fit to take care of herself!"

"I forgot that."

"So did I, but I promised to watch over her, and I must. Which way did they go?" demanded Rose, wrapping the white mantle about her, and running her eye over the little boats moored below.

"You will follow her?"

"Yes."

"I'll be your guide then. They went toward the lighthouse; it is too far to row; I am at your service. Oh, say yes," cried Done, leaping into his own skiff and offering his hand persuasively.

She hesitated an instant and looked at him. He was always pale, and the moonlight seemed to increase this pallor, but his hat brim hid his eyes, and his voice was very quiet. A loud peal of laughter floated over the water, and as if the sound decided her, she gave him her hand and entered the boat. Done smiled triumphantly as he shook out the sail, which caught the freshening wind, and sent the boat dancing along a path of light.

How lovely it was! All the indescribable allurements of a perfect summer night surrounded them: balmy airs, enchanting moonlight, distant music, and, close at hand, the delicious atmosphere of love, which made itself felt in the eloquent silences that fell between them. Rose seemed to yield to the subtle charm, and leaned back on the cushioned seat with her beautiful head uncovered, her face full of dreamy softness, and her hands lying loosely clasped before her. She seldom spoke, showed no further anxiety for Belle, and soon seemed to forget the object of her search, so absorbed was she in some delicious thought which wrapped her in its peace.

Done sat opposite, flushed now, restless, and excited, for his eyes glittered; the hand on the rudder shook, and his voice sounded intense and passionate, even in the utterance of the simplest words. He talked continually and with unusual brilliancy, for, though a man of many accomplishments, he was too indolent or too fastidious to exert himself, except among his peers. Rose seemed to look without seeing, to listen without hearing, and though she smiled blissfully, the smiles were evidently not for him.

On they sailed, scarcely heeding the bank of black cloud piled up in the horizon, the rising wind, or the silence which proved their solitude. Rose moved once or twice, and lifted her hand as if to speak, but sank back mutely, and the hand fell again as if it had not energy enough to enforce her wish. A cloud sweeping over the moon, a distant growl of thunder, and the slight gust that struck the sail seemed to rouse her. Done was singing now like one inspired, his hat at his feet, hair in disorder, and a strangely rapturous expression in his eyes, which were fixed on her. She started, shivered, and seemed to recover herself with an effort.

"Where are they?" she asked, looking vainly for the island heights and the other boat.

"They have gone to the beach, I fancy, but we will follow." As Done leaned forward to speak, she saw his face and shrank back with a sudden flush, for in it she read clearly what she had felt, yet doubted until now. He saw the telltale blush and gesture, and said impetuously, "You know it now; you cannot deceive me longer, or daunt me with your pride! Rose, I love you, and dare tell you so tonight!"

"Not now—not here—I will not listen. Turn back, and be silent, I entreat you, Mr. Done," she said hurriedly.

He laughed a defiant laugh and took her hand in his, which was burning and throbbing with the rapid heat of his pulse.

"No, I *will* have my answer here, and now, and never turn back till you give it; you have been a thorny Rose, and given me many wounds. I'll be paid for my heartache with sweet words, tender looks, and frank confessions of love, for proud as you are, you do love me, and dare not deny it."

Something in his tone terrified her; she snatched her hand away and drew beyond his reach, trying to speak calmly, and to meet coldly the ardent glances of the eyes which were strangely darkened and dilated with uncontrollable emotion.

"You forget yourself. I shall give no answer to an avowal made in such terms. Take me home instantly," she said in a tone of command.

"Confess you love me, Rose."

"Never!"

"Ah! I'll have a kinder answer, or—" Done half rose and put out his hand to grasp and draw her to him, but the cry she uttered seemed to arrest him with a sort of shock. He dropped into his seat, passed his hand over his eyes, and shivered nervously as he muttered in an altered tone, "I meant nothing; it's the moonlight; sit down, I'll control my-self—upon my soul I will!"

"If you do not, I shall go overboard. Are you mad, sir?" cried Rose, trembling with indignation.

"Then I shall follow you, for I *am* mad, Rose, with love—hash-ish!"

His voice sank to a whisper, but the last word thrilled along her nerves, as no sound of fear had ever done before. An instant she regarded him with a look which took in every sign of unnatural excitement, then she clasped her hands with an imploring gesture, saying, in a tone of despair, "Why did I come! How will it end? Oh, Mark, take me home before it is too late!"

"Hush! Be calm; don't thwart me, or I may get wild again. My thoughts are not clear, but I understand you. There, take my knife, and if I forget myself, kill me. Don't go overboard; you are too beautiful to die, my Rose!"

He threw her the slender hunting knife he wore, looked at her a moment with a far-off look, and trimmed the sail like one moving in a dream. Rose took the weapon, wrapped her cloak closely about her, and crouching as far away as possible, kept her eye on him, with a face in which watchful terror contended with some secret trouble and bewilderment more powerful than her fear.

The boat moved round and began to beat up against wind and tide; spray flew from her bow; the sail bent and strained in the gusts that struck it with perilous fitfulness. The moon was nearly hidden by scudding clouds, and one-half the sky was black with the gathering storm. Rose looked from threatening heavens to treacherous sea, and tried to be ready for any danger, but her calm had been sadly broken, and she could not recover it. Done sat motionless, uttering no word of encouragement, though the frequent flaws almost tore the rope from his hand, and the water often dashed over him.

"Are we in any danger?" asked Rose at last, unable to bear the silence, for he looked like a ghostly helmsman seen by the fitful light, pale now, wild-eyed, and speechless.

"Yes, great danger."

"I thought you were a skillful boatman."

"I am when I am myself; now I am rapidly losing the control of my will, and the strange quiet is coming over me. If I had been alone I should have given up sooner, but for your sake I've kept on."

"Can't you work the boat?" asked Rose, terror-struck by the changed tone of his voice, the slow, uncertain movements of his hands.

"No. I see everything through a thick cloud; your voice sounds far away, and my one desire is to lay my head down and sleep."

"Let me steer—I can, I must!" she cried, springing toward him and laying her hand on the rudder.

He smiled and kissed the little hand, saying dreamily, "You could not hold it a minute; sit by me, love; let us turn the boat again, and drift away together—anywhere, anywhere out of the world."

"Oh, heaven, what will become of us!" and Rose wrung her hands in real despair. "Mr. Done—Mark—dear Mark, rouse yourself and listen to me. Turn, as you say, for it is certain death to go on so. Turn, and let us drift down to the lighthouse; they will hear and help us. Quick, take down the sail, get out the oars, and let us try to reach there before the storm breaks."

As Rose spoke, he obeyed her like a dumb animal; love for her was stronger even than the instinct of self-preservation, and for her sake he fought against the treacherous lethargy which was swiftly overpowering him. The sail was lowered, the boat brought round, and with little help from the ill-pulled oars it drifted rapidly out to sea with the ebbing tide.

As she caught her breath after this dangerous maneuver was accomplished, Rose asked, in a quiet tone she vainly tried to render natural, "How much hashish did you take?"

"All that Meredith threw me. Too much; but I was possessed to do it, so I hid the roll and tried it," he answered, peering at her with a weird laugh.

"Let us talk; our safety lies in keeping awake, and I dare not let you sleep," continued Rose, dashing water on her own hot forehead with a sort of desperation.

"Say you love me; that would wake me from my lost sleep, I think.

I have hoped and feared, waited and suffered so long. Be pitiful, and answer, Rose."

"I do; but I should not own it now."

So low was the soft reply he scarcely heard it, but he felt it and made a strong effort to break from the hateful spell that bound him. Leaning forward, he tried to read her face in a ray of moonlight breaking through the clouds; he saw a new and tender warmth in it, for all the pride was gone, and no fear marred the eloquence of those soft, Southern eyes.

"Kiss me, Rose, then I shall believe it. I feel lost in a dream, and you, so changed, so kind, may be only a fair phantom. Kiss me, love, and make it real."

As if swayed by a power more potent than her will, Rose bent to meet his lips. But the ardent pressure seemed to startle her from a momentary oblivion of everything but love. She covered up her face and sank down, as if overwhelmed with shame, sobbing through passionate tears, "Oh, what am I doing? I am mad, for I, too, have taken hashish."

What he answered she never heard, for a rattling peal of thunder drowned his voice, and then the storm broke loose. Rain fell in torrents, the wind blew fiercely, sky and sea were black as ink, and the boat tossed from wave to wave almost at their mercy. Giving herself up for lost, Rose crept to her lover's side and clung there, conscious only that they would bide together through the perils their own folly brought them. Done's excitement was quite gone now; he sat like a statue, shielding the frail creature whom he loved with a smile on his face, which looked awfully emotionless when the lightning gave her glimpses of its white immobility. Drenched, exhausted, and half senseless with danger, fear, and exposure, Rose saw at last a welcome glimmer through the gloom, and roused herself to cry for help.

"Mark, wake and help me! Shout, for God's sake—shout and call them, for we are lost if we drift by!" she cried, lifting his head from his breast, and forcing him to see the brilliant beacons streaming far across the troubled water.

"Springing up, he uttered shout after shout, like one demented. Fortunately, the storm had lulled a little, and the lighthouse keeper heard them and answered."

He understood her, and springing up, uttered shout after shout like one demented. Fortunately, the storm had lulled a little; the lighthouse keeper heard and answered. Rose seized the helm, Done the oars, and with one frantic effort guided the boat into quieter waters, where it was met by the keeper, who towed it to the rocky nook which served as harbor.

The moment a strong, steady face met her eyes, and a gruff, cheery voice hailed her, Rose gave way, and was carried up to the house, looking more like a beautiful drowned Ophelia than a living woman.

"Here, Sally, see to the poor thing; she's had a rough time on't. I'll take care of her sweetheart—and a nice job I'll have, I reckon, for if he ain't mad or drunk, he's had a stroke of lightnin', and looks as if he wouldn't get his hearin' in a hurry," said the old man as he housed his unexpected guests and stood staring at Done, who looked about him like one dazed. "You jest turn in yonder and sleep it off, mate. We'll see to the lady, and right up your boat in the morning," the old man added.

"Be kind to Rose. I frightened her. I'll not forget you. Yes, let me sleep and get over this cursed folly as soon as possible," muttered this strange visitor.

Done threw himself down on the rough couch and tried to sleep, but every nerve was overstrained, every pulse beating like a trip-hammer, and everything about him was intensified and exaggerated with awful power. The thundershower seemed a wild hurricane, the quaint room a wilderness peopled with tormenting phantoms, and all the events of his life passed before him in an endless procession, which nearly maddened him. The old man looked weird and gigantic, his own voice sounded shrill and discordant, and the ceaseless murmur of Rose's incoherent wanderings haunted him like parts of a grotesque but dreadful dream.

All night he lay motionless, with staring eyes, feverish lips, and a mind on the rack, for the delicate machinery which had been tampered with revenged the wrong by torturing the foolish experimenter. All night Rose wept and sang, talked and cried for help in a piteous state of nervous excitement, for with her the trance came first, and the after-agitation was increased by the events of the evening. She slept at last, lulled by the old woman's motherly care, and Done was spared one tormenting fear, for he dreaded the consequences of this folly on her, more than upon himself.

As day dawned he rose, haggard and faint, and staggered out. At the door he met the keeper, who stopped him to report that the boat was in order, and a fair day coming. Seeing doubt and perplexity in the old man's eye, Done told him the truth, and added that he was going to the beach for a plunge, hoping by that simple tonic to restore his unstrung nerves.

He came back feeling like himself again, except for a dull headache, and a heavy sense of remorse weighing on his spirits, for he distinctly recollected all the events of the night. The old woman made him eat and drink, and in an hour he felt ready for the homeward trip.

Rose slept late, and when she woke soon recovered herself, for her dose had been a small one. When she had breakfasted and made a hasty toilet, she professed herself anxious to return at once. She dreaded yet longed to see Done, and when the time came armed herself with pride, feeling all a woman's shame at what had passed, and resolving to feign forgetfulness of the incidents of the previous night. Pale and cold as a statue she met him, but the moment he began to say humbly, "Forgive me, Rose," she silenced him with an imperious gesture and the command "Don't speak of it; I only remember that it was very horrible, and wish to forget it all as soon as possible."

"All, Rose?" he asked, significantly.

"Yes, *all*. No one would care to recall the follies of a hashish dream," she answered, turning hastily to hide the scarlet flush that would rise, and the eyes that would fall before his own.

"*I* never can forget, but I will be silent if you bid me."

"I do. Let us go. What will they think at the island? Mr. Done, give me your promise to tell no one, now or ever, that I tried that dangerous experiment. I will guard your secret also." She spoke eagerly and looked up imploringly.

"I promise," and he gave her his hand, holding her own with a wistful glance, till she drew it away and begged him to take her home.

Leaving hearty thanks and a generous token of their gratitude, they sailed away with a fair wind, finding in the freshness of the morning a speedy cure for tired bodies and excited minds. They said little, but it was impossible for Rose to preserve her coldness. The memory of the past night broke down her pride, and Done's tender glances touched her heart. She half hid her face behind her hand, and tried to compose herself for the scene to come, for as she approached the island, she saw Belle and her party waiting for them on the shore.

"Oh, Mr. Done, screen me from their eyes and questions as much as you can! I'm so worn out and nervous, I shall betray myself. You will help me?" And she turned to him with a confiding look, strangely at variance with her usual calm self-possession.

"I'll shield you with my life, if you will tell me why you took the hashish," he said, bent on knowing his fate.

"I hoped it would make me soft and lovable, like other women. I'm tired of being a lonely statue," she faltered, as if the truth was wrung from her by a power stronger than her will.

"And I took it to gain courage to tell my love. Rose, we have been near death together; let us share life together, and neither of us be any more lonely or afraid?"

He stretched his hand to her with his heart in his face, and she gave him hers with a look of tender submission, as he said ardently, "Heaven bless hashish, if its dreams end like this!"

PART IV

Remembering Louisa May Alcott:

Essays, Photographs, Drawings, and a Poem

FROM "WHEN LOUISA ALCOTT WAS A GIRL"

BY EDWARD W. EMERSON

IN THE YEAR 1840 A REMARKABLE FAMILY MOVED TO CONCORD; high-minded, cultivated, exceedingly poor, despised by most persons, welcomed by one or two; apparently so ill fitted to fight the world's fight that failure was sure. Yet they won, in the end, respect, recognition, success, and their name is honorably associated with that of the town.

The head of that family, Amos Bronson Alcott, began life as a peddler, but a call came so strongly to him, like that which Jesus gave to certain poor fishers to become teachers of a better life than they found, that he felt justified in obeying the Master's command to them: "Take no thought, saying, What shall we eat? or, What shall we drink? or, Wherewithal shall we be clothed?" . . .

The Alcotts' Humble Home in Concord

MR. ALCOTT began to teach in a better sense than the schools of New England then recognized. He appealed to the intellect, the conscience, the imagination, discovering for himself methods that advanced teachers strive to introduce to-day, held to these at a loss, and finally had his Boston school wrecked and was himself almost mobbed for being in advance of his day. In his school, and later, on a day of public shame, he bravely espoused, even at the risk of influence and of life, the cause of the poor slaves.

It is of his family that I am to tell here, but their extraordinary nurture and home surroundings must be known to rightly value their interesting personalities and their life together . . . In the glimpses that I shall give of this family this point is best worth heeding: that with beliefs, tastes and aims differing so widely as to make domestic harmony seem impossible, courage, respect for each other and love won the day, and kept father, mother and children a united family, and if with suffering, also with happiness. After the loss of his school Mr. Alcott brought his noble wife . . . and his four little daughters to Concord. He gardened, let himself out for day's work to farmers, and gave conversations as opportunity offered. Because of poverty, and also of his brave attempt, in a world not bred to Golden Age methods, to revive that blameless life, and live on the herb of the soil and the fruit of the tree, with water from the spring; and clothe the body in linen wrought from the blue-flowered flax, not murdering, robbing nor enslaving the animals, nor yet becoming partners in human slavery by the use of sugar, spice and cotton—all stimulants whatever were also forborne—their housekeeping was not easy for the wife to manage, and alarmingly frugal for a cold zone. The conditions of family life were hard. As a compensation its simplicity saved time for purposes that were worth while. Mrs. Alcott made it a rule to rise early enough in the morning to get through all the work in the forenoon, so that after dinner was cleared away she should have a long afternoon to devote to her children. She meant that life should be rich enough in the gifts that the woods, the flowers, the skies, stories and games and poems had for them to make up for what they had not, so that poverty should not darken their young lives. She was not only loving and sympathetic, but she had a well-stored, fertile mind. From her they learned to depend on themselves for good times, and their imaginations were quickened.

Louisa Alcott's Gifts Were Early Disclosed

LOUISA when very young used to tell fairy stories to my sister in the woods, and later wrote others and sent them to her. These were gathered in her first book, "Flower Fables." A great taste for acting and skill in devising and producing wonderful romantic plays soon showed itself. Love, despair, witchcraft, villainy, fairy intervention, triumphant right, held sway in turn. In those days a red scarf, a long cloak, a big hat with a plume stolen from a bonnet, a paper-knife dagger, a scrap of tinsel from a button-card, a little gold paper for Royalty, tissue paper stretched on wire hoops for fairy wings, produced superb effects. Sheets pinned on the clothesline, a clotheshorse, a sarcenet-cambric curtain, a few little pine trees in stands, supplemented by proper common-sense in the audience, would give castles, enchanted forests, caves and ladies' bowers. Barns, because of their well-known possibilities for desperate but safe leaps from beams, and the advantages for disappearance offered by mangers, were the first theatres. The zeal of the mother in helping on her children's little plans appears in a touching sentence in a story of Louisa's, where she describes the preparation for a school masquerade such as we had later. The fathers might grudge expense, "But the mothers, whose interest in their children's pleasure is a sort of evergreen that no frost of time can kill, sewed spangles by the bushel, made wildernesses of tissue paper blossom as the rose, kept tempers sweet, stomachs full, and domestic machinery working smoothly through it all by that maternal magic which makes them the human Providences of this naughty world."

The Friends and Companions of the Alcott Girls

FROM TRAGEDY and melodrama the girls were led to comedy by the delights of Dickens, and thereafter they especially shone in dramatized bits of his work. As they grew up they fully appreciated the humorous side of the strange specimens, communists, anti-money and anti-marriage men, sun-believers and the like, who came to their door and tarried for a time, for Mr. Alcott had a most catholic hospitality. It was especially at Fruitlands, a Golden Age community of philosophers that wilted at winter's first frost (by no means golden, however, for poor Mrs. Alcott), that these pilgrims gathered. Thence the family, with fortune at lowest ebb, returned to Concord, but left it in 1848 and lived for a time in Boston, and then in Walpole, New Hampshire; but Anna and Louisa tried their fortunes as teachers in Syracuse and Boston, and so saw something of the world.

In the autumn of 1857 the Alcotts returned to Concord, but in sadness, for Lizzie, the good girl of whom one of her playmates lately spoke to me as "all conscience," was fading away after an attack of scarlet fever in Walpole, where her mother had gone to the aid of a poor family afflicted with the dreadful sickness, to see that the children were not neglected. The loss of their daughter, the following spring, was, as has been well said, "the result of one of those generous acts which the Alcotts performed as constantly and as inevitably as most persons perform acts of self-interest" . . .

A Home That Delighted the Mind and Eye

THE ALCOTTS had bought a small piece of land, and a farmhouse, once good, but fallen into decay, on the "Great Road" to Boston, a mile east of the village. They made some repairs and a small addition, greatly improving its appearance, and moved into it the following summer. The situation was extremely picturesque. It was backed by a range of hills clothed in the rich green of pines relieved by a tracery of gray birch. A superb elm served as a great parasol in summer, and besides there were apple trees, pink and white in May, and red and yellow in September, which commended the place to the fruit-loving father, who called it Orchard House. In front, between the house and the wooded hills about Walden, stretched a broad meadow, said to have been an ancient bed of Concord River. A charming wood path led up a little pass among the hills behind the house, sweet with the hot breath of pine. Mr. Alcott's hands, unaided but by taste and skill, greatly beautified the place by a little terracing of the sunny slope here and there, the planting of woodbine on the porch, and the building, out of sticks cut on the place, of a rustic fence and gates, a seat around the spurs of the elm by the door, and pretty arbors and trellises out of gnarled pitch-pine boughs, over which the Concord grapevines should run, giving fragrance twice a year, fruit once, and grace all the time . . .

The True Charm of the Alcott Cottage

. . . A LADY who remembered well their home in the days of their extreme poverty after the collapse of the Fruitlands community, said that "Even then the Alcotts' rooms were distinguished looking." Mrs. Alcott had sense and taste, and was a woman of expedients. What was the secret of the pleasant effect produced on the guests on entering? First, there was light and air; second, there was rest for the eye instead of confusion; third, the things were for use for body and for spirit— the furniture being plain and unpretentious, the few engravings, drawings and woodcuts good in subject and interesting, the books classics or else individual in character, and showing use. To give a few details: each window did not have two kinds of curtains, two kinds of shades, with all the fixtures, ribbons, cords and tassels involved, besides shutters, wire nettings and blinds—seven lines of fortification against sun and air! The trees outside tempered the light, the blinds could help at need, and pretty muslin curtains, made out of old party dresses, did the rest . . .

The woodland gate that led into the Alcott and Hawthorne woodlands in a drawing by May Alcott. Here, Louisa, chin in hand, gazes toward the picturesque family manse of which her father was so—justly—proud.

A Memorable Evening at the Alcotts' House

THE ALCOTT GIRLS, self-helpful, kindly and bright, came among the young people of Concord and made themselves felt at once. But they helped their good mother and did their part at home, and however little the girls followed their father's philosophical flights or grahamite and vegetarian practices (which after they grew up they abandoned), they were a loving and loyal family. On one occasion, Mr. Alcott probably being away, a friend who called to see him found the girls shoveling in a ton of coal to the cellar. They did not flinch nor apologize for their unusual work, but said with pretended boastfulness, "See what vegetables will do. It's all vegetables!"

One evening, a few months after their return to Concord, my sister and I accompanied our mother on a call on the Alcotts. Mr. Alcott was in the study, but we were cordially received by his wife, and the girls were summoned. Louisa was fine looking, had the most regular features of the family, and very handsome, wavy brown hair like her mother's. She had always a rather masculine air, and a twinkle woke constantly in her eye at the comic side of things, a characteristic that carries many persons through hard experiences that crush or sour others. Her talk was always full of little catches from her favorite Dickens. I remember that her assent always took the form of "Barkis is willin'." Anna, the eldest, was plain, but so friendly and sweet-tempered a person that the beauty of expression made up for the lack of it in her features; but she had a quick sense of humor, without the ingredient of tartness that Louisa's sometimes had. Anna had a wonderful dramatic gift. May, the youngest, the darling of the family (Amy of the stories), was a tall, well-made blonde, the lower part of her face irregular, but she had beautiful blue eyes and brilliant yellow hair. She was overflowing with spirits and energy, danced well, and rode recklessly whenever she could, by rare chance, come by a saddle-horse for an hour.

Before we left, Louisa was persuaded by her mother to do something for our amusement. She disappeared and soon came in transformed. Her hair, which girls in those days wore brushed low and braided, was twisted up into a little knob on her head so tight that she could hardly wink. The broad collar, white undersleeves and hoopskirt of the day were gone, and she appeared in an ugly, scant, brown calico dress, with bloomer trousers to match, blue stockings and coarse shoes. She had a manuscript in one hand, and a pen in the other, which she thrust behind her ear and began a harangue on the "Rights of Woman," and offered and at once proceeded to read in strident tones a gem of thought which she had just turned out, called "Hoots of a Distracted Soul in the Wilderness." She then passed on to other confirmatory manuscripts that she professed to be editing—travesties on her father's writings, I think—certainly on those of my father under the name of Rolf Walden Emerboy. Mr. Alcott came in from his study to hear, and however little he could understand such manifestations of the spirit of prophecy, he seemed to feel the pride of a parent in his daughter's wit . . .

The Way Many Delightful Evenings Were Passed

THE EVENINGS at the Alcotts' house have . . . left delightful memories. Although these involved a long walk the bait was good enough to draw the girls and boys often. The hearty and motherly quality of Mrs. Alcott's welcome was something to remember. The too prevalent custom—in bad taste, too—of young girls at once retiring with their callers into a room apart from the elders was never practiced there. There was a piano, by no means too good to use, and May, in the highest spirits, would swoop to the stool, and all would fall to dancing, the mother herself often joining us. One of the guests would relieve May, who then had her gay turn. Then, with or without voices, we stood by the piano and sang, "Rolling Home," *"Ubi sunt, O pocula,"* "Juanita," "Music in the Air," and, after the war began, "The Battle-

Hymn of the Republic," "John Brown," "Marching Along," and other stirring songs fresh from the camp. Short stories on the porch might follow as twilight deepened into dark, and they were sufficiently "creepy." Perhaps chestnuts, Rhode Island greenings or Northern spies ended the evening, and we went home by ten at the latest.

This was the epoch when Dr. Dio Lewis had introduced a calisthenic revival, and his classes gave great sport, in which children and elders took part. Matches of pin-running, or, much better, of bean-bag tossing and passing between two carefully chosen sides, had passed from the classes to private houses, and were wildly exciting. We never played cards on these occasions, and let it be said that in those days to play for a prize was unheard of. We played for fun, the best of prizes, and thus there was no unwholesome excitement . . .

The Useful Lesson of Those Joyous Times

I HAVE THOUGHT that in these days, when the tendency of life in America is to become more complicated, not only in business but in household life and amusements, it might be well to call up some pleasant pictures of the past that may have a lesson. Great pleasure may be had very simply and cheaply. Good nature, self-help, mother-wit and independence are such good ingredients that a cake baked with them is safe to turn out well. Riches must not set the pace for us all, for they are confined to a small number, and these change. We cannot all begin where our fathers left off. The family whose beautiful life I celebrate first made themselves happy in adversity by their methods, and later hundreds of others. One trait remains which I have hardly emphasized enough. I have never known a family who equaled the Alcotts in generosity, even in their poverty. Later, when better times came, mainly by Louisa's devoted work, whatever they had they gladly shared . . .

◆ ◆ ◆ ◆ ◆ ◆ ◆ ◆ ◆ ◆ ◆ ◆ ◆ ◆ ◆ ◆ ◆ ◆ ◆ ◆

FROM "BETH ALCOTT'S PLAYMATE: A GLIMPSE OF CONCORD TOWN IN THE DAYS OF *LITTLE WOMEN*"

BY LYDIA HOSMER WOOD

The Spirit of Neighborliness & the Trip Abroad

M RS. ALCOTT, WHO CAME FROM TWO OF THE OLDEST FAMILIES in Boston—the Sewalls and the Mays—had to learn through bitter experience to conquer her pride and to accept gifts from friends who understood her needs as the wife of an impractical idealist. Her husband, Bronson Alcott, was one of the most lovable men one could ever hope to meet, so kind and so wise, but he did not know how to make money, and as a consequence, when his dear wife's dowry was all gone there was no further source of income. Money meant nothing to him and he never seemed to understand why they didn't have any. He did teach school at different times, but never with any financial success . . .

When they lived in the cottage near our home and when the children were very young, Amy a baby, some friends offered to take him abroad with them. He accepted with alacrity and the whole family seemed delighted at the opportunity; if they thought about their means of subsistence at all, it was probably with the conclusion that "Heaven would provide," and surely it was with that thought, if with any, that the father ordered a new suit at a Boston tailor's shortly before sailing. When it was sent home he turned to his wife and said in his delightful, absent-minded way: "I don't believe that I paid for that suit, but if I didn't you will attend to it, will you not, my dear?"

In answer, she only smiled in her quiet, patient way, never mentioning the fact that all they had in the world to live upon was a box of oatmeal standing upon the pantry shelf.

In spite of the poverty, theirs was one of the most hospitable households I ever knew. We always felt welcome and happy in this home which fairly radiated sweetness and wholesomeness. The house may have been scantily furnished, but it was always neat, and whatever they had was good and pretty. As the mother and the girls had to do all the housework themselves (the Hannah of the March household was a myth in the Alcott home), they were always very busy about the house, but never too busy to romp and play.

Louisa, of course, was always the leader in the fun; it seems to me that she was always romping and racing down the street, usually with a hoople higher than her head. That was the best way in which she could give vent to the exuberance of her spirits, I suppose.

She was continually shocking people, just as Jo does in the book, by her tomboyish, natural, and independent ways. Somewhere, in one of her earlier books, little read to-day, she tells the story of how she went down to the fields one day, to talk to some men who were hoeing potatoes. As they were chewing tobacco, Louisa, always curious and never afraid, wanted to know what it was they were chewing, and asked for a quid. When they gave it to her, she chewed it so vigorously that she had to be carried home in a wheelbarrow . . .

A Novel Bath

WHILE WE ARE on the subject of their frugality and their natural ways, which to others might have seemed shocking, let me tell you of the novel method of taking a bath adopted by the Alcott girls. As rain water is commonly known to be a great beautifier and as systems of plumbing such as we have to-day were practically unknown then, what did they do but take a shower out on the little back piazza, facing the grove and completely hidden from the gaze of the passer-by, in nature's most approved fashion, whenever it rained . . .

They were such a dear, conscientious family, so harmonious and so lovable. The atmosphere of their house was almost sanctified, so much better did you feel for having been in it. There was so much love in their make-up, and love was the only medium through which the parents ruled and disciplined their children.

Louisa and May (Amy) were the unruly ones; Anna and Lizzie were by nature more quiet and subdued. Whenever they did anything distasteful or naughty, instead of rebuking them with words, Mr. or Mrs. Alcott would write them little notes which they tucked under their pillows at night. After due deliberation over their sins, the children then sent their answers. It was a lesson in humility, self-chastisement, and self-expression, and it always seems to have had the desired effect.

Another method of punishment which Mr. Alcott sometimes used was to serve a meal, and then, without eating anything himself, he would rise and leave the table. Naturally the child with a conscience guilty with the thought of having caused her father sufficient unhappiness to make him lose his appetite would lose hers too, and until a reconciliation could be effected felt thoroughly ashamed and disgraced.

"Remembering to Be Good"

THE "BON-BOX" was another device the Alcotts had for remembering to be good. Inside the front door of their house stood a box which served as the symbol of an honor system, for into it, at the end of each day, the child who had been good and hadn't disregarded a single rule of conduct dropped a little slip bearing her name and the code-word

"Bon" with three crosses after it, like this: X X X. It was such a distinction to be a depositor at the end of the day, that I asked whether I might be allowed to work for it, too. I do not remember how often my name went into that box attached to a Bon-slip, but I do know that I used to examine my stock of virtues very carefully in those days . . .

FROM "THE WOMAN WHO WROTE *LITTLE WOMEN*"

BY JULIAN HAWTHORNE

WHEN IN THE 1860'S YOU THOUGHT OF THE ALCOTTS YOU thought of Louisa; and some malign wit said that she was her father's best contribution to literature. Even before she wrote *Little Women*, she was eminent in her family, though none of the other members of it was negligible. She was a big, lovable, tender-hearted, generous girl, with black hair, thick and long, and flashing, humorous black eyes. Humor she had, and wit too, and dramatic talent; and in spite of what Henry James once told her—I shall tell that story by and by—she did have genius . . .

Three Famous Neighbor Families

OUR PLACE and the Alcotts' adjoined, the houses themselves being less than two hundred yards apart; and when we came back from Europe, in June of 1860, we naturally fraternized with our neighbors, and my two sisters and myself and the Alcott girls were in and out of one another's houses all the time, almost forming one family. And the three Emerson children, Ellen, Edith and Edward, being but ten minutes' distant in space and even nearer in amity, were not long in getting into the game—nine of us in all, while our elders looked on approvingly. It was a fine nucleus for good society, and it is surprising, in the retrospect, that so little romance evolved from such a situation. But there were only two males in the combination, and as a matter of fact, the love-making, such as it was, and it was very mild, was restricted to Abby [May] and myself. We kept it secret, and it is now for the first time disclosed.

Anne [Anna] Alcott married a fellow altogether admirable, whom we called John, and if I ever knew his other name I have forgotten it. Abby [May] became the wife of an artist, I believe, long afterward. Edith Emerson married a fine young gentleman, Forbes by name, whose father was rich; Ellen never married, but devoted her life to taking care of her father. My sister Una died unmarried; Rose, in 1860, was less than ten years old. Edward Emerson, after graduating from Harvard, married a Concord girl, Annie Keyes, and he may, for what I know and hope, be living yet, a veteran approaching eighty. That leaves only Louisa and myself to be accounted for; I found a wife in 1870, and Louisa lived and died a maid in 1888. Like Ellen Emerson, she devoted herself to her father and mother—and to the myriad little women and men who read and loved her books.

In no young woman that ever I knew was strength of character more manifest than in Louisa Alcott. Ellen Emerson, of the Concord girls, was nearest her in that respect; but Ellen was aristocratic, while Louisa was a true democrat. Ellen was deep, but narrow; Louisa was both deep and broad; her sympathies were world-wide. Ellen, for all her noble self-dedication to her father, was always conscious of herself; Louisa—aside from her dignity of womanhood—never considered herself at all. Nobody ever ventured to take liberties with the woman, but as Louisa she was hand in glove with us all. Her spirit was high and courageous. She was great in comedy, laughed and inspired laughter, but for a heart so tender as hers tragedy was always near, though she was resolute to smile her tears down for others' sake. Did she ever have a love affair? We never knew; yet how could a nature so imaginative, romantic and passionate escape it? But her control was greater than her passion, and she could put aside personal felicity for what she deemed just cause. The Alcott girls were society in themselves, and Concord would have been crippled without them. Anne, when she could be spared from her own married sphere, was a precious element; Abby's enjoyment gave joy to others; and Louisa was the hub of the little universe and kept the wheel in constant activity.

Abby Alcott's Startling Question

MY FIRST INTERVIEW with Abby Alcott was on a June day just after our return from Europe. She and I stood on the path skirting the base of the hill between our abodes; we had lately been introduced and she was helping me along, I being a bashful nondescript of fourteen, seven or eight years her junior, and ignorant of American civilization. Abby began by asking me whether I didn't think it was nice for "ladies and gentlemen to go bathing together."

Those were her words. Dear, honest girl, she never suspected the voluptuous shock that her inquiry produced upon my innocent but not unimaginative nature. My conceptions of bathing had till then been confined to the severe isolation of bathrooms, or to hardly less unsocial English sea beaches, where the sexes were rigorously segregated, boxed up in bathing machines—tiny huts on wheels—and clad from neck to heel in shapeless, dark flannel robes; bobbing up and down, thus, in chilly splashings of gray waves, solitary and miserable . . . I glanced at Abby's well-turned figure, her clustered yellow ringlets, her cheerful and inviting expression; she was older than I and must know best; one must follow the customs of the country. I stammered, I blushed . . .

Fortunately, she continued: "We and the Emersons often go over to Walden this hot weather—to the cove where Thoreau used to live; there's a tent for the girls. We're going next Thursday *and* you could have John's bathing dress; *it would* be awfully nice!"

. . . I have no recollection of the rest of the conversation, but I

"Hermitage at Walden Pond," a drawing by May Alcott of the now legendary haunt of that "independent of independents," Henry David Thoreau. "He seemed," said Bronson of his dear, irascible companion, "one with things, of nature's essence and core, knit of strong timbers,—like a wood and its inhabitants."

have no doubt that the Hawthorne children were splashing in Thoreau's cove that Thursday, with other tritons and naiads, properly draped . . .

It was not with the tall, dark-flashing Louisa, however, that I fell in love; she must have been close upon thirty by that time, and besides I had seen Abby first; I was content with an adoring younger-brother attitude toward Louisa. Adoration is not too strong a word; she always equaled and often surpassed anticipation. The Civil War so kindled her that no one was astonished, or ventured to remonstrate, when she took the almost unheard-of decision to volunteer as nurse behind the lines. But it brought the war home to Concord as even the departure of the Concord volunteers for the front, a year before, had hardly done.

After she had gone, our thoughts and love followed her, and almost every week a letter came from her. Wonderful letters they were; they were published afterward, but not in the same form in which we had listened to them as Mrs. Alcott, in a voice tremulous sometimes with laughter, sometimes with tears, read them out to us, grouped around the porch of Apple Slump in those fierce, emotional first passages of the war.

Louisa put her heart and soul into them, as she was putting heart and soul into her work in the hospitals. The pathos and the humor both were there; she felt them to her marrow, and in her homely narratives she made us feel them. And this devoted and heroic figure was our Louisa! She seemed enlarged into something greater than we had suspected. What a dauntless temper, what tenderness and sympathy! Into what scenes of horror and tragedy had she entered, after the ancient peace and amenity of Concord!

Louisa Alcott as a War Nurse

ONE WEEK the customary letter did not arrive, and a hush of suspense fell upon us. Then came an official dispatch from the front: Miss Louisa Alcott had caught the fever, and was being invalided home.

The homeward journey was long, and to our misgivings it was almost like a funeral, with the pain of uncertainty to boot. On my way home from school I would call at the house for news, and go away heavy hearted. Mrs. Alcott would shake her head, pale and sad, and Abby's eyelids were red and her smiles gone.

She came at last, a white, tragic mask of what she had been, but with a glimmer of a smile in the depths of her sunken eyes. Her spirit was indomitable, and it pulled her through. After some weeks she could be carried out of the house to sit in the sunshine; she got well, and her cheeriness and social animation returned, but there were occasional tones in her voice and expressions of eyes and mouth that indicated depths of which she could not speak . . .

The Insufferable English Visitor

. . . PILGRIMS OCCASIONALLY came from foreign parts to taste the transcendental springs at their source—Anthony Trollope and others; but they couldn't divert the attention of us young folks from one another. One episode, however, touched me nearly.

For some days Abby and Louisa had been letting fall obscure allusions to the anticipated visit at Apple Slump of some relative of theirs, a young Englishman of rank, as I gathered, and distinguished in the London fashionable set. They seemed quite excited about it, Abby especially; he was said to be handsome and fascinating, and what was termed in those days "a sad dog." As has been stated, I was in love with Abby myself, and I didn't like her hardly disguised interest in the expected visitor; but I tried to calm myself with the reflection that he would be more apt to admire Louisa.

The date of his arrival was not fixed; March came and went and there was no news of him. I began to hope that his plans might have been changed. On the first day of the next month the school had to play an important match game of hockey; it was not decided till near sunset, and by the time I came abreast of Apple Slump on my way home it was dusk. At the gate, chatting with Abby, I descried a figure who could be no other than the Englishman. Abby beckoned me to approach.

Much as my jealousy bristled against this person, I couldn't deny his grace, charm and high-society bearing. He was slender and dark, and wore a black broad-cloth suit and soft black felt hat. His waistcoat and cravat, however, were rather too decorative for my taste; he twirled an absurd switch cane and occasionally caressed the points of a tiny black mustache; and as I came up, rough and disheveled in my hockey rig, he inserted a monocle in his right eye and fixed me with what Tennyson would have called "a stony British stare."

I didn't like him, the rather that in putting up the monocle he relinquished Abby's hand, which he couldn't have been holding without her consent.

On being introduced, however, he greeted me with insufferable condescension, and spoke in an airy, smiling tone, with marked English intonations. Meanwhile, by a quick contraction of the eye, he projected the monocle from its place, and with the easiest air imaginable slipped his arm round Abby's waist. Nor did she flinch from him; on the contrary! I asked her where Louisa was. She said Louisa had to change her dress.

I felt sure I could thrash this fellow—he wasn't so big as I; but my tenderness for Abby had been kept secret from the world, and one cannot protect the girl he cares for if she obviously does not want to be protected. I stepped back, and haughtily said that I guessed I'd be going home.

"Oh, I say, don't be in a hurry, my dear child," drawled this intolerable creature, flirting his cane with an effeminate gesture. "Do you know, I find you quite amusing."

I stepped up to him again with my fists clenched; my wrath must have been visible in my crimson and distorted countenance. "Child" indeed!

He snatched off his hat and tossed it up in the air, thereby letting a thick mass of black hair fall down to his waist. He and Abby burst into shouts of laughter, and with arms around each other performed a wild saraband.

Then, enchanted with the success of her masquerade, and perhaps embarrassed at her pantaloons, Louisa fled up the path and into the house, "April fool!" coming back to me over her shoulder. Abby leaned against the gate, breathless and giggling; my own emotions were mingled and indescribable. There was not even anybody to be thrashed! . . .

Her Meeting with Henry James

I SAID I would tell the story of her meeting with Henry James. It was in the winter after the publication of *Little Women*, and Louisa was running the gantlet of receptions and dinners given her by important people in Boston and elsewhere, and her wit and charm won her great popularity, which, however, never turned her head; she kept her own very modest estimate of her achievement.

At one of the first dinners she attended, Henry James was present, and his seat was beside her.

Henry was born in 1843, and was therefore eleven years younger than Louisa, but his gravity and reserve were portentous and amply bridged the gap; in fact, he was one of those who get younger and more approachable as their years increase. He was already a reviewer for the *New York Nation*, and his first novel, entitled *Watch and Ward*, had either been published or was running serially in *The Atlantic*.

He took his literature seriously, almost prayerfully, and felt the obligation laid upon him to warn and to command, more than to comfort, his contemporaries in the venerated craft.

The literary fashions of Boston fifty years ago do not appear to our generation frivolous, but to James they were so, and he strove by example and precept to stem and divert the shallow, glittering stream. I doubt whether he had found it possible actually to read *Little Women*, but he had, as it were, scented it, and his conscience compelled him to let Louisa know that he was unable to join in the vulgar chorus of approval.

He was silent during the opening stages of the dinner, and his gravity deepened as he overheard the compliments which Louisa was absorbing with her wonted humorous discrimination; the ego in her cosmos, as I have intimated, having been long ago licked into modesty by the buffetings of chance, success to her was a happy accident, and laudation nine-tenths whipsillabub. She laughed and smiled, hoped her good luck might continue, and was resolved to do her best to be not undeserving of it.

At length Henry, from the height of his five-and-twenty winters, felt that it was time to act. He bent toward her and spoke thus: "Louisa—m-my dear girl—er—when you hear people—ah—telling you you're a genius you mustn't believe them; er—what I mean is, it isn't true!"

Then he relapsed, spoke no more, and—er—declined the pudding.

The Last Talk with Her

LOUISA'S MIMETIC FACULTY enabled us to see and hear the judge in Apple Slump sitting room, as he handed down his decision. Years afterward, as he and I walked on Hastings Esplanade, in England, I told him the anecdote. He made inarticulate murmurs and smiled thoughtfully, and looked up at the gray sky and along the populous promenade, and he observed, after due consideration, that he couldn't fix the episode.

"But—well," he added, rubbing his chin through his clipped dark beard, conscientious to the last, "you know, after all, dear Louisa isn't."

But at any rate, Louisa had a delightful talent, and the greater part of human nature, as of the pyramids at Gizeh, is on the lower levels. Those vast underlying courses support the apex and exist for that purpose, though knowing and caring little about it. Moreover, the apex, sublime though it appears, is the first part of the structure to wear away, and when it is cast down it has no honor. Henry James has written exquisite books of which the man in the street knows nothing; but something of whatever is good and sound in the man in the street he owes to influences such as Louisa's stories bring him.

A dozen years and more after *Little Women* had become part of American household furniture, I had returned from Europe to New England and was spending a summer at Nonquitt on Buzzards Bay. Louisa came to visit a friend there, and I walked over to the cottage and sat an hour with her on the veranda.

She was the same tall, rather rustic looking woman, dressed in black silk, her shoulders a little bent, her cheeks somewhat thin, her big black eyes sparkling now and then with humor or irony. The contours of her face had begun to sag a trifle, making her powerful chin more noticeable than of old. She seemed to be happy; she had lived a hard-working, generous life, returning good measure for all she had received. But it seemed to me that I discerned beneath her cheerfulness some veiled sadness; the bright and lively pattern that she showed the world did not wholly hide the pensive background.

"There has never been anything else like our nights at Apple Slump," I said.

After her smile the corners of her mouth drooped. "Everything belonging to us, that can be seen and touched, drops away," she said, "till nothing is left. But maybe the things we wanted and never got are more real than the others and the rest is just padding."

"And perhaps the things we never got are waiting for us somewhere?"

"I'll ask father about that someday—he ought to know!"

I thought of the blameless Sage, blinking blandly round at his little circle [of acolytes]—he ought to know; but would he? [I let the] subject drop.

THE ALCOTTS

BY CHARLES IVES

IF THE DICTAGRAPH HAD BEEN PERFECTED IN BRONSON Alcott's time, he might now be a great writer. As it is, he goes down as Concord's greatest talker. "Great expecter," says Thoreau; "great feller," says Sam Staples, "for talkin' big . . . but his daughters is the gals though—always *doin'* somethin'." Old Man Alcott, however, was usually "doin' somethin' " within. An internal grandiloquence made him melodious without; an exuberant, irrepressible, visionary absorbed with philosophy *as* such; to him it was a kind of transcendental business, the profits of which supported his inner man rather than his family. Apparently his deep interest in spiritual physics, rather than metaphysics, gave a kind of hypnotic mellifluous effect to his voice when he sang his oracles; a manner something of a cross between an inside pompous self-assertion and an outside serious benevolence. But he was sincere and kindly intentioned in his eagerness to extend what he could of the better influence of the philosophic world as he saw it. In fact, there is a strong didactic streak in both father and daughter. Louisa May seldom misses a chance to bring out the moral of a homely virtue. The power of repetition was to them a natural means of illustration. It is said that the elder Alcott, while teaching school, would frequently whip himself when the scholars misbehaved, to show that the Divine Teacher—God—was pained when his children of the earth were bad. Quite often the boy next to the bad boy was punished, to show how sin involved the guiltless. And Miss Alcott is fond of working her story around, so that she can better rub in a moral precept—and the moral sometimes browbeats the story. But with all the elder Alcott's vehement, impracticable, visionary qualities, there was a sturdiness and a courage—at least, we like to think so. A Yankee boy who would cheerfully travel in those days, when distances were long and unmotored, as far from Connecticut as the Carolinas, earning his way by peddling, laying down his pack to teach school when opportunity offered, must possess a basic sturdiness. This was apparently not very evident when he got to preaching his idealism. An incident in Alcott's life helps confirm a theory—not a popular one—that men accustomed to wander around in the visionary unknown are the quickest and strongest when occasion requires ready action of the lower virtues. It often appears that a contemplative mind is more capable of action than an actively objective one. Dr. Emerson says: "It is good to know that it has been recorded of Alcott, the benign idealist, that when the Rev. Thomas Wentworth Higginson, heading the rush on the U.S. Court House in Boston, to rescue a fugitive slave, looked back for his following at the court-room door, only the apostolic philosopher was there cane in hand." So it seems that his idealism had some substantial virtues, even if he couldn't make a living.

The daughter does not accept the father as a prototype—she seems to have but few of her father's qualities "in female." She supported the family and at the same time enriched the lives of a large part of young America, starting off many little minds with wholesome thoughts and many little hearts with wholesome emotions. She leaves memory-word-pictures of healthy, New England childhood days,—pictures which are turned to with affection by middle-aged children,—pictures, that bear a sentiment, a leaven, that middle-aged America needs nowadays more than we care to admit.

Concord village, itself, reminds one of that common virtue lying at the height and root of all the Concord divinities. As one walks down the broad-arched street, passing the white house of Emerson—ascetic guard of a former prophetic beauty—he comes presently beneath the old elms overspreading the Alcott house. It seems to stand as a kind of homely but beautiful witness of Concord's common virtue—it seems to bear a consciousness that its past *is living,* that the "mosses of the Old Manse" and the hickories of Walden are not far away. Here is the home of the "Marches"—all pervaded with the trials and happiness of the family and telling, in a simple way, the story of "the richness of not having." Within the house, on every side, lie remembrances of what imagination can do for the better amusement of fortunate children who have to do for themselves—much-needed lessons in these days of automatic, ready-made, easy entertainment which deaden rather than stimulate the creative faculty. And there sits the little old spinet-piano Sophia Thoreau gave to the Alcott children, on which Beth played the old Scotch airs, and played at the *Fifth Symphony.*

There is a commonplace beauty about "Orchard House"—a kind of spiritual sturdiness underlying its quaint picturesqueness—a kind of common triad of the New England homestead, whose overtones tell us that there must have been something aesthetic fibered in the Puritan severity—the self-sacrificing part of the ideal—a value that seems to stir a deeper feeling, a stronger sense of being nearer some perfect truth than a Gothic cathedral or an Etruscan villa. All around you, under the Concord sky, there still floats the influence of that human faith melody, transcendent and sentimental enough for the enthusiast or the cynic respectively, reflecting an innate hope—a common interest in common things and common men—a tune the Concord bards are ever playing, while they pound away at the immensities with a Beethovenlike sublimity, and with, may we say, a vehemence and perseverance—for that part of greatness is not so difficult to emulate.

We dare not attempt to follow the philosophic raptures of Bronson Alcott—unless you will assume that his apotheosis will show how "practical" his vision in this world would be in the next. And so we

The Orchard House. Home of A. Bronson Alcott.

"There is a commonplace beauty about 'Orchard House'—a kind of spiritual sturdiness," wrote Charles Ives. In 1884, Julian Hawthorne recalled a "low, brown, gabled, irregular structure with a lazy wink of wise old windows," which, beneath enormous, embowering elms, "reclines, rather than stands . . . forty yards or so back from the road . . ."

won't try to reconcile the music sketch of the Alcotts with much besides the memory of that home under the elms—the Scotch songs and the family hymns that were sung at the end of each day—though there may be an attempt to catch something of that common sentiment (which we have tried to suggest above)—a strength of hope that never gives way to despair—a conviction in the power of the common soul which, when all is said and done, may be as typical as any theme of Concord and its transcendentalists.

LOUISA ALCOTT

BY G. K. CHESTERTON

I T IS VERY GOOD FOR A MAN TO TALK ABOUT WHAT HE DOES NOT understand; as long as he understands that he does not understand it. Agnosticism (which has, I am sorry to say, almost entirely disappeared from the modern world) is always an admirable thing, so long as it admits that the thing which it does not understand may be much superior to the mind which does not understand it. Thus if you say that the cosmos is incomprehensible, and really mean (as most moderns do) that it is not worth comprehending; then it would be much better for your Greek agnosticism if it were called by its Latin name of ignorance. But there is one thing that any man can fairly consider incomprehensible, and yet in some ways superior. There is one thing that any man may worry about, and still respect; I mean any woman. The deadly and divine cleavage between the sexes has compelled every woman and every man, age after age, to believe without understanding; to have faith without any knowledge.

Upon the same principle it is a good thing for any man to have to review a book which he cannot review. It is a good thing for his agnosticism and his humility to consider a book which may be much better than he can ever understand. It is good for a man who has seen many books which he could not review because they were so silly, to review one book which he cannot review because it is so wise. For wisdom, first and last, is the characteristic of women. They are often silly, they are always wise. Commonsense is uncommon among men; but commonsense is really and literally a common sense among women. And the sagacity of women, like the sagacity of saints, or that of donkeys, is something outside all questions of ordinary cleverness and ambition. The whole truth of the matter was revealed to Mr. Rudyard Kipling when the spirit of truth suddenly descended on him and he said: "Any woman can manage a clever man; but it requires a rather clever woman to manage a fool."

The wisdom of women is different; and this alone makes the review of such books by a man difficult. But the case is stronger. I for one will willingly confess that the only thing on earth I am frightfully afraid of is a little girl. Female children, she babies, girls up to the age of five are perfectly reasonable; but then all babies are reasonable. Grown girls and women give us at least glimpses of their meaning. But the whole of the period between a girl who is six years old and a girl who is sixteen is to me an abyss not only of mystery, but of terror. If the Prussians were invading England, and I were holding a solitary outpost, the best thing they could do would be to send a long rank or regiment of Prussian girls of twelve, from which I should fly, screaming.

Now the famous books of Miss Alcott are all about little girls. Therefore, my first impulse was to fly screaming. But I resisted this impulse, and I read the books; and I discovered, to my immeasurable astonishment, that they were extremely good. *Little Women* was written by a woman for women—for little women. Consequently it anticipated realism by twenty or thirty years; just as Jane Austen anticipated it by at least a hundred years. For women are the only realists; their whole object in life is to pit their realism against the extravagant, excessive, and occasionally drunken idealism of men. I do not hesitate. I am not ashamed to name Miss Alcott and Miss Austen. There is, indeed, a vast division in the matter of literature (an unimportant matter), but there is the same silent and unexplained assumption of the feminine point of view. There is no pretence, as most unfortunately occurred in the case of another woman of genius, George Eliot, that the writer is anything else but a woman, writing to amuse other women, with her awful womanly irony. Jane Austen did not call herself George Austen; nor Louisa Alcott call herself George Alcott. These women refrained from that abject submission to the male sex which we have since been distressed to see; the weak demand for masculine names and for a part in merely masculine frivolities; parliaments, for instance. These were strong women; they classed parliament with the public-house. But for another and better reason, I do not hesitate to name Miss Alcott by the side of Jane Austen; because her talent, though doubtless inferior, was of exactly the same kind. There is an unmistakable material truth about the thing; if that material truth were not the chief female characteristic, we should most of us find our houses burnt down when we went back to them. To take but one instance out of many, and an instance that a man can understand, because a man was involved, the account of the quite sudden and quite blundering proposal, acceptance, and engagement between Jo and the German professor under the umbrella, with parcels falling off them, so to speak, every minute, is one of the really human things in human literature; when you read it you feel sure that human beings have experienced it often; you almost feel that you have experienced it yourself. There is something true to all our own private diaries in the fact that our happiest moments have happened in the rain, or under some absurd impediment of absurd luggage. The same is true of a hundred other elements in the story. The whole affair of the children acting the different parts in *Pickwick*, forming a childish club under strict restrictions, in order to do so; all that is really life, even where it is not literature. And as a final touch of human truth, nothing could be better than the way in which Miss Alcott suggests the borders and the sensitive privacy of such an experiment. All the little girls have become interested, as they would in real life, in the lonely little boy next door;

but when one of them introduces him into their private club in imitation of *Pickwick*, there is a general stir of resistance; these family fictions do not endure being considered from the outside.

All that is profoundly true; and something more than that is profoundly true. For just as the boy was an intruder in that club of girls, so any masculine reader is really an intruder among this pile of books. There runs through the whole series a certain moral philosophy, which a man can never really get the hang of. For instance, the girls are always doing something, pleasant or unpleasant. In fact, when they have not to do something unpleasant, they deliberately do something else. A great part, perhaps the more godlike part, of a boy's life, is passed in doing nothing at all. Real selfishness, which is the simplest thing in the world to a boy or man, is practically left out of the calculation. The girls may conceivably oppress and torture each other; but they will not indulge or even enjoy themselves—not, at least, as men understand indulgence or enjoyment. The strangest things are taken for granted; as that it is wrong in itself to drink champagne. But two things are quite certain; first, that even from a masculine standpoint, the books are very good; and second, that from a feminine standpoint they are so good that their admirers have really lost sight even of their goodness. I have never known, or hardly ever known, a really admirable woman who did not confess to having read these books. Haughty ladies confessed (under torture) that they liked them still. Stately Suffragettes rose rustling from the sofa and dropped *Little Women* on the floor, covering them with public shame. At learned ladies' colleges, it is, I firmly believe, handed about secretly, like a dangerous drug. I cannot understand this strange and simple world, in which unselfishness is natural, in which spite is easier than self-indulgence. I am the male intruder, like poor Mr. Laurence and I withdraw. I back out hastily, bowing. But I am sure that I leave a very interesting world behind me.

FROM "RECOLLECTIONS OF LOUISA MAY ALCOTT"

BY MARIA S. PORTER

. . . MISS ALCOTT HAD THE KEENEST INSIGHT INTO CHARACTER. SHE WAS rarely mistaken in her judgment of people. She was intolerant of all shams, and despised pretentious persons. Often in her pleasant rooms at the Bellevue have I listened to her estimates of people whom we knew. She was sometimes almost ruthless in her denunciation of society, so called. I remember what she said as we sat together at a private ball, where many of the butterflies of fashion and leaders of society were assembled. As with her clear, keen eyes she viewed the pageant, she exclaimed: "Society in New York and in Boston, as we have seen it to-night, is corrupt. Such immodest dressing, such flirtations of some of these married women with young men whose mothers they might be, so far as age is concerned, such drinking of champagne—I loathe it all! If I can only live long enough I mean to write a book whose characters will be drawn from life. Mrs. ———— [naming a person present] shall be prominent as the society leader, and the fidelity of the picture shall leave no one in doubt as to the original."

She always bitterly denounced all unwomanliness. Her standard of morality was a high one, and the same for men as for women. She was an earnest advocate of woman suffrage and college education for girls,

Mar. 21st

Dear Miss Anthony,

Many thanks for the book. I was too ill to attend to it when your sister wrote me.

The other volumes are shut up in our house in Concord & I do not remember the color of the covers. Will see about it later.

In this touching letter to Susan B. Anthony, Alcott reaffirms her commitment to woman suffrage: "I am very proud of the good people with whom I may claim kindred, & wish I could do more to help on the noble work they began. But my chore was a private one, & health went in the doing of it, so now I can only look on & say God speed!"

because she devoutly believed that woman should do whatever she could do well, in church or school or state. When I was elected a member of the school committee of Melrose in 1874, she wrote:—

I rejoice greatly thereat, and hope that the first thing that you and Mrs. Sewall propose in your first meeting will be to reduce the salary of the head master of the High School, and increase the salary of the first woman assistant, whose work is quite as good as his, and even harder; to make the pay equal. I believe in the same pay for the same good work. Don't you? In future let woman do whatever she can do; let men place no more impediments in the way; above all things let's have fair play,— let *simple justice* be done, say I. Let us hear no more of "woman's sphere" either from our wise (?) legislators beneath the State House dome, or from our clergymen in their pulpits. I am tired, year after year, of hearing such twaddle about sturdy oaks and clinging vines and man's chivalric protection of woman. Let woman find out her own limitations, and if, as is so confidently asserted, nature has defined her sphere, she will be guided accordingly; but in heaven's name give her a chance! Let the professions be open to her; let fifty years of college education be hers, and then we shall see what we shall see. Then, and not until then, shall we be able to say what women can and what she cannot do, and coming generations will know and be able to define more clearly what is a "woman's sphere" than these benighted men who now try to do it.

During Miss Alcott's last illness she wrote:—

When I get upon my feet I am going (D.V.) to devote myself to settling poor souls who need a helping hand in hard times.

. . . Miss Alcott had a keen sense of humor, and her friends recall with delight her sallies of wit and caustic descriptions of the School of

Philosophy, the "unfathomable wisdom," the "metaphysical pyro-technics," the strange vagaries of some of the devotees. She would sometimes enclose such nonsense rhymes as these to her intimate friends:—

> *Philosophers sit in their sylvan hall*
> *And talk of the duties of man,*
> *Of Chaos and Cosmos, Hegel and Kant,*
> *With the Oversoul well in the van;*
> *All on their hobbies they amble away,*
> *And a terrible dust they make;*
> *Disciples devout both gaze and adore,*
> *As daily they listen, and bake!*

The "sylvan hall" was, as I know from bitter experience while attending the sessions of the School of Philosophy, the hottest place in historic old Concord . . .

From the time that the success of "Little Women" established her reputation as a writer, until the last day of her life, her absolute devotion to her family continued. Her mother's declining years were soothed with every care and comfort that filial love could bestow; she died in Louisa's arms, and for her she performed all the last offices of affection,—no stranger hands touched the beloved form. The most beautiful of her poems was written at this time, in memory of her mother, and was called, "Transfiguration." A short time after her mother's death, her sister May, who had married Mr. Ernest Nieriker, a Swiss gentleman, living in Paris, died after the birth of her child. Of this Louisa wrote me in reply to a letter of sympathy:—

I mourn and mourn by day and night for May. Of all the griefs in my life, and I have had many, this is the bitterest. I try so hard to be brave, but the tears will come, and I go off and cry and cry; the dear little baby may comfort Ernest, but what can comfort us? May called her two years of marriage perfect happiness, and said: "If I die when baby is born, don't mourn, for I have had in these two years more happiness than comes to many in a lifetime." The baby is named for me, and is to be given to me as my very own. What a sad but precious legacy!

The little golden-haired Lulu was brought to her by its aunt, Miss Sophie Nieriker, and she was indeed a great comfort to Miss Alcott for the remainder of her life.

In 1886, Miss Alcott took a furnished house on Louisburg Square in Boston, and although her health was still very delicate she anticipated much quiet happiness in the family life. In the autumn and winter she suffered much from indigestion, sleeplessness, and general debility. Early in December she told me how very much she was suffering, and added, "I mean if possible to keep up until after Christmas, and then I am sure I shall break down." When I went to carry her a Christmas gift, she showed me the Christmas tree, and seemed so bright and happy that I was not prepared to hear soon after that she had gone out to the restful quiet of a home in Dunreath Place, at the Highlands, where she could be tenderly cared for under the direction of her friend, Dr. Rhoda Lawrence, to whom she dedicated one of her books. She was too weak to bear even the pleasurable excitement of her own home, and called Dr. Lawrence's house, "Saint's Rest." The following summer she went with Dr. Lawrence to Princeton, but on her return in the autumn her illness took an alarming character, and she was unable to see her friends, and only occasionally the members of her family. On her last birthday, November 29, she received many gifts, and as I had remembered her, the following characteristic letter came to me, the last but one that she sent me:—

Thanks for the flowers and for the kind thought that sent them to the poor old exile. I had seven boxes of flowers, two baskets, and three plants, forty gifts in all, and at night I lay in a room that looked like a small fair, with its five tables covered with pretty things, borders of posies, and your noble roses towering in state over all the rest. That red one was so delicious that I revelled in it like a big bee, and felt it might almost do for a body—I am so thin now. Everybody was very kind, and my solitary day was made happy by so much love. Illness and exile have their bright side, I find, and I hope to come out in the spring a gay old butterfly. My rest-and-milk cure is doing well, and I am an obedient oyster since I have learned that patience and time are my best helps.

In February, 1888, Mr. Alcott was taken with what proved to be his last illness. Louisa knew that the end was near, and as often as she was able came into town to see him. On Thursday morning, March 2, I chanced to be at the house, where I had gone to inquire for Mr. Alcott and Louisa. While talking with Mrs. Pratt, her sister, the door opened, and Louisa, who had come in from the Highlands to see her father, entered. I had not seen her for months, and the sight of her thin, wan face and sad look shocked me, and I felt for the first time that she was hopelessly ill. After a few affectionate words of greeting she passed through the open doors of the next room. The scene that followed was most pathetic. There lay the dear old father, stricken with death, his face illumined with the radiance that comes but once,—with uplifted gaze he heeded her not. Kneeling by his bedside, she took his hand, kissed it and placed in it the pansies she had brought, saying, "It is Weedy" (her pet name). Then after a moment's silence she asked, "What are you thinking of, dear?" He replied, looking upward, "Up there; you come too!" Then with a kiss she said, "I wish I could go," bowing her head as if in prayer. After a little came the "Good by," the last kiss, and like a shadow she glided from the room. The following day I wrote her at the "Saint's Rest," enclosing a photograph of her sister May, that I found among some old letters of her own. Referring to my meeting with her the day before, I said:—

I hope you will be able to bear the impending event with the same brave philosophy that was yours when your dear mother died.

She received my note on Saturday morning, together with one from her sister. Early in the morning she replied to her sister's note, telling of a dull pain and a weight like iron on her head. Later, she wrote me the last words she ever penned; and in the evening came the fatal stroke of apoplexy, followed by unconsciousness. Her letter to me was as follows:—

DEAR MRS. PORTER,—Thanks for the picture. I am very glad to have it. No philosophy is needed for the impending event. I shall be very glad when the dear old man falls asleep after his long and innocent life. Sorrow has no place at such times, and death is never terrible when it comes as now in the likeness of a friend.

Yours truly,
L. M. A.

P.S. I have another year to stay in my "Saint's Rest," and then I am promised twenty years of health. I don't want so many, and I have no idea I shall see them. But as I don't live for myself, I hold on for others, and shall find time to die some day, I hope.

Mr. Alcott died on Sunday morning, March 4, and on Tuesday morning, March 6, death, "in the likeness of a friend," came to Louisa. Mr. Alcott's funeral took place on Tuesday morning, and many of the friends there assembled were met with the tidings of Louisa's death. Miss Alcott had made every arrangement for her funeral. It was her desire that only those near and dear to her should be present, that the service should be simple, and that only friends should take part. The

358 ◆ REMEMBERING LOUISA MAY ALCOTT

services were indeed simple, but most impressive . . . Mrs. Cheney read the sonnet written by Mr. Alcott, which refers to her as "Duty's faithful child." Mrs. Harriet Winslow Sewall, a very dear cousin, read with her sweet voice and in a tender manner that most beautiful of Louisa's poems, "Transfiguration," written in memory of her mother. I had carried my simple tribute of verse, but could not control voice or emotion sufficiently to read it, and laid it with a bunch of white Cherokee roses on the casket.

TO LOUISA MAY ALCOTT BY HER FATHER

BY BRONSON ALCOTT

When I remember with what buoyant heart,
    Midst war's alarms and woes of civil strife,
In youthful eagerness thou didst depart,
    At peril of thy safety, peace and life,
To nurse the wounded soldier, swathe the dead,—
    How piercèd soon by fever's poisoned dart,
And brought unconscious home, with 'wildered head,
    Thou ever since, mid languor and dull pain,
To conquer fortune, cherish kindred dear,
    Hast with great studies vexed a sprightly brain,
In myriad households kindled love and cheer,
    Ne'er from thyself by Fame's loud trump beguiled,
Sounding in this and the farther hemisphere,
    I press thee to my heart as Duty's faithful child.

The publisher's proof for the frontispiece to Ednah D. Cheney's reverential memorial,
Louisa May Alcott, The Children's Friend *(1888). Addressing the youth of*
America, Cheney closes her little volume with a somewhat deflating homily: "My
little friends, you may not one of you have the great talents which made Miss Alcott
famous, *but every one of you can try to have her spirit of love and duty, can follow*
in the paths she has pointed out . . ."

SUGGESTIONS FOR FURTHER READING

BIOGRAPHY

ALCOTT, AMOS BRONSON. *The Journals of Bronson Alcott.* Selected and edited by Odell Shepard. Boston: Little, Brown and Company, 1938. An engrossing volume, culled from Bronson's staggeringly voluminous journal (estimated to weigh in at some five million words), which also includes some powerful excerpts from Abba's journal. Both were very shrewd judges of character. Here is Abba on her second-born, when that difficult child was not quite ten: "United to great firmness of purpose and resolution, there is at times the greatest volatility and wretchedness of spirit—no hope, no heart for anything, sad, solemn, and desponding. Fine generous feelings, no selfishness, great good will to all, and strong attachment to a few."

ALCOTT, LOUISA MAY. *The Journals of Louisa May Alcott.* Edited by Joel Myerson and Daniel Shealy; Associate Editor: Madeleine B. Stern. With an introduction by Madeleine B. Stern. Boston: Little, Brown and Company, 1989. The chronicle of a writer's life, assembled from both published and unpublished sources, with annotations, chronology, and an excellent introduction. Alcott left instructions that her journals be destroyed upon her death. One can only be thankful that her wishes were ignored.

ALCOTT, LOUISA MAY. *The Selected Letters of Louisa May Alcott*. Edited by Joel Myerson and Daniel Shealy; Associate Editor: Madeleine B. Stern. With an introduction by Madeleine B. Stern. Boston: Little, Brown and Company, 1987. Witty, warm, lively, and marvelously observant letters to family, friends, publishers, and even some lucky admirers (from Europe, she is forced to tell her mother to stop forwarding any more letters from the *"so cracked* girls" who continued to bombard the Concord P.O. in her absence, adding that "the rampant infants must wait"). Again, Stern's introduction is a model of its kind.

BARTON, CYNTHIA H. *Transcendental Wife: The Life of Abigail May Alcott*. Lanham, Md.: University Press of America, 1996. A biographical study of Alcott's mother, who was at least as wonderful as "Marmee" in *Little Women*, but much more interesting.

BEDELL, MADELON. *The Alcotts: Biography of a Family*. New York: Clarkson N. Potter, 1980. An elegant study in which the Alcotts and their age are brought vibrantly to life with rich detail, insight, and compassion. A splendid achievement.

CHENEY, EDNAH DOW. *Louisa May Alcott: Her Life, Letters and Journals*. Boston: Roberts Brothers, 1889. In this admixture of biography and Alcott's private writings (carefully edited), the high-minded Mrs. Cheney sculpted an idealized portrait of "Duty's Faithful Child" that would prove to be greatly influential. Very important because it preserves material that otherwise would have been lost. Reprinted several times (there is a 1980 edition, published by Chelsea House, with an introduction by Ann Douglas) and still well worth seeking out.

SAXTON, MARTHA. *Louisa May: A Modern Biography of Louisa May Alcott*. Boston: Houghton Mifflin Company, 1977. A compelling, if rather overheated, portrait of the Concord Scheherazade, which goes after the "good daughter" myth with a vengeance. As the jacket copy of the Noonday Press 1995 reissue of this book has it, Saxton gives an "arresting account of the disparity between the sweet family story Louisa May Alcott is remembered for and the poignant reality of her oppressive father and stifling spinsterhood." One comes away from this evocative, often very witty, and often unduly harsh book thinking, "Oh, if only she had had a good therapist . . ."

SHEPARD, ODELL. *Pedlar's Progress: The Life of Bronson Alcott.* Boston: Little, Brown and Company, 1937. The standard biography of the Sage of Concord.

STERN, MADELEINE B. *Louisa May Alcott.* Norman, Okla.: University of Oklahoma Press, 1950. The classic biography by the doyenne of Alcott scholars. Republished by Random House in 1996 with an updated bibliography of Alcott's writings, now numbering 314(!) items. Stern set out to re-create Alcott as "a living, breathing, extremely *human* being," and that is exactly what she did. Essential.

CRITICISM

BROPHY, BRIGID. "Sentimentality and Louisa M. Alcott," in *Don't Never Forget: Collected Views and Reviews.* London: Jonathan Cape, 1966. The English novelist and critic finds herself "driven back" to Alcott after catching the George Cukor–Katharine Hepburn version of *Little Women* on the BBC—and though she herself is an "almost wholly unsentimental writer," Brophy succumbs yet again to the saga of the Marches, just as she had at fourteen. Having blown her nose, she penned this wicked article, which apparently caused quite a ruckus when it made its debut, in a slightly shorter form, in *The New York Times Book Review* (original title: "A Masterpiece, and Dreadful").

DOUGLAS, ANN. "Louisa May Alcott, 1832–1888," in *American Writers: A Collection of Literary Biographies.* Supplement I, Part 1. New York: Charles Scribner's Sons, 1979. An excellent essay by the author of *The Feminization of American Culture* (1977), the now classic study (also highly recommended) of the sentimentalization of theological and secular culture in nineteenth-century America.

ELBERT, SARAH. *A Hunger for Home: Louisa May Alcott and* Little Women. Philadelphia, Pa.: Temple University Press, 1984. A perceptive reading of Alcott's life and work, which, taken together, as they must be, "demonstrate the full range of feminist concerns in the nineteenth century."

KING, STEPHEN. "Blood and Thunder in Concord," in *The New York Times Book Review*, September 10, 1995. A master of blood-and-thunder tales, twentieth-century style, reviews, with admiration and finesse, the recently discovered Alcott shocker *A Long Fatal Love Chase*, which was dusted off and published by Random House in 1995, one hundred and thirty years after Alcott was told by her publisher that it was too lurid to see the light of day. King is more discerning.

O'FAOLÁIN, SEÁN. "This Is Your Life . . . Louisa May Alcott," in *Holiday*, November 1968. A clever article by the Irish novelist and biographer.

STERN, MADELEINE B., ed. *Critical Essays on Louisa May Alcott*. Boston, Mass.: G. K. Hall & Company, 1985. A compilation of contemporary notices (for the most part anonymous, as was common in the nineteenth century), later appraisals and reappraisals, and essays commissioned especially for the volume. There are some wonderful things here by— to name just a few of the contributors—Henry James, Elizabeth Vincent, Leo Lerman, Cornelia L. Meigs, Lavinia Russ, Elizabeth Janeway, Nina Auerbach, and Madelon Bedell. Also, works by four authors recommended here (Chesterton, Douglas, O'Faoláin, and Brophy) are to be found in this collection, if in variant or abbreviated state.

OF RELATED INTEREST

BUNYAN, JOHN. *The Pilgrim's Progress*. Available in a number of editions, but the Oxford University Press (World's Classics) paperback has an illuminating introduction by N. H. Keeble, a chronology of Bunyan's life, explanatory notes, bibliography, a glossary, and a very useful index. This masterwork of spirituality (and English prose) was greatly cherished by Bronson Alcott; and like her father's, Louisa's admiration for *The Pilgrim's Progress* was lifelong. It was a key text for both. In her introduction to the Centennial Edition of *Little Women* (which, of course, takes many of its chapter headings from Bunyan), Cornelia L. Meigs suggested that if one were to select Louisa May Alcott's counterpart in *The Pilgrim's Progress*, it would have to be Mr. Valiant-for-Truth.

MILLER, PENNY. *The American Transcendentalists, Their Poetry and Prose.* Garden City, N.Y.: Doubleday/Anchor Books, 1957. A classic anthology of writings by Thoreau, Emerson, Margaret Fuller, Theodore Parker, Bronson Alcott, and other advanced souls, some of whom Louisa May Alcott knew well and most of whom she admired greatly. This "poetic sampling" of transcendental genius, which is much enlivened by Miller's superb commentaries, was reissued in paperback by the Johns Hopkins University Press in 1981.

STEEGMULLER, FRANCIS. "House of Little Women," in *Holiday*, March 1960. A charming tour of Orchard House, the "venerable, brown-painted clapboard dwelling beside the road in Concord, with the lilacs at the door," which, much to Alcott's amazement and eventual annoyance, *Little Women* made famous round the world.

CHECKLIST OF
ILLUSTRATIONS

All of the illustrations in this edition are from the collections of The New York Public Library's Center for the Humanities, and, unless otherwise noted, are located in the Henry W. and Albert A. Berg Collection of English and American Literature.

Page xvii: Portrait photograph (cabinet photograph) of Louisa May Alcott by Conly of Boston, ca. mid 1870s.
Miriam and Ira D. Wallach Division of Art, Prints, and Photographs

Page xix: Portrait photograph (cabinet photograph) of Amos Bronson Alcott by Warren of Boston, ca. 1860s.
Wallach Division

Page xxiv: "North Main Street, Concord, Massachusetts, at 12 o'clock noon." Stereograph, ca. 1870s.
Wallach Division

Pages xxvi, 313: Cover of the November 1876 issue of *Frank Leslie's Popular Monthly* ("The Cheapest Magazine Published in the World") and an illustration for "Perilous Play" from the same issue.
General Research Division

Page xxxi: Full-page illustration (wood engraving) from the August 14, 1880, issue of *Frank Leslie's Illustrated Newspaper*, featuring portraits of four luminaries of American letters (Ralph Waldo Emerson, A. Bronson Alcott, Louisa Alcott, John G. Whittier); sketches of the Concord School of Philosophy and "The Home of Miss Alcott"; and a depiction of the interior of the school's chapel during a lecture by Bronson Alcott (all engraved after the sketches of W. Parker Bodfish).

Page xxxv: Cover of *V.V.: or, Plots and Counterplots* by A. M. Barnard (i.e., Louisa May Alcott) (Boston: Thomes & Talbot, ca. 1870, no. 80 in the firm's series of Ten Cent Novelettes of Standard American Authors). *Rare Books Division*

Page 7: Portrait of Ralph Waldo Emerson by Gibbs Mason (in color), ca. 1873, set into the inside front cover of an elaborately tooled and gilded Levant morocco book-shaped case commissioned by Charles Eliot Norton to hold the holograph manuscript of Emerson's essay "Immortality," which was presented to Norton by Emerson's daughter Edith Emerson Forbes, in 1886.

Page 28: Fruitlands, from a photograph in *Lost Utopias* by Harriet Ellen O'Brien (Boston: Perry Walton, 1929). *General Research Division*

Pages 85, 106: Two illustrations from *Hospital Sketches and Camp and Fireside Stories* by Louisa May Alcott (Boston: Roberts Brothers, 1869). *General Research Division*

Pages 128, 324, 335: Three illustrations (photogravures) by May Alcott Nieriker from *Concord Sketches* (Boston: Fields, Osgood & Co., 1869): "The Wayside," "Woodland Gate," and "Hermitage at Walden Pond." *General Research Division*

Page 130: Manuscript collection of early poems by Louisa May Alcott, copied out by her into a blue exercise book and presented, with a dedicatory letter on its first page, to Miss Sophia Foord (also spelled "Ford"), sometime after 1850.

Page 139: "Mother of Miss L. M. Alcott at Home" by Thomas Lewis. Stereograph, ca. early–mid-1870s.
Wallach Division

Page 147: Autograph manuscript of Louisa May Alcott's poem "The Hawthorne," ca. late 1862–early 1863.

Page 150: Daguerreotype portrait of Henry David Thoreau by Benjamin Maxham, 1856.

Page 155: Autograph manuscript of Louisa May Alcott's poem "Most Women Do Whatever They Can," enclosed by her in an envelope addressed to G. J. Whittlesbury *Esq.* of Elmira, New York (envelope postmarked March 18, [18]84).

Page 157: "The North Bridge in Concord, Massachusetts, with a view of Daniel Chester French's Minuteman." Stereograph, ca. late 1870s.
Wallach Division

Page 163: "Louisa M. Alcott's Famous Books," an advertisement featuring "Jo in a Vortex." One of eight pages of advertisements bound into the back of her *Silver Pitchers: and Independence, a Centennial Love Story* (Boston: Roberts Brothers, 1877).
General Research Division

Page 168: The Union Hotel Hospital at Georgetown, from a wood engraving published in the July 6, 1861, issue of *Frank Leslie's Illustrated Newspaper.*
General Research Division

Page 176: "Full Course Ticket" to the Concord School of Philosophy for the year 1884, issued to and signed by David A. Wells.
Manuscripts and Archives Division

Page 179: Portrait photograph (*carte-de-visite*) of May Alcott Nieriker, ca. mid–late 1860s.

Pages 192, 208: Two illustrations (wood engravings) that accompanied the publication of Part I of Louisa May Alcott's two-part prize-winning story, "Pauline's Passion and Punishment," in the January 3, 1863, issue of *Frank Leslie's Illustrated Newspaper*.
General Research Division

Page 263: "Mrs. Sairey Gamp Bursting in upon the Artist in His Studio," a drawing by "Phiz" (Hablot K. Browne). This served as a document of authentication for a series of forty original watercolor drawings illustrating scenes from Charles Dickens's *The Life and Adventures of Martin Chuzzlewit*), which Browne executed for Frederick William Cosens in 1866.

Page 345: Photograph (cyanotype) of Orchard House, ca. late nineteenth century.
Wallach Division

Page 352: Autograph letter from Louisa May Alcott to Susan B. Anthony, March 21, [1885?].

Page 360: " 'Louise Alcott,' The Children's Friend" by Lizbeth B. Comins. This chromolithograph (proof) by L. Prang & Company, ca. 1888, served as the frontispiece to Ednah D. Cheney's *Louisa May Alcott, The Children's Friend*, published by Prang in 1888; it also appeared in the firm's "Louisa May Alcott Calendar."
Wallach Division